INSIDE THE THIRD

Book #2 in the Roll Call Trilogy

GWEN MANSFIELD

https://rollcalltrilogy.wordpress.com

gwenmansfield.com

ISBN-13: 9781545192993
ISBN: 1545192995

Cover design by Sherri Miller
Cover photos by Sherri Miller
Author photo by Andie Avery Photography
Map illustration by Denise Cormier Mahoney and Sherri Miller

To

Phil, Ellie, Natalie, and Zoe

You stood by my declaration: "I am a writer."
You knew what that meant, and you still loved me.

REVIEWS FOR
ROLL CALL

- "*Roll Call* strikes at the fundamental nature of the human story. With humor, imagination, and gripping realism, Mansfield transports us to a world in which essential myths of our time play out and we are compelled to reexamine where we are as a society."—Valerie Veatch, Director *Love Child* (HBO 2014) and *Me @ the Zoo* (HBO 2012). Sundance Film Festival 2012, 2014.

- "Mansfield begins her new trilogy by dropping readers into a future that's as propulsive as it is miserable. In marvelous, staccato prose, she describes Avery's world as 'Gray. The sky. The factory. The conveyor belt. The little pills that feed us, heal us, alter us—stabilize us.' The GEBS are reminiscent of the pod people in *Invasion of the Body Snatchers*, but are used so cleverly here that they feel totally fresh. Although the novel is aimed at young adults, sophisticated jolts of turmoil charge the narrative as when Avery has 'lost the time to let beauty perform its work on [her] spirit.' Overall, this masterful series opener is in better company with William Gibson's *Neuromancer* than the safer fare such as *The Hunger Games.* An exhilarating ride full of sheer drops and whiplash curves."—Kirkus Reviews

- "Gwen's writing style is concise, never dawdling for unnecessary information that would clutter her action-packed adventure. The manner in which she designs her 'post-apocalyptic' zone is a bit too credible for comfort with the current environmental changes we see in the news daily (tornadoes, earthquakes, tsunamis in unusual locales, etc), but with the author's attention to detail and to character development it is obvious that that is her intention. In a relatively short novel Gwen has placed all the characters that will define a trilogy clearly in context and has allowed us to know them, care about them, feel the discovery of love amidst the devastation they face, most important for a proposed trilogy, glued us to their futures and the development of the plot she has so carefully carved. A fine Young Adult novel, this."—Grady Harp Hall of Fame Top 100 Reviewer VINE VOICE

PROLOGUE
COLONY G
AVERY DETORNADA

It seems a curtain's drawn back each time I step across the threshold from the colony space I share with Chapman. I am quite aware of this divider, invisible to others, and when I pass through the makeshift door, leaving my boy behind, I leave the *me* that is the *mother* with him. I step out of the knee-high leather mukluks that all of us in the colonies of the New Coastline wear and place my feet firmly in the steel-toed boots of a commander on the front. Urgent strategy, these constant preparations for war. The Third is barking at the moon over our colony, and I hear them howling. Tomorrow their eyes may be so close, glowing, searching for Colony G, and we might feel their hot breath on the back of our necks. We know they're coming, and it's a hefty risk, this waiting.

For years, after escaping Reichel, we chose the running option. The first two and a half years as Colony A we dodged capture in the familiarity of the transplanted forest on the New Coastline. We hid among the boughs and branches of trees not all that different from our once strong command center, Red Grove. Living from the content of our packs, which were ever by our sides, a simple swing up to our shoulders positioned our belongings for the next escape. The exodus routine commanded our schedule, dominated our strategy and directed our relationships. This son of mine, Chapman, thought pack-grab in the middle of the night was a game. He kept his lips tight as we rappelled the trees, comrades with the darkness of midnight, settling into the rhythm of the run, the hides around our feet laced to the knees and begging us for quiet among the branches.

The year we first began our life as Colony A, declaring freedom from The Third, Chapman jostled on my back, but as time marched and Chapman grew, he found his running legs. Lean and strong, this boy's been built in the immediacy of the chase, trained by the threat of capture. A mother waits for her son's first word, thinking "mama" might grace his lips. Chapman uttered "go," and the second word, close behind the first to form a sentence: "now." "Go now, mama." I didn't mind too much being third in line.

Our fledgling rebel country hardly posed a threat, even though by then the number of those identified as loyal surpassed 7,000, spread out and hidden in abandoned housing subdivisions, underground bunkers of old air bases and gas stations of towns that never had significant populations. We advance the Colony letters (now we are at "G") each time we find a place to settle and hope, unlike the past, that *home* will include a location where bags might be unpacked and gardens given time to grow. With Colony B we moved inland, closer to what was left of the four remaining lakes, no longer "Great" by former standards, but shrunken to a fraction of their former length by *Jurbay's* hot breath. We avoided The Third's detection in an underground parking garage, and were all quite sure The Third had lost interest in The 28 United. We were residents there for months, until infrared tracked us below the earth, sensed our heat. Our fortune that day was that The Third had no reinforcements. We killed all six of them, but not before they communicated to their own that the target had been located. Again, we were running, hunted, our hair grown long and flying behind us, the leaves and branches clinging to our tresses, reminding us of our connection to the forest.

Sometimes when we ran the land smelled clean, void of the odor that previously permeated the air after our population had been exterminated, or at least diminished, by one of the 14 Deadlies. Why was one section, like the New Coastline, seemingly cleansed of the stink of death and another still filled with the bones of annihilation? How did enormous sections, hundreds of square miles, rid themselves of death and disease? Was someone helping the process along? No clues, ever. Was I right that when we strategized a move to an area, it appeared skeleton-free, but when we made a spontaneous decision to travel an unplanned route it was laden with piles of bones? In this uncharted world, coincidence seems rational and fate a fantasy.

I wouldn't call our other attempts at colonies (C, D, E and F) settlements. In one case, we'd hardly moved in to an abandoned twenty-six story office building at the center of a forsaken city before we were discovered by the enemy. It took just one mistake by a small group of children. They exited through a side door instead of the underground electrical storage room. Sighted again. Just like the time when we were in the deserted sports arena that used to house cheering communities, and the occasion when we dared to lay our heads for a night in the theater where actors once told grand stories to those who paid to listen. And there was the night we rested in the government legislative building where God's ten laws were written boldly on the marble walls, cracking, the text barely readable. Each time, each place—detection. Commander Dorsey would send teams in to scout for us, six Elite soldiers at a time. They would unearth our hiding, and we, in turn, would eradicate their scouting with our Z-Colts, and our SE454s and our DR93s. Then we moved on—and on—and on.

But now The Third seems more concerned about their plans to expand their reign than our presence, if indeed they believe we even exist anymore. And we, at last, have settled, burrowed into the acres of an abandoned zoo to the northwest of the Waters of Erie, a lake much smaller now since *Jurbay* ate half our nation for lunch. We are now Colony G. In this place, a few of our citizens have been tempted to whisper the word *home*. But my job is to be the one who reminds them that we are still in a battle for existence. A fight where if we win, justice and equality will top the pyramid of government, and if we lose...well, wolves hunt in packs to take down larger prey, and we are getting larger by the day. The ultimate war is coming, and we rise as a fierce and vigilant enemy. No more running.

Chapter 1
THE CLEANER
DEGNAN

2077

When one of the 14 Deadlies took a city down, it was stomach-churning lunacy. A massive hit, quick and devastating. The Deadlies were unlike the blast site of a dirty bomb that mangled the victims in split seconds, less than a full breath, and unlike the ground zero of an atomic bomb that fried a population between the beat of the heart and the next beat. With the Deadlies there was a macabre and fatal waiting period, inhumane as the Deadly itself. A chain reaction, like dominos stacked in a line for miles, waiting for the designer of the line to tap the back of a solo domino, igniting it into motion. Once that connection—that touch—that simple push occurred, there was no stopping the progression of that single domino from hitting the next and each consecutively cascading forward until the last one had fallen away and the line lay still.

Deadly #8 hit its victims through the puff of a perfume atomizer. Everyone in the exclusive European gem store lay in the collapsed domino line which wove its way past *his* protective-suited leg and onto the sidewalk where, one by one, the people fell to the ground in a ten second death dance. He held the bottle in his hand, finger poised to continue the squirt, if necessary. It wasn't. The victims' eyes exploded from their sockets, and their tongues swelled with elephantiasis-like girth that obstructed their mouths, choking and strangling the victims. Never mind that fingers and toes scorched to charcoal. Some fell off, rolling away as the victims hit the pavement. However, an even greater horror came in the waiting. Those moments of time when the Deadly hit others and those watching knew it was coming for them. Twenty feet away from victims or halfway down the city block, they saw it approaching. The Deadly #8 rolled toward them in a domino knockdown that was unavoidable. Some ran as it approached, but most grabbed the person next to them—that "goodbye" embrace strangers have when they know the end is coming, and they share a final torturous breath.

He dropped the perfume bottle to the sidewalk and walked away through the carnage, hearing the crunch of charred appendages crackle underneath the safeguard of his boots, the only one standing in the midst of it all. He took mental notes to later enter into the scientific records that would fill the holograms of The Third. Documentation of population annihilation that would set The Third's plan for world control into action. Oh, there would be survivors—those who weren't in the path of the Deadly or perhaps held some unexplainable immunity to the toxic release. But those left would be yearning for any help The Third might send in the years following these attacks. Ironically, countries would open their doors for help from the very nation that put them in this position in the first place. That was the plan.

The plan, however, was incomplete, flawed at best. The Third turned loose the 14 Deadlies on the world, attempting to grab power without antidotes in place to counteract the evil. The Deadlies hopped across the water and settled in on their own country. The 14 Deadlies changed more than just the population number. *Jurbay*, that falling asteroid that already reduced the populace in the nation to half, had left those in the 28 remaining states as orphans or childless or in families sliced half through by the disaster. But the 14 Deadlies went far beyond the death count of *Jurbay*, leaving rotting corpses with all sorts of thriving bacteria, lying in wait for surviving settlers to arrive in the area.

———

2083

Now that The Third had abandoned Reichel, or rather were chased away by sinkholes, it needed a cleanup of the 28 remaining states in the worst of ways. The Third chose to focus the cleanup in one city only—the city of Ash to the northeast of Erie—just like Commander Dorsey had done with Reichel, the Children's Garden and the forest surrounding Reichel. They would eliminate the rot one city at a time and expand their kingdom as they sanitized. The Third went looking for someone to do it, thinking it would take decades to complete the task. They were fully aware that by the time a cleanup was done there could be so much new disease from the filth of decaying corpses that a cleanup might not be worth it, but they had to try.

It didn't take long for them to find the person for the job. The Cleaner. After all, he'd already sanitized the New Coastline as a test area for his invention. He and his mammoth crew swept into the half-eaten state that somehow survived *Jurbay* by clinging to what was left of the lake called Huron, now more of a saltwater bay, merging with the seas of the New Coastline. The only fresh water left from Huron was a tiny section, separated from what used to be the lake by a giant mudslide. They called it the "Anteater's Nose." The severed state also held fast to the reduced Waters of Erie. Superior and Michigan were gone completely. So, the Cleaner and his crew came in riding float cars like bucking broncos. They were cowboys of sorts, rescuing the New Coastline of its disease as it clung desperately to the remaining states. Perhaps the Cleaner that commanded the float cars truly wanted to sanitize the area for The 28 United's arrival when they pushed north, leaving Reichel and The Third behind, or maybe he just wanted to test his sanitation revelations before advertising them to The Third as the ultimate solution. But more likely, the man saw the value of cleaning the land and the rot upon it as his first preparation to build a market only he could conceive. He intended to suspend it forty-five feet deep in the receded Waters of Erie. The remaining lake, thirty-five miles long with an average depth of sixty-two feet, waited for his lucrative development. The Cleaner's tattoo of his submerged commerce map ran from his left wrist up the outside of his arm, wrapping around his shoulder and resting on his right clavicle. No mistake that it bore incredible accuracy, outlining the Anteater's Nose and the altered coastlines of Huron, Erie and Ontario.

What kind of a man pulled the trigger to spark the 14 Deadlies, then came back with an ironic diligence to clean it all up? One who had detached and cast away the remaining shreds of morality that begged him not to be discarded. One who in the name of science or financial gain or glory said, *I'll do more than pull the trigger. I'll create a Deadly, or a pack of them, and like Medea, send them into action—a necessary evil to accomplish an ordained plan.* The kind of man who threw a vial of Deadlies into a pool to kill a child and sent vipers down holes in an underground hideout just to see if Avery DeTornada and her comrades could fend the vipers off. Degnan. As brilliant in his scientific prowess as he was in his lack of moral code, he foresaw the problem of sanitation long before there was a reason to sanitize, long before The Third proclaimed their desperation and came to him for help.

After the Deadlies easily eradicated the larger part of The Third's citizens, they had to have someone to blame for the disease gaining a foothold right in their own country. Might as well be Degnan, the creator of the Deadlies. So, for a time, they sent him off beyond their sanitized city of Reichel to the Children's Garden, proclaiming his new rank as "pocket watch." His job: caregiver for the sons of those in command, in a remote and dilapidated library. It seemed punishment enough. But sometimes in an attempt to bury brilliance, it replicates itself and breeds a grand and risky business plan. The Third could not have imagined that at a time in the future they would need his help, for Reichel would be gone and a new city would be needed for their rule. A clean city.

———

2084

Degnan stood before a pretentious mansion, enormous in size with groomed artistic gardens and walkways leading to the twelve-foot double entry door at the center of the stately, four-story house. He noticed the effusive use of color, gushing from every bush and tree. Apparently, The Third's Commander enjoyed the variety of hues even as he demanded gray be the operative color of uniforms, housing units and factories for the populous.

Degnan stood in calm control surrounded by three buff men and one buffer woman, forming his bodyguard. This highly skilled protective squad held their brainy weapons on alert, fingers primed on triggers and eyes scouting potential targets that might threaten their employer. They were loyal to the death, and he treated them well, allowing them to eat with him when they were off-shift and providing everything they needed for a comfortable existence. He didn't need *locasa* to command devotion; manipulation through reward and a share of the vision worked just as well. And for added protection, if all else failed, two brain-swappers cuddled in his polished, leather messenger bag that hung unassumingly off his right shoulder.

He was one of the few medical experts left that understood how to swap the brains of one living organism for another, and then manipulate the gene structure of each into lethal varieties the Creator had never even thought of. His two newest treasures were half Indian red scorpion and half poison dart frog. The creatures—scorpodarts—displayed a deep burgundy on their scorpion body with extra frog legs extending from their back quarter designed to leap on targets. These blue legs allowed for jumping great distances, and the poison embedded in the frog's skin increased the threat of death, should the sting of the scorpion miss its mark. Both scorpodarts responded exclusively to a Degnan voice command.

No one rang the bell of the imposing, well-manicured building. It would be foolish. The VATs, video-audio trails installed by Commander Dorsey, were impeccable and captured every possible image outside each entry to his estate from any angle, including above and below.

A thin girl dressed in the gray uniform of The Third opened the door, flanked by two brain-swappers of her own, much bigger than Degnan's concealed scorpodarts. Commander Dorsey, too, had maximized the use of swappers to add to his defense from any unforeseen circumstance. These two swappers, nimble and sleek like leopards, flaunted T-Rex heads, both an admirable and formidable result of genome design. These two leprexes swayed their upper bodies in perfect unison, like they were listening to music, keeping their sinewy lower bodies still. "Here for what reason?" she asked with a voice so hoarse it sounded raw and far too husky for girl of her frail demeanor. Accompanying her question, two purrs emerged from the caverns of the leprexes' throats. All three sets of eyes focused on the man in the middle of the protective squad.

"Tell Dorsey the Cleaner's here," said Degnan.

"Wait," she said and turned to go, but Degnan would have nothing of the wait.

"Dorsey gets once chance. *He* invited *me*. I'm sure you know this." The swappers were swishing their leopard tails in irritated synchronization. "I follow you now, or Dorsey can get another lunch guest." The leprexes' purrs turned to the subtlest of growls, and the girl's steel gray eyes showed no significant acknowledgment. Nonetheless, she had to be processing. The slightest nod Degnan's way indicated he may follow.

Degnan and his squad tracked the tails of the swappers through a foyer that ended at a huge archway, an entry to another room. The girl stopped just under the arch and said, "Commander, the Cleaner's here." Degnan stepped two paces forward, close enough to see Dorsey raise his hand, using only his fingers to beckon Degnan in.

Commander Dorsey was a continued picture of the fitness of command, his silver hair picking up a glint from the sun that shone through the open French doors at the side of the room. The light, filtering through the early morning, fell upon a small table with a linen tablecloth. It was immaculately set, with a centerpiece of mustard-colored tulips standing erect in a cut crystal vase. The silver plates and cutlery were polished to the point of reflection. Dorsey stood as Degnan entered the room, offering him a glass of cognac.

"Hennessy?" questioned Degnan.

"Your favorite," responded Dorsey.

"Appropriate for the finest of agreements," said Degnan with the slightest smile of arrogance sliding to the corners of his mouth like a racehorse easing to the gate, anticipating the sound of the starter gun. Degnan watched Dorsey, and without a break in their locked-in eye contact, he said, "Thank you, Dorsey."

He studied Dorsey, looking for the "tell." Most people had one. He knew that through playing poker with Avery, McGinty and Shaw, and through playing gin rummy with Pasha, Ulysses and Pepper. That giveaway detail imperceptible to others—that clue, that habit that tipped his hand and pitched the game one way or the other. Years of employment inside The Third gave Degnan constant opportunity to observe the Commander, memorizing the details of the muscle action in his face, recording the mannerisms most would say were only part of the normalcy of life. And there it was, ever so slight, that pulsing thin vein at the side of his temple, probably caused from an indecipherable clenched jaw. Small, minute. But it was there, and Degnan recognized the tell the second he'd addressed Dorsey without the proper title of "Commander."

Degnan knew no one called Dorsey by his first name. Maybe he didn't have one, like many of them, himself included. Some had adopted monikers or had gone so long by a last name that the first had become irrelevant.

Always referred to as "Commander Dorsey," the casual greeting Degnan had the audacity to use irked this man in command, and Degnan saw it. The tell told everything. This was going to be fun.

"Have a seat," said Dorsey and sat down, not waiting for Degnan to sit first. Degnan didn't sit at all, crossing slowly to the open doors and looking out on the perfectly trimmed gardens.

"Degnan?" asked the man of beauty, his silvery hair just short enough to spike, and his black eyes attempting to bore through Degnan's back, but falling short. "What kind of payment are you looking for to sanitize—"

"Sanitize what?" Degnan turned to face Dorsey. "Sanitize it all?"

"Only the 28 remaining states—our part of the world. The rest of the world, I'll take care of in a decade when they need me most desperately."

"That's a large order." Dorsey's muscular frame tightened, like he wanted to throw a punch. He didn't like Degnan playing with him, and he just wanted a straight answer. Degnan knew Dorsey would never take a swing, and that Dorsey realized Degnan was no longer the drugged-out pocket watch of half a decade ago, babysitting Dorsey's brat of a kid, Raghill, and his little minions Morris and Carles. In fact, in the year since Reichel fell, Degnan had reinvented himself—his look, his presence, his power. Now Degnan had Dorsey by the throat, and he wasn't about to let go.

"Not looking for payment," said Degnan as he walked to his designated side of the table. "I barter what's due me." They were only six feet apart, glaring at one another across the tips of the corralled tulips, sitting in the vase in the middle of the table. Degnan couldn't help but notice the Commander wore the customary gray of all The Third's citizens, but his Nehru jacket was braided around the high collar with silver strands of thread, and the string of buttons cascading down the front of the jacket were fashioned with black diamonds set in a circle of mother-of-pearl. His silk pants were so gray they were almost black, sewn from a fabric Degnan knew Dorsey had obtained from a nation he'd invaded with the Deadlies a few years before. But this hard-assed warrior had nothing on Degnan, whose khaki-colored suit and red tie would have commanded a $3500 price tag pre-*Jurbay*. They both shared an enjoyment of the spoils of war—Dorsey with his direct involvement as a commander and Degnan always enlightened with the spill-over. That's what Degnan's market was all about.

"Barter what?" Dorsey asked and expected an immediate answer. Degnan gave him none, making Dorsey wait. He didn't like it. Dorsey's stare never wavered from its hold on Degnan, but there was something significant about Degnan's return gaze—a smirk behind his eyes. Dorsey urgently needed Degnan, and they both knew it.

Degnan took a hefty swig of the cognac and said to Dorsey, "I want you to build me this." Then he tossed an intricately designed, underwater market blueprint on the table top between them. Dorsey's fingers twitched. Degnan knew Dorsey wanted to pick up the paper immediately and was sure the Commander was trying to restrain himself, feigning indifference and attempting to show control. Finally, with finesse, Dorsey picked up the market drawing and studied it.

"An underwater market?" Degnan nodded to his question. "What's the point?"

"Clean. Hanging there in Erie, suspended. Forty-five feet submerged, connecting the East with the states left in the West. Out of the way. Out of war."

"There is no war."

"Not now, but there will be. You know it. You have your own little kingdom on land, like you always have, and I control the hanging commerce. We stay out of each other's way." Degnan paused, letting the division of power sink in.

Dorsey stopped looking at Degnan for the first time since he had arrived. Now all he focused on was the design. Then, after a full two minutes of study, he folded the paper to a quarter of its size. He twirled it in and out of his fingers, from the little finger to the ring finger to the middle to the pointer, and then back again. Each time he did this, the crease at the center of his brow furrowed and etched a deeper wrinkle than the moment before. Degnan knew the concept of sharing power, even if Degnan's power was submerged, was one Dorsey was not accustomed to.

As the design flipped by Dorsey's ring finger, he grabbed it between his thumb and pointer finger, extending it at Degnan. "If I accept this trade—your underwater kingdom—you're going to have to give me more of your plan."

"Ha. More information? I cleaned the New Coastline while you were playing commander of a sinkhole in Reichel." He spoke with that one-up attitude that he knew would drive Dorsey crazy. "I cleaned your city of Ash and swept away the filth and rot of the entire surrounding state so you could have a place to settle your empire after the sinkholes in Reichel sucked that city to the underground. You don't need 'more' information."

"But how? How do you clean a nation?" asked Dorsey.

"You don't get that answer. You get the finished product—or lack of it—because all of it—the rotting—the disease—they just go away."

"Completion date?" asked Dorsey. "And I want a guarantee."

"Two years, three at the most. The entire nation."

"And your market?" asked Dorsey.

"My market?" Degnan pushed away from the table and crossed to the archway at the edge of the room where his four sentinels stood at attention. "Well, you can start building tomorrow." He placed himself inside the rectangle of the four protectors. "It's kind of like the pyramids. You get enough people working on a project, you're going to see steady progress. But unlike the pyramids, it's not going to take ten years to build. This pharaoh's going to be operating in his market by the time your nation's antiseptic."

They struck the deal in under an hour without the necessity of releasing one bullet, a scorpodart or a leprex.

This was the first of two deals Degnan would proctor for his market. But the second deal, years down the road, and the person Degnan would strike it with—now, that would be much more difficult.

Chapter 2
BEHIND THE MARKET
AVERY DETORNADA

2088

Five years ago, we left Reichel burning behind us, sucked under by the sinkholes that reminded us we were susceptible to *Jurbay's* lasting temperament. Now, our scouting party is thirty miles from the zoo. Shaw and the mappers had been here earlier in the week and wanted us to see the damage the 14 Deadlies had done years before. We hadn't seen that in our previous explorations. Besides Shaw and me, our explorers include Morris, now fifteen, taller and looking older, but still every bit the scholar; Raghill, the same age as Morris, muscular and buffed up far beyond what a teen should be; and Annalynn, thirteen, her curly brown hair flying wild around her dark skin, and her clichés now flavored with the sarcasm of an adulthood she has yet to see. They are part of

Shaw's teenage mappers. Ulysses, one of the GEBs who had won our confidence and proven his loyalty to The 28 United, is on his first scouting trip with us. And of course, McGinty journeys by my side to contribute his weapons expertise, but everyone knows it's more than that. We're inseparable in command and like glue in our personal lives. Shaw, McGinty, Pasha and I have been friends for a decade—training together, living together, warring together. To hide the relationship between McGinty and me that has intensified from trusted friend to loyal confidant, and now to unshakeable love is not possible in the company of those who know us so well.

Another travels with us. On this longest scouting expedition beyond the New Coastline, *he* waits for me. I don't have to see him to know he's there. I sense his presence.

We approach a city southwest of Huron, and without warning the landscape changes. We find it necessary to side-step the bones of the 14 Deadlies' carnage. While much of the land we encountered had been sanitized, there are still pockets like these that serve as reminders of the viciousness of The Third. Years ago, when we all ran from the sinking Reichel, Clef, Old Soul and the minstrels led hundreds of The 28 United north to the New Coastline. Yet, they'd seen none of this rotting display we now confront. Back then it seemed as if our pathway to the New Coastline, and the area we ended up inhabiting, had either been whitewashed by some unexplainable messiah, or that section of the world had mysteriously avoided the invasion of the 14 Deadlies—hardly likely as the population would have remained. And like everywhere else on our pathway away from Reichel, we'd discovered any remains of citizens were gone as well. Here, while the flesh no longer clings to the bones, dissolved by the toxins and picked apart by buzzards, the bacteria rages, waiting to host the next devastation. We wear our protective masks and gloves, our pants tightly tucked in the edges of our boots.

Two hours later, on the outskirts of a city we can't find a name for, the bones disappear and a thin coat of ash emerges. A grayish powder lingers on the vehicles rusted from lack of use, collects on fallen street signs and occasionally swirls up from the city streets, disturbed by the marching of our feet or the breath of an unexpected wind. We take off our masks and gloves. There is no disease here. Sanitized.

About a mile past the housing units of the abandoned city, several stands of magnolia trees line a slow-flowing river. We draw closer.

"I'll keep watch," says Shaw. He always prefers to shoulder a brainy and an anti-brainy rather than manage water purification peps and canteens needing a fill-up. I allow my gear to slide off my shoulder and lift out two purification peps from the side pocket of my pack, one for Shaw's canteen and one for mine. My canteen glides through the water. The coolness of the liquid covers my hands and refreshes me, easing for a moment my thoughts that there may be a party from The Third lurking anywhere. The breeze lifts my escaping wisps of hair and interrupts my vision with strands of dusty brown, lots of ginger highlights in the mix, reminding me of Quinn's russet curls. Our genetic connection evidenced in the smallest of ways. I miss her. Chapman and I haven't seen her in almost a year. A boy needs his grandmother.

I smell him first. Not really *him*, but that constant extension of his persona, the Hennessy. Annoying pricks of fear cover my torso. I wonder how anyone could have gotten past Shaw. He's always on the ready.

And now, here he is. I force myself to turn slowly and face—Degnan. Degnan. Standing eight feet from me. He points his Z-colt straight-armed at my head, and in his other hand a battered tin cup is raised in salute to me.

"Drink?" he asks. I see the others in my party standing sixty paces behind him, trapped both by the threat of what he might do to me, but also by a contingent of three fit, aggressive men and one woman, who I imagine are completely prepared to take my comrades down. To get this close to us is almost impossible. McGinty, Shaw, and I have been Elite trained, and while I lost my Elite training to *locasa*, five years has given me ample time to train and regain most of what was taken from me. We are always ready for surprise attacks from The Third. We know their maneuvers, but Degnan and his independent protectorate are new to us. We haven't seen him since we lost track of him in the forest when we escaped from Reichel. My guess is that Degnan's guards came in from above us, maybe utilizing the trees. We will not be surprised by him again.

I look at Shaw, his machismo deflated, and his brainy disarmed. McGinty, held back by Ulysses, appears bent on getting his hands on Degnan in spite of the arsenal pointed at him and the others. Degnan has us. What can I do? I take the tin cup from Degnan and motion him to join me by some boulders clustered at the edge of the river. He follows me, returning his Z-Colt to his shoulder holster, extracting a flask from the inside pocket of his jacket and joining me by the river for a drink. The others start to move my way, but I motion them to remain.

"Where's your son?" asks Degnan

"Far away from you," I answer.

"That's no way to talk to Uncle Degnan."

"Humans aren't related to reptilians."

"I can tell we're going to need more than one drink." The arrogant smirk on his face that I remember decorates his demeanor.

We sit facing each other, taking more than sips of Hennessey. Then, for a while we gaze at the river. The searing pain he's branded in my memories boils up, haunting every part of me, my body cold, yet sweating from brow to palms. I count off the list of personal losses he was directly responsible for. Prospero, a library boy we'd befriended, his flesh scorched off his body by Degnan's toss of a Deadly in the boy's direction. Degnan sent the vipers slithering down the ceiling holes of the horseshoe tunnel in Reichel, venom ready for attack, just to see if we could defend ourselves when snakes outnumbered us all. The father of the 14 Deadlies changed the context of our world forever. The rage and injustice of it all begins to overtake me and my heart, so filled with anger, like an over-stretched wine skin ready to burst, now pricked by needle-sharp reminders of the paradox Degnan has become. Each pin-prick is a different set of memories, contrasting the ones of horror and momentarily defusing the hatred I feel for this man. Degnan led us to the underground horseshoe tunnel that allowed the destruction of the GEB recipes and the demolition of the hundreds of GEBs that lay in wait for activation. Degnan gave Ulysses and Pepper their beginnings— their personalities—strange and frequently unbalanced, but family to us. Degnan saved my life from a viper with open jaws ready to puncture my jugular. I want to forget those memories, but time and destiny will not allow it. Suddenly my heart doesn't feel so stretched anymore.

After minutes of silence I ask him, "Why track us down? We were done—you and me. You've got everything you'll ever need. Everything you could want in this world."

His laugh unmistakably targets me with his conceit, as only he can do. "Track you down?" mocks Degnan,

"Don't flatter yourself. I've been one step ahead of you since we parted on our way out of Reichel." And now, in this moment, with horrifying awareness, *I know* that the eerie premonition that has hung over me the entire time we've been scouting is motivated and real. Suddenly I imagine seeing Degnan's fingerprints in the gray ash of our march through this city—his handprints on the rooftops of the decaying cars we'd passed, his footprints on the collection of powdery deposits at the base of street lights—he's imprinted everywhere. Somehow, in his Degnan way, that I always think I understand but never do, he makes the bones, the skeletons, the bacteria, the carnage disappear. Degnan reads my thoughts. I hate that.

He says, "Disease breeds more disease, and I get rid of it before it grabs hold of command and scores a victory. I clean the rotting human garbage."

"How could you clean it all?"

He lounges on a stack of boulders like a king on a cushioned throne. "Still underestimating me, are you, Avery?" I say nothing. "Since before we burned Reichel I had the formula to spray the death away. Poof." His eyes confidently dance with mischief both childlike and demon-like. "I hold power, and that means The Third hates me and adores me in the same breath."

The crack of a brainy fills the air. This is not a shot from Degnan's protectorate, so it must be The Third. Degnan and I both dive for cover behind the boulders, even though I know hiding will be completely useless 'cause a brainy bullet tracks its target until it makes bone-shattering contact. A brainy fires more like a shotgun with a single pop, not like an assault weapon with a spray of multiple rounds. It will chase the target around a corner, up a tree, in a hole, even on the backside of a boulder. The first brainy finds its mark. It drills one of the three men from Degnan's force.

I see Shaw and McGinty dive for their weapons stacked against a tree by Degnan's people who had previously disarmed them. Now, Degnan's troops don't stop Shaw or McGinty from grabbing their weapons. They know McGinty is the inventor of the anti-brainy, and he'd mounted the brainy and the anti-brainy in tandem: same weapon, separate barrels, independent triggers. I hear the crack of two more brainies fill the air and then counter shots by Shaw and McGinty who pop off two anti-brainy rounds. McGinty fires a third. Now our bullets chase The Third's, and our anti-brainies hunt their brainies in a race for our lives.

Degnan's three remaining people scale the trunks of the trees to scout the attackers. I know McGinty's invention works because I can see the anti-brainies track and collide with the brainies, causing mini-explosions in the air, one right above my head, so close I feel the heat. I see Morris and Annalynn run for cover in the grove of trees. Ulysses follows at a distance, looking nothing like a soldier and every bit the weird GEB he is. A volatile target with his bald head and brightly colored kaftan waving around his legs.

One more time, I hear that unmistakable high piercing zing of the brainies, coming for us. One brief second ticks before Shaw and McGinty send their counter shots our way. Degnan and I fire our Z-Colts, hoping to create some diversion so that Ulysses can at least be out of visual contact from our attackers, but I know brainies don't discriminante, don't need to see their targets.

I yell at Degnan, "Tell your people not use their brainies or our anti-brainies will shut them down too. Choose another weapon."

"They don't need telling," he shouts back and nods his acknowledgement of willingness to cover me as I race for Ulysses, joining Morris, Raghill and Annalynn in an effort to get him beyond the tree line. His feet don't get a chance to work as we drag him over rocks and debris. Just before we reach the grove of trees, I see the mini-explosion five feet away in the air as an anti-brainy outwits a brainy, then another burst of fire, cancelling a second brainy right before it should have connected with Ulysses.

There's one more brainy out there, and I see it speeding toward us, the anti-brainy in pursuit. Just as the anti-brainy is about to combat the brainy, it hits Ulysses' thigh, burrowing in his skin. His eyes are enormous, but he's a GEB with an inhuman pain tolerance. Annalynn takes his hand. "Just repeat with me, 'There's no place like home. There's no place…'" Morris covers her mouth to shut her up and the grove is silent. No more shots.

Shaw and McGinty rush to Ulysses, followed by Raghill. I hear and count six single shots at the south side of the tree line, and Degnan says, "Bye-bye, Elite scouts."

The anti-brainy that should be diving after the brainy slows to a floating position directly above Ulysses' leg. The only thing worse than the brainy consuming Ulysses' leg would be the anti-brainy making chase and blowing up inside his leg. But it doesn't. It hovers. Then right before our eyes it sucks the brainy from Ulysses' leg, drawing it fifteen feet into the air and exploding it.

It's several seconds before anyone speaks. Then Degnan says, "I've never seen that before."

"Been perfecting the design," says McGinty.

"I guess," I murmur, staring at him in disbelief and watching Morris tend to Ulysses' injury.

Annalynn strokes Ulysses' bald head. Tears roll down his face, and he whispers, "There's no place like home." He looks at me with deep sincerity. "I wish it was Valentine's Day." We all wait for more. "Send cards, not bullets."

I look suspiciously at Annalynn. "Valentine's Day has been archived for years."

"I'm a history scholar," says Annalynn.

"You're a culture junkie," says McGinty, "And the queen of clichés."

"There's nothing wrong with passing a little history onto the good-guy-GEB-citizens of The 28 United," says Annalynn.

Ulysses pulls himself together, getting to his feet. "Pepper will be worried."

Shaw pats Ulysses on the shoulder a little too roughly, stowing away his unused knife.

McGinty places his hand on Ulysses' bald head for a brief second. McGinty is an expert at brief but lasting blessings. I help Morris rip some gauze cloth from the first aid bag, and he ties it around Ulysses' leg. I wonder why he doesn't use the cauterization tool, but then I notice there is a surprising lack of blood. Not sure if that's something Degnan and Pasha designed when they were handing out the activation traits for Ulysses and Pepper, or if it has something to do with McGinty's anti-brainy experiments.

"Ow," says Ulysses as Raghill gives the tie on Morris' bandage a secure knot.

"Hush," I say. "You don't have the same nerve sensors as we do. That didn't really hurt."

"You're supposed to say 'ow.'"

"No, you're supposed to say nothing. We're on a mission." I try to sound firm, but these GEBs, even though ridiculously related to Raben, by genetic recipe, have gotten under my skin and into my heart. For five years, Pepper and Ulysses have proved their allegiance and helped The 28 United in ways no human could.

How ironic that Raben, as a GEB, almost took down the entire 28 United, yet these two have become a part of our mongrel heritage. We keep inviting the strange and unique to take a seat at our family table. I would never change that.

Degnan's three remaining protectorates drag the six dead soldiers of The Third in our direction, piling them together about thrity feet away. The woman opens a gear bag and takes out an oblong container with a nozzle on the front. She pulls down a face mask from her helmet that seals at the neck so that nothing is exposed on her body.

Degnan calls to her, "Miranda, any communication on their coms as to what they're to do next?"

"None," she says. Degnan nods. She releases a trigger by the nozzle, and a gas is slowly emitted from the container. It covers the pile of bodies, teeming like a swarm of bees. I start to pull Morris and Annalynn back, but Degnan raises his hand for me to stop. "Its range is only four feet," he says. We watch the pile disintegrate, and all that's left is a grayish ash, dissipating in the wind.

"Like I said: 'poof.' There's bound to be hidden pockets, overlooked, like the one you encountered today on your scouting party. We'll take care of it before we go."

"The bodies?"

"The bodies, the bacteria, the disease waiting for curiosity-seekers, the ash. All gone. A pure 28 United once again—with the exception of the impurity of The Third, of course. That's an issue of character, not science."

"Character's not in your wheelhouse. So, no comment." I walk to the river bank, hiding a smile that flirts on the edge of admiration for this man I've always despised. I sense he follows me.

"Let me guess," I say, "You have a network."

"Always."

I turn to him. "A network completely loyal to you."

"To the core."

"They'd do anything for you—"

"'Cause I've done everything for them." Now he's climbed the boulders, assuming a position of power.

"And I know Dorsey paid you to do his 'cleaning' with something much more valuable than extinct currency or newly formed trade coupons." I climb toward him up the pinnacle, steady, confident. I stand in front of him, opening the inside pocket of his vest and extracting the flask of Hennessy. I sense there is a bargain lurking at the forefront of his mind, and I am sure it involves me. I pour myself another, then retreat down to my riverside rock, getting as far away from him as possible, yet still in earshot and looking up at him for the next move.

"Let's just say while my pockets are lined with the contracts of The Third, I value my life more. They're flaky—"

"*They're* flaky? So, what is it? You got your own military as a back door if they turn on you?"

"I abhor violence, Avery," he says with a complete calm that would make a stranger believe him in a flash, but I'm no stranger. "I'm not interested in a military coup. I've assembled a trade network and that is all." I wait for more. "A very *large* trade network."

"And that includes your cleaning team?" I laugh at the absurdity of it all, but it's Degnan, and he did dig the tunnel that gave us access to Reichel's secrets. Nothing is inconceivable.

"Exactly. But we didn't use any brooms or dustpans. Much more high tech than that."

"Of course."

"We made quick work of it, the destruction of human remains. The sanitation of cities, roadsides, office buildings. The disappearance of the afterlife of disease, the purification of our world for—for us. This work force belongs exclusively to me. Not The Third."

"Do they know that?"

"Of course they do."

"Where'd you ever get the workforce for the scope of cleaning an entire nation?"

"Not everyone swears allegiance to The 28 United, Avery. And not everyone is subjected to The Third." The sheer magnitude of that statement that there might be thousands—tens of thousands of people with no allegiance to anything or anyone thrills me. Terrifies me. We have the potential of shutting down a selfish tyranny and bringing justice back to government. We could offer protection to the thousands of the anonymous that live invisibly in regions we haven't scouted yet, maybe even in areas we might have walked right past, not knowing they exist. Perhaps they hide in fear of us as much as the terror of The Third. There must be a way to change that.

Degnan draws my mind back to the immediate as he hatches his plan. "I've been thinking of alliances," he says.

"And the fact that we don't have one?"

"And the fact that we should have one." I take a final sip of the Hennessy. The aroma almost relaxes me, but I remember that in spite of a quiet river and a couple of shared drinks, with Degnan there is no peace.

"My trade network—" he begins.

"Oh, you've finally got the market you always wanted? I don't want to imagine what you're selling. I'd call it a Dark Market, but it'd be an understatement."

"I'm providing services, Avery. The market has something for everyone—even you."

I study him while he sits on the crest of the rock pile. There's something distinctly different about him. Clean. Fit. Self-possessed. Right now, I don't find it difficult to imagine him as an officer in The Third, though I know he's much too independent to ever work under their rule again. He's hardly the image of the Degnan I'd met six years ago, when he was a drugged-out pocket watch, trying to take care of the abandoned children belonging to the officers and commanders of The Third in the Foxglove Library of Reichel.

"So, what?" I ask. "You want to hire us as your market's protective detail for the next decade or two? Keep your market safe from the changing whims of Dorsey?"

"Maybe. Even though I've groomed a few brain-swappers to help with that job." He pulls a folded paper from the chest pocket of his armored vest, glances at it with an irritatingly haughty smile and lets it flutter to the ground, landing by my feet. I'm not used to seeing paper, and this piece is aged and worn.

"Look at it," he says.

"Only 'cause I like your Hennessy." I pick the paper up, then find a smooth, flat rock to sit on, a distance away from Degnan. I study the paper.

"You'll never change, DeTornada."

"Oh, I've changed. Seeing your husband die while you hold a Z-Colt in one hand and your newborn in the other does that to a person."

"Put Raben to rest. GEBs don't die. They're just recycled."

I pull my Z-Colt from its shoulder holster and shoot a bullet off the boulder directly below where he stands before he even has a chance to draw on me again. "I assume you need both feet?"

"That would be my first choice."

"Then watch your mouth." Did he flinch? I don't think so.

"Look at the paper," he says, once again lounging on his stone kingdom, sipping from his flask while he stares at me. I'm a specimen for his humor and a target for his plan.

As I study the paper, I understand right away I'm looking at a sketch of his market. "Okay, so I get it. You didn't want your market in some cave or back alley. You went classy on us, and had Dorsey build you something to serve the upper tier clients. But why underwater? You sanitized all the land. You can take whatever you want. You always do anyway."

"Careful..." says Degnan, and kicks a loose stone in my direction.

"Why underwater?"

"You really think this world will get by without another 14 Deadlies attack?"

"Not as long as you're alive."

"I'll never create another Deadly."

"Oh, found your moral compass, have you?"

"I've always had a moral compass. You and I just define it differently."

I let that sink in for a second and say, "My compass pulls me toward justice. Yours pulls you toward Degnan."

"Good calls to good, Avery."

"I'm supposed to know what that means?"

"This deal—this trade—works for both of us."

"Yeah? Well, you've got us trapped here so spill it. What is this 'trade' you're talking about? Make it quick. We've got things to do."

"I know. You're saving the world," he says. I stare at him. "This fits your job description, Avery." He points at the paper in my hand. "For you and The 28 United, it's not what's incorporated in the blueprint of the market. It's what's not included. Behind the market."

"Tell me."

"You see how there's a series of cars—like the old subway cars only streamlined, lightweight, durable? Then running parallel to the cars of the market, from end to end of the lake—thirty-five miles—a transport system."

I analyze the map again. "I see the commerce cars—your *Dark Market*." I emphasize the words just so he knows that no matter how classy his location is, his market is still for the pleasure and profit of Degnan only. "And I see the transport system."

He is silent for a moment then says, "Yes. Transport tubes—or glides. They carry customers and military from the city of Ash all the way to the other end of the lake—just to the east of where your little hideaway exists." My breathing stops, but I do not give away the fear I feel that Degnan might actually know where we have settled. I realize The Third occasionally searches for us, but I also know they are unaware of where The 28 United is. *Could Degnan really know?*

"Your little hideaway where animals, once caged for observation, are now long gone, their former habitat grown over, camouflaged with the flora and fauna of the

New Coastline." *He knows,* He stares at me and I can feel his eyes watching, hesitating, perhaps to see if I will flare at him or question him, but I do neither. Then, maybe trying to reassure me that he has no evil intent, he says, "Avery, I don't think like The Third. They don't know where you settled."

I ignore him. "You said 'good' for both of us. All I see here is a market where all the benefits belong to you."

"On the back side of the commerce section—the market section—is a third parallel set of cars."

"I don't see it on the design."

"That's the point. You're holding the blueprints I showed Dorsey. You and I are discussing the design that's up here." He points to his forehead. "I call it the Warrior Strip. And when I say *warrior,* I mean you. And yours, of course."

"Why?"

"You need a way to get to Ash, to send in more sub-terraneans and a way to check in with the ones you already planted inside." There he goes again. How does he know about our subterraneans? Still, I give away none of my concerns and insecurities. "I need protection. Protection for my market," Degnan says.

"I thought you had protection!" I march with anger to the bottom of the stack of boulders, sick of this banter, sick of the mystery—sick of him. My voice rises, my irritation evident. "You said you had your pet brain-swappers and your market guards—your people. You don't need us." I glance over at the others. McGinty and Shaw, their weapons on the ready. Morris, Raghill and Annalynn fussing over Ulyssess. Degnan's guards. All are now motionless, staring in our directions. Can they hear us?

Degnan stands and begins to climb down the boulders. "I have a small protective force. It's not enough. When the war erupts—" I open my mouth to argue, but he continues. "—and it *will* erupt. I want your unconditional protection for the market. For me. No arguments, no new deals, no negotiable trades—just unquestionable protection in exchange for daily access to Ash through the Warrior Strip, without the threat of discovery. Their secrets can be your secrets for a simple exchange." I knew when we were running for shelter in Red Grove five years ago, and I was trying to convince my son Chapman to stall his birth until we found a way to reach the New Coastline—I knew that sometime Degnan and I would meet again. There's way too much history between us and too many unsettled accounts for him to just fade away. He wanted a dominant position in The Third's trade community. He wanted their dependence on him. He got both, but Degnan, like me, knows The Third can molt and shed the camaraderie of commerce for a new coat of war. They are chameleons transforming to any identity that serves them. Degnan knows that, and his plan from the beginning lay not only in the Dark Market itself, but behind the Dark Market in the Warrior Strip—his guarantee, through me, that in the midst of conflict his own domain would remain protected. Degnan's always wanted control on his own terms. Maybe Morris should tell him humans don't control destiny.

"This *Warrior Strip*? It's got its own transportation? Its own set of glides?"

"No. It has its own entrance and exit—underwater, with some options here and there, but quick transport from one end of the market to the other is by glide."

"With the customers? The military?"

"Exactly. You dress like them. Uniforms. Nondescript—"

"I remember."

"And you'll make sure you never ride in the same transport glide with any of them. You go in with your own people. That's it. No one will know."

"How soon until you build this Warrior Strip and give us access to behind the market?" I ask. Degnan nods at his protective squad. Miranda reaches into a large military duffel and begins to toss packages at us, wrapped in reflective material. Shaw, McGinty and I all get one. The others do not.

"Open them," says Degnan. "It's Christmas."

"What's Christmas?" asks Ulysses.

"Reindeer, red noses and fat guys," says Annalynn, but before she can continue, Morris shuts her down with a look equivalent to Shaw's ten-inch blade.

From my package, I pull the all-too-familiar drab coverall, restyled to look more like a uniform. The Third's uniform. Five years ago, we ran from Reichel with its flames burning at our backs, and I swore I would never put that uniform on again, no matter what. I hold the uniform up, realizing it's my exact size. I look at Shaw and McGinty, and all I can say is, "Gray."

Chapter 3
THROUGH A GLASS DARKLY
AVERY DETORNADA

Less than a week after Degnan tossed us our uniforms, I stand, dressed as a soldier of The Third, before a door to a tool shed in an uninhabited residential district nine miles from the zoo. McGinty's by my side. Our Council had agreed with my proposal that the two of us scout the underwater Dark Market first, report back to them, and we would all discuss how Degnan's offer might be used to our advantage. Tapping more information about The Third from our discoveries in the Warrior Strip of the market would definitely be a plus. I have found our Council invaluable. While I am considered the leader of The 28 United and continue to hone my sixth sense as part of my assets, the combined wisdom of Clef, Old

Soul, McGinty, Shaw, Pasha, Morris and Quinn (when she's around) have proven a strong combination to protect us from rash decisions and personal agendas. Our debates and arguments are lively, but our conclusions generally end in a unanimous decision based on facts, track record and gut instinct.

McGinty opens the door to the tool shed, and we step inside a small, dirty space with stacks of old rags, worn garden tools, and (as promised) under one of the piles, a rusted manhole cover. McGinty finds an iron hook with a long handle and we pry the cover up and climb down a steel ladder into a cramped waterproof room. McGinty tugs at the cover above him, allowing the aged hinge to release and latch and secure the lid for the manhole.

Every inch of the low ceiling and walls shine with a coating of polished metal, immaculately clean, and on the far wall just six feet away from where we entered, a hatch is mounted. It had been vividly described to us by Miranda, one of Degnan's four personal guards we'd encountered by the riverbank outside the unnamed city. Miranda stands six foot one, a muscular specimen, with skin like a pit bull, no extra anywhere on her body. I recited her descriptions of what to expect so many times last night that Chapman began to recite them with me. *There will be no swim gear or breathing tubes. The hatch opens below the market on the back side—the side without windows. When you exit the holding room beneath the tool shed, you will be on the north side of Erie, sixty feet underwater and fifty feet away from the entry hatch of the Warrior Strip at the beginning of the market.*

McGinty and I prepare exactly as Miranda instructed. We breathe deeply, slowly prepping our lungs for the length of time needed to hold our breath. The prep is not just for the distance we will swim from where we are now to the underwater tubular entrance leading to the Warrior Strip, but we hold our breath for the opening of this hatch that will fill the underground holding room rapidly and release us into Erie. I am terrified. I know what it means to open this circular exit—the churning water soon to spill in, consuming the space with its power and force. I can't help but think about the battle in the History Labyrinth pool, pregnant with Chapman and so enormous with hate for Borden. Together my mother and I killed him in the pools. Irony once again weaves its way through the water, throwing me a challenge I'd rather not take.

McGinty clutches my hand for a moment, definitely not part of Miranda's instructions. Then he turns the wheel on the hatch as I press my back against the ladder leading to the sealed manhole cover above. All the breathing preparations are going out the window as nerves fight to constrict my windpipe. The clogs inside the hatch click with each turn of the wheel. Water seeps in around the entry. My breathing turns from deep, steady, consistent, to quick and erratic. And then it doesn't matter.

The water surges in with a force that crushes, but only for the twenty seconds it takes to fill the transition room. I feel McGinty's hand squeeze mine with that same kind of power, but I can't see him through the turbulence of Erie as she swirls to fill the empty space with a reminder of her supremacy. As soon as the water stills we swim through the hatch. McGinty, as instructed, turns a small dial on the outside of the entrance. Miranda promised it would drain the interior room of excess water and reseal the hatch. I go first, pushing away from the hatch, feeling the strength of my legs and arms working together. I frog-kick my way through Erie. My panic eases and, even though I know I only have so much breath to reach the market entrance, calm settles over me. McGinty has caught up and is swimming by my side.

Searching for the entrance at the bottom of the market, I remember Miranda saying, "You'll know it when you see it."

"Specifics?" I asked her, but Degnan had called her to another room, and she was gone with incredible speed the second she heard his voice. My question remained unanswered, and my curiosity stirred, but at the same time the worries I always felt when leaving Chapman confronted me—unsure if I would return.

Urgent, out of breath, we swim along the hull of each car. Hidden behind the Dark Market, no one would ever expect this Warrior Strip existed. If anyone should ever choose to go looking, they would find no windows here on the backside. It simply appears to be the outside shell that supports the relevant part of the structure, the market itself.

Where is the entrance? My lungs are burning. Then I point at a white circle on the underside of the hanging market. It is a child-like painting of what is left of our nation. The 28 remaining states with their new coastline sculpted out and still looking strange to me. Of course, inside the circle there are no words indicating this is our symbol. We don't have to see the words to remember the way the artists had painted them on the canvas hanging two stories high in the Red Grove command center. *The 28 United* was engraved on our spirits. While to anyone else it might look just like a map of what remains, it is our emblem—those 28 connected states hanging onto one another as the Pacific laps at the new shore to the west of our nation. This is our image, our entrance.

I splash through the entry tube to the Warrior Strip. I gasp for air, McGinty close behind.

"You okay?" McGinty asks as he holds my face in his hands, demanding my focus on his eyes.

"Okay," I say, staring at him through clumps of wet hair.

"Make it through without thinking about Borden?"

"Who?" I quip.

"Yeah, that's what I thought." I want to put the memory of Borden behind me now, like I've tried so many other times. McGinty and I face the waiting vacuum suck and are dry in seconds. "You could let the memory drown," he says.

"It's that easy?" I ask.

"I didn't mean to say it was easy."

"Your suggestions on how to do that—drown the memory?" His face is close to mine now.

"Think about something very pleasant." I don't move my face away.

"Like?"

"Your future."

I break away from him. "Oh, so now we all have a future? When did that happen?" I move a short distance from the hatch to the wall of the Warrior Strip, where I see a framed design of the Dark Market secured in a water-tight container made of a material we've been making as a substitute for plastic for over a year at the Energy Concourse several miles beyond the zoo. Yet here's that same material utilized in Degnan's market. Later I will question him about that. This design I study of the market is more intricate than the one Degnan tossed me at the river, and at last I see his full intentions.

McGinty crosses to the units lining one wall of the Warrior Strip. Every unit is a locker with exactly enough space for the identical gear bags that rest in each. A name plate is screwed to every unit and awaits a name, except for the five units already labeled for myself, McGinty, Pasha and Shaw and Raghill. *Why Raghill?* I wonder. McGinty pushes the button by his name plate and mine, and three claws appear from the sides of each locker, activating and loading the packs with dried fruit, explosives, weapons, ammunition, rope, water, a scanner, first aid supplies, and a hologram cylinder. While I continue to pour over the design plans, he opens the units and grabs our gear bags, handing me mine.

He glances over my shoulder at the framed design. "I can't believe there's a thirty-five-mile submerged market hanging out in Erie," says McGinty, "forty-five feet under water. How can anyone fill thirty-five miles with sellable items?"

"Oh, it's not just a market," I respond, roaming the car and scrutinizing its solid construction. "This train of tubular cars is very deceptive. Degnan-deceptive. He's got several cars of market, then unmarked cars—lots of them— then market again, then unmarked again. I can only guess what fills the unmarked cars of this Dark Market."

"Yeah, I have some guesses," says McGinty as his finger travels from our end of the market to the other, tracing the long pathway of Degnan's commercial kingdom. "Just like Degnan said, he's constructed three sections running parallel to each other, lengthwise through every car. The center space for the market, and on the outside of the market the transport glides run along the front."

McGinty seems mesmerized by the map's complexity. He says, "And here is our little Warrior Strip hideaway—tucked neatly on the backside of the market." His face is inches away from the framed design. "Give me a minute. I need to commit it to memory."

I run my hand along the side of the car. "Our Warrior Strip shares a wall with the market," I say.

McGinty finishes his inspection of the design and explores the second car adjacent to ours, easily accessed through an archway. "Something tells me Degnan's built a way to close these connecting doors on command." McGinty stands in car #2 and runs his hand down the panel to the side of the archway. A metal partition immediately rolls down from the top of the arch, separating McGinty from me. I rush to the arch and try to open it. I hold my palm against the threshold, and it activates and opens the door. I enter car #2, joining McGinty and ask, "What'd you think that's all about?"

"I think he's got it activated to his palm code and to all of us who have our names on those lockers. That's five of us so far."

"How could he do that without getting our imprints?"

"We opened the packages that held our uniforms. That's the way he thinks."

"I hate him."

"Yeah, I know. Now Raghill? I'm not sure why the kid is coded in here and has a locker already." Now McGinty stares at the common wall the Warrior Strip shares with the Dark Market. I follow his gaze, moving closer to the wall, realizing it's not just a metal structure separating the two cars.

We say together, "Two-way mirror." I continue, "That's why the light's so dim in here. We can see everything in the market, but they can't see us." I place my hand against the two-way mirror, imagining the information we might mine from this perfect subterranean setup. "We've got to bring the mappers here," I say.

"Yeah, Shaw needs to map all the details from our perspective in the Warrior Strip. In the meantime—" McGinty opens the chipster in his bicep, loading in information— "I'll record as much data as I can so next time we come out here we'll have a baseline of info."

"You mean tomorrow?"

"Yeah, tomorrow. Guess someone will be here every day from here on out."

"It's a goldmine," I say, looking closely at the window in car #2 of the Dark Market. "What would Annalynn say?"

McGinty smiles. "We hit pay-dirt, baby. The Motherlode."

"Yeah, that." I'm intent on observing the action in the market, but as I gaze through the window's surface to the other side, I catch my own reflection. A faint memory. Morris' voice. After the library burned, Morris didn't ever want to risk letting any of the information burn again. So what was left, he and Raghill memorized. One of his ancient recitations flits in and out of my thoughts. *For now we see through a glass, darkly, but then face-to-face.*

Maybe looking through this glass would bring me face-to-face with the destruction of The Third. How strange to hear Morris' voice at this moment, but he had a way of unintentionally haunting me with his quips and arguments. Now fifteen, he's still beyond my intellect in many ways. The principles of bio-chem that he whispers in his sleep. The mechanical engineering stats he recites for pleasure. The calculus equations that evoke his rare smile. Though I'll never understand it all, I trust him to collect, carry, and safeguard it. Fate left Morris in my care when Borden, entwined in The Third, turned his back on his only son. I have always treated Morris as Chapman's brother, and I guess that means I also treat Morris as my son. *For now we see through a glass, darkly.* I pull myself back to the task at hand, looking beyond my own reflection.

Down the center of this submerged car the Dark Market pulses. McGinty, glances up from his chipster and says, "Well, they're not selling anything gray."

"That's how we know it's upper-tier trade here," I comment. "All these people are in Dorsey's closest ring of protection, his strategy makers or their relatives or those who are connected to the relatives."

"And they can't wait to get their hands on color."

"Do you blame them?" I focus my attention on one strong woman behind a counter. "Hey—the one selling the merchandise—she look familiar to you?"

"Not really."

"That's 'cause she had her DR93 pointed at the back of your head while Degnan offered me cognac by the river."

"You got the better deal." He takes a closer look at her. "Okay. That's Miranda, one of Degnan's top four—or top three—since he lost one by the river."

I scan the framework of the mirror, locating a hologram panel. After I activate the volume control for the inside of the market, I note the sign above the alcove leading from the market to the transport platform outside. It reads: *Sculpting—Design Your Own.* Your own what? I wonder.

It's a hub of activity, hard to sort out. Miranda is dressed in the uniform of Degnan's own: sharp khaki with a red insignia on the right shoulder—a scorpod-art. The patrons wear the gray of The Third, but not the coverall of Reichel. These are fitted uniforms, and most of these people carry their jackets, with their torsos covered by dark gray tank tops, fitted as well. I find that strange. Miranda has a full uniform on and shows no sign of overheating, not a bead of sweat anywhere. Why are these people so stripped down, sweat glistening over their bodies?

There are shelves surrounding this market car, and each shelf is loaded with glass jars about a foot high, the interior filled with some sort of solution, either rose- or amber-colored. Inside the clear containers are an assortment of amoeba-like creatures, looking similar to a jellyfish, some chestnut-sized, others as large as a child's fist.

I watch a man who grotesquely displays his muscles for two girls and a boy who stroke the man's biceps in admiration. His skin is stretched so tight over the muscle that it is bruised and tiny rivulets of blood ooze through areas where the skin is cracked, no longer able to hold the muscle in. The two girls and the boy lose interest and begin comparing the size of their arms.

"McGinty? You notice anything strange about the patrons?"

He looks up from his chipster and through the mirror. "You mean that every person in there is either bursting with the bulge or emaciated beyond sanity?"

"Yeah, but it's how they got that way. Watch." The three pre-teens approach a machine sending input through a hologram. They measure the circumference of their wasted arms, obtaining three measurements—bicep, forearm and wrist. The girls jump up and down squealing with delight at their results, but the boy seems dejected, disappointed. The girls take him to the shelf with the amber jars and point at the contents inside. He gingerly lifts the jar and steps under an arch, standing on a metal dais. The boy pulls out a small brass disc from his pocket and holds it to the scanner. A flash occurs. Then he steps out of the arch, his purchase finalized. The girls run to him and insist he opens the jar. He does, slipping his hand inside, grabbing one of the moving creatures, lifting it to his mouth and swallowing it whole. The girls cheer, one taking the jar from him as his body contracts quickly and then he's involuntarily flung against the wall, slamming hard, then again and once more, until he collapses on the floor. One girl offers him her hand, so he can pull himself to his feet. He's wobbling, unstable.

They all put on their uniform jackets and button them up. The far side of the car is glass, and I can see them step out of the car archway to the transport platform. In seconds a small transparent rectangle appears, hovering as they climb inside. A metal contraption emerges from the floor of the craft and connects a leg iron to each customer's left ankle, holding them in place. They grip onto a bar above them for additional support. The glide door slides shut and they are off at an amazing speed.

The sculpting car with the glass jars is now packed full of patrons all clamoring to touch the rose and amber jars. They know the merchandise they want.

"Oh, that craving," Degnan's voice startles me. "Amazing what one will do to attain an idolized body image." I turn to see him behind us, looking through the two-way mirror, admiring his creation.

"Perverted," says McGinty, closing his chipster and staring at Degnan. "What do those blobs they swallowed do? Sculpt them from the inside out?"

"Accurate description. Of course, later today they'll visit another car for the pain."

"Still providing essential services for the masses?" I ask.

"Ah, hasty words before you reap the benefits of what the market has for you." Degnan opens car three and beckons us to follow him.

"Information at the cost of what you're doing to those people? That's not a trade I'm willing to make."

"You already made that trade. We're partners. Information for protection. Couldn't be clearer. Follow me."

We pass through three more cars named *Pain Cavity*, *Personality Waiver*, *Space Adjustment*. In the next car, *Upside Eye*, we watch in safety from the Warrior Strip, and see clients writhing in excitement. It takes only a moment to figure out their eye-readers are tuned to revolting pictures, demeaning humans in unimaginable ways, I'm sure. Images that McGinty says should be illegal, but upper tiers with a disc of trade and a medical chip for medicinal pleasure push their way into Degnan's depraved tube of horrors, looking for a decadent fix.

Degnan cups his hand around McGinty's cheek. "I can have your eye-readers hooked up in less than 30 seconds." The speed at which McGinty moves his knife from his belt to Degnan's neck reminds me that McGinty is every bit a warrior, Elite trained. I have come to know a gentler, more compassionate side of him, but that is private. This is public. I hear a clicking from inside Degnan's messenger bag, then a hiss, and I see a rippling movement.

"I wouldn't put your smut in my eyes for anything," says McGinty. "That was never part of the deal." He spits his words in Degnan's face, and I see a bit of a flinch from this man who controls these cars of perversion.

Degnan speaks slow, deliberate. "Telson and Dart are twins. Smart brain-swappers. Scorpodarts that will crawl out of my bag by voice command. My voice." He's sweating now, but so is McGinty. The selfish in me hungers for McGinty to slit Degnan's throat. The commander in me knows I need Degnan, and he needs us. I want to let him sweat as long as possible.

He continues. "In under three seconds, after the scorpion part of my little pets stings you with its tail, your throat starts to swell, and as the back legs of the poison dart frog rub against your sin—anywhere on your skin really—its poison paralyses you while your head explodes with pain—"

"Stop it!" I say, pulling McGinty's arm away from Degnan's neck.

"Ready for a drink?" asks Degnan as he straightens his jacket. "My quarters cover the next few cars."

"I don't want a drink. Give me something on The Third."

"You don't want to see my little abode? Come on, now. Just for a moment."

Degnan leads us through an archway heavily guarded by three of his personal guards. As I follow him into his quarters I hear McGinty whisper in my ear, "You want to rethink this alliance?"

"Not a choice. Let's go." We step into his lair. I determine this day won't end until I retrieve some sort of significant information about Dorsey.

Chapter 4
THE CHANT
AVERY DETORNADA

"They're homebodies," says Degnan as the two scorpodarts rattle out of his messenger bag, down his leg
and up the side of his lush, midnight-blue sofa placed
artistically behind an expensive Persian rug. Both
McGinty and I lurch when the scorpodarts jump from
one end of the sofa to the other using the frog part
of their bodies to propel them. These little monsters
are easy to track with their burgundy-colored bodies
scurrying, and their bright blue frog legs extending
just under the raised venomous tails, stingers upturned
for action.

The entire ceiling and the front of the sitting room
look out at the transport tube through clear glass windows. The lighting accentuates the beauty of the water,
but reminds me that we are completely encased.

"Stunning, isn't it?" Degnan asks, gesturing at the walls of water, and I notice a glide waits for us beyond the transport platform on the other side of the window. Miranda is inside the glide on alert, weapon ready. Degnan opens his bag, taking out two hooded caps. He throws one at McGinty and one at me. The scorpodarts make quick work of scoping out the room, like the hounds at airport drug-checks in the days before *Jurbay*. They race back across the floor, up his pant leg, reentering their habitat.

"The water temperature is cooler this time of year. We don't heat the transports. Makes these look legitimate. Put them on." We place the close-fitting knit caps on our heads, pulling the bottom part up to below our noses and pulling down the top, covering our foreheads. "You're not going to want anyone recognizing you. At least, not this early in the game."

He activates the hologram in the alcove by the front window, and the glass wall retracts into a metal frame, allowing us to step on the transport platform.

Degnan ducks into the glider, followed by McGinty. I go last into the transport, my hooded cap in place, rough against my skin. As the door closes, McGinty and I instinctively grab onto the bars above our heads. Designed to keep travelers stable, these bars allow us to lift ourselves inches off the glide floor, retracting our feet and avoiding the lock of the ankle cuff. It clasps around air instead of our ankles.

"That lock was for your own protection," says Degnan. "These transports don't float. They torpedo at 200 miles per hour."

"We always had the strongest grip in the Elite. Pasha made sure of that," says McGinty.

"How is the old girl, anyway? I kind of miss her compulsive idiocy."

"She's the most brilliant neurosurgeon we have left," I say.

"No, that'd be me."

A strut attached to the transport platform gives our glide a thrust and detaches us from the docking area, sending us on our way, hooked only to the cables above. We are indeed submerged. This entire transport tube is a twelve-foot corridor suspended in the Waters of Erie and broad enough to allow one glider to overtake another from behind, or for two gliders going in opposite directions to pass each other with a few feet between. They move at such a rapid pace that no one traveling could tell who's in the passing glide, and the only time an identifying glimpse might be gained is when the glides pull into a transport platform for docking and passengers debark from the glide. There is no reason for us to look suspicious. While Degnan and Miranda are dressed in the uniform of Degnan's marketeers, everyone else is dressed the same, and most are wearing the hooded knit caps, due to the cold.

My eyes meet McGinty's. I can tell he's as fascinated as I am by these gliders. "Exhilarating," he says. I try to hold back my laughter, but for a brief moment some sneaks out. The thought of enjoying this ride when danger surrounds us is, well, absurd.

Our glide passes car after car, many unmarked. I know there's got to be more in all these cars other than Degnan's living quarters and the cars of retail sales. I'm determined to find out what fills the unmarked cars.

When our glide begins to slow, I see a transport platform coming into view. Two armed Elite soldiers guard the entrance to a car without windows. In front of the docking mechanism, our glide stops, lining up our door with the platform door and opening instantly. Miranda stays in the glide while Degnan exits. The Elite guards let him pass without question. We follow.

"Stockpile," says Degnan after the door closes behind us. In this car there are four torpedo-like weapons positioned in a row, allowing room for us to walk behind the fin-like back end of the weapon. Their payload muzzles point down toward individual exit hatches on the floor. "We call them fishborns, and once The Third gets the energy to deploy them, they're coming after you—or whoever else is out there."

"Great," McGinty says. "While we've been harvesting wind and chicken poop at the Energy Concourse, they've been building weapons."

"Don't play the integrity card with me, McGinty. I know your solar cells and wind blocks will one day fuel your fleet of planes that can drop a payload of their own. You're no more a pacifist than I am."

"Defensive weapons," I argue.

"No one gets rid of The Third with defense. You know that." I am silent. He's right. The winners of this war win the offensive battle. I hate that.

McGinty and I both examine the steel weapons that seem a throw-back to a century ago.

"Archaic," I say.

"Hardly," counters Degnan. "They're not what they look like."

McGinty asks, "So they store them here and haul them when they're needed—where? To a plane?"

"Ha. The Third's air fleet is dead. No energy. No mechanics. No pilots."

"Then they load them all on military trucks?"

"Guess again." Degnan watches me inspect the pointed end of the weapon that carries the explosives, and now I get it.

"They're not hauling them anywhere," I say. "This is no storage facility. They're going to deploy from here, aren't they?"

"So if we were to attack by air," says McGinty, "we would never think they had any weapons stored. We'd be looking above ground and would never guess they were suspended in a launch car in Erie."

"You just scored," Degnan says, looking at me, "your first benefit of the Warrior Strip."

"Yeah, but now we do know," I say. "And we can destroy them from above."

"You know, but you'll have to find another way to stop these fishborns. You're under contract, DeTornada." I see a slight smile emerge from the corners of his mouth. I raise my hand for a swift slap at his face, but he catches my forearm, preventing the connection.

"You're every bit the devil you've always been," I accuse him and pull my arm away. I begin pacing around the weapons, arranged uniformly, neat and trim, awaiting the command for destruction. Waiting for a metal mouth to open and spew them to their destiny—and ours. "You've got us contracted to protect you and your market, yet your market houses the very launch cars that will destroy our colonies."

"The Third's got some experimenting to do. It'll be some time before these are functioning weapons, let alone ready for a launch. By that time you'll be sailing above, dropping your own version of destruction."

"They're going to need energy. A lot of energy." McGinty pauses, I think because he may not want to probe further, but he has to. "Do they have energy? Our subterraneans tell us their power's always going out."

"No," says Degnan. "No energy. Eventually they'll try to trade me for my energy source."

"Which is?" I ask.

"Very close to home," Degnan sneers.

"Well you need to keep it away from them."

"See, DeTornada? It didn't take that long for us to agree on something."

"Where are you getting your energy?"

"You forget that my knowledge and creativity have always been one step ahead of Pasha."

"You have energy mines of your own hidden, where?" asks McGinty.

Degnan laughs as he always does when he thinks he's outsmarted us. "Why create more when someone else has already done the work?"

I grab his arm and demand, "Are you siphoning our power?"

He makes no attempt to take my hand off his arm or deny my accusation. He enjoys this game of "cat and mouse," and thinks, of course, he's the cat. "We're in business now, Avery, so it shouldn't make any difference. But just in case you find and shut down our siphon—no more Warrior Strip for you."

I let his arm go. I don't want to agree with him, but the need for information on The Third buries any hope I have of ending my alliance with Degnan and blowing these weapon cars out of the water. "Okay, for now, but not forever."

"Let's work on tomorrow first, before we move on to forever."

"How many of these cars hold The Third's weapons?" McGinty asks.

"Thirty-one. Four in each car. Each honed in on a target area to the south and to the west of Erie."

That number is staggering to me, and I sit down on the mechanism that braces the fishborns, keeping them in place. I whisper, "That's 124 weapons."

"I did the math," says Degnan. "Say something new. Use that sixth sense of yours to solve the fate of the good guys you're supposed to be commanding. I have my market. I'm content to be a businessman. There's nothing I'd like more than to have the fishborns gone and the military presence out of here."

"Now you're growing a conscience?"

"It's always been there."

"Debatable."

McGinty and I approach the archway to the next car, when I notice Degnan has stopped. "We're in car one hundred," he says.

"And...?" I ask.

"You looked at the diagram of the Warrior Strip?"

"So?"

"So, its car one hundred. You never were good at homework, DeTornada."

McGinty is on his hands and knees in the back-right corner of the car, behind a fishborn. He says, "Every fifty cars of the Warrior Strip, there's an exit for emergencies.

Palm code-activated, and I know my palm is in that code. Yours too, Avery—" But before he can finish speaking, the floor opens wide enough for McGinty to go feet first down a cylindrical tube. I squat by the opening to take a closer look.

Degnan says, "After you." I follow McGinty, sliding a short distance down the tube and crawling out into the Warrior Strip. Degnan is right behind. As he climbs out, he says, "Quite the little playground I made for you two."

We walk for minutes through the Warrior Strip, passing in and out of cars without a two-way mirror, but now we know they are loaded with fishborns, waiting for breath from a solar cell or a wind block. We come upon a conference car with the familiar two-way mirror separating the Warrior Strip from the car. This conference space is empty. It has no furniture other than an oblong table that runs the length of the room, surrounded by vacant chair slats. Degnan lounges against the wall of the Warrior Strip, watching the empty room from our side of the two-way.

"What?" asks McGinty. "We're taking a break?"

"Just wait. The entertainment's about to begin," says Degnan.

"It's an empty room," I say, anxious to return to our Council back at Colony G and report the weapon count.

"Patience." No sooner has he spoken then the entry arch opens, and the car begins to fill with men and women dressed in The Third's military uniforms. "Dorsey's officers," says Degnan. They may be officers assembled for a meeting, but they are heavily outfitted with extensive military gear and weaponry.

As the officers take their places at the table, I'm struck by the hollowness of the moment. Between Shaw, McGinty, Pasha and me, even in the stress of recon or the dangers of being the hunted, there is a dysfunctional banter back and forth that identifies us as comrades, as friends—as family. We fight, like siblings vying for the last potato in the bowl, and we laugh at each other and the ridiculousness of what life's come to. We have each other's backs for the sake of The 28 United, and it is also intensely personal. But in this room, there is a void of any familiarity that makes a rotten life tolerable, or allows a soldier to think at the end of the day there might be a comradery that exists that goes beyond the work week. I don't have to see the #14 on their right wrists to know that *locasa* squeezes its sterile hold on these warriors' hearts. Every face, void of expression. No one yawns from a late night, or jokes with a comrade next to him or even straightens a weapon belt or the collar of a uniform. The Third used *locasa* to take the passion from these officers. They may have children somewhere in the city of Ash, but they are unaware that they even have families. Kids living in some indistinguishable housing unit, having their basic needs met by some pocketwatch of a caretaker under direct command to feed and shelter, but not to touch. Pasha has worked years on the concept of reverse-*locasa* to return the memories and re-unite the familes. We have an agreement that she will not use it again on anyone as an experiment like she did with Quinn, but I wonder—could she experiment in this room, with these men and women? Would they be any worse off than they are now?

Two guards step in through the entry and posi-tion themselves, one on each side of the arch. I recog-nize the guard on the left. Frederick, the Elite soldier I used the reverse-*locasa* on as a last resort weapon when I was pregnant with Chapman and racing to the History Labyrinth to uncover the Third's secrets. Frederick's finger had been on the trigger of his DR93 to take down some dump-picker children. I didn't hesitate to bury reverse-*locasa* in the back of his neck. Pasha stud-ied Frederick carefully over the following weeks as he travelled with us, skirting The Third in the forests of the New Coastline. The effects of reversing *locasa* were many, including erratic and dangerous behavior, muscles that failed to demonstrate muscle memory and a con-tinual misfire of tasks that seemed normal to others, like using an upside-down fork to eat or putting a right boot on a left foot. Frederick was a mess, and it took an in-credible amount of our time to monitor his condition, and when he disappeared we were disappointed we could no longer follow his progress, or lack of it. At this stage of reverse-*locasa* we cannot risk releasing more problems on the world through a mass reverse-*locasa* strategy, but someday Pasha will get it right and unlock the isolation, return the passion of not just these soldiers, but all the citizens of The Third. She'll get it right. Maybe someday these Elite will find their children, locate their spouses and, when their shifts have ended, have a reason to find home.

Now, Frederick seems unaffected by reverse-*locasa*. I haven't seen him in over four years, but it looks like he's as much embedded in the ranks of The Third as he always was. If Pasha could have achieved the positive results of reverse-*locasa* on Frederick, we could have had a subterranean entrenched inside The Third right at the top of the ranks—guarding Dorsey.

Through the archway comes Commander Dorsey. Everyone in the room stands. He strides to one end of the oblong table, turns and addresses those gathered. "At ease, officers." They all sit, but remain attentive, stiff.

"There will be a virtual test of a weapon today." The conceit in his attitude assaults those present in the room. He seems tense, belligerent. Quinn told me stories about when he gets like this, and I sense he's about to tear someone apart. The vein in his right temple pulses. "You know what that means, Templeton?"

"It means we won't waste energy if it's virtual, Commander," answers the man right in front of the two-way. *Is that a slight wince on Dorsey's face? What's that about?*

"What else, Abbott?" Dorsey turns his glare across the table to another man.

Abbott sounds sure of his response, "We get one more opportunity to prove that these weapons can skim the ground and directly hit the coordinates of any target we program."

"True, but not the best answer." The wince is almost imperceptible, but I have studied this man extensively. I see it. Dorsey holds his finger on top of his ear, like he wants to shut the sound out, shut the pain out. He scans the room with his eyes and settles on a third man. "Olson?"

Olson says, "It's not 'one more opportunity,' it's the *final* opportunity. Reassignments will follow."

Dorsey carries a dead branch in the shape of a Y, patting it rhythmically on his leg, reminding me of stories I'd read in the History Labyrinth about pioneers and their one-room schoolhouses where whipping children for their indiscretions was commonplace. He paces around the table, slow and deliberate, heading toward the two-way mirror, his face unseen by the officers. He's avoiding them, and I wonder why. A master communicator, Dorsey proves an expert at using all the presentational skills that he's honed, including every muscle on his face. "Yes, a final opportunity," says Dorsey. I can only imagine how these men and women must be sweating in their gear, fearing the eyes of the despot that might bore deep through their steel gray uniforms. Yet, now that Dorsey is in front of the two-way, I see he is the one sweating. He keeps his finger to his ear. "The virtual test will be monitored in launch car #78 of the market. Attendance required by everyone. Abbott, is everything in car #78 ready for the launch?" This time he leaves out the word "virtual." Knowing this man's active imagination, I'm sure he's already thinking in terms of an *actual* launch, and I can only hope that spot on the timeline is a ways off.

Abbott replies, "The hologram is loaded and fully operational. Ready for use, Commander." *Right answer this time, Abbott*, I think.

"One more thing." The Elite stand in unison, very much at attention. Inches from the two-way glass, I wait for the final gem of information. It has been a productive day. Dorsey commands the devotion of these military representatives who will in turn carry out his dictates to the next level of officers, who will then deliver the orders to the multitudes of soldiers and forces, acting on behalf of this Commander. Now we can return to our own ranks with more information than we came with, and our objective will be to interrupt Dorsey's seemingly flawless chain of command in a very lethal way. We must continue to ready our air fleet and surprise The Third from above, before their virtual test becomes a deployment that's way too real.

The sweat increases, dripping down Dorsey's chin, staining the collar of his uniform. If the mirror wasn't there, if the wall did not exist between the conference room and the Warrior Strip, he'd be face to face with me. Eyes straight ahead, straining for focus, the vein in his temple dancing in and out at a rapid rate. He repeats himself for emphasis, "Just one more thing." His lips part. His breathing is notably faster. I feel my own heart rate mounting. If I could just reach through this glass and end all this with a clear, straight shot of my Z-Colt, I would. "We never forget—" Dorsey pauses, waiting for the group of fifteen officers to respond in unison with him.

"DeTornada!" They shout together. A war cry! I move a few steps back from the mirror, shocked to hear my name. McGinty's body tenses, but Degnan's unflappable, his composure intact.

"We are always aware—" says Dorsey.

"She has not been captured," respond the officers, like a terrifying choral reading group.

"Goal at the top of the list?"

"DeTornada."

"Won't stop looking until we find—"

"DeTornada."

"Dismissed," Dorsey says. The officers chant my name as they leave. Their husky voices at full volume cause the car to shake. *No, that's my imagination*, I think, *That's me shaking.*

Two by two they go through the exit, like the animals in Morris' story about the ark. On the other side of the arch they will load the submerged transports, gliding away at an intense speed, leaving Dorsey to his own reflections. He has not moved from the mirror, transfixed by his own image reflected in the glass. But just after the last soldier leaves the room, he swipes at his sopping forehead. There is too much moisture for his hand to make a difference. He reaches his palms to his ears in an effort to quiet something we do not hear. He whispers, "DeTornada." And then, he too leaves followed by his private guard. The room is empty once more.

I breathe again and wonder how long it's been since I took a breath. Since I heard them chant my name. We three are quiet for the moment. Maybe it is a time of silence, commemorating my inevitable death. After all, an entire nation is on the hunt for me.

Degnan says, "Pull it together, DeTornada. This really shouldn't come as a surprise to you. You drowned one of his top officers, took in his son as your own and you command the only existing threat against him. Of course they're going to chant your name. Get on your feet and chant back."

McGinty steps forward, placing a strong hold on Degnan's shoulder, but I waylay any further force by removing McGinty's hand, saying to Degnan, "I'm on my feet, but I'll do more than chant."

———

Thirty minutes later McGinty and I are back in the first car at the west end of Erie, preparing to return to the underground hatch, the waterproof room, the zoo, the Council and life as we know it. Today we've unearthed information that might have taken us months to retrieve through our small army of subterraneans undercover in the daily life of The Third. I'm anxious to report to the Council—to see Chapman, hold him.

After my gear bag is off my back, I try to hang it in the locker marked with my name, but my hands still shake violently. In my head, I still hear the *DeTornada* chant from the officers of The Third. McGinty places his hands over mine, stilling the movement. The shaking does not return. He takes my pack and hangs it in my locker, pushing the button and sending the clear covering into place. He wraps his arms around me, and I embrace him as well. "You know how to leave a legacy, DeTornada." I attempt a laugh, but it is not convincing.

We continue to hold each other. I'm tired of the running, exhausted from the chase, but for this moment I am not a DeTornada. I am Avery. A woman who just wants to raise her boy in a world unobstructed by the darkness of power. I am settling, calming in the arms of McGinty. In my mind, I lift a hopeful thought for the death of Dorsey and the destruction of The Third. Then, with a sudden realization, the shaking begins again. It's horrific who I am! My hope should be for peace or justice or a world where children can play with their volume turned up to uninhibited. I wonder why my hopes are always about destruction and the annihilation of evil. If there was no Dorsey, no Degnan, no Third—what would I hope for then? My perspective is calloused with the blood of a necessary victory, and I disgust myself. I need to figure out what hopes I should be whispering into the night, as I face my own identity.

Raghill bursts through the open hatch from the Waters of Erie into the entrance of the Warrior Strip, bringing gallons of water with him. Raghill, breathing hard from his journey, his curly mop of brown ringlets sopping with lake water, shouts, "Avery! We need you back at the colony."

"Chapman?"

"He's fine, but we need you."

"I've only been gone a few hours. Clef and Old Soul can handle anything that's up. You don't need me to do it all. That's what they're trained for."

He pulls himself up through the hatch, dripping and splashing all over me. "You don't understand." He seems worried and desperate as he grabs my shoulders. "It's Pasha. She's acting weird."

I laugh, shaking his arms away from me. "Pasha's weird? There's nothing I can do about that."

"No, this is not the normal weird!" And without warning, this fifteen-year-old who's buffed up far beyond his years grabs my arm and pulls me downward through the tube and into the water. I frog-kick my way back to the land hatch and the waterproof room. I can't even begin to guess what "not-the-normal-weird" might mean with regards to Pasha.

Chapter 5
THE ROAR
PASHA

The quarters Pasha had claimed at Colony G formerly belonged to the zoo vet and his crew. A year ago, when The 28 United established Colony G, Pasha had placed her sleeping mat below the only unbroken window in the entire zoo because she thought it was anomaly, like her. The mat, two blankets from the defunct gift store stuffed with leaves and sewn together with range grass around the edges, provided all the comfort she needed. It didn't bother her that one blanket was leopard print and the other zebra. She connected with mismatches.

She paced erratically from one side of her small area to the other whispering, "Hear that roar. Got to figure it out. Right now. Right now. Right now. Roar." A big white slime of pigeon poo fell from the metal roof beam, just missing her head and falling on her boot. Pasha jerked her head upward to find Herman staring at her. She warned him. "Don't try to play innocent. You know better." Taking a pillow from her mat she threw it with the biggest thrust she could muster, missing Herman by several feet. "You're an idiot! There's broken windows all over this place. Fly outside and do that." Herman and his mate Orbit, cooed in response, and Pasha remembered a time when she only spoke sweet words to her pets. Rummaging through the piles on the floor, she found the cuff of a worn-out shirt and wiped the poo from her boot.

That nervous stomach, now a common factor in the anxiety of her persona, stirred. She lifted her hands to rub her head, but stopped when she felt the bald spots that had already been picked away. Making a path through the piles of clutter on the floor, she stood before a mosaic of broken mirror pieces that she had reassembled to create an entire reflective surface. She studied her image. Fractured in so many ways.

"Bald spots are the worst," she spoke to herself, which was common. Herman and Orbit continued to gaze at her, but when she opened her threadbare gear bag and raised her right hand in command, they knew their orders. Flying directly into the bag, they nestled obediently. Pasha moved the pack to the floor by the curtained archway and felt comforted by the cooing noises resonating from the khaki depths. Her hair, the color of chestnut, frizzed in a natural fro, hardly covered the bald patches that speckled her dark-colored scalp. This troubled Pasha. Sometimes she could go for weeks without compulsively rubbing her head during the day, but by morning, tufts covered her pillow.

"Got to stop fidgeting. Annoying. Obsessive. Must be taken seriously." Pasha's room was heavily strewn with eclectic discards. She didn't bring these items on purpose to place them on a shelf or a windowsill for décor or sentiment. Each item had a purpose when she had initially picked it up, but by the time she arrived home she'd been visited by a string of divergent ideas and, still clutching the object, was unable to remember why she'd brought it to her quarters in the first place. So, promptly it was discarded, only to be moved again if a pathway from one side of the room to the other needed clearing. These mounds of disorder Pasha found most comforting, and convinced Herman and Orbit that the hoards were collected for their nesting pleasure.

Pasha dropped to her knees, rooting through a clump of clothing. She thought she might find her uniform. The uniform of The Third.

She wondered if there were any others who, at thirty years old, had accomplished as much as she had. Still a skilled neurologist, over the last year she had become the *creator of energy wonders* and was solely responsible for the vision and construction oversight of the Energy Concourse. An enclosed four-mile-long, three-story structure birthed by her imagination and a gigantic workforce. The Concourse, located on the outskirts of Colony G, had a thin-skin covering offering a more advanced version than the one that camouflaged Red Grove and what used to be The 28 United's headquarters outside the city of Reichel. This edition covered the entire Energy Concourse, providing hidden protection should an enemy scouting party end up in the area. The hypothesis for energy mining had roamed around Pasha's brain for years, and when it finally came time to turn visions and experiments into the production of sustainable energy she was ready to innovate and demonstrate, once again, her prowess in scientific advancement.

A year ago, Clef, the chief musician and one of the original Council members, had asked the Council if there was any new business. His empty eye sockets reminded Pasha of the cruelty of The Third and how Avery and The 28 United were taking forever to develop a strong enough offensive posture to end the tyranny of the current government.

That particular meeting was no exception to the dozens before. Pasha immediately jumped to her feet when new business was approached and presented her concept for the Energy Concourse. However, she no longer kept her eyes glued to the ground or on the wall or at the ceiling as she used to. No, she had studied the Council members. They used impeccable eye contact when presenting their side of an argument. Focused. *I'm a genius*, she thought, *I can learn to do the same.* So, while her nature led her to carry on short, blunt conversations composed of incomplete sentences pronounced at the dirt, she learned to match the other Council members' stares with an intimidating one of her own.

"That's an over-the-cliff idea," Avery had said of Pasha's proposal for the Concourse. "Surely you can't expect us to risk putting hundreds of workers on open highways and range land to develop energy. We might be spotted by Elite patrols." It gnawed at Pasha that Avery found it necessary to stand when she questioned Pasha's plan. It was Pasha that had the floor, not Avery.

"Not going 'over the cliff.' We're running up to the edge and holding ground. You think we can beat a monster by not taking a risk?"

"I think they won't need to destroy us if we kill ourselves free-falling off the jagged edge."

This memory made Pasha smirk as she dug the rumpled uniform from the bottom of the pile she'd been rooting through. Pasha had won the Council vote, and even though Avery had mentioned more than once how the Energy Concourse was the right decision, Pasha thought back on the Council meeting. *Typical, Avery. Too cautious. She'll keep the 28 United running forever. Action needed.* Trying to shake the wrinkles from the uniform, she gave up, stuffing it in her gear bag next to Orbit.

Pasha pulled her hand from the pack, holding reverse-*locasa*. She'd been instructed by Avery to pursue its perfection, but not to touch another human subject with it until she was certain of its success—no side-effects. The short, cylindrical component had become a compulsive challenge to Pasha. *Locasa*, originally stolen by The Third from Catalonia almost a decade earlier, had been designed to eliminate traumatic memories from victims' minds. The intension was that, once the memory was extracted, therapy would be provided for the victims and when they were ready to receive the memories back and deal with them, the memories would be replaced. This final stage would be accomplished when *locasa* was perfected. Before this could occur, The Third captured the device, using it to extract all reminiscences of family and home from its citizens, assuring their complete devotion, without question, to The Third.

Pasha sat cross-legged in the middle of the mess on her quarters' floor, twirling reverse-*locasa* in her hands. She knew the Third had used *locasa* on her. Pasha could remember when Quinn took her in as a teen and trained her to work for The 28 United. She remembered being a subterranean, undercover, receiving training to become an Elite soldier of The Third. But the memories in the gap—between residence with Quinn and training as an Elite—were gone. Nothing but empty.

Lifting the reverse-*locasa* to the base of her own skull, her hand hovered, shaking. It had only been used on two other people. Avery had used reverse-*locasa* as a weapon on Frederick, an Elite guard of The Third; as protection for herself, her unborn baby and the dump-picker children captured by Frederick. Then, there was Quinn, Avery's mother. Quinn asked Pasha to return the memories of her husband Carles that *locasa* had stolen. The memories of the original leader of The 28 United came back with the passion of her love for him, but also all the images of his murder in the presence of his daughter and wife in a cathedral in Catalonia. Quinn said it was worth it. *Maybe*, Pasha thought, *it would be worth it for me*. Quinn also said there were side-effects. This did not worry Pasha. Experiments always involved risk, trial, error.

She pulled reverse-*locasa* away from the nape of her neck without engaging it, dropping it in her lap and thrusting her palms to her ears, chanting, "Avery, out of my head. Out. Will use reverse-*locasa* when I want. Not when you say it's ready." Her pointer finger poked erratically at the device. First a poke—then a jab—then holding it firmly in her hand—then moving it slow motion to her skull—then yanking it back to her lap. Indecision. Follow orders or pursue scientific hypothesis? She picked up the device, placed it on the back of her neck and turned it on. After all, she was a scientist.

The effect was immediate and uncontrollable. Shaking so violently the movement sent her to the floor. The cracked linoleum pressed hard on her cheek, and her hip bone became the victim of banging and bruising against the floor. The shake turned to a tremor and finally to an occasional minor contraction. And then the flashing pictures inside her brain started clicking away at a rapid pace. *Wrapped in the arms of a man. She couldn't see his face. He was gentle with the jacket of a soldier covering his shoulders. Then guiding a small toddler to Pasha. The girl climbed into Pasha's lap, careful not to disturb the baby that rested in Pasha's arms. They were a huddle of bodies. A funny, scrunched together pile. Sweet laughter without restraint. Uncontrolled. Raucous. Hysterical. Then quiet. Dark. Silence.* No pictures left. No sound. Silence hurt. Pasha wanted the pictures back. She wanted to see the faces.

When Pasha sat up she didn't know how long she'd been crying. Once again, the roar was back. When she heard the tapping at the window she scrambled to find reverse-*locasa* and slipped it back in her gear bag, making sure the cover was secure. Her skull pulsed with pain, and she struggled to get her breath. Her fists rubbed her scalp with a fury, unrestrained. The tapping turned to a hard knock. Pasha yelled, "Who?"

Morris slid open the window, climbed in her room and stepped on her mat, announcing, "Libraries will return to haunt the ignorant."

"I have a door." She pulled her hands away from her hair, hoping he hadn't seen her plucking.

"You learn so much more about a person's character when you surprise them," said Morris in a hold-over British accent from when he lived in the library and romped through Shakespeare's canon.

"You're not British. Talk normal."

"And you're a doctor—be normal."

"Too late."

Morris, accent gone, repeated, "Libraries will return to haunt the ignorant."

"Have eye scanners. Don't need libraries."

"Besides, you have me." Pasha thought about Morris and how he'd been flying float cars and debating with Old Soul and Clef in the Council meetings of The 28 United since he was age ten. Now, at fifteen, he had enough child left in him to know how to provoke her beyond her breaking point. Breaking point. She'd been beyond for a while.

"Twenty minutes ago, by the acacia trees, we were in a stimulating conversation and you just walked away."

"Who's we? You were in a conversation with your-self." Pasha put her hands to her ears, patting them, pulling at them. "Hearing something in my head." She threw Morris a disgusted look. "It's not you."

"Well what is it?" Morris moved around her quar-ters, straightening one pile at a time.

"Leave my stuff alone."

"This isn't your stuff. It's everyone else's stuff that you've collected." Pasha noticed Morris was trying to listen to what she might be hearing. He said, "Hey, I don't hear it. Whatever you're hearing—I don't hear it." She said nothing, checking the contents of her gear bag. He squatted beside her. "I'm trying really hard to hear it, due to the fact that you're supposed to be my mentor, and my agenda is to learn from you, but I don't hear a thing."

"You don't have the intelligence to hear it." Pasha dug through disorganized heaps on a search for something.

"What kind of sound did you hear? Wind? Waves?" She was silent. "Tell me!"

"It's a roar."

There was another knock at the window and Annalynn entered without an invitation, stepping on Pasha's mat. "What's up, Buttercup?" The queen of clichés arrived, now thirteen, but no less irritating to Pasha than when she was eight. Annalynn was dressed in leg-warmers that used to be orange before she wore them out, and a homemade helmet, covered with metal debris.

"Pasha hears a 'roar,'" said Morris.

"Probably a throwback nightmare from *Jurbay*."

Pasha threw an entire pile of clutter at them from the floor. "Get out. My quarters. Find your own."

"So, lion?" asked Annalynn. "Sound like a tiger? Ocelot?"

Pasha collapsed on a pile of old appliances, shuffling them from spot to spot, still trying to locate an item she was determined to find. She said quietly, "More like a human roar. Not an animal."

"You're speaking metaphorically I presume?"

"No!" she yelled and stood facing them. "The dictionary. What's it say about 'roar'?" She looked at Morris, waiting. "You have the dictionary memorized—"

"Not all of it," Morris said.

"Well, quote from the part you know."

He quoted, "'To utter a loud, deep, prolonged sound, typically because of anger, pain or excitement.'"

"Try the *Urban Dictionary*," said Annalynn, lounging on Pasha's mat, pounding it in various spots to rearrange the contents to better fit her body.

"The *Urban Dictionary* is not a dictionary," said Morris. "It's a joke, filled with local color, slang and urban legends."

"Who died and made you God?" asked Annaylynn and stood to face Morris, both of them posturing with hands on hips.

"There you go again. You can hardly make it through a sentence without discharging a cliché."

"Radical, right? Okay, here goes. 'Roar: to vomit, to spew, to throw up.' That's a very different definition that yours." She turned to Pasha, "So which one's it gonna be?"

Pasha stopped foraging through her junk, holding their gazes with her own, like a tiger contemplating dinner. She stood and walked toward them, each word accentuated by her steps. She yelled, "'To utter a loud, deep, prolonged sound, typically because of anger or pain.'" And then she roared. Deep, prolonged, angry. "*That's* what's in my head."

"Well, okay then," said Morris.

Annalynn climbed out the window and said to him as she left, "Pure fear. I'm sayin', she's pure fear."

"Idiots. I can hear you," said Pasha. Now her quest for the missing item became more urgent.

This time there was no knock on the window. In climbed Chapman, Avery's five-year-old son. "What, you? Got a convention going on here," Pasha grumbled, and she noticed the kid moved silently, stepping on her mat like an animal who knew how to hunt, using all his senses to lead him to discoveries. "You're here—why?"

Chapman went immediately to Pasha's gear bag, quickly unzipping it and pulling out Orbit, stroking her head. "Bag packed, Auntie Pasha. Don't take the pigeons," said Chapman.

Pasha yanked Orbit out of Chapman's hands, returning her to the pack. "I'm not your 'auntie.'"

Morris grabbed Pasha's arm, whispering, "Lay off, he's just a kid."

She pulled her arm away. "I don't trust him. He's half GEB."

"He's Avery's son, and he's five. How can you not trust him?"

Pasha returned to her hunt. "Gotta find, gotta find, gotta find."

"I'll help you, Pasha. What are you looking for?" asked Morris.

"It cuts."

Morris joined her quest. "A knife? A saw? A-a-a-a..." He pulled out a pizza slicer from the bottom of a stack. "I don't know what this is."

Pasha started to growl, impatient with the search until she turned around and saw Chapman, holding up a battery-operated razor. For a moment, no one moved. Pasha thought, *How'd he know what I wanted? Where'd he find it? How'd he know?* Then she rushed over, grabbed the razor from Chapman and knelt before the mosaic mirror.

She commanded Morris, "Shave it." Morris took the razor, turning it on to see if it worked. It did. "Don't need any compulsive ticks where I'm going," she said

"Changing locations doesn't make you less compulsive," said Morris.

"I can hide it."

"You never have before."

"Changed."

"If you say so." He examined the razor.

"Get the alcohol."

"I don't drink."

She pointed to her gear bag. "The kind that sterilizes. In my pack."

Morris went to the cooing bag. "Why do you have Herman and Orbit packed up?"

"Go everywhere with me. Going to scout."

He looked in the bag. "And how long of a scout trip are you planning?

"Long as it takes."

"Where are you going?" She didn't answer. "I could go with you."

"And what? Talk dawn to dusk? Like my quiet."

"You talk to yourself all the time. That's not quiet."

"Not the same thing as bringing the human dictionary with me."

Morris began the haircut. It took a long time to buzz off strips of the fuzzy mess, then find a rusted can of shave cream (buried in a stack by her mat) and the straight razor (under her pillow). He swiped her skull bald. When finished, Pasha couldn't tell which were the places she'd rubbed raw and which spots were the ones caused by Morris' lack of barber skills.

Pasha stood before the fractured mirror, watching dozens of split images reflect her new look. A sly half smile parted her lips, rare indeed. Her hands did not return to rub or pluck, but remained by her sides.

She grabbed her gear bag and headed for the window above the bed, opening it and climbing out. Morris called after her. "Thank you?" He ran to the window and yelled out, "I get no thank you?" She made no reply. He turned to Chapman, who had not moved since he found the razor. "Go home, Chapman." Morris stepped out the window, but then leaned back in and said, "Chapman, be careful." Chapman remained motionless. Morris followed after Pasha.

Chapman stared at the window for almost a minute, then got up from his position on the floor, pushing a crate in front of the mirror. He crawled up on top of it, placing himself in a sitting position, like Pasha had posed for her haircut. Careful, cautious, deliberate, he picked up the razor with one hand and pushed his hair away from his face with the other. He lifted the razor to his hairline and began to buzz his own shoulder-length locks with the precision of someone who had barbered all his life.

Chapter 6
CIRCLES
AVERY DETORNADA

It is almost dark when McGinty and I hit the fringe of the grasslands on the zoo's perimeter. I'm exhausted from the trip to the Warrior Strip—the entrance and exit through the water—and the chanting of my name. I crave sleep, but my dulled senses awake when I see Old Soul waiting for us. I do not expect him. He and Clef had been tasked to watch Chapman for the day. Only a couple pinstripes on Old Soul's denim bell bottoms remain; the rest faded away from constant wear and tear. He adjusts the round metal frames of his glasses continually, a nervous tick that I rarely see him yield to.

"Where's Chapman?" I run past him in the direction of my quarters, leaving him behind, trotting in my wake in an attempt to catch up. "Is he all right?"

McGinty jogs beside me and says, "You go ahead to Chapman. I'll find Pasha. Get a read on what's going on. See what Raghill means by 'weird' behavior."

"Thanks," I say. He's off in the opposite direction, and I'm grateful for the many times he's covered "business" while I've covered "kid."

"Now, Avery, I don't want you to be upset," Old Soul puffs hard, trying to balance running and speaking. I can't even begin to think of what new thing Chapman might have done to cause me to be upset. He already sneaks out the second a caretaker turns her back, and eerily returns to our quarters without a scrape or bruise anywhere on his body.

"Is he hurt?" I see the pampas grass that camouflages my quarters in the distance.

"No. Not hurt."

"Well, what is it this time? He's off on another unknown journey?"

"Well, yes, he did escape for a while." I can tell Old Soul doesn't want to get to the point. "But he's back. He's back. Now."

The pampas grass sways as I weave my way to the curtained entrance of my quarters, pushing back the hanging piece of fabric that represents my door. I freeze and gape at my bald boy. No hair. None. I realize the deep attachment I have felt to his blond-brown locks. Chapman looks strangely more petite without the fullness of the thick tresses swinging around his face and shoulders. "Chapman—" I prod, careful not to say anything that would send him out the door on another escape. "Who shaved your head?"

He looks at me with innocence. Sweet and sincere, he says, "I did."

"By yourself?"

"Just like Auntie Pasha." He rubs his head, seeming to like his new look.

"Pasha shaved her head?"

"Morris did it for her. Just before she left." I move to sit beside him, intent on finding out more about Pasha's departure than his missing hair.

"Where did 'Auntie Pasha' go?"

"I'm not supposed to call her 'auntie.'"

"Where did Pasha go?" I hear the rising tension in my voice as Chapman turns his eyes from mine, continuing to rub his smooth head.

"Tired of mis-mis-mis-man-age-ment." He struggles to pronounce the word, and I am sure he is quoting Pasha. It does not surprise me that she would complain about my leadership, even to my own child. We have a friendship that cannot be characterized by the common definition. After all these years, I am often able to look past her abrasive attitude and caustic tongue to recognize her extraordinary abilities. And while she cannot verbalize it, I muse that she sees my strengths as well.

"Took Herman and Orbit in the big bag. I miss pigeons."

I want nothing more than to scoop him up in my lap for a story time, but I can't. I say, "What kind of a 'big bag'?"

"Has everything," he says, and I wonder if he's keeping bits of information from me, pushing my buttons. But I discard that idea. He's only five.

"What was in Pasha's bag?"

"Pigeons. Two. Energy stuff."

"You mean like wind blocks and solar cells?"

"That. And food." I hear Old Soul and Clef shifting positions by the door, Old Soul's denim pants rustling. They probably sense, like me, that Pasha is traveling somewhere with her energy inventions, and we'd better find out where.

"What else did she pack?"

Chapman turns my way and seems to, quite deliberately, give me an answer I don't want to hear. "Clothes. Gray clothes. Maybe like the uniform Morris told the story about."

I turn to Old Soul and Clef, knowing tomorrow Pasha's disappearance will be first on the Council agenda. "It's almost dark. Let's all get some sleep." I gather Chapman up, moving him to the comfort of his sleeping mat, positioned a few feet from mine. "Early in the morning, the Council will meet, and we'll put the pieces together. We'll figure out where she went. It's not the first time she's left for a few hours unannounced—"

"Never packed a bag before," Chapman says. "Not with pigeons. They always ride on her shoulders." I cover him with a blanket.

"We'll make a plan to find her." I sense Old Soul and Clef's concern as they back out the door.

Later that night, Chapman thinks I'm asleep and crawls on my mat beside me. He knows I will ask him to return to his own mat if he is discovered. He is unaware I relish time to hold him, for all too soon the dawn will spread, and I will become every inch a commander.

Chapman wriggles close to me, so close that I feel his heart rhythmically beating. His breath smells clean from the mint he chewed before bed. The herb grows among the grasses of the man-made streams in the replicated African savanna area of the defunct zoo. I drape my arm over him, surrounding his back and shoulder with a moment of protection before I rouse myself in preparation for military strategies and the casting of visions. Hope for an entire world, seemingly unattainable.

Without warning, Chapman jerks to a standing position in the middle of my grass mattress. Not breathing. His chest is still, and his eyes wide open. I have seen this before. Many times. But still, I cannot avoid an audible gasp that brings McGinty through the curtain on my door faster than if I had time to call for him. In the moonlight McGinty's eyes are alert and focused, yet his body hesitates, as if waiting for instructions. His Catalonian skin blends olive with the midnight blue of nighttime, making the whites of his eyes penetrating, captivating.

"He will be all right," I whisper.

"Breathing?" McGinty asks.

"No." I gently place the palm of my hand on the small of Chapman's back, more for my reassurance than his.

"How long?"

"Just started."

"Worried?'

"Always." McGinty's and my eyes are locked like they are so many times when we share trauma or possibility. He is across the room from me, yet his presence comforts without a touch. I force myself to look back at Chapman. "The longest he's gone is twelve minutes."

"I remember. He slept all day after that."

"He'll be okay." I try to convince myself.

"I'll wait by the door." McGinty takes up a station on the inside of the draped entrance to my quarters. I would tell him it's not necessary, but it wouldn't matter. He'll stay until it's over. I'm glad.

And now Chapman turns in a small circle, spinning, and in my head I rage against The Third for placing genetically engineered beings, GEBs, into our world. I desperately want this boy, my boy, to be normal. But what is normal in this world? With parentage half GEB from Raben and half reticent commander from me, what would "normal" be for Chapman? Yet, he's only five and has years to find a pathway to whole. I will guide him through it all. McGinty, Shaw and the others will help him—maybe not Pasha, I don't know. And then, there's my mother Quinn. Chapman needs so much of what she has to give.

Quinn. Such a sage advisor and interesting grand-mother. Perfect for Chapman. She could still outrun me and pull the triggers of an anti-brainy and a brainy al-most simultaneously. Her discarded silver locks of The Third's commander position were never missed, and I celebrated the hair that replaced her former subterra-nean look with her natural auburn tresses now faintly painted with graying strands. She'd hardly aged, and took on her role of grandmother with grace and the spirit of a teacher. How she loved my boy, and how Chapman loved his *nonnie*. Perhaps we might not have the luxury of photographic snapshots like families did in decades past, or of holograms for personal reflection, or a record of Chapman's history and growth in our eye scanners (there's always a way for The Third to track that sort of sentiment), but nonetheless I have snapshots in my mind.

Snapshot One: Quinn rocked Chapman as a newborn in a metal-framed chair formed from reconstructed piec-es of a crashed float car and bound together with slashes of dried, braided ivy that had wound up forest redwoods with the wild purpose of reaching the tip-top branch. Quinn whispered in Chapman's ear, "Your grandfather died in battle. Watch your mother for example. The 28

United waits for you to match steps with a family of warriors who walked before you. Bring peace, Chapman. End this running."

Snapshot Two: At three, the age when toddlers think legs might make a difference, Chapman snuck up on Quinn while she slept, pulled the covers from her mat and simply watched her before light consumed the morning. She feigned sleep for the benefit of Chapman.

"Nonnie," he said, "I'll beat you past the scrap pile and cement heap. Beat you." Well, it was Quinn, and she never turned down a challenge, even from a child. Of course, she was always on the ready and dressed for the unexpected, so she wasted no words on discussion, timing or plans.

Snapshot Three: Quinn ran. Chapman chased. She leaped from the mat, Chapman right behind her. Words interrupt my snapshots with cynicism and taunts. *His father was a GEB. His father was a GEB.*

I would shut this snapshot tour down right now, but I can't. It would mean The Third achieved victory over my mind. Do they really think I can't raise this boy to have the integrity of The 28 United? I want to scream at Dorsey. *He's not* all *his father. He's not* all *GEB. He's half DeTornada. He's part me.*

Snapshot Four: Quinn dressed for the hunt, Chapman by her side. She'd determined Chapman would be a competent child able to track anyone or anything. At times, I see him as a gift, a combination of all the assets from the other children in my life, with the vocabulary of Morris, the faithfulness of Raghill and the humor of Annalynn. Perhaps he will be the DeTornada to usher in peace and the rule of The 28 United. Maybe he will be the one to witness the demise of tyranny and the end of The Third. Maybe that too will be a gift.

I look at the timepiece in the cuff of my sleeve. It has the picture of an elephant across its digital read. Seems silly for a commander, but it was better than the other choices remaining in the deserted gift shop of the zoo—a monkey or an ostrich. In choosing the timepiece, I didn't want to be thought of as a jokester or someone with their head in the ground. But elephants, they're massive and strong. Sweet irony that The Third issued the abandonment proclamation for all zoos and our discovery of this one gave us food, water and shelter, resulting from the command and actions of the very source that hates us. Zoos are extinct while The 28 United thrives.

My timepiece reads twenty-seven minutes since Chapman began the spinning, in circles. I sit on my bed facing him, my hand brushing lightly on his shoulder each time he turns. McGinty slips in my bed beside me, his arms encircling me from behind, encouraging me to never tire of making my presence known to Chapman in this GEB-oriented ritual. McGinty, always the steadfast support. The most reliable friend I know. I feel his hand move from my shoulder to my hair, smoothing away the worry as we share these remarkable and horror-filled minutes that no one else can know exist. We'll protect him, McGinty and me. Even after five years and our destruction of the hundreds of non-activated GEBs in Reichel, our citizens remember the activated GEBs we killed. Their innards spewed across the ground. Their right ventricles cut out and destroyed so that their data collection sites could never be accessed. Raben was one of those. All it will take is one person seeing Chapman spinning in his breathless circles to accuse him of being a storage GEB undercover for The Third. I'm sure he isn't storing a thing. After all, he's half my boy too.

With Chapman, I feel like each day is an experiment in motherhood. Not the good kind of adventure that one walks through, discovering the newness of a child, but an exploration that taunts: *you'll never know what tomorrow holds for you or for Chapman.* That taunt is intolerable, yet I must tolerate it, protecting him from himself and from others that might want to end the life of a child they think is far more like his father than his mother. *He's only five. He's only five. He's only five.*

My boy still spins, his breathing nonexistent. I call up the memories of him that will help me transform the terrifying into the bearable of the ordinary.

———

"What's the story, mama?" His voice was hazy from the interruption of morning, but he was never able to disguise the curiosity that began his day. Last night I'd promised him a story in the morning, and he never forgot a promise.

I answered him, "One you haven't heard before."

"Am I in it?"

"Of course, you're always the hero."

"Then tell it quick." He sat on crates braced up against the cement walls, where the feeders used to prepare the food for families of lions. Just through the iron bars of an open doorway was a small hall that led to the African savanna and several platforms sculpted into the hillside. Draped off the front of the iron gate surrounding the savanna was a pitiful rusted sign held in place by a single bolt, causing the sign to lean dramatically to one side. It read: "Do not feed the lions."

I staged my story in front of Chapman, acting out each detail as the storyteller, the townspeople and the evil painter. He only played one part. He knew it by heart, even when the story changed each time I told a new one. A savior always knew the right things to say.

I proceeded with the drama. "There was a night darker and longer than any other. It sucked the color from the world. It stole the memory of sunset and no one could ever recall the dawn."

"I would have protected the color," Chapman said bravely. "I would have hidden it away so no one could steal it."

"Hidden is an interesting word, Chapman. 'Cause 'hiding' is what this entire town did."

"Everyone except the hero."

I nodded my head and looked at him as only a proud mama could. "Yes, everyone except the hero." We both said the name of the hero together: "Chapman." Out the window I saw the silhouette of hills, defining themselves through the approaching rays of dawn, a very dramatic background for our story.

I continued. "The Dark Painter came daily to surround the town with the blackest paint from his buckets. "

"What did Chapman do?"

"Made a plan. A secret plan. A surprise plan. He spread the word to everyone in the city to find anything they had of color. Items from their past—scarves, toys, blankets. 'Pile them in the middle of the town,' the hero said."

"How could they see to find the color? It was dark." Chapman leaped from the crates to my bed.

"That's exactly what the people asked the hero." I threw a blanket around Chapman's back and tied it under his chin. He clawed at its roughness. It tickled his ears, and finally he positioned his cape just the way he liked it. "What do you think was the hero's answer?"

There was no delay in Chapman's reply. Rising slowly to his feet, he fully embraced the hero's lines. "Remember how it felt, when you could see the color.

You remember an orange scarf with blue pears. Was it smooth and silky, or cottony and stiff? Where did you leave it last? Feel your way to it. You don't need your eyes. Use your fingers and your mind. Remember."

I thought: *A five-year-old with a sixth sense.* It scared me. Fascinated me. Intrigued me that he should have the same sixth sense of his mother and his grandmother, and that it would manifest itself so early. He also inherited my big feet and sarcastic wit. Nonetheless, both were a part of me. What part of his father would I detect next? I already saw Raben in the depths of Chapman's hazel eyes, and I saw Raben in the strands of gold woven in Chapman's light brown hair, now missing, shaved, lying in a heap on Pasha's floor.

"Well, they did go looking," I said. "Every person in the town worked for days in the darkness, remembering what things looked like, how things felt. They stumbled their way over chairs, through doors, inside of trunks and bags and baskets." I sensed Chapman's body tense with every new sentence I pronounced. Was he imagining what it was like to find these treasures himself? I pondered what this story meant to him, and then was brutally jolted back to the story by Chapman beating violently on my arm, pounding on my shoulder.

"What's next?" he yelled. "Stop daydreaming! Tell me the rest of the story." His blows, even though from a young child, were strong and painful to me, and I instinctively protected myself from his assaults. I grabbed his forearms and held him still. We glared at each other, face to face. I would teach this imp the meaning of control, the purpose of patience. He couldn't hit his mother. But then I released his arms, remembering his age. Years ago, I had no patience at all, none. I didn't want to lose what little I'd developed. And even though he's only five, I could hear what Quinn would say: "He's not too young for high expectations. He'll be needed much earlier than what you might think." And to that, I'm sure I would respond, "He's a child." Then she'd retort with the knockout line, "Battle calls who's ready. Age is an irrelevant benchmark that yields nothing but confusion." *Age is an irrelevant benchmark.* While I have come to love her as my mother, I still hated it when she was right.

———

Chapman's hair is gone now, like the story. Sweet and thick replaced by smooth and bald. Just like Pasha's, so he said. She's gone missing, and we don't know where she is. I'm still wondering if I want her back.

Since his breathing stopped thirty-six minutes ago, he has spun, armed with energy, but like a chipster needing a solar cell, he's running down. His legs begin to wobble, and he collapses in a heap in the middle of the covers on my mat. His body violently jerks in one extreme movement, like a giant hand has fallen, resuscitating his heart. He breathes again, steadily. And I wonder if this stoppage of breathing is a prelude to his death or a GEB anomaly leading to ours. Could he be storing information during these spinning moments? Or is his DNA so confused it takes this action to try to right itself? Am I raising a son or a weapon pointing at me?

McGinty covers Chapman and says, "I know what you're thinking. He's just a child. Give him a chance."

"That's right," I say.

From the other colonies, splayed out across the land like a fan to the south and west of us, a sound lifts its head, drifting through the open areas of my quarters. So soft, so comforting, a community whisper. I recognize it as a lullaby my father Carles sang to me. A lullaby I've sung night after night to Chapman. I smile in the dark where no one sees, partly from the embarrassment that somewhere others have heard me singing, learned the song and the lyrics and the tenderness. It's a brief misstep of ridiculous pride that makes me wish I'd kept my mouth shut. Very brief though, 'cause I can't help but sing along.

> *The wind says quietly, "be still."*
> *The waves whisper, "children, all is well."*
> *The stars call you to your night of peace,*
> *Sleep, sleep, children; be at ease.*
> *Sleep, sleep, children; be at ease.*

I think of these words: *your night of peace.* Maybe tomorrow. I can hope.

The three of us sleep, knowing a few hours will need to be enough.

———

Several hours later, I hear McGinty outside the quarters, beginning the ceremonies of the morning. The chopping of wood. Stacking of the kindling in a teepee tower. Blowing on a spark. Crackling of first flame. Then, coffee cups assembled, clacking. Finally, the smell of the boiling brew, welcoming the dawn. Chapman crawls on my lap. He shivers, and I pull him close, his back to my chest. He says he likes to feel my heartbeat. He raises his chin just a little, positioning himself for a perfect view out the hole that used to have a pane of glass, used to have a frame, used to be a window. I stare over his shoulder with expectancy. The sunrise never disappoints.

Shaw calls from outside my quarters door, "Avery! Avery." I leave Chapman on the bed, grabbing my boots. Chapman and his caretakers know what to do when the commander in me rises to attention. He will be cared for, if they're able to keep their eyes on him.

I burst through the fabric petition covering the entrance. The entire Council waits for me, what's left of it. "She's definitely gone," states Shaw, stomping around the campfire, livid at Pasha's disappearance.

"Morris, Raghill, Annalynn—" says Clef.

"What about them?" I ask.

"They're gone too."

"Didn't show up for mapping assignments," says Shaw.

"And something else," adds Old Soul, his nervousness once again apparent. "All four of them were spotted out in a deserted cul-de-sac by the Waters of Erie."

McGinty and I exchange a knowing glance. We're the only ones so far that have traveled to the Warrior Strip—us and Raghill, but we know Degnan has already palm-coded in Pasha and Shaw. Shaw was with us when I cut the deal with Degnan. He picked up the uniform, just like McGinty and I did, but Pasha wasn't there. Raghill wasn't there. They didn't touch any uniforms like we did, but somehow Degnan, the great puppet master, is by design deciding who is coded-in and who is not.

Chapman peaks out the curtain from the quarters. He says, "Tired of mismanage-ment." This time he's not quite so hesitant in his pronunciation.

"Okay," I say, lacing my boots. "We know the drill. Rescue. Even if it means rescuing Pasha from herself. She doesn't have any orders to launch any sort of plan that involves her leaving The 28 United and possibly—"

"Going inside The Third?" asks McGinty, finishing my thought.

"She can't do that!" yells Shaw. "There's no Council plan for that. Our strategy from the beginning has been to build energy for the air fleet. Surprise The Third—attack from the air when they don't expect it. Gain command of Ash. When she went inside The Third—she risked everything."

"So, let's go get her," I say, leading the way, on a run, to the cul-de-sac tool shed. And I wonder if I am repeating my own mother's priority list: Duty first. Motherhood—somewhere down the list of an itemized agenda.

Chapter 7
RABBIT TRAILS
PASHA

"So you put reverse-*locasa* on the base of your skull?" Annalynn asked, and stepped on the heels of Pasha's boot. Annalynn was always too close.

"Didn't say I put it anywhere," barked Pasha. "You said that. Stop following me. Stop talking to me. Stop stepping on me." She made no attempt to confront Annalynn, Morris and Raghill even though they'd been trailing after her for miles. Pasha rehashed events in her mind. It was her fault they'd tracked her. She'd opened that opportunity. Pasha's own agenda had replaced caution. *Shouldn't have packed Herman and Orbit so soon in the quarters. Should have hid my gear bag and not put it by the door. Should have remembered Morris is snoopy. Annalynn's irritating. Raghill follows everywhere. Should have been careful.* The three of them had been clever at first—sly in the way they shadowed Pasha, using the training they'd received from Shaw.

Morris ran to the front of their four-person caravan. Side by side, he matched Pasha's steps. "You can't abandon us. We need your expertise." She quickened her pace, but all three kept up. "There are details at the Energy Concourse that still need problem-solving. You designed it. You were there for the construction, and you oversee repairs." No response from Pasha as they approached a toolshed that formerly serviced a string of housing units in a cul-de-sac now deserted. Pasha set her bag on the ground and lifted Herman from inside.

"Hey, what are you doing?" said Annalynn. The three watched solemnly as Pasha held the pigeon in her hands, her arms extending straight in front of her body. "Colony G," she whispered and released the pigeon. Pasha loved the sound, the melodic flapping of her pigeon's wings as he soared on the route she'd trained him to fly. It was home to Herman. Home to Orbit. And even though Avery wouldn't let them call it that, it was the closest thing most of them had to *home*—even pigeons.

"You must be serious about not coming back if you're sending Herman off," Annalynn said.

"I'm always serious," said Pasha, and she released Orbit in the same fashion, watching her fly away.

Raghill tried to reassure Pasha. "Chapman will find them. People will take care of them." Pasha ignored

Raghill, pushing on the door to the tool shed that was warped and stuck against the cement floor.

"Listen to me," called Annalynn.

"You're thirteen. Not listening," Pasha responded.

"You're headed after a rabbit trail here." Even though Pasha ignored her, slamming her shoulder against the tool shed door, trying to release it, Annalynn was not deterred. "You know—a rabbit trail. It's like when a dog is hunting a rabbit, and he loses the scent, sniffing around in circles."

"You're ignorant. The best trained hounds don't lose the scent, even on a rabbit trail."

Annalynn countered, "Rabbits turn sharply from side to side. You don't know what you're trailing. You don't know what they're going to do, and you don't know what you're in for."

"Rabbits are clever. Evasive," Morris joined in, placing his face directly in front of Pasha's. "You may think this is a good idea—trying to get inside The Third— but the rabbit that led you down this trail probably has something else in mind."

"If a hound keeps his nose to the ground," argued Pasha, "he won't ever lose the scent. It's when he lifts his head that the wind takes it away. I keep my head to the ground. Always." The tool shed door gave way.

"You can't leave us. We're family!" Raghill yelled. She knew he was the one who could not function without a leader. He'd be desperate for her to stay, but Pasha didn't listen to the quietest of the three. She swung around to confront them, her face sweating in spite of the crisp morning air. The moisture rolled down her newly-shaved head, like tributaries rushing for an open sea.

"Family?" she shouted. Then her voice quieted to its normal grumpy. "You three weren't even born when real families existed." She opened the door to the tool shed and entered, her trackers close behind. "You don't know what it was like to have parents or to be a parent or—"

"Hey!" Annalynn might have been the only person who would ever have the guts to grab Pasha's arm, and she did. "Morris said he saw you with reverse-*locasa* in your quarters. You used it, didn't you? Were you a parent? Was that what reverse-*locasa* did to you? Showed you what you're missing?"

Pasha pulled her arm away and kicked at the piles of tools and left-over flower bulbs from years before, exposing a manhole cover, like what used to be on city streets before the 14 Deadlies took away the population that needed streets.

"Help me with this," Pasha said, and Raghill immediately rushed to assist her. Morris pawed at Raghill's arm, and Pasha thought Morris was trying to remind Raghill that they needed to deter Pasha, not facilitate her plan, or lack of it, but Raghill labored anyway to get the manhole cover up.

Pasha started down a ladder to whatever was located below, and just before her head disappeared she whispered, "Families mean nothing if we can't remove The Third from power. Done hiding." And then she disappeared through the hole, following the scent of the rabbit.

Morris said, "She never said she *didn't* use reverse-*locasa*."

"She never said we *weren't* her family," said Annalynn.

"But," Raghill added, "She *did* say she was done hiding, and that means…"

Together they said, "She's going in." Then, without discussion and led by Morris, the three descended the ladder, trailing after Pasha to whatever waited below.

The shiny metal chamber was a notable contrast to the dark, filthy tool shed above. Pasha, standing in the area opposite the ladder, turned a wheel to a hatch. Water was trickling in around the gasket. "What is that?" Annalynn asked as she dropped to the floor, skipping the last few rungs of the ladder. "What are you doing?"

Tension filled the sterile room as the water began spilling in around the perimeter of the hatch, picking up volume and power. By the time Raghill dropped from the ladder and all three were looking at Pasha for an explanation, Pasha said, "Don't follow me." The water from Erie smashed into the room and the cries of shock and fear from Morris, Raghill and Annalynn were quickly swallowed by the raging water that filled the transition room. The three swirled with Pasha through the hatch, kicking with all their might.

Pasha emerged from Erie into the Warrior Strip, let the vacuum suck dry her and entered car #2 by holding her palm to the side of the archway—there was no sign of Morris, Annalynn and Raghill. Since they hadn't made it into the market after her, they probably choose swimming to the surface of Erie as the option to drowning. She tried to convince herself. *Strong swimmers. Smart kids.* Inside her stomach she felt a screw tightening, like someone wanted to strip the threads, make it dysfunctional, broken. What if the three didn't make it to the surface? What if she was responsible for their deaths the way Degnan had been responsible for Prospero's death in the forest pool when they were running from The Third? Was she Degnan's protégé? Had she learned his evil? No. She was here to try to embed herself into the upper tier of The Third, to become a convincing master negotiator. A subterranean for The 28 United, even though she had no orders from Avery and no dictates from the Council to do so. Someone needed to take the bold step to implant herself where it would make a difference, give them the edge against The Third, find out what they were using for weapons and shut them down. Not a worker from a plant of The Third. Not a soldier in their forces, but someone next to Dorsey's side. *Try.* She thought. *Have to try.*

She reached her hands to her head, but refused to touch the smooth surface of her skull still spattered with the scabs of nervous energy and the jerks from Morris' razor technique. Breathing slowly, she focused on controlling every muscle that shivered with anxiety. Dorsey had no reason to keep her alive. She needed to give him one. After she allowed his Elite to capture her, she must be, to them, a convincing surgeon and an inventive scientist, but nothing more, certainly not a mastermind behind ending the deployment opportunities of The Third and allowing The 28 United to invade with a full feet of energy-driven aircraft. She didn't have the skills to manipulate humans, she could hardly control herself. She'd always insisted on her own way because she thought herself brilliant. Everyone should listen to her, follow her lead. Her blunt form of arrogance alienated those who didn't know her well. She believed The 28 United's salvation hung on her ability to convince Dorsey she had something to offer that no one else could give him. She knew she was indispensable. Could she convince him?

The fingers of her right hand rummaged through her gear bag, locating reverse-*locasa*, sliding along the command buttons on its cylindrical sides. *Not again. There are probably carloads of weapons waiting with a payload to be powered and slammed down the throats of The 28 United. Not now.* She lifted the device from her bag, her knees shaking. *Don't.* She collapsed against the wall of the Warrior Strip, uninterested in what the two-way mirror might reveal about the market, only thinking about the fleeting images from her recent experiment with reverse-*locasa*. And now that ever-widening gap between her compulsion to get inside The Third and be the world's savior, and her obsession to use reverse-*locasa* to reconnect her past, were driving her in polar opposite directions. She must harness one direction into compliance with the other, or they would tear her apart.

Not now. Nose on the trail. Don't let the wind take the scent away. Nose on the trail. But her fingers, like a knee-jerk reaction to the little hammer of a doctor's reflex check, lurched on the button that sent her tumbling toward her past.

———

When The Third stole *locasa* from the Catalonians, Pasha had been one of the doctors working at the clinic in Reichel where The Third's citizens thought they were coming to receive an immunization against the 14 Deadlies. The #14 tattooed on their right wrists actually indicated that locasa had been used on them, stripping any memory of family and home from their minds, allowing their complete devotion to The Third.

"Dr. Lutnik," said one of her fellow doctors at the clinic lab where she'd gone to get more of the tattoo ink for the inoculation procedure. "Your turn," he said, holding *locasa* in his hand. One of the two Elite guards that accompanied him pointed his weapon in the direction of a chair slat on the wall at the side of a storage rack. She sat. Pasha thought how she and the other subterraneans lived in a world filled with life-or-death options. As *locasa* touched the back of her neck and sent its relaxing vibes through her crania, she didn't fight it, so her anonymity as a subterranean might be preserved. But her allegiance to The 28 United, unlike the hordes of people naively receiving *locasa*, would never be replaced by devotion to The Third.

Yes, they took Pasha's family like they had most other citizens. They sent her off to Elite training where she met up with Avery after years of not seeing her, both of them in subterranean status. She knew they'd taken something, she just couldn't remember what it was. Little did The Third know that when they used *locasa* effectively on the masses of unsuspecting innocents, they had also ignited a personal vendetta inside a seemingly powerless doctor.

———

Once again, she allowed the cylinder to plunge into her skull, and the effects of reverse-*locasa* slammed her body against the Warrior Strip wall. Then it started. The rapid-fire screenshots began. She longed to see them. She was not afraid.

Her hair was long, frizzy, laden with the perspiration of childbirth. His hand, skin darker than her own, holding tight in futile assurance. Contractions wracked her body beyond where she thought pain could go, and her intellectual control of any situation had been stripped from existence. This hurt like hell. Pasha floated on the sidelines of this memory, trying to force fuzzy images of faces into focus. Not yet.

As soon as a frame blinked black in her mind, another filled its spot. *Together the man with strong arms held both of them—her and the newly birthed miracle. The miracle was a boy. The man's tears dropped from his face and merged with her own that fell upon on the baby's forehead.* Then she felt her own tears falling. Not the tears in a screenshot's image, but her own tears. And they were tears of joy. No faces. *The man held her and they, together held him—the baby boy.*

Pasha shuddered awake from reverse-*locasa*, and staring her in the face were two little wicked scorpodarts with their blue legs pulsing inches from her skin, and the stingers on their tails raised for action.

"Telson! Dart! Come," commanded Degnan. The scorpodarts backed off Pasha's face and neck, their blue legs avoiding the touch of her skin. She heard the sound of their arachnid claws rubbing together, creating the stridulate sound that terrified her as they climbed the side of the two-way mirror and perched on either corner, waiting for further instructions.

"Not as scary as looking at the fangs in the mouth of a striking viper," said Pasha.

"You haven't seen their full potential." Pasha noticed Degnan held reverse-*locasa* in his hand. "It's a weapon. I'll keep it for a while."

She pushed herself to her feet, and evaluated her lack of muscle control. She wondered if she would recover from these effects, or if this was her lifetime punishment for using a device still in the incomplete stages of research. If she got inside The Third and lived, she would need a secret access to a lab undetectable by others, where she could continue to perfect reverse-*locasa*. A lab that would not only free her memories, but would free the memories of the citizens of The Third as well.

Degnan attempted to slip the reverse-*locasa* inside his messenger bag, as Telson and Dart made a quick entry, burrowing their poisonous bodies out of sight, but Pasha grabbed his arm and took the device back. He made no attempt to stop her. Perhaps he was pushing at her raw nerves, testing just what kind of subterranean she would be. Her nerves—already frayed by another encounter with reverse-*locasa*.

He led the way, car after car, through the Warrior Strip. At car #50 Pasha followed Degnan up a tube and into the market car that shared a wall with the Warrior Strip. They ended up in a dressing room of an upper tier clothing car. He grabbed a fur coat discarded on the floor and wrapped it around Pasha's shoulders, leaving the dressing room behind, and entering the crowed merchandise room. Then he escorted her to a sitting area attached to the transport platform. His hand bound her forearm, and she was glad for that. She thought he must have seen the effects of reverse-*locasa* on her, her instability, or maybe she was just his prisoner.

When the glide arrived and two guards exited, standing at attention, Degnan motioned Pasha to enter first. One guard handed him a Z-Colt just before the glide door sealed them in. Degnan aimed it at her head. She was way too short to grab the stability bar above her, so she had no choice but to let the ankle cuff slide around her foot. Degnan stroked the Z-Colt. "Funny how a weapon can legitimize most anything in the eyes of The Third." He used his free hand to slap her face with a force so strong she could not have stood if it wasn't for the holds on her ankles. "An injury creates the effect of struggle to those looking for evidence. We'll need that." Pasha moved her hand to the spot on the corner of her mouth where blood ran down. She wiped it away, but as soon as she did another stream flowed, and she felt the warm dribble continue.

"Big points from Dorsey if you catch the doctor of The 28 United." He placed his hand on her chin and manipulated it so he could get the best view of her injury. "I don't need the points, but blood is very effective when trying to make an impression and..." he nodded upwards to a small camera, "…the video-audio trails record my efforts and your pain."

"So you think you're part of my plan now?" She forced herself to speak in complete sentences.

"No, *you're* part of *my* plan," insisted Degnan. Pasha shook her head away from him. "Granted, an unexpected part of my plan, but an appreciated addition nonetheless."

"We're not working together."

"The 28 United and Avery owes me. It's contractual. Whether you like it or not, we're partners."

Pasha spit the blood from her mouth on his shoe. She expected another hit, but he didn't strike. He laughed.

Just before the guard pushed the release for their glide, Degnan said, "961. Remember the number, doctor." Pasha's mind spun, like a kaleidoscope trying to move jumbled beads to assemble a design. Mixing shreds of memories from reverse-*locasa*, with her brash move to get inside the Third, with the haunting memory of three teenagers in the Waters of Erie, with the pounding on her skull from the blow Degnan dealt her, and—still— still—that sound she'd heard back at the zoo—that roar in her head.

Chapter 8
SOUNDS LIKE PINK COMMANDER DORSEY

One glide sailed silently through the transport space fifty feet in front of Dorsey's private glide and another trailed fifty feet behind. The six Elite soldiers of his assigned guard were distributed for his safety—three in the forward transports and three in the aft. They understood Commander Dorsey's protocol: protection at all costs.

The leprexes curled lazily at Dorsey's feet, their left ankle bracelets secure as a safeguard. To Dorsey, the purring from the depths of their mutated esophagi proved insufferable. He craved quiet. He needed to think. The brain-swappers kneaded their claws in momentary comfort, scratching against the metal of the glider floor. Reverberation. Sound waves bouncing erratically from one clear glass side of the transport to the other and then settling on Dorsey's earlobes and hopping into his ear canal.

"Stop it," Dorsey whispered to the swappers, not wanting his own voice to add to the discord. Then louder. "Stop it!" Retracting their claws the leprexes yawned, rising to their feet, readjusting positions. Dorsey placed his hand on the scruff of the neck of the monster on his right. His hand was shaking as he squeezed violently. "Your heavy breathing is getting most annoying. Shut up." The creature blinked its eyes at Dorsey, rolling over, turning its back on the Commander.

Deep breath. Several deep breaths. He watched the transport in the front of him dock and the three soldiers step into the transition space, their weapons held on alert, their bodies attentive to the task. His glide docked. The door slid open, and Dorsey made a mental note, as he approached his conference room and private quarters, to remind his assistant to fix his transport immediately. These glides were to be noiseless, even at docking, but the clanging in his ears at the moment the transport connected with the dock and the unforgiving clanking when the door opened did not meet his expectations. Degnan had guaranteed the Commander that these three cars designed for his transport through the market, to his weapon stash and to his private quarters would be more than sound-proofed. Sound was to be extinct. This noise—exceedingly unacceptable to Dorsey.

The footsteps of the leprexes followed Dorsey onto the platform of the transition space with a heaviness that milled around his ears in chaos. He stopped abruptly. With the quietest of his commander voices he spoke to the soldier closest to the archway leading to his hideaway. "Keep the swappers here."

"Yes, Commander," said Frederick, the Elite in charge, and the other two soldiers guarding the private glider slipped their fingers under the collars of the swappers and attached a leash to each.

The Commander entered his conference room and private quarters by palm code, leaving the swappers and three soldiers to wait on the small platform for an undesignated period of time. The other three soldiers in the aft glider were abandoned, staying on duty and suspended in the Waters of Erie.

At last Commander Dorsey was alone. He crossed the luxurious brown carpet, past the copper colored sofas and chairs, plucking a gardenia from a three-foot-high arrangement on the polished brass end table. The smell was heavenly. Calming. He followed a familiar path to the bar and around the back of it where the well-stocked booze bottles called him to face the enormous mirror on the wall behind. The Third hung very few mirrors. There were none in the citizens' units. *All hair is to be worn buzzed and black. Five gray uniforms will be provided at the beginning of each month, delivered with the regular pep allotment. Place the uniforms daily in the laundry drop.* No reason for mirrors. Dorsey had no such restrictions on his attire, or his hair. While he was faithful to eat his allotted peps, he also enjoyed the privileges that came with command.

Transfixed. Couldn't take his eyes off—himself. He had mirrors in most rooms. They were polished and waiting for the reflection of his power. He ran his hand over the bottles of wine that rested in brass racks on the counter under the mirror. All reds. He perused the pinot noir, the merlots, as well as a few malbecs and cabernets. His choice, a merlot with a hint of blackberry, plum and cherry. One of his favorites, and hard to get now that the western states, their wineries and vintners were all entombed in the Pacific. He'd drink it slow, honor the victims of *Jurbay*, that raging asteroid that had paid no attention to the points awarded fine wines. After all, their compassion-soaked survivors were the ones that placed his father and The Third in power two decades ago. No complaints from Dorsey. He'd been able to walk right into the seat of power in his father's place. A comfortable arrangement.

The corkscrew grated against the cork. He knew what was coming next, and he hated it. The cork popped out. That horrible sound! Disgusting what he was willing to listen to for the pleasure of tasting an excellent wine. The goblets were brass, and he chose a big one, stuffing his finger in one ear to stunt the sound of the lapping wine as he filled the glass. Carrying the wine with him to the sofa at the center of the room, he sat. At last the silence. He sipped. The noise of the wine touching his lips was so disappointing. He tried to think of something else other than the sounds.

At first, when Dorsey was diagnosed with hyperacusis, an unrestrained sensitivity to sound, the disease presented itself to Dorsey in such an extraordinary fashion, it seemed a gift. Another tool in his extensive commander's toolbox, providing uncanny insight. For several years, he'd relished this sensitivity that was imperceptible to others. When soldiers were asleep and unconscious from the rigors of responsibility and the weariness of war, he'd listen in the darkness. While they'd slept, he walked among the exhausted workers in their open barracks, disguised like Shakespeare's Henry V. He'd heard which soldiers told bits of stories in their sleep, secrets no one else had heard. He saw who turned from side to side in fits of nightmares that tormented their unconsciousness.

However, in the last months, the gift transformed into a curse. Whispers turned into taunting cacophonies, hacking away at his vigor, lacerating his confidence, and there were no sutures in sight. Now he was like a nervous Caesar in the minutes before the Ides of March. Dorsey struggled to find the calm he used to feel surrounding him. In the midst of the chaos, he somehow rallied each day like a turtle driven to the beach for nesting and birth. Yet, the tranquil spaces he'd retained for his retreat, so he might hide this disability, were getting fewer, noisier. More often than not, he felt he'd climbed onto a precipice, overlooking the sea, standing by the cliff's edge, toying with temptation. He begged the screaming noises to stop.

Dorsey's private quarters in the market, submerged in the quiet of Erie, was one of the few places left to leave the noise behind, but tonight the sounds had followed him. His private physician planned ahead, knowing there may come a time when sleep would elude Dorsey and the demons of night might consume him by the morning. He crossed to the wall where the physician had arranged for a medication hub to be installed. Dorsey sat on the chair slat in the small alcove and activated a hologram. He inserted his arm into a medicine cuff. He'd been promised five hours of sleep. It was all he needed. The pant legs of his uniform rustled against each other, further unraveling his nerves. The wine lost its flavor. In the hologram a message from his doctor appeared, requesting confirmation. Dorsey proceeded.

When the prick of relief struck the vein in his arm, he sighed, unhooked his arm, stood and faced the cushions of the sofa. Stumbling to the edge of the couch, he collapsed mid-breath, half on the sofa, half off, his uniform jacket lying disheveled on the floor. The noise disappeared. Deep sleep. Thinking of nothing.

————

What woke him was the sound of her breathing. Calm. Taunting him to open his eyes. He did. The shine from her ginger hair competed with the brass and copper in the room. Dorsey had never seen her hair red before, only the silver of command. Quinn.

She held his uniform jacket on her lap, smoothing the arm, petting it in a hypnotizing fashion. "No need to look at your timepiece," Quinn said. "It's 4:00. Those injections used to lay you out for five hours. Now—three hours and fifty minutes." As always, she exhibited steady control. "What are you going to do when the injections don't work anymore?"

Dorsey brought himself to a sitting position, still dazed from sleep. "Degnan has cars full of alternative concoctions." He knew she might have a weapon pointed at his heart under the jacket she held. "Whisper in my presence," he commanded. He studied her, sitting there, straight-backed and smug. How long had she been watching him? He reached for his wine glass, but she whisked it away before he had a chance to touch it.

"I'll get you another." Quinn wore The Third's uniform well, the gray jacket hugging her muscular torso. Her knitted cap lay resting on the sofa. He figured she was in disguise and had somehow gained access to his quarters. He would mark all six of his Elite private guard and send them to the interrogation chamber before the night was over. If there was a leak, his interrogators would find it; after all, he had personally trained them.

Quinn handed Dorsey the refill. He tried to take the glass, but Quinn did not release it. She held onto it for another few seconds, forcing his visual engagement. He said, "You've been gone five years. I should call the guards. I should call the leprexes." His own voice made him wince. And though he tried to hide his auditory feebleness from her, she was still the master observer.

Quinn released the glass, her combat boots a din on the carpet as she walked to a brown leather chair. While her back was to him, he raised his fingers to his ears to plug them, stop the noise, but she turned, just before she sat, and caught him in the act of his weakness. "You know there's a way to stop that, don't you?" The initial danger stage was over for her. Dorsey wasn't going to call the guards or the swappers or any other of his protective provisions. She always had the answers that he wanted. Before, when she worked for him as second in command of The Third, she was instinctive, strategic, focused and capable of separating their very personal life from the demands of duty. Now, did she really have a way to strip this noise from inside his head and free him from the flaw that would eventually gobble up his ability to command?

"Hyperacusis." Quinn stood, and manipulated her sleek body Dorsey's way, winding around the back of the sofa, standing behind him. He let her move wherever she liked. "Over-sensitivity to sound frequencies." She touched the temples of his head with her fingers.

He flinched in response, then relaxed. But as she rubbed each side of his head in a circular motion, the noise stirred up again. For a moment, Dorsey didn't care. He remembered her age. Ten years his senior, but she never looked it. Alluring. He closed his eyes. The smell on her skin was nothing more than *clean*. Everything he'd missed. There were many other women over the last half a decade. Women purchased. Women eager to please the Commander. Women unlike Quinn. She matched the commander in him but picked at his emotions from the inside out.

She traced a line from his right ear to the top of his head. Her fingers, rustling through his short, silver spikes of hair, sounded like violent waves pounding the shore. Impossible noise. Captivating touch. "What you've got going on here is a brain processing issue." Her voice was raging now and he grabbed her arm, applying the pressure of a vice.

"Whisper," he demanded again. She did.

"Damage to the olivocochlear bundle of nerves. Cerebral processing interrupted." Dorsey released Quinn's arm. Taking her other hand away from his head, she moved around the sofa to stand in front of him. From a pocket just above her right knee, she eased out a small leather case. As she did, Dorsey's body tensed until she gestured that she meant no harm. The small gray box was nondescript, yet she offered it to him as a rare treasure. Dorsey watched her collar bone rise and fall with each controlled breath. The sounds were horrifying, but every movement, gesture and nuance of Quinn, mesmerized.

"Open it," she whispered. Dorsey stared at her. "It's old-fashioned, but it works." Cautiously, he reached one hand forward and lifted the box from her hands. Easing the lid up, he expected some uncanny weapon but hoped she'd brought a cure. Small ear inserts rested in the middle of a miniature velvet divot. "Pink noise." She knelt before him, gently taking the first insert and placing it in his left ear.

"There's a buzz," Dorsey said.

"Flat? Like ocean waves? Empty TV station at the History Labyrinth?" Dorsey nodded. After she'd inserted the cure in his right ear, Quinn clapped her hands and there was no flinch from Dorsey, no wrinkling of pain in his face. Snapped fingers. Clicked tongue. Wine glass lifted up and then down, loudly, on the table.

"Nothing," he said as he stood for the first time in her presence. He kissed her with passion, without gentleness. "You can't run out on command, Quinn, disappear for five years and stroll back, expecting no consequences." His movement to the room's entrance was quick, decisive. Activating the hologram to the side of the archway he said, "Voice command."

"Consequences," she said with the steel of authority he recognized instantly, "can be negated by gifts you can't attain anywhere else. Call me a consultant. I'm no longer interested in power."

"Send in the swappers." The metal plates in the archway ascended and Quinn leaped to stand on the bar, drawing a wicked hatchet from the back of her uniform, sleek, sparkling, sharp.

The leprexes used their leopard bodies to slink to the front of the bar, one on each side, in ready position. They growled with an ugly desire to be let loose on behalf of their master. Their mouths opened, displaying their menacing teeth, the drool detaching from their tongues and rolling to the ground.

Dorsey took note that, while she protected herself from the brain-swappers, there didn't seem to be one crack in her control as she attempted manipulation of the circumstances. She said, "You have no complaint. I returned."

"I have no trust in grandmothers," he said.

"I'd hardly call me that. I have a relationship with the boy that will one day work to your advantage. I'm an independent contractor."

Adjusting his right earpiece, he said, "Like Degnan?"

"Like Degnan."

"That involves a considerable amount of hate on my part." Dorsey snapped his fingers and both leprexes leaped to his side, sitting instantly at attention. The bar called him. Quinn called him. He walked in her direction, extending both arms upward to her where she stood on the bar, clasping her waist in his hands. He lifted Quinn to the ground. She took his hand and guided him over to the sofa where she had draped his jacket. Gingerly lifting it, she opened the uniform and held it up, offering assistance to Dorsey. He turned his back on her and slipped his arms through the armholes, then faced her again. She buttoned the jacket front and adjusted the collar for him.

The robotic announcement from Dorsey's guard came through several speakers in his private car. "Commander Dorsey. A problem has been detected, and we have it contained in the conference room."

"Take care of it," barked Dorsey, adjusting the earpiece in his left ear.

"Commander, you'll want to see this yourself."

Dorsey gestured toward Quinn to remain. "Wait here," he said. "Over by the archway," he pointed to the hologram, "you can watch and listen."

"I will," Quinn said. The leprexes followed the Commander to the door and planted themselves as centurions on either side of the archway, licking their lips and continuing their guttural growl, never taking their eyes off Quinn's neck.

Dorsey's hand rested in the hologram control and Quinn asked, "You leaving both those swappers here?"

"They're a matched set." He adjusted both his earpieces at once. For the first time, he smiled. It was insincere and filled with deceit, but nonetheless, a smile. "Think of them as guards for valuable contraband, not sentinels watching a proven traitor." When he opened the archway, he added, "They haven't been fed today." He left for the conference room.

Quinn stepped toward the hologram to activate the video-audio trails, but instantly froze when the leprexes jumped to their feet and snapped their swapper mouths open, showing oversized jagged teeth. The hologram automatically activated with a live feed. No need for Quinn to do any activation, Dorsey had guaranteed she'd be watching. Images fluttered into focus from the adjoining car, revealing Pasha standing, defiant, under guard, her bald head shining and her gear bag still on her back. Other guards pushed in three teenagers, dripping wet, looking terrified, like they'd rather be anywhere then in the presence of Dorsey, the Commander of The Third.

Frederick said, "We fished these three out of Erie." Dorsey momentarily ignored them, placing all his focus on Pasha. "Well, well," Dorsey said, his sarcasm flashing and hardly seeming like a man who an hour ago faced the madness of noise. Ear inserts gave him back his sanity.

Degnan was there too, his smirk competing with Dorsey's. Degnan ran his hand over Pasha's bald head and said, "Consider her a gift." Pasha shook her head away from him.

"'Thank you would be premature."

"We'll see."

Dorsey appraised Pasha, her size laughable, and her delegation of teenage misfits a joke. While he didn't recognize the young girl with Pasha, he'd confronted

Morris before as Borden's son, and the other boy—well, the Commander took extra time with his examination of Raghill. He mused at the grand mismatch between himself and his son. Some divine creator had made an unspeakable error. He asked Pasha, "Are these three yours?" She didn't answer him, turning to the three, throwing them a wicked look. Then, bringing her attention back to Dorsey, she nodded. He said, "And this is what The 28 sent as a contingent of war?"

"I have a proposal," said Pasha.

"Well that solves your reason for being here"—he gestured at Raghill—"and I know this one will follow anyone anywhere."

"Wouldn't follow you," blurted the young girl.

Raghill whispered instantly to her, "Shut up." His words were unnecessary as the Elite guard reached his arm around her neck with a stranglehold. The girl shut up.

"But you," Dorsey prowled his way to Morris, his wine-laced breath spilling over Morris' space and beyond, "Borden's son."

"I have a name," Morris said. Spit flew from his mouth and took a direct route to land on Dorsey's uniform. "Borden's dead. He no longer has a son, and I never had a father."

Without needing instructions, Frederick approached Dorsey and wiped the spittle off his jacket. Dorsey, unfazed by Morris' spit, was content to treat Morris as he had all the commanders' and officers' sons that had been sent to the library years ago, without individuality. Considering he'd dressed everyone in gray for over a decade, it was no surprise. "Borden's son wouldn't follow without a reason." Dorsey pushed his fingers against Morris' chest. "What's your reason?"

Pasha distracted Dorsey with her words. "You need help," she said. Dorsey laughed. "You're in way over your head, Commander."

The vein in Dorsey's temple pulsed with a tempo that matched the speed of Pasha's voice. "You've got car after car in this market filled with weapons collecting dust. Not only are you low on energy in Ash, but you don't even have the energy to open an exit door for those weapons, let alone launch."

Pasha slammed her gear bag on the table, unzipping it and displaying her bait piece by piece. "Solar cell," she said. Dorsey's eyes widened as she lifted a perfect rectangle from her bag and arranged it on the table top. "Wind block." She slid out a small gray square, slightly bigger than the Rubik's cubes from the History Labrinth, and placed it next to the solar cell. Pasha lifted a third item from the bag, a ball eight inches in diameter, and lined it up next to the other two items. "And a poo-ball. Has the stink of chicken manure that matches something I smell here."

Dorsey stared at Pasha's collection without so much as a cringe or a wince from the briskness of her voice.

Pink in his ears was working. He was glad. Pasha brought something he had to have and all distractions must be avoided.

"You want the energy?" she continued. "Then I'll work for you." Dorsey noticed she purposely took the slightest of pause, insuring the drama of her next comment. "My terms."

"I'm a very good listener," said Dorsey. He was also an excellent liar.

"You'd better be a good listener 'cause I'm only gonna say this once." She lifted the cell, the block and the ball with purpose back into her bag, one by one, accentuating her words with each repacking. "My safety here will never be in question." She zipped closed the opening to the bag, and demanded, "You provide a lab for me with every resource I need—available immediately." In an instant, with a strength way beyond her slight frame, Pasha used her Elite training and grabbed the weapon from Dorsey's soldier, targeting the muzzle directly at Dorsey's head. "And just one more thing."

Dorsey smiled at her and shrugged his shoulders. "I *am* listening," he said.

"Don't ever touch my minions again." The guards tightened their holds on Morris and the girl as they tried to wriggle away. Raghill remained still. Dorsey nodded at the guards who released the three of them. Pasha stood directly in front of him, and he thought she tried to make her 4'11" frame look taller than it was. "You need me, and I need them for what you want."

Dorsey scrutinized the captured again, eyes coming to rest on Raghill. "Finally back to where you belong, son?"

Pasha yanked Dorsey's arm, sending Frederick to restrain her again. "Raghill belongs with me," said Pasha.

Dorsey smirked, "Well, good, it's a group package. All for one and all that." He crossed to the alcove that led to his quarters, touching the hologram and opening the archway. "Why? I thought you and Avery DeTornada were joined at the hip."

She waited a long time before she answered. "I don't ever want to follow any one again."

"Fine. I'll just give you a few minutes with those DR93s pointed at you and your 'minions' to make absolutely sure I've got your energy and your loyalty on all of this. Then, we can get started." He left and the archway slid closed behind him.

———

Dorsey faced Quinn, who sat across the room on the bar. Immediately he noticed the uniform was gone, and she was dressed in civilian clothes. Khaki pants, brown boots laced to her knees and a simple black turtleneck tucked into the waist of her pants, leaving her weapons belt unobstructed. She stared at the screen in the alcove connected to the VATs. He knew she'd been watching Pasha pitch her deal. He knew Quinn wouldn't miss a beat, and he wanted Quinn's advice. Had to have it. "In less than a paragraph…your thoughts?" he asked.

Everything about her seemed seductive in the strategy of war. When she spoke, everyone listened. It had always been that way when she was a commander and worked with him before. The before…when they were intimate, involved on a personal level, yet distant, clinical within the realms of rulership. In spite of all their disagreements and the fact she'd disappeared for five years, he knew they still had a strategic connection. If they decided in union, the results would be stronger than if they were decisively apart. It had worked in the past. Could he trust her? He'd keep his guard up. Let her in a little at a time. He owed her that. She'd brought him healing.

Quinn—closer to him than anyone he'd ever known, other than Degnan, whom he hated. Instinctive, she could always put forth a challenge that evoked logic, elicited power. Quinn was almost his equal. And Dorsey liked the newer version of her—the russet hair, a faint, silver strand blended in here and there—the lack of a uniform. So when Quinn spoke, even after her long disappearance, the lengthy void in their connection—he listened.

She said, "Degnan and Pasha are tops in their field. No one comes close. You've got Degnan in your pocket.

You need Pasha. Keep a tight watch on her, but she doesn't have the social skills to deceive anyone. And she doesn't have the military background to plot any sort of a take-over. Science motivates her. Her ego motivates her. But as a threat to you—to Ash—to The Third— she's neutral. Lock this down, Asher Dorsey. Lock it down now." Dorsey thought Quinn might be the only one who knew his first name, Asher. She slipped off the bar and moved toward him. He met her halfway across the room. They were so close he imagined her breathing heightened in pace from the excitement of working with him again. So close he could feel her breath, warm and inviting, on his cheek. He said, "I love it when you call my name."

———

When Dorsey returned to the conference car, no one had moved. The three minions and Pasha were still under guard, but Pasha continued holding the weapon she'd liberated from the soldier and pointed at Dorsey.

Dorsey stared at Pasha, knowing he wanted her cutting-edge inventiveness, and as long as he gave her the freedom to create, she would pose no threat. He craved the power of the solar cells and the mystique of the wind blocks. He was prepared to give poo-balls the opportunity to activate his weapons, but most of all he knew Pasha to be the sharpest inventor in what was left of the world. Dorsey touched his hand to his ear. Pasha was also a beyond-brilliant neurosurgeon. He'd already gotten acclimated to the pink buzz, the calming noise in his ears, already felt the control he'd lacked for so many months returning, but it wouldn't last forever. Good. He'd have her work on deploying the weapons of the market, and in the meantime, surgically deploy healing for both his ears.

"Set them up with quarters," Dorsey commanded his Elite. "Under 24/7 guard. For awhile." He took several intimidating steps toward Pasha, and was right in her face, checking her out with his capacity to detect a liar. "How'd you know I'd take you in? How'd you know I even needed energy?" Dorsey thought for sure she was ready to fire off one of her rude, sarcastic clips.

"That's easy, Commander Dorsey," Pasha said, staring him down. "Easy. I heard you roar."

Chapter 9
ROOM FOR SIX
AVERY

In the Warrior Strip of the market, I stand with my contingent of nineteen, watching Frederick, one of Dorsey's Elite guards, enter the conference room with his weapon poised. He makes a sweep of the car, assuring it is safe. He passes by the window less than a foot from me. He doesn't know I'm here on the other side. Do I see his eyes dart my way? Might he still be a subterranean after all these years? Is he informed as to the power behind this glass, waiting to be unleashed at the precise moment we are needed? I'm quite sure I have imagined his slight acknowledgement of our presence. Surely reverse-*locasa* had no permanent effect on Frederick, and he remembered nothing from those brief days he traveled with us in forest when we were on the run, after Red Grove fell.

The hologram on the archway entrance at both ends of the strategy car activates, and from one end, several Elite soldiers enter, using their weapons to nudge forward two of their own men whose hands are pinned at the wrists in front of them. These prisoners have been stripped down to the waist, their bodies showing signs of beatings. The flinch I feel in my composure is collective. Our entire group of soldiers standing with me cringe, and McGinty grabs my forearm, saying, "Their —"

"Some of ours," I finish his sentence.

Following the Elite guard are Pasha, Morris, Raghill and Annalynn. Confirmed. Not only is Pasha an idiot for going inside The Third herself, but a bigger idiot for taking three teenagers with her. From the opposite end of the car Dorsey rushes in, grumbling his discontent, "What?" Frederick seems hesitant to speak. "What? I don't like being disturbed." I want to rush them all with the nineteen men and women that stand behind me. Bust through to the other side and take Dorsey and The Third down, but twenty of us can't do it alone.

Raghill rushes forward to Dorsey and blurts out the information. "Commander, they're subterraneans for The 28 United." I see the shock on Morris and Annalynn's faces, and I feel that disbelief myself. How did this faithful boy who I rescued from a burning library and who has lived with us as family for so long turn on our own? Has he always been this desperate to win a father?

Pasha's face remains unreadable as Dorsey address-es Raghill. "And you know this—how?" But before Raghill can answer, I see her. My mother Quinn walks through the archway from Dorsey's quarters. I long for her, but the hole in my heart—Chapman's heart—that she dug with her unannounced disappearance a year and a half ago reminds me not to make the mistake of caring again.

She stands alert but comfortable just behind Dorsey's shoulder, like a prompter ready for action on opening night. Out of uniform, she no longer shares the com-mand of leadership as before, but I sense they still share something, and I am eager to find out what it is. I do not question her loyalty. She may desert family and abandon those she's claimed to love, but she will never turn her back on The 28 United. It has always been her passionate mission. I am left with the disappointment of knowing she is and always will be an independent contractor.

"Speak up," demands Dorsey, and I hear him clearly from my side of the glass. "You know this how?"

Frederick answers, "We got a tip from uniform ser-vices. Unlikely that anyone would see it, on the inside of the bicep and all, but I guess someone caught a glimpse when they ditched their shirts to the laundry suck."

"Go on," says the Commander.

"But that's not the only way we knew." Dorsey stares at Frederick, expecting the rest of the answer. "Raghill recognized them."

My stomach sickens while I watch two of the armed Elite guards twist the bare arms of the prisoners upward to reveal a small, unobtrusive circle tatted with The 28 United's patch.

"How foolish," I whisper before I can stop myself.

McGinty, standing beside me, argues, "How bold."

"What? A tat is worth dying for when they could have continued to be subterraneans working undercover in there for us?"

"They didn't know, when they got those tats, they'd ever be subterraneans," says McGinty, "But, yes, worth dying for." I'm ashamed that I let my honest comments slip. It seems my first thoughts are always how to use another's life as strategy, while McGinty thinks first of the quality of life. Maybe that's why I'm a commander, and he's a person of integrity. I'd trade positions with him in a heartbeat.

"Shoot them." Dorsey's voice is ice and his eyes colder. Frederick doesn't hesitate and drills the first soldier in the head with a bullet from his Z-Colt. McGinty and I both jerk in reflex. Our subterranean falls to the ground. Is Frederick's game-face really that good that he can murder so quickly and without response? This is just one more imperfection of reverse-*locasa*. It appears to work, but is short-lived. A family man like Frederick whose memories had come back after reverse-*locasa* would never purposely return to the emotional void needed to be an Elite. No one's that good. My eyes travel from

Frederick and the fallen soldier to Quinn at Dorsey's shoulder. Every muscle controlled, her face unreadable even by me. No, I'm wrong. *She's* that good.

Frederick points his raised weapon at the second soldier, but Dorsey says, "No, stop." He takes a few steps toward Raghill. Some of my men and women standing behind me run for the two-way mirror, one of them shouting, "No, don't make him!" They know what's coming. McGinty puts his hand on my shoulder. Steady. "You do it," says Dorsey, looking straight into Raghill's eyes. Dorsey's cruel command, a counter-point to my whispered hope.

I say, "Don't do it, Raghill. Don't."

This teenage boy, one of our own, whose been through unspeakable horrors of abandonment by his father, the murder of most of his friends, the killing of the two closest to him by brain-swapper and deadlies—this boy, Raghill, takes the Z-Colt from Frederick. Sweat, like a leaking levy, darkens the collar of his shirt, and with his hand quivering, he holds the barrel to the soldier's temple and pulls the trigger.

Some of my troops, formerly clinging to the window in a raging, unheard protest, sink back away from the two-way. I hear the wretch of someone inconsolable. The smell of vomit spreads and fills the air space of the car. I shut the part of me away that wants to comfort.

I say, "Raghill might have just given us another six months of opportunity—inside The Third. Let's not waste it." I activate the palm code, open the archway and lead our troops to the secret entrance of the Warrior Strip. There, we'll plunge to the depths of Erie, finding our way to the zoo and the Energy Concourse, where Pasha's inventions will one day spin our planes in the air for an all-out assault on the one that commands a boy to murder.

———

I stand at the edge of the hatch that leads me back to the frigid Waters of Erie and then to the underground entry of the tool shed at the end of the cul-de-sac. Staccato breaths begin, yet I know I need the adagio pace that dictates control. I cannot find it, and there is McGinty, unafraid to place his hand on mine when eighteen soldiers stand at our rear.

I say, "Even if I can't breathe right, with you there's peace." We should only be thinking of Raghill, consumed in grief for him, but we have all learned to place the horror in a locked container to be opened and dealt with at a future time. McGinty knows this well, avoiding Raghill's memory and reminding me of the memory of another.

"Sometimes I think I compete with *him* even after he's long gone."

I take a quick curt breath, like when the air's so cold I think my lungs might collapse. "You have never competed with Raben. You and I were friends when I was married to him. He betrayed me. He betrayed us all." I cling to McGinty's hand. "Count the years we've had together: over a decade of friendship…and now much more."

Shaw pushes his way between us and jumps in the water. His head reappears for a moment. "Hey, love-birds, we've got a world to save here." He slips below the surface, and I jump in to follow him.

It is this exit that I hate, partially because there are no other choices, but mostly because of the haunting ter-ror that Borden might be reborn, coming to grab my an-kles again and dragging me to the life-and-death battle that only one can win.

I kick with the muscles in my legs and feet. I create bubbles that surround me, fizzing as I race by them for the hatch. I sense McGinty at my side before I see him in my peripheral vision. The way to the exit is familiar now. I will make it. We will make it.

When we swim into the chamber below the tool shed there is room for six of us. I must hold my breath until three more follow Shaw, McGinty and me. The fi-nal woman to enter slams the hatch and turns the dial quickly, triggering the sucking action that clears the room of water. We all gasp in unity, and Shaw immedi-ately releases the manhole cover above the ladder lead-ing to the tool shed. I let the other five go first. They hurry. We all know that there are many more of our soldiers, holding their breath, waiting in the Waters of Erie to enter the chamber. Probably no one from above is counting how many of us have climbed the stairs, and in their rush, just as I move toward the ladder, someone latches the manhole cover above me. I open my mouth to scream, but it goes unheard, as simultaneously the hatch to the Waters of Erie bursts and releases hundreds of gallons of tumbling lake over me.

The chamber fills for the arrival of the next group of six that were behind us. The churning liquid rolls over me before I have time to plan a breath. I am overcome with the thrust of Erie claiming the space that she is compelled to fill. Fighting for calm, I will myself to think of the moment the room will clear, and I will breathe in all the air I need, but no one has even entered the chamber yet. The pressure of the lake weighs heavy on my chest, pressing me without mercy against the walls of this transition space. I try to fight the volume of this monster I oppose, but there is no competition, and it pushes my hands flat against the shiny steel walls. I can't breathe. Spots start to flash before my eyes even as I see the first soldier enter. I have been in this position before when I wrestled Borden for life in the History Labyrinth pool. I know what's coming. The black is coming. The black is here.

Chapter 10
BREATH IN THE UNDERGROUND
AVERY

Everything around me moves, but my legs—arms—shoulders—neck—can find no movement. I feel like I'm floating on an ever-advancing stream of memories. The water that carries me is on the verge of freezing, but it is electrifying, stimulating. I ride along the ripples on my back, thinking I might reminisce about the truly significant things of life. My father. Quinn. Raben. Chapman. McGinty. But everything of import swirls away with the bobbing leaves and sticks, drifting by my head. Far away I hear someone say, Take her to the caves. *I think it is McGinty's voice, but I don't know where he is, or what caves. I float on the water. Cool. My mind drifting back—way back.*

Only once did I have a pet. Pets, according to Quinn, were a "frivolous emotional taxation," but my father was a master negotiator. "Bling" arrived as a puppy. Quinn had his vocal chords removed. A barking dog might draw attention to Carles and Quinn's secret operations. A man dressed in Bermuda shorts and sun glasses delivered Bling. He didn't fool me a bit, even at seven. I'd seen him in military uniform at the lengthy strategy meetings when the round table was up and running in the basement of our home. Quinn wanted to name the pup Scofield. Carles suggested Rex. But the pup's eyes "shone like jewels," I said, and pronounced him "Bling." Quinn opened her mouth to argue her case for Scofield, but a look from my father confirmed his status as my advocate. Bling. Ridiculous name, I know, but I was seven. Later that month, the three of us were on a plane east to attend a military ball honoring Carles, leaving Bling with Bermuda Shorts. Two days after we left, *Jurbay* fell, and Bling joined everyone else we left behind in the ocean plunge that sealed their fate. Quinn was right, of course: *a frivolous emotional taxation*. I never thought of pets again.

Then came Gizzie. Of course, it was Pasha who found her. Our gazelle, Gizzie, curled up in the grasslands of the zoo's savanna. Half dead, she was unable to reach water, and her front right hoof was torn away, blood dripping and barely attached. Pasha figured the gazelle was almost ten years old, and that was quite a feat for the thin survivor. Gizzie was the only animal we ever encountered from the zoo. She was a bit of a metaphor for our own destiny, surviving the odds but not without injury and damage. More than a pet, she occasionally brought messages from those on the perimeter (when Herman and Orbit were busy elsewhere already in flight), sending word of approaching scout parties from The Third.

There've been two times I've allowed Gizzie to sleep on the mat next to Chapman. The first when Chapman cried inconsolably from the loss of his muskrat, shot by friendly fire when the critter scrambled past a perimeter guard. Chapman made it clear that was my fault for not letting the muskrat sleep with him each night. I was amazed that a child could heap that much guilt on his mother. The second time Gizzie curled beside Chapman resulted from a selfish relinquishment on my part. McGinty and I held each other close just outside the quarters, dancing to the chipster music in his arm, Gizzie was an endearing diversion to Chapman. That night, when I drew the curtain aside, returning to my bed by Chapman, he sat cross-legged, petting Gizzie's head, staring into the distance. He said, "Why don't you just bring the music inside?" Then he leaped through the window, followed by Gizzie, into the night. I didn't stop him or shadow him through the darkness. Chapman could trek the path of nightfall with surety, and I knew he would be back. Strange for a five-year-old? Motherhood most times confused me. Or was it just that I didn't understand the pioneering life of mothering a half-GEB child?

———

The water evaporates. I am no longer floating. The darkness engulfs every part of me. I want to open my eyes, but they are glued shut. I feel a scratchy garment against my face. It smells of campfire smoke and the grass from the savanna. Up and down, it rubs against my cheek, up and down. The steps of the one carrying me move with even strides. I hear the word caves *again. It reverberates and mixes chaotically with other words.* Hurry. Minstrels. Pepper. *No longer floating. No…longer…floating. My chest hurts. No, it's something deeper. Lungs. On my cheek a tuft of air— and another, maybe breathing, maybe an open door. No door. Outside? I hear trickles of water, not waterfalls, but gentle, tumbling gracefully from somewhere. I tell my eyes to open, but they will not. Notes are everywhere. Beautiful melodies from haunting flutes. The sound of drums grabs at my heart, and I feel the strength of beating. And so many strings! I try to picture them in my mind, decide how many different instruments there must be, but every time I try to count I am carried away by the beauty of sound, by the deep, deep peace. For a time, I cannot remember who I am, I only hear the music. I only want to hear the music.*

———

My eyes finally open. I hear a whisper in my head. It says: *Commander.* It says: *Commander, come.* I know this voice. It is the voice of my father. It is clear. I know where I am. I am in the caves of healing. Clef is here, with his musicians bringing their own kind of medicine. I will stay here until The Third is defeated. I am safe. I can rest. My gaze is stuck on the ceiling of this cave. Those artists! They are ever-present, but so often I do not see them face to face. I see their handprints, remaining in the ragged remnants of their craft. Even in the dimness of this underground retreat, there is the color and the magnificence, the result of trained and brilliant hands. I see the blue of skies scattered on the cave's upper limits, created for my enjoyment, and clouds so white their lightness calls me to take a ride. Depicted in one section is a man with long hair, a peaceful man, with twelve others gathered around him, eating. Then, there are the animals in the paintings, like I have only seen in eye-readers hooked into the History Labyrinth. Mighty elephant warriors in the savanna grasses where they belong. Stunning cats leaping with muscular power and others lying in the grass cuddled with sheep and rabbits and pit bulls and donkeys.

And then I see another painting in the corner. The artists perched on their scaffolding apply the finishing touches. I stare, overwhelmed. Tears roll out the corners of my eyes, slipping down my cheek and pooling on the ridge of my collarbone. *I am on the ceiling. I am there.* And in the painting, I am not a warrior. Not a woman in command. No combat boots, just bare feet. I am curled up on my side in a field of daisies, warm yellow centers perfectly placed amid white petals. Snuggled in the curve of my body is Gizzie, our gazelle. I look for Chapman in the painting, but he is not there.

Suddenly, I feel my arms again. I remember McGinty dripping wet, his lips on mine, breathing for me, into me, and the heavy hand of Shaw on my chest, beating the rhythm of life back into my body. That is memory. This is real. My hand touches something soft, and I turn to my side and see Gizzie's huge brown eyes staring back at me. I wrap my arms around her neck and hold her tight. She breathes with my rhythm, and I sob. It hurts my lungs to weep, and yet...I sob.

———

Somewhere in my past—before eye-readers and peps and the falling *Jurbay*—there were movies I watched with Carles, my father. We laughed raucously, Bling running off to the back room, disturbed by our noise. Movies sometimes were not to be laughed at because they were "classics," and some were filled with war. Infirmaries displaying images of uncountable rows of damaged people. Blood soaking through bandages. Nurses scrambling in the wake of a shortage of doctors. Human limbs absent from their bodies, never to be found. People incomplete. Why they called some of these films that show the horrors of war "classics," I'm not sure.

Here in the caves I see an infirmary of sorts. We call this the Healing Caves, but until now I have never been here. Our war schedules no time for healing or to experiment with music and art. This place is not like the movies. Nonetheless, it is our place of healing. The blood-soaked bandages are replaced by the empty eyes of children born into a constant life of running. I note there are very few parents here, their memories buried by *Jurbay* or banished by *locasa*. Clef, our Council member with the ebony skin, empty eye sockets and sage-like wisdom, strums a lute. The children sing, and just like in the war films, our minstrels are missing fingers, hands, tongues, eyes. Victims of The Third's abuse. But the children—they are intact physically. I notice they jump at the slightest sound beyond the music. If a stalactite cracks, getting ready for a fall that takes a century to unfold, these terrified kids cling in masses to the drummers, to the flautists and to anyone who wears the cross of red looming over the patch of The 28 United. When the children shrink with horror away from jarring sounds, the minstrels play louder, but never frantically—always steady, dependable.

And then the stories begin. Stories of warriors carving out a place in the world for refugees. Stories of children, looking like circus clowns and escaping a burning library only to grow up strong and become warriors themselves. Stories of children who had the guts to escape their pocket-watch caretakers in the hope they'd find a home with a substitute family for the ones they'd lost. Stories of a nation assembled from dump-pickers and minstrels and girls too young to lead and assemble an army. The Raghills, the Annalynns and the Morrises who walked into this crumbling world before these little ones of the caves faced a no-future life, a no-hope existence. If stories heal, this is where they are told, in hopes that the children of the caves might one day have a story of their own.

Across the cavern, I see Pepper sitting cross-legged and leaning against the moist cave walls. She has her hand on her nine-month-pregnant belly, and her GEB face is filled with the sorrow of the world. I think of her as a mother in waiting. Pepper has been pregnant for almost a year and a half. Perhaps if I give Degan the benefit of the doubt, I might convince Pepper that he was just about to problem-solve the fact that he gave her and Ulysses the ability to create life, but never got around to providing the connections that allow delivery and birth. But it's Degnan, and there is no benefit of the doubt. Her appearance indicates she is a GEB in progress. Unlike those that infiltrated The 28 United as weapons of The Third, Pepper and her husband Ulysses were liberated from Reichel and received their human attributes on the run from the malicious

Degnan and the ever-mischievous Pasha. So, Pepper's lack of eyebrows and eyelashes, her pale white skin and missing fingernails point to a non-human status that we've protected in our Colony. In the city of Ash, she wouldn't do so well.

No one has to tell me she is here for the healing of chronic trauma. The nine-month-old child within her isn't growing anymore, just breathing and waiting for Degnan to finish what he began. A toddler barely walking waddles up to Pepper, draping himself over her lap, reaching up to her Marilyn Monroe wig, petting the platinum and tracing the bow in her hair. She readjusts the blanket on her lap to include him and then welcomes several other children to surround her with kisses and patty-cakes and silly sing-song poems.

> *Pepper, Pepper, in a tree,*
> *Won't you come and rescue me?*
> *Please come down,*
> *Don't make a sound.*
> *We'll be together,*
> *Don't you see?*
> *Then we'll all climb up this tree.*

Pepper smiles faintly and stretches her blanket to extend to the furthest child who clings to a corner of the fabric. It is enough. She answers their rhyme with one of her own, in a quiet frail voice.

Children, children by my tree,
Won't you come and rescue me?
I'll come down.
Without a sound,
We'll be together,
Don't you see?
Then we'll all…

And everyone yells together, *Climb up this tree!* There is much giggling, and together they transform the blanket into a sail, then an ocean, and finally a monster complete with only sounds children can create. My face is wet with silent tears.

From my nest on the cave floor, I glance upward one more time at my towering portrait-in-progress. Then I right myself, feeling very unsteady on my feet. I wonder how long I have laid here in recovery, soaking up restoration. Nuzzling my hand, Gizzie is vigilant at my side, unwilling to let me take a step without matching me, her hooves clicking on the slick floor, my hand clutching the skin on the back of her neck. She doesn't seem to mind.

I cross to Pepper's side, unnoticed by her and her crew. I drop down beside her, sitting close. She seems uncomfortable to see me. "Commander," she says.

"You've always called me 'Avery.' What's changed?"

Pepper takes her time looking around the caves. "Brokenness…" she turns to look at me "…it lives here."

"You could also say the breath of healing lives here."

"You could, but then you have Chapman."

I place my hand on the top of her baby bump. "You're a mother too."

"No. I'm a landlord."

"I'll find Degnan. He'll come and finish what he started. You'll have your baby."

Pepper pulls away from me. "He hasn't had time."

"He'll make time" I guarantee. "With Degnan I have much to trade."

"Don't make that promise, Avery. Birth is a promise that hasn't been kept, and I can't take any more broken ones." She turns her face away from me, gazing out into nothingness. "I'm going to live here forever, Avery."

"Just for a time, Pepper." I try to take her hand, but she resists.

She drags her heavy pregnant body to stand. "No! Not for a time. Forever." The realistic human tears she was programmed to have now fall. We don't touch, as friends do. Pepper will not allow it. Not even a glance into one another's eyes. She can't face me. I understand. But I cry with her. This GEB and I share what only a GEB mother and the mother of a half-GEB might comprehend. And so, with nothing else in our arsenal to combat the trauma, the sorrow, and the broken hearts, we weep. Yet, I feel the stone-face of battle creeping back into my spirit.

I watch her hobble off, followed by an entourage of children. Pepper is their leader, their mother. They are seeking wholeness in these caves, away from a world that can only hurt them. But Pepper and I both know The Third can find you anywhere, even underground. Pretending that won't happen offers only artificial peace and a distant longing, never to be satisfied.

A child tackles me from the side then wraps his arms around me. A matted mess of cornrows frame the face of an eleven-year-old boy. "Remember me, Commander?"

"Of course I remember you, Carles. After all, I gave you the name of my father." The boy is small for his age, looking almost malnourished. Like many of the children staying in the caves, eating is not always their first priority. Sometimes there is no appetite for healing. He hugs me tighter, prodding my memory with images of a burning library where we lost most of the library boys, the sons of the leaders of Reichel. Carles helped me forge wooden crosses and line them up in what was left of a scorched garden, trying to create a moment of honor in a world that had so little. The Littlest Librarian asked for a name, and I gave it to him, willingly passing my heritage to him. And yet, here he is in the caves, clinging to the hands of healing like a mountain climber, holding fast to avoid a plunge in the middle of a raging avalanche. Carles is here.

I let go of Carles and once again find my arm curled around Gizzie's neck, and I hear her snort a murmur of what I think must be her approval.

Carles says, "I love the music, Avery." He reaches up to my face, holding my head in his hands, looking into my eyes. I cringe at the horror of my responsibility, its weight unbearable. I want to rest with him here—lay a hand on his shoulder, lift a prayer to heaven, whisper a song in his ear and stay for as long as forever lasts. But my boots are sturdy, and I cannot exchange them for the comfort of slippers. My boots are accustomed to the rigors of the run, and they have wear left in them, lots of wear. They must march against an enemy I have fought for way too long. And I wonder if I've changed at all in the last five years since I was that stubborn girl of twenty-two, wanting desperately to say "no" to the job of leader, the job my father did so well. I perceive his presence in these caves. Carles DeTornada. I sense him in the healing. For me, courage is not the decision to stay and help these through the healing. There are others here who do that well. Much better than any effort I might make. Courage is the boldness to step out of the caves and continue to carry the weapons of revolt. To make peace, I have to fill my life with war. These residents of healing need more than a momentary political asylum for refugees on the run. More than a temporary camp where the breath of the enemy is hot on their necks. More than a zoo camouflaged by savanna grass and acacia trees. More than a Warrior Strip where we watch evil and plan against it. They need a place we can call *home*. A place where the injured step out of an underground cave and into the light of justice. It's time for me to leave the caves.

Clef is sitting beside a small cluster of children. They all hold simple reed flutes and their small fingers pop up and down on the holes, following the exercises Clef has given. They chant the names of the notes as they pat the appropriate hole. C-D-E-F-G, A-B. C-D-E-F-G, A-B. And I know that with every note they speak, a drop of healing is washing over their souls. Allegra, by his side, plays a similar instrument. She has learned to play past her missing fingers and her diminished spirit. She revels in blowing the notes the children learn to play. She is leading, leading the way to wellness.

The minstrel without hands moves his elbows on the skin of his drum to create a soft lullaby of steadiness. A girl of eight shyly lifts her eyes to him, and with his eyes he beckons her to drum. She lays her reed on the blanket where she sits and timidly walks to join him. For minutes she gazes at his elbows, watching him play. She has hands. Can she find the way to the music too? The girl strikes the drum, barely registering a noise. Then again, stronger. Once more. Now both hands pound creating chaotic sound with no rhythm at all—until the minstrel stops his playing. She follows suit with stillness. Then as he begins again, her left hand strikes the drum skin each time his left elbow strikes. Then she mimics in the same way, her right hand following his right elbow. She discovers the beat. The girl giggles, drawing the other children near, each clutching their reed. Allegra beings her song again, and now the children join. Six young kids utilizing fingers to squeak out the first notes of a song they've just begun to learn. It is frenzied, a joke, a horrifying collection of sound waves that should send people running, but not here. A crowd of others gathers, clapping the strange rhythm with the drummers. Together they find strength in a symbiotic symphony.

Clef acknowledges me as I stand by the entrance to the cave. I'd like to say he *sees* me, but I know his empty sockets are incapable of vision. Yet he knows where I am, he faces me, he nods his head in my direction. It is a different kind of seeing. "Breathing okay?" he asks.

"My lungs hurt."

"It shouldn't take more than a few days for you to heal. These kind of injuries"—he gestures to the others—"take longer."

"I'm sure I have both kinds, but I don't have the schedule to heal from either." I love this mighty Council member who chooses to spend his days and many of his nights teaching children to play again, to sing. He knows the steps of healing.

I turn my back on Clef and the clusters of injured. And suddenly, in unison, melodies and harmonies gently roll over me. The instruments play and the singers sing our lullaby, Chapman's and mine.

The wind says quietly, "Be still."
The waves whisper, "Children, all is well."
The stars call you to a night of peace.
Sleep, sleep, children; be at ease.
Sleep, sleep, children; be at ease.

By the entrance to the cave in a pile knee high, I notice a stack of weapons. Not traditional. No DR93s or SE454s. No Z-Colts in the random collection. Rusted pipes, homemade dump-picker claws, pieces of glass, fragments of metal with serrated edges. Items scavenged from a life of running, a life of war. These children here in the caves came willingly or were brought by those who cared for them. No weapons in the caves may be active in the process of healing. The arsenals wait. I want to believe when these kids are well they won't pick them up again. They'll leave them behind. Yet long before there was a need for Healing Caves, I became aware, as a naïve child, that some thought there was a necessity to prepare children for war. A horrifying concept, especially when the inventor of the idea was my mother.

I think back on the time Pasha was fifteen and living with us, my mother recognizing Pasha's scientific abilities and providing an environment where she was free to create. Pasha herself was one of my mother's experiments. One night in our basement another secret meeting of The 28 United's leadership took place. Pasha and

I were old enough then to be interested in the strategic planning to defeat The Third. Usually when we hid at the back of a basement brick wall, unseen by those present, we heard the military options laid out. Not this time. A delegation of Catalonians for peace confronted Quinn, who stood in front of them, powerful and statuesque, Carles calmly at her side.

She said, "I understand your concern with us using children to conduct research, but these are exceptional children. Young scientists, if you will."

"Madame DeTornada," said the Catalonian ambassador, "you know I'm not speaking of scientists. I'm addressing our concerns about your children warriors."

"I have no children warriors."

"You're training them."

My father spoke up, "We're not placing children into battle. We're preparing *some* children for the inevitability of all-out-war."

"Be realistic, Ambassador," said Quinn, "It's our duty. We're all going to want children ready when the time comes."

In all of Quinn's military brilliance and instinctive sixth sense, she never perceived that children do not see with the wisdom of experience. They act with childlike impulses. This heap of weapons by our cave entrance represents more than those who came for healing. It characterizes the hundreds of other children in The 28 United who've grown up with the idea that they *are* at war, and behind the backs of wise adults, many of them have become angry.

At times, I've been so consumed with the abnormalities of Chapman, I've failed to comprehend the slow-moving tidal wave of children who cannot reconcile their childlike instinct to play with their adultlike passion to fight for whatever they believe. I know there have been others out there, like Clef and Old Soul, who've been called upon to settle skirmishes among the children. I asked about it once not long ago, and Shaw said, "We got it, Avery. You've got other things to do." And so, I pursued my agenda as Commander, and let the others play the role of mediators for the children.

Yet, in the last months, I've sensed a festering sore of open rage in certain children. I asked again, this time of McGinty. I knew he would be honest. "What's going on with the Colony kids? I was in the southern section yesterday," I said. "They looked like they'd set up their own living quarters outside their assigned families. They had weapons hanging off their belts, and when I asked why they weren't working at the Energy Concourse, they backed away from me, leaving one kid to speak for all of them."

"Well, what'd he say?" asked McGinty.

"He said, 'We're in training to help you anyway we can.'"

"And you told them—what?"

"To get their rears back to the Energy Concourse."

"Did they go?"

"Yeah, but they dragged their feet, and I doubt they ever made it there."

"There's a group of them who have war in their blood," said McGinty, "and that's all I know. But we're going to have to deal with this before someone gets hurt."

"Someone's already hurt," I said. "Look in their eyes."

I pick up one of the dump-picker claws from the pile of weapons, thinking back to over a decade ago when I overheard the comments of Quinn. I call Clef to my side and say. "I want this pile of weapons destroyed. I don't want them waiting here as a temptation for these kids when they leave the caves."

"With respect, Commander," says Clef, "I want them to be strong enough to resist the temptation." Of course, he's right. What good is hiding weapons from them? They need to find their way to healing, accepting the peace that goes with it, trusting our soldiers to do the rest of it.

I leave through the entrance of the caves. The dripping walls remain behind, yet the images of those seeking wellness travels with me. The memory of me holding onto Gizzie settles in my soul. Only a few feet away from the caves, the music has disappeared. The Third would never track this place based on the proximity of sound. And yet, I hear every note in my head so clearly.

Chapter 11
WAR OF THE CHILDREN AVERY

Just outside the caves, I see the others on their horses, waiting for me in a grove of sycamore trees. My horse, held in check by McGinty, is impatient, pawing at the ground. He's a dapple gray, an odd color for a horse of mine, considering I've done everything I can to get away from the drab. McGinty rides a stallion—black, muscular and lusty for the fight. Shaw's steed is a dirty white, dancing around, anxious to get going. It's not our habit to ride—much easier to be hidden on two legs than six—but when speed is needed, we some-times take the risk. Shortly after we discovered the zoo and the mappers began to explore the surround-ing area, they spotted the herd. Wild and majestic, they may have been broken at one point, but we were sure they'd been on their own since the inhabitants of the cities had disappeared with the cleansing of the 14 Deadlies.

Even as I leap on the back of Dapple I sense a pressing urgency. So many times, I've found that leadership is riding on the backs of those who know what they're doing. I'm surrounded by highly trained, courageous risk-takers, and I wouldn't have it any other way. Dapple stands firm, allowing me to take the reins from McGinty. We'd trained all the horses by trying anything Morris and Raghill might remember from the library books they'd memorized, but mostly by trial and error. Once the horses had been broken for saddle, they seemed a part of us, connected, treated kindly and embraced as members of Colony G. I hope someday Chapman will ride with me, but each time I try to approach Dapple with my child the horse riles and fights the idea of a child in the saddle. I'm sure we will succeed eventually.

Our horses in a gallop, Shaw and McGinty update me up as we go, yelling over the pounding hooves. "The children are at war again," says McGinty. "At the Concourse." Tension throbs through my body, and I tighten my grip on the reins, barreling toward the Energy Concourse with all the speed I know my horse is capable of.

Shaw says, "None of us have time for this. These kids are wasting my time." He jabs the ribs of his dirty-white, taking the lead at a full speed, the Concourse minutes away.

McGinty and his black stallion stay neck and neck with Dapple and me. In my head, I remember his comment: *There's a group of them that have war in their blood.* These children are always trying to claim their spot as warriors. And while Carles' and Quinn's training of children warriors was derailed, we've given kids the thirst for battle. We did that to them. They didn't need any training.

———

The camouflaged entry to the Energy Concourse slides open for brief seconds as our train of three speed through. We dismount and leave our reins in the hands of those trained to ready the horses for a quick departure.

I hear the warring children before I see them, screaming like wild animals caught in the snare of trappers. We run through a forest of twelve-foot-high windmills that spin so fast the blades are blurred and can't be distinguished. Giant turbines mounted sixty feet above us blow powerful gusts twenty-four hours a day.

On the far side of the windmills, we reach the children's war. On the rise of a small hill, I pause for a brief moment to gain perspective. This is a battle for blood. A mace swings in the hand of a younger teen, crafted of rusted bolts and set into a hardened mud center. The girl he tries to bludgeon defends herself with a spear made of a sharpened metal bar. Small boys and girls stand back-to-back, rotating in a circle, gaining a 360-degree view as they hold their pieces of jagged iron in their hands. Coming at them from the outside of the circle are older kids, threatening with their sacks of palm-sized rocks. Violence has a smell of open wounds and fresh cut skin. This place stinks. For a fleeting moment, I wonder if this war started as a childish skirmish—someone called another a name or chose the wrong person for a competitive game. However, a spray of blood across my leg, coming from a slice in the arm of a nine-year-old kid, slaps me with reality. These battles are the real thing, regardless of the motivation. Again, our fault. They'd learned their passion and opinionated concepts from us. We never lacked an appetite for argument and our evenings were often filled with the entertainment of debate. But we did not raise our weapons at one another. We saved that for the enemy.

The three of us throw ourselves in the middle of the battle-raged children. Their weapons are everywhere—hammers, picker claws, clubs with nails banged in half-way that caused malicious injuries that no one should ever have to look at, let alone create. Standing to the side, helpless and without weapons, are Clef, Old Soul and several artists. Everywhere, there is blood.

Shaw separates cluster after cluster of children, disarming them and herding them, with his ten-inch knife blade, to the artists who hold the kids in check, refusing to let them reenter the fray.

McGinty helps too, but instead of using a knife, like Shaw, he stares the warrior children down. Maybe McGinty corrals these kids with a mere glance because they remember he was the creator of the brainy and anti-brainy weapons. Then he funnels them to the mappers, the ones that Shaw works with and trains most days. These mappers now recant their error of egging on the warrior children as they fought.

I separate two children, a girl of about six and a boy who seems eight years old. I grab them by their upper arms and drag them to the small rise on a knoll of the battlefield. When I shout at the crowd of twenty or so fighting children and the scores of spectators, no one has a problem hearing my voice.

"If you want to fight like men and women, then you will be jailed like men and women."

My grip tightens on the boy as he tries his best to squirm away, but I am more determined than he is and my strength surges at this rebellious imp. "We're ready to fight with you now!" he yells, rallying the crowd of children. Regardless of which side they were on moments ago, they all cheer together, anxious for any enemy, any war.

I throw both the boy and girl to the ground, and security points their DR93s at the heads of children. I am both horrified and righteous in the same breath. "No one fights for The 28 United without the control of battle under their skin. Without patience and timing, we fail. It is a skill to wait for the right moment." Now I have their attention. Finally, they are still and stare at me. "Warriors are not made of spit-fire rebels that let their rage boil over at disagreement or self-righteous quarrels. You break each other—you break us—you break our world." Maybe these kids expected a scolding, like a parent training a child, but I am not their mother. "Send them all to jail," I command. Each one starts to cry, to whimper, to wail—they are children, after all. I hear murmurings from the adults in the crowd, maybe questioning my decision, maybe concluding I am too tough on sandbox kids and school-age children.

"But for how long?" asks Clef. "How long in jail?"

"Until they're ready to learn. Clean them up, then feed them and place them in separate cells. Make sure there's warm blankets. And we'll see. We'll see how long." I make my way through the bloodied kids, trying not to look at their faces wet with tears, but out of the corner of my eye I see my own child, Chapman. Blood covers his bare leg where his pants have been torn away. In my brief glance, I notice there isn't much blood elsewhere, and I wonder how a five-year-old could have managed not to get the worst of it. *Doesn't matter. I can't separate him out from the rest and take him home and hold him like a mother should.* The crowd separates for me, and as I pass through, I wonder if there are those who whisper as I pass, "She's just like Quinn." I may even be whispering it to myself.

Moving quickly away from the scene, I hear turmoil tramping behind me—McGinty's footsteps. As we pass back through the windmill orchards, he runs by my side. "You can't leave Chapman in the jail overnight." I see the passion in his eyes. He is always an advocate for justice, reminding me I need to be too.

"Do you think I want to leave him?" I ask, and the look McGinty throws at me convinces me he isn't sure if I want to or not. "I can't give him special treatment because he's the Commander's son. He was right in the thick of it. He was throwing punches too. He chose to do that."

McGinty grabs my arm, bringing me to a stop and refusing to let me escape his questioning. "He's five years old, Avery. He's the youngest one. He'll fall apart in prison. He needs his mother."

"And I need him." I pull away from McGinty, keenly aware of how much he cares for my son. "Our prisons are not like The Third's. They'll take good care of him. I'll get him soon."

We pass between the platforms that house the solar panels. We are minuscule below their towering heights. "I need an update on the energy production from the harvest office," I say, but as I am hustling down the path, McGinty cuts me off again, standing in my way.

"I can get those updates, for you—the same updates Avery DeTornada can get. But being a mother? That's on you."

An enormous explosion throws us to the ground, rocking the entire Energy Concourse. There's no debris, so the explosion must be further down the Concourse. Soldiers in full combat gear fly by us. I know they are ours. They have all the gear necessary to be combat ready, but no uniforms, just items assembled from an assortment of scavenged surplus. They run in the direction that is most probably the blast site, and McGinty and I follow them.

We enter the section of the Concourse where the energy experiments are conducted. There are hundreds of chicken coops in this section, and we have only passed a few rows before the blast site becomes apparent. A yawning hole in the thin-skin ceiling, a hundred yards wide, welcomes an aerial view of our energy operations to anyone with aircraft. It is daunting, threatening our security with a profound overstatement, placing the secrecy of our projects and the future of our offensive war against The Third in jeopardy.

Over half of the chicken coops, the processing plant and part of the lab are destroyed. McGinty quickly takes a tally of our losses, and our guards set up a perimeter. Some hoist others sixty feet up to the roof hole, scouting and making sure no one will attack from above.

The coops are blown apart, but the only people I see around are a woman, shaken up by the blast and holding her hands to her ears, and a few children near her. "What happened here?" I ask.

The woman rocks back and forth, not hearing what I am saying. One of the children with her withdraws his hands from his ears and shouts, "Methane blew the coops right up to the ceiling." Tears form in the kid's eyes. "Killed a lot of our chickens." I'm shaken by the irony and contrast of a child caring so deeply for scrawny poultry with rigid beaks when I just left children who were in the process of cutting each other to pieces with the implements of war.

"Where are the other children?"

"Just got off work and left for their quarters." I'm grateful for that.

McGinty yells at the guards investigating the hole in the ceiling. "Can any of you fix that hole?" No one responds.

One girl, covered with chicken manure says, "Pasha could."

"Once again, Pasha's kept her knowledge to herself, and that doesn't help us now." My remark is confidential and meant only for McGinty. However, I see one of the little chicken ranchers running away, waving his hand in the air for me to follow, and I think maybe he overheard my comment about Pasha.

"Commander DeTornada," he calls. "Follow me. You'll see. You'll see." What choice do I have? I trail after him.

McGinty and I stoop into a chicken coop after the child who is dirty with manure, but alive and responsive after the blast. I stand full height once I enter the coop, and the top of my head is a couple of inches from the ceiling, but McGinty ducks to avoid the boards that form the roof. I'm struck by the cleanliness of the coop on the inside. As if reading my mind, the kid says, "They're not all like this, Commander." He kneels in front of one of the chickens, chasing the squawking hen off her nest. Uncovering a small pewter box, he lifts the lid, revealing a mechanical device. We stare, expecting an explanation. "Call the chipsters," he says, then adds, "Pasha said."

My touch on the top of the box activates a hologram that displays Pasha, her bald head and irritating arrogance. Through the hologram she speaks. "See, you're still fighting to be half as smart as me." How typical of her, flaunting her abilities. "Before I left, in case of emergency, I created this opportunity for you to call our subterraneans inside The Third and let them know if you need to step up our attack schedule. It's connected to our eye-readers only. You're gonna be able to use this once—maybe two or three times—and then The Third will be on to you, big time." The hologram snaps away, and I am left with a very slight amount of remorse that I'd trashed Pasha about keeping info to herself.

McGinty activates the mechanical device and types my message as I speak it. *Accidental explosion busted hole in ceiling of thin-skin. Security threat. Need to meet with subterraneans inside The Third to assess moving up attack date. Meet—abandoned butcher shop, north end of the city. Midnight tomorrow.*

McGinty asks, "You finished?" I nod at him, and he doesn't have to ask if he should send it. He does.

McGinty tucks the device away in his bag, ducks his head through the door of the coop and I follow, taking a deep breath of air outside the shed. It still stinks from the explosion that blasted chicken poo everywhere.

When we finally take stock of the situation outside the coop, we see the soldiers who had investigated the hole in the thin-skin, the woman holding her ears and the few children who were with her. They are motionless, staring up at the hole. And there they are, descending.

The balloon-techs float through the ceiling of our Energy Concourse, camouflaged like the sky. If I hadn't seen them before, I wouldn't be able to detect that they were there. For those of us who gaze above, we know what to look for. Circular crafts, built from materials made of the manioc plants that replaced lightweight plastic. These small flying machines are big enough to hold a medium-sized adult and one passenger.

As the balloon-techs sail silently downward, their exterior colors transform from the color of the sky to the changing environment. If we weren't looking, they would remain unseen, but their pilots are noisy, talking incessantly and making no attempt to surprise us. All the pilots have their face-spaces open, speaking nonstop and waving to us through the small window openings. What might be used as stealth spy-units descend with annoying verbal visitors. I'm sure Checkmate is leading the aerial scouts.

The balloon-tech pilots are part of a citizen's colony in the outer regions, south of Erie, and beyond where our mappers have yet to advance. They have no allegiance to The 28 United or The Third, and they have posed no threat to us. However, they are not at all what I want to deal with in the middle of a crisis. These lone rangers always talk the speed of aircraft and can keep at their conversations for hours, sometimes days. So as not to offend them, we created a rotating schedule among our colony members. Men and women, who were experts at keeping meaningless conversations going, took turns, participating in chat with the b-tech pilots and protecting the schedules of those of us who had work to do. When exchanges became necessary for reasons of trade, I'd step into dialogue with their leader, Checkmate.

I don't know where he got his chess board. Maybe the balloon-techs have their own brand of history labyrinth, but he carts the game with him everywhere. A chipped marble knight, two pawns and a lopsided queen, whose left side is missing, are still intact, but all the other pieces are crudely fashioned from river rock or tree bark. Checkmate was the first b-tech I'd met. I've never travelled to his colonies, and I can't help but wonder how he can find time for games.

Drifting easily into our Concourse, the pilots' faces become visible through the one foot by two foot rectangular windows at the forward section of the balloon-techs. Their chameleon outer covering switches seamlessly to the colors they pass in such a fascinating manner I find it difficult to turn my eyes away, even though I know I need to avoid meaningless conversations.

Through the face-space of the first b-tech to land, I see a man of Asian descent smiling and waving. His lips move rapidly, even though there is no one with him in the craft. No avoiding it. Conversation imminent. It's Checkmate.

He's a wiry man under five feet tall. His long, strangely colored platinum hair is braided and wrapped around two small wire circles on the top of wooden sticks that extend four inches above his head, looking like the antenna of a beetle or a termite. Climbing out of the balloon-tech he says, "Commander DeTornada, how quaint that your disguised energy experiments have now been exposed to the light of day."

"So what?" I ask. "You've just been hovering up there for months to find a way to get in here?"

Checkmate does a few calisthenics to limber up from his ride. "Well, of course, we occasionally patrol your section of the grid from above."

"We don't have a grid."

"Well, anyway, we noticed unequal moments of light distribution, and we've been waiting for some big discovery in your little section of the world. Thanks to your recent explosive moment—we found our revelation." He scans the area, turns up his nose at the stink and waves his hand in front of his face, trying to get the smell to dissipate. "I was hoping for an increased trade deal with you, Commander, but I don't want to trade anything that smells like this."

Our guards have Checkmate and his other five pilots (who have not left their balloon-techs) under heavy guard. I head down the path toward the other end of the Concourse. "Listen, I'd love to talk, but I have a hole to patch."

"Not willing to trade anymore, Commander? Trade with me is to your colony what the exchanges were like with the survivalists of old—a century ago. It is a healthy sharing of resources, a vital way to communicate with those colonies unlike your own. It's a—" Okay, he keeps using the word "trade," and it does perk my interest. Trade is always on my mind.

"Trade for what?" I ask. "Be brief."

"Need energy. You have some. I want it. Brief enough?"

"How much?"

"A slab of wind blocks and a palette of solar cells." He sniffs the air. "We'll pass on the poo-balls until you perfect the product." *How did he know about any of our energy mining and experiments?* He answers before I have time to ask. "Oh," he says, adjusting the circles of braids on his head, "of course you're wondering how I know about your exploits in your little invisible dome. Let's just say my camouflaged flying machine trumps your camouflaged energy mushroom, hands down." He pauses and looks at me through his World War II flying goggles. "Make sure you tell Dr. Lutnik that."

"Oh, I will." I take a few steps closer to him, my hand on my Z-Colt. "Will this trade agreement you're proposing guarantee me I won't see you around for a while?"

"I'll miss our lengthy conversations, but yes."

My eyes ascend to the hovering balloon-techs. My decision is quick. "Okay. I'll trade you a slab of wind blocks and a palette of solar cell for…one flying balloon-tech."

Checkmate sizes me up, probably wondering how far he can go to advance his trade. "These balloon-techs are pretty valuable—"

"Not without energy they aren't."

"You would do well to get yourself a fleet of these things. Sneak in on the enemy of Ash undetected."

"Maybe someday. I'm pretty sure *we* could keep our mouths shut, so the chameleon effect might actually work for us."

"We did pretty good getting a beat on what you're doing in here."

"Checkmate."

"Ha. You won't believe what it's like to ride in one of these. I could strap you in right now. You'd be safe. You'd be thrilled. You'd be convinced that it's the only way to travel...want to take a ride and get a demonstration of what you're trading for?"

"I'm a little busy for a demonstration. Do you want the trade or not?"

"It's a deal if you throw in another palette. Then, we'll call it even."

"Done." I call two of our guards over and address them. "Help Checkmate tether one of his balloon-techs up at the west end of the Concourse by the horses. Make sure he gets his worthy trade. Count it out. Be sure it's fair." I nod my goodbye to Checkmate, but he has already begun a one-sided conversation with the guards about the color perspectives of chameleons.

I jog down the path, but am stopped by the boy who took us to the chipster mechanical device in the chicken coop. He tugs on the back of my jacket. "You gonna copy that balloon-tech design, Commander? Build us a fleet of them?"

"Maybe," I reply.

McGinty says, "I can see strategy wheels whirling in your head—what else? What else are you going to do with one balloon-tech, Commander?"

"I don't know. I was thinking maybe I'd do some trading of my own."

I start back down the path, but this time I hear Checkmate calling after me. "'Till next time, Commander. 'Course, according to our agreement, that'd be a long time from now." I catch sight of McGinty waving an acknowledgement to Checkmate, but I do not. It is dusk and I have an appointment with a prison guard.

Chapter 12
THE WATERS OF FAMILY AVERY

Chapman will be brought to me from Prison #3. I arrive at the meeting place, a section of the Energy Concourse where the forest of windmills makes way for an idyllic pond. Of course, we know whose idea that was: the artists. To them, there needed to be hints of beauty in the middle of the mundane rows of energy makers, wave after wave of solar panels and strips of chicken coops. If they did not remember to paint pictures on cave ceilings and etch out ponds in the middle of progress, the rest of us might forget. Sycamore trees encircle the pond and spill over into a neatly clustered grove. Beside each grouping sits a wooden bench. I've been told that resting on one of the benches and meditating on the pond might calm the spirit. I need calm.

I try to sit, but am instantly on my feet when I see a figure approaching. I didn't know what to expect, but it wasn't a guard carrying Chapman in his arms. My little five-year-old's hands lie limp at his sides, bouncing from the movement of the guard advancing. My son is shaking, and as they come closer I realize sobs accompany his trembling. The guard rolls Chapman from his own arms into mine.

"Should I wait, Commander?" asks the guard.

"No. He won't be going back with you." I answer. I can see the relief on the guard's face.

"Not right having a jail for children."

I shoot back an answer in my defense, "Not right that children do things so unspeakable they need a jail."

"Still, there ought to be an age limit or something,"

"What's your name, soldier?"

"Baxter."

"Baxter, you talk this way to all your officers?" I am irritated, yet a bit impressed.

"No." He waits a moment, but I know he'll speak again. "Only to the powerful ones who can declare an age limit."

"How about no one under six goes to jail?" I run my hand over the rough stubble on the top of Chapman's shaved head, wondering what provokes a five-year-old to give himself a haircut. His hair was long, to his shoulders, the color of his father's.

"That's a good limit, Commander. Thank you." He turns and walks away, and I look down into Chapman's eyes flooded with tears.

"Am I your prisoner now, Mama?" His innocence is jarring, considering hours ago he was covered with the blood of other children. I sit with him. The splintered wood of the bench rubs through my pants, and I think we should assign a work patrol from the children's prison to do some sanding. The wind whispers through my wisps of hair while I hold Chapman tight.

"No, sweet boy, you are not my prisoner." I reposition him, setting him on the bench and tucking the military blanket that's around his shoulders under his chin. Walking a few steps to the pond, I soak a clean cloth from my bag and wipe the blood from his face. "Who taught you to fight?" I prod him.

"I learned from watching you."

No conversation like this should ever exist between a mother and her son. I want to pick him up, rock him and sing our lullaby together, but something keeps me from touching him again. Many times, in the last months since we arrived at the zoo, Chapman has spoken to me with the vocabulary from an adult world. In moments like those, my little one turned wise, spewing sage phrases through the air, like a child slings skipping stones across a creek. Now he reaches up to my hair, tracing the copper highlights on a few strands. Even when he was a baby he loved to touch the shiny color. "What?" he asks. "You don't think you've ever taken me along into a battle?"

I stand, backing away from him. "I *never* have." The pendulum begins to swing from child to adult, and I hate that this is happening to him.

Chapman brings himself to a standing position on the bench. His movements shift to slow-motion. He addresses me with cool analysis. "'In battle' doesn't just mean pilots and ground troops and warriors finding underwater entrances to secret places." It troubles me, this reference to the Waters of Erie. This information of the Warrior Strip is known only to the members of the Council and to the twenty of us with military clearance. I can't help wondering who Chapman has overheard. He continues. "When you put a bullet in the chamber of your Z-Colt and blew out the brains of some soldier tracking us down, I rode in the carrier on your back."

"I saved your life!" I will not let my own child question my methods as a commander or as a mother.

"A week later, you told me, 'Hold tight to the back of my belt, so they don't see you.' Then you decapitated three of *Dorsey's* guards with the force of your brainy."

I charge forward at him, stopping inches before the bench. "I stepped in the line of fire for you," I say. "I will do anything to protect my family." I want to slap him.

"Including strangling Morris' father in the pool at the History Labyrinth?" I grab him in my arms—not a gentle hug, but one of desperation. He needs to stop.

"You couldn't know that," I say, directly in his ear. "You heard that from others. You were in my womb when that happened."

And in my ear he whispers back. "I felt his kick against your belly …"

"Stop it…"

"Felt the pulsing of your muscles, holding him under…"

"Stop it…"

"The final stillness when it was over."

"Please. Stop." He pulls away from my embrace, his childhood back, riding the pendulum that's slicing my heart apart and hovering in the innocence of his eyes. The analytical man now gone.

"I don't want to be your prisoner, Mama." Now he hugs me, careful, so frail.

"You're not. You aren't." And as I stare over his shoulder, I see, on the other side of the sycamore grove, a band of soldiers from The 28 United, watching uncomfortably to see how their commander will navigate the waters of family.

———

Tonight, we are all in my bed, McGinty on one side, me on the other, and Chapman curled up in the middle with Gizzie our gazelle, holding tightly to her neck. Maybe we are trying to cement a family together within the four corners of a sleeping mat. It's only the third time I've ever let Chapman sleep with Gizzie. Tonight, it seems only right for a boy of five who's been to war with children, spilt blood with innocent hands and who's been cooped up in a prison—all in the same day.

Chapter 13
DATE WITH DEPLOYMENT PASHA

If anyone were to enter stockpile car #84 of the Dark Market, they would never know Pasha Lutnik was there, squeezed behind two of the identical fishborn weapons in an unmarked car containing some of Dorsey's military stash waiting for deployment. Her body curled into a fetal ball, Pasha's tiny frame hardly looked human. The hands of this subterranean scientist were fisted and rubbing her bald scalp with a fury. She chanted, *Speak complete. Hands away from head. Control. Outside. Inside. All over. Speak complete. Must try.* The warm blood broke through her skin and oozed just above her right ear. Flinging herself out of her contracted position, she yanked her hands off her head and pinned them tightly behind her back against the wall. *Take control. Hands be still.* Her breathing jumped back and forth between erratic and chopped to slow and measured. She must decide which pace would win the jurisdiction in her lungs. *Three big breaths. Fill lungs with oxygen.* She obeyed her own voice, and then it came, a simple sentence, complete. *They think everything about me is impotent, except my mind.* Now her breaths were even, filling her lungs with a steady rhythm. *They are wrong.* She reached for her gear bag, touching the clasp, expecting Herman and Orbit to pick their way out of their temporary home and nuzzle against her shoulder. She caught herself. No comfort from a bag without pigeons.

Even as she slipped into the glide encased by Erie's waters and headed east toward Ash, her mind spun through the stories she pitched every day to Dorsey, regarding the supposed advancement of her energy experiments. Simultaneously she worked in a secret lab in the early hours just past midnight, calculating her errors in each failed attempt to perfect reverse-*locasa*. She felt the device rubbing against her ribs in the side pocket of her jacket, a reminder that she hadn't been able to leave her personal experiments alone. Locating the device, her muscle memory kicked in. Pasha pushed the button.

Each time she placed the device on the back of her skull, she yearned to float outside the memories in clinical observance, but all sorts of images interrupted her fact-finding mission, and it became personal. There were sounds and smells too, and always emotions. The most prevalent was confusion, but a close second was warmth, a longing that she desperately wanted to explain. She wasn't sure how to describe it any clearer because there was no frame of reference in her own life for gentle moments that seemed to be a part of her history.

Baby now walks with stumbling first steps. Man strokes Pasha's frizzed hair with a gentle hand. Words in a jumble. Letters search for the order of language. Hold the baby. Want to hold the baby. Odors permeate. Familiar. Baby powder. A boiling soup of lentils and venison. Gun oil. Man's hands move from Pasha's hair to an item lying in his lap. Z-Colt. Man and the weapon disappear. Time rolls backwards. Now baby, too small to walk. Mother in rocking chair. Newborn. Holds newborn. Whispers its name, but the word is skewed by letters tumbling out of order. Face of the child still unclear. One moment Pasha felt the baby-smooth skin, the next she could not feel it. She knew touch was running away from her fractured memories. Pasha heard herself say, *"No, don't go."* All images diffused except a pile lying in the center of the floor—a scythe, a hoe and a bag of lentils, the contents spilling out onto the floor.

Annalynn tapped the toe of her boot on the transition platform, waiting for Pasha's glide as it docked and unhooked. Pasha thought the stance Annalynn took, arms crossed in impatient frustration, mirrored something familiar in Pasha's own mannerisms. She tromped past Annalynn without acknowledgment, prompting Annalynn to catch up and yell, "Patience is a virtue and you make it impossible to be good." Pasha snorted as Annalynn walked by her side. "Pasha, when you take these little trips away—you think it's easy trying to be you?"

"Impossible," snapped Pasha, widening the gait of her childlike steps, but Annalynn kept up, reaching her hand to the side of Pasha's head, rubbing its baldness. Elite training from Pasha's past kicked in, and she grabbed Annalynn's arm, twisting it around her back. She was never very good at it, but good enough to threaten Annalynn. Why did it feel so good to use her training? She was much more suited for the creation of scientific impossibilities—for beakers and petri dishes and digital input. Those were a perfect fit, but bashing another's head in—not so much. She moved her hold from Annalynn's arm to her neck and tightened the grip, just because she could.

"Hey, stop that! I'm thirteen."

"Thirteen and impertinent."

"Hey, you almost spoke in a whole sentence," said Annalynn. "Transformation of the un-transformable."

"Shut up." Pasha felt the creepers staring. Those small collections of people that hung out in the dim and often darkened outskirts of the city. The ones unwelcomed by The Third, whether they'd outgrown their usefulness or would rather take their chances with hunting than eating manufactured peps. Perhaps they just wanted a taste of a life without curfew, but more likely they were the few that had escaped *locasa* and knew what they'd be in for if they went back to the city. They'd chosen scrounging and bare survival instead of loss of memories and family. Those that lurked behind the boarded-up windows, broken doorways and crumbling sidewalks would never be found trading in the Dark Market with Degnan's upper tier clientele, but Pasha guessed Degnan might walk these areas at times. He was good at sniffing out a deal.

Annalynn shoved Pasha around a corner of an alley barely lit by what was left of a street light. Shadows hovered on the building walls, mixing Pasha and Annalyn's own gray shapes, enlarged by faint rays of light, making them look like giants on the hard surfaces of alley buildings. Pasha punched Annalynn in the shoulder, sending her to her backside in a puddle.

"You need to come with me," whispered Annalynn. "Someone needs to see you." Pasha stood immovable, silent and offering no agreement to follow Annalynn.

"She who learns from her mentor's bag of tricks," said Annalyn, "comes back to haunt the mentor with a trick of her own."

"You ought to trust culture to create clichés…"

"I'm proactive. You say something enough it becomes a cliché."

"I don't want to hear that one more than once," said Pasha and walked away.

"Look up, Pasha."

Pasha felt a shiver ripple through her body, and she quickly stopped. A curious impulse badgered her to look skyward, and she could not quell the curiosity. She peered above.

"What?" asked Pasha.

"Don't see anything?"

"Is this a joke? There's nothing."

"Joke's on you, noble one. Wanna take a ride?" Annalynn opened the chipster in her leg, coded in and lifted her knuckles above her head. The hook-up immediately slung down to grab the back of her uniform, and she was headed upward just as the thin-skin above opened a small entryway to a pitiful copy of Pasha's zips that had provided Reichel (before it disappeared in a suck of sludge) with energy efficient transport for years. Annalynn shouted back to Pasha, "I share that adjective you use so often on yourself: 'brilliant.'"

"Copying doesn't qualify as brilliant. How'd you get that chipster? Who came up with the thin-skin, and why was I kept in the dark about it all?"

"You know everyone has chipsters now. "

"Not everyone thirteen."

"The Third—not so good at original products—but very competent at stealing the ideas of others. Their motto: Copy now. Create later."

"That's your motto too."

"Oh, this isn't mine. Remember I've only been here as long as you. This copy of your zips belongs to the subterraneans." Annalynn hangs, gawking down at Pasha. "You're their hero."

Annalynn zipped upward one story, headed to the top of the thirteenth floor of the building that now displayed only Pasha's shadow, not Annalynn's. "Don't let your pride," Annalynn shouted at Pasha, "stop you from taking a ride. The code's in. The attachment's already installed in your uniform. Just lift your knuckles—"

"I know how it works." Pasha hooked in and swung erratically from the ground upward, then zipped across the distance between buildings and ended up beside Annalynn. "Lousy construction," she said to Annalynn.

"You try skidding around Dorsey and his Elite mega-men to build a masterpiece."

"I do. Every day." There was an unspoken moment between the two when the gravity of daily danger overwhelmed their banter, and it was quiet. Rare for the two of them.

They zipped on the piece of cable running from one building to the next and leaped to a second roof. Pasha asked, "And what about the thin-skin that hides this zip?"

Annalynn worked quickly to unhook the mechanism and re-hook to the next zip. "Some of the subterraneans had assignments in the labs. You don't really think if they figured out how to do something great like thin-skin, they wouldn't do it just because you did it first?"

"I didn't think anyone but me would ever figure it out."

"And that's why you're in the dark about a lot of things right now. Let's go. Someone's waiting. And by the way, arrogance proceeds annihilation." Annalynn zipped away.

Pasha shouted after her, "That'll never be a cliché. Nobody'll ever repeat that!" Annalynn mimed a funky dance move midair, as she sailed across the chasm between buildings, saluting Pasha all the way. Pasha followed, mumbling to herself a list of the ways she could send Annalynn back to Colony G and the zoo where she belonged.

When the two of them plopped on the roof of the fourth building, completing their ride on the three shabbily constructed sections of zips, Pasha's foot entangled with a broken tile on the roof. She tripped. Unable to stick the landing, she rolled several times, finally resting on her stomach and looking at the spit-shine of someone's boots. Degnan sneered down at her, offering no hand up. She didn't need one.

Pasha scrambled to her feet. Degnan perched himself on the brick half-wall that edged the roof, gesturing to Pasha to take a seat, and since Pasha didn't take the offer, Annalynn did, right next to him. Scooting several feet away from Annalynn, Degnan resettled.

"So, what?" asked Pasha. "Dorsey sent his reception committee to haul me back to work?"

"Not really," he said. "They don't even know you're gone, thanks to Morris. He's been busy negotiating for you." Something about his tone said that this wasn't a chat, but an information teaser—the kind he always employed right before he dumped the bomb of information he knew would shake up the mix—just before he spit out the facts that she couldn't live without.

Pasha turned her back on him, unhooking from the zip. "What's that supposed to mean? Morris negotiating? You mean he put his foot in his mouth again?"

"To the contrary. Dorsey and Morris are waiting for you this very moment to demonstrate the deployment of a fishborn. One explosion as an example of the power they will have once you've provided the energy the Third needs to release their arsenal."

"No! Part of my plan is the stall. Dorsey *thinks* I'm going to demonstrate a launch, but I've been stalling. Morris can't control where that fishborn goes without making Dorsey suspicious. I was going to get enough info about this place to Avery, so when we come in above for the kill they'd never expect it." She looked cautiously at Degnan. "But then you know all that already. After all, you and Avery have a contract."

Pasha thought he was irritated now, pacing the roof. "You know nothing about strategy. Even though Avery and I don't see eye to eye all the time, at least she—"

"Never," Annalynn clarified, and Degnan looked hard at her for the interpretation. "You and Avery *never* see eye to eye."

"At least DeTornada knows strategy," said Degnan. "Why are you even here?"

Pasha was blunt and said, "I ask the same of you."

"I'm protecting my investments."

"You mean that serpent of a Dark Market, slithering through the water? How noble." Degnan clutched her arm, pulling her off the ground, forcing her to face him.

"Listen. While you've been off on one of your experiments, chasing your past, Morris has been trying to keep Dorsey believing that you're doing everything in your power to take your cells and blocks and provide a consistent bottomless supply of energy for the deployment of his weapons. And the best way Morris could do that was to promise a test run. He'll be deploying one weapon, two hours from now at the launch site in car #78. Consider this your invitation."

He released her, hooked up and zipped off in the direction he had come from. The subterraneans might only have managed to string three zips, but they worked well for the area.

Mirroring Degnan's zip trip was Checkmate in a balloon-tech. When Degnan finally realized there was some unknown contraption flying beside him, he slowed the zip, taking a closer look. While Pasha couldn't hear a word Degnan said, she knew no one else but Avery and

Colony G even knew what a balloon-tech was, which meant Degnan had never seen one. Which also meant, now that he knew, he'd have to find a way to get one or two or a fleet of them for himself. She couldn't imagine why Checkmate would've flown a balloon-tech directly in front of Degnan, purposely allowing discovery. To Pasha this whole "chance" meeting between Degnan and that b-tech seemed a little too staged. And she knew the real expert of staging in the tit-for-tat relationship with Degnan was Avery. *Good one, Avery,* she thought. *Checkmate.*

Staring after Degnan, Pasha thought about Morris and his "negotiations" with Commander Dorsey while she was away. She whispered, "Morris had no right."

The staircase that led to the inside of the building was easily accessed, and Annalynn already had the door opened for a quick exit. She slung a final comment back at Pasha. "Don't underestimate Morris. He's only 15, but you put him in front of the wisest of the world, and he'll win any argument. He can win it with bland facts and no emotion or passionate rhetoric, but he will win."

"And that's important...why?"

"He's the leader you can't be."

"You're a rebel."

"Yeah, just like you. Except for one thing."

"Yeah?"

"By studying warfare, I've learned the premise of peace. You never learned it." Annalynn began her descent.

Pasha wanted the last word. "One weapon could wipe out most of our colony."

Popping her head back outside the door, Annalynn countered, "While your head's stuck in science and yourself, we're turning off the history lessons in our eye-readers and making history of our own."

"I have what Dorsey wants, and I can stall him—"

"You forced Morris to back up your 'stall' with action. If he didn't promise a launch, our cover would be blown." They stared at each other for way too long. "You think Morris is just an irritating kid, but words fall from his mouth like a clever weapon locked on a target."

"Another cliché?"

"Fact." Annalynn clamored down the stairs, leaving Pasha alone on the roof to imagine how she would stop the weapon launch about to shatter a section of the world that needed a leader on the inside to save it. She still believed it was her.

———

The official lab Dorsey had set up for Pasha detailed perfection. White with sanitation and stark with the essentials of science, the room seemed small. Pasha liked it that way. She could listen to anyone assigned to work with her. There would be no secrets kept from her like the kind she withheld from Commander Dorsey. Already the subterraneans had figured out her formula for thin-skin and implemented it on the outskirts of the city to cover the three zips. A caution rose inside her. Even if she wasn't working on reverse-*locasa* here where there were some who might discover her efforts, Pasha had to admit that her preoccupation with perfecting reverse-*locasa* had tinted the glasses with which she viewed her self-appointed mission.

"Almost time for the demonstration of the fishborn deployment," said one of the three Elites appointed to guard her in the lab. Pasha wasn't sure if they were there to protect her valuable services from harm, or if they were there to keep her from escape, but in any case, they drove her crazy—more crazy. Turning from her calculations regarding fishborn #1, she laughed at what she saw. Pasha mused at how unfamiliar she was with laughter. The trio of Elites that faced her looked like a singing group from a century ago. Dressed identical in the gray camouflage uniforms of The Third's Elite, they were heavily armed, but all three wore assigned lab coats over their uniforms. The coats could not withstand the pressure of the taut muscles bulging from inside the fabric, and the seams were already ripping. The men—Heck, Maven and Bly—wore black barrettes, set off to the side of their heads and stared through their oversized lab glasses at Pasha. The one in charge repeated, "Almost time for the demonstration of the fishborn deployment. Prepare."

Pasha's laugh turned maniacal and she stood, presenting her four-foot-eleven self to face off against three six-foot-plus muscled frames.

The leader reprimanded. "This is no laughing matter to our Commander, Dr. Lutnik." She wasn't ready for the glint of mockery in the corner of his eyes. Was he mocking her or The Third? She wasn't sure, but she'd seen so little emotion from any Elite soldier that it caught her off guard. With a nod of his head, he dismissed the other two saying, "I'll escort her to the site."

After the other two left the lab, Maven relaxed a little. "My name is Maven." *Oh, here it comes*, she thought. *That ridiculous need for chit-chat.* Then in Pasha's memory an intrusive image of Annalynn appeared, instructing Pasha (as she had so many times through the years) with a lesson on developing relationships with strangers. Annalynn insisted that development would pay off to Pasha's advantage in the future. Frequently Annalynn emphasized to Pasha that it was not always the best choice to alienate others with opening remarks.

Pasha tried. "Nice last name," Pasha said and groaned inside, immediately regretting saying it. *Awkward being polite and cordial.* She thought. *Not used to it.* Annalynn's smart-mouthed comments rang in Pasha's ears. "Dr. Lutnik, if I were to describe you flat out, you'd be 'a short, out-of-control ebony pest ready for a fight.' However, add a little tact, a bit of calculated jargon, and you become 'a small but power-packed woman of African descent, ready to take on the world.'" Pasha made a second attempt at cushioning the way for some manipulation later.

"Nice last name, soldier Maven." Pasha said, the compliment feeling awkward in her mouth.

"It's my first."

"First what?" She growled. "First time to hear somebody say something nice?"

"No, it's my first name." She felt like an idiot. She'd never be polite again.

"What's your last name?" she asked.

"Not allowed to say two names."

"Stupid rule."

"I'd think twice about calling The Third 'stupid,' doctor."

"Truth's an elixir."

"Or a poison," Maven countered.

"Well. I can tell who's been feeding you your medicine."

Her quips didn't faze him, and the mirth was still lurking in his black-brown eyes, set deeply in his inky-colored skin. He stepped closer to her, and she didn't move away. "You know, if you need someone to practice being nice to—just so you don't offend Commander Dorsey—you can practice on me."

"You'd be here long past shift change."

"Wouldn't mind." Her brain was begging her to look away from him, but she couldn't. His appearance was too stunning for a soldier, dark eyes playing with her emotions, laughing at her, teasing her like a playful kid, yet he was physically commanding like a weapon of war. Pasha was unglued.

Finally, she broke past him, but as she did he reached up to her shaved head saying, "Hey, lighten up." And as he spoke he balled his hand into a fist and rubbed the side of her head. Quick as a crack of lightening interrupting the night, they jumped apart, both freezing in an eerie momentary chill that hovered over the lab, suspended over them. Pasha stared at Maven, sensing he felt the same churning familiarity passing between them, encircling with an otherworldly haunt. Both pairs of eyes waited for acknowledgement from the other, a recognition of shared seconds of…of what? Memory?

Maven straightened to his full height of training, allowing military decorum to march between them, ending any potential for a discussion of what just happened. He said, "I'll escort you to the deployment."

———

In her head, Pasha chanted the reasons Morris should be kidnapped by The 28 United and sent back to mapping school with Shaw where he belonged. Raghill and Morris sat in front of a huge hologram screen eight feet tall and split in half, showing simultaneously the underwater openings where the fishborns were to be launched and the deserted outskirts of the city. With the control of the hologram in Raghill's hands, Pasha was unable to tell if the grasslands shown on the hologram were south of the city where she knew the balloon-techs had colonies, or if it was to the west where The 28 United's colonies had been established and the Energy Concourse remained hidden under the security of thin-skin.

Around the strategy table sat Dorsey's appointed officers, all engaged in Morris' explanation of the deployment. Pasha tried to force her focus on Morris, but images of Maven and their brief connecting moment in the lab kept prodding her to consider not only the effects of reverse-*locasa* on herself, but the power of the lost memories that belonged to those that received *locasa* originally. Were those memories so strong in someone like Maven that they were tapping on the door of his brain, begging for entrance and return?

Morris said, "We've developed enough wind blocks and solar cells to, we think, deploy one fishborn as an experiment. Not fire it—just send it."

"We'll see," said one of Dorsey's advisors. The right screen image flipped now and showed plant workers loading over a hundred blocks and cells into slots on the side of the weapon.

The left screen zoomed in on the grasslands and the entire frame filled with Gizzie's big brown eyes. The same advisor spoke again. "Stop. There's an animal.

That's almost as good as people. Target that." Pasha wasn't sure how she kept her game face on, but she managed to signal Morris with her eyes. *Choose another location*. However, it wasn't Morris controlling the hologram and launch coordinates. It was Raghill. Dressed in the uniform of The Third, his long curly brown locks were now shaved in a close crop, and Pasha recognized for the first time in Raghill, a younger version of his father. They shared a sharp, square jaw, perfectly shaped nose, and eyes so black the pupils were indecipherable. For the six years she'd known Raghill, he'd always been the carefree, spirited kid she'd met from the library where Dorsey and the other leaders abandoned their sons to a drugged-out caretaker, a pocket-watch named Degnan. This post-*Jurbay* world left kids skipping childhood and stepping into the oversized shoes of adults, misfit to feet that would stumble and often fall.

Commander Dorsey paced back and forth over the length of the deployment car, his hand to his ear, wincing. He called Pasha over and asked, "Why aren't you up there explaining your own energy masterpiece?"

"Not good with crowds," she hated herself for responding without a full sentence.

"I noticed." He lowered his voice to a whisper. "You and I have a date in my private surgery room tomorrow."

"That depends," she blurted. "Does that fishborn have a payload, or are we just checking out its ability to deploy?

"It shouldn't matter to you."

"Then it shouldn't matter to you if you get a permanent fix to those sounds pounding on the inside of your head." She could tell by the way he flinched that the pink noise inserts he'd been wearing in his ears were predictably losing their effectiveness.

Moving even closer to her face he said, "Shut up. You'll do the surgery tomorrow."

"Have you locked those launch coordinates in yet?" Morris asked Raghill, and Pasha knew the question was meant to catch her up on what she'd missed.

"Just about to do that," said Raghill, but as his hands moved to make the final lock, the lights in the launch car blinked and went black.

"Not again," Pasha heard Morris say, and she imagined him controlling the blackouts for the last week, so that when this one happened it was no surprise to those present. The lights flickered on, then held strong. As Pasha expected, the screen continued to show the grasslands, but there was no Gizzie in the image. Morris had shifted the launch site.

While all attention was on the hologram of the launch, Dorsey tried to hide his pain, turning away from the group and retreating to the far edge of the room, the palm of one hand covering his entire right ear.

Raghill reached for the hologram controls, saying, "Looks like these shifted in the blackout. I'll make the corrections, so we're good to go."

Morris placed his hand on Raghill's forearm, interrupting his adjustments. Morris' voice was soft-spoken, unheard by the others carrying on their own conversations. "The Commander said there was no payload on that fishborn. Is this thing armed?"

Pasha looked at Raghill as he directed his gaze at Morris. She thought there was nothing left of The 28 United in his eyes, and he was every bit a fledgling of The Third. She moved closer to hear Morris repeat, "Is this thing armed?"

"It shouldn't matter to you," Raghill quoted his father. Pasha held Morris responsible for this, and firmly placed the guilt on him for believing Dorsey, that he wasn't going to waste ammunition on a payload that was only a test. She knew that if she'd been here doing her job, she could have stalled this launch—tried to appease Dorsey—tempting him to wait for all the energy she'd promised to deliver a complete and legitimate launch. But she hadn't been here. If this fishborn was armed, it could hit any part of Colony G.

Raghill was a fresh recruit for Dorsey, a follower who she was sure hadn't made a plan to enter the service of The Third when he, Morris and Annalynn had followed her here. He must still have emotional ties to The 28 United—to Morris, to Annalynn—to her. While the conversations of fishborn power gained volume behind them at the strategy table, Pasha whispered to Raghill, "You didn't tell him about Colony G, did you?" He didn't answer. "We're your family." She was desperate to reach him.

"I'll never tell him," Raghill whispered. "But I might lock down coordinates that would prove myself as valuable to the father I never had." To the horror of Pasha and Morris, Raghill locked in the coordinates. She hoped he was targeting a warning explosion that would be close enough to alert The 28 United without destroying it, but reality hung on the images in her mind, images of Colony G after the launch. None of the images painted a picture of "warning."

In and out of the hologram, Raghill moved his hands, activating codes as Morris spun the details of the experiment to the officers. Pasha had to admit Morris was polished and smooth. Somewhere back in her mind, she remembered him presenting his persuasive argument for marriage to Avery and Raben. Morris had flipped The Third's ban on marriage upside down. He replaced their proclamations that marriage was an antiquated institution with his own revolutionary ideas that marriage was a renewed commitment to family and home. He was the one that initiated a marriage plan as a tactic to be used against The Third, shutting down their idea that any commitment outside of one to The Third was treason. Avery and Raben were the first of many to enact that tactic, but ultimately their commitment failed through Raben's deceit and violent death.

Once, after Raben's death, Pasha argued with Morris about marriage and said, "I bet you regret that argument." Morris looked at her, surprised, and answered.

"Their marriage brought every result we wanted—a stand against The Third."

"Their marriage and Raben's presence almost took down the entire 28 United."

"Things are different now. Better now because of it. I have no regrets." He was fourteen when they had that conversation, and Pasha was twenty-nine. Still, his arguments sent her away grumbling, wishing she'd had one more comment to fling the last word his way.

And here he was making *her* speech to the top ranks of The Third. Fitting. While she thought she'd called the shots on this mission, it was Morris who put the details of this experimental launch together, thinking he'd bought them enough time to let Avery plan an attack. In reality they were now on the verge of dumping a devastating explosion in the middle of the Energy Concourse. Pasha recognized that Morris was a wordsmith in every way, but whether or not he cared to admit it, he was also still a child, and children shouldn't play outside their own backyards.

Pasha knew she still had a last resort. Maybe she couldn't stop the launch by using the eye-reader mechanism hooked only to the chipsters of The 28 United, but she could warn Avery—get her and all the workers at the Energy Concourse to bail out of the area before Raghill ripped the Concourse to shreds and converted their chances of launching an air attack on Ash into rubble. But there was no guarantee that the chipster application would function. Only those in The 28 United had chipsters with this function, and she knew it was only powerful enough to work for two or three messages. Avery had just activated it to call a meeting of subterraneans inside The Third. Pasha pictured Gizzie and Chapman back at the colony, Avery, McGinty, Shaw, Herman and Orbit and all the others she loosely considered family. She had to do this. Nonchalantly opening the chipster in her forearm, she mimed the rechecking of Raghill's coordinates, all the time sending an eye-reader message that would go only to those in The 28 United. *Fishborn coming at Concourse now. Abort all work and head west.* She activated the message.

Chapter 14
EVACUATE AVERY

"The pressing need to round up Pasha and get her back here can't go on tomorrow's agenda," I argue with McGinty in the middle of the zoo's deserted underground room where reptiles used to wander. It is now the Council chambers, currently a haven for negotiation. However, we are all keenly aware that within the weeks to come this room will become a hotbed of strategy for the inevitable assault on Ash. We are currently in the conversations that foreshadow either the end of The Third or the demolishment of The 28 United.

McGinty says, "Pasha knows we're coming inside The Third to meet with the subterraneans tomorrow night. We'll find out from her then if we can coordinate the air attack with whatever her strategy is. We can talk about her plan then."

"She has no plan," I say.

"Call it what you want, but she's inside, and she might have intel that could help us."

"It's not up for discussion. Those choices are not in her hands. Those are my decision—*our* decisions as a Council. She has no experience in formulating strategy, especially when she has no input from the Council—no input from anyone."

"Morris is there. Raghill. Annalynn."

"Are you kidding? Annalynn's thirteen and the others fifteen. And how's Raghill supposed to keep our subterranean protocol when he's living around the father that abandoned him to a deserted library? He's a kid."

Old Soul enters the debate. "Avery's right. Pasha is instrumental to all of our energy research here, and for her to take matters into her own hands without discussing it with us was careless."

"It was stupid," I say. "Rash. One more time she thinks of herself and no one else. We've had a strategy since we arrived at the zoo. Mine the energy, put the fleet together, fly into Ash, destroy it, eliminate The Third—and bring justice back."

The eye-reader message from Pasha comes unexpected to all of us, like an electrical shock through our bodies and a psychedelic wave inside our heads. As a group, we stand immediately and snap to attention with a jerk, a spasmodic slap. Simultaneously we read it. *Fishborn coming at Concourse now. Abort all work and head west.*

We run in unison to the exit, each shouting instinctively how we will manage the evacuation. Clef has the caves. Old Soul—the children's prison. Shaw—the mappers, and McGinty will collect the children throughout the Energy Concourse. I will ride through the trails shouting the escape plan like a contemporary Paul Revere with a lot less organization. There are no Council members other than us. Quinn is on a sabbatical from being a mother and a grandparent—Pasha on a self-appointed mission to save our world—and Morris, the only kid on the Council, has decided to spread his wings as a rebel, following Pasha, claiming subterranean status.

The soldier Baxter stands outside the Council door holding the reins of Dapple. I'm grateful I don't have to look far for my horse. I take the reins from Baxter. "Thanks."

"Need any help, Commander?"

"No, but McGinty does. Go with him and rescue the children." As I gallop off I call back, "See you on the west side of the Concourse." The air pushes hard against Dapple's mane and my face as he carries me the length of the Concourse. I shout to the children, "To the west side. Now. No questions. To the west. Help each other. Run." All I can think about is what Pasha can possibly mean by *Fishborn coming now*. Does "now" mean we have thirty minutes, or twenty, or half a day or is it *any* minute?

After Dapple and I run the Concourse once, we run it again. This time there is no one left in the east section. The heavy concentration of people now push their way over the last mile at the far edge of our Energy Concourse. I pass McGinty. A child clings to the mane of McGinty's stallion, leaning forward, his chest flat on the horse's neck. Holding onto McGinty's from the back and clinging to his belt is another child, Chapman, just old enough to know he can't let go or he'll end up on the ground. I'd left Chapman with his caregiver this morning asleep under his quilt, but my boy has a reputation for wandering. So, I'm not surprised that McGinty found him on the Concourse.

Right behind McGinty, the children workers fan out to the sides, their numbers growing as they draw closer to the west end. They breathe hard, but they are fit and the concept of escape is not new to them. The children from the prison carry other kids on their backs, encouraging them with desperate phrases like "hold tight" and "you can't let go now." Today these prison kids can find nothing to fight about.

I realize our instincts were right. If we had tried to herd everyone from inside the Concourse out toward the east exit, we would have wasted valuable time and headed in the direction of the fishborn, coming from Ash. Instead we are trying to put as much distance as possible between us and an imminent blast.

When we arrive on the west side, hundreds of us cram against the end wall, made of thin-skin. The horses stand loose, but perfectly still. Perhaps we think the tighter we press against each other, the better chance we have avoiding a direct hit from a fishborn. Maybe Shaw, McGinty, Clef, Old Soul and I think if we stand in front of the children, it will prevent them from destruction. Death is about to shoot along the ground, or under it, at any minute and explode in our faces.

The one thing I know about this weapon is that its sleek nose can bore through the earth, skimming just below ground level, sensing the most potent potential impact. But before I can process the impending ramifications of this disaster, it starts. A shimmering comes first, like a shiver when the air is unpredictably cold. Then, more powerful. A shake, throwing us from side to side, bringing all of us to the ground. Then we see it, like a giant worm inching its way through the dirt less than a foot underground—a hundred yards away. I feel myself trembling with the weapon's force. Now, fifty yards from us. The fishborn starts to veer above the ground, its nose like a bloodhound seeking a scent. Something seems to be putting a drag on it, slowing it down. Its nose is now uncovered, traveling in slow motion and gigantic with payload, twenty yards from us. Then it stops. This fishborn tilts upwards at an angle, frozen and exposing its tip armed with an explosive package.

In a voice, with a shake of its own, but loud, I say, "You're going to follow Shaw and the Council—slow, careful, quiet—back to the east end of the Concourse, to the exit." In total silence, they do as they are told, stepping gingerly. Every forward motion they make, every jar of the ground may be the movement that triggers a blast that will blow them apart. I'm herding those last in line when my eyes glance up at the top of the fishborn's nose. There is Chapman. The terror I feel, seeing him where no one wants to be, is unmatchable to anything I've ever felt. More intense than killing Borden. More horrific than seeing Raben's chest cut open and his ventricle remains lying on the ground. Worse than seeing Lear eaten by a brain-swapper and Prospero's flesh torn away by a Deadly. Chapman lies on the nose of the fishborn, tinkering, disassembling it, one piece at a time, as if he knows the ins and outs of stopping the power of this weapon.

His concentration does not surprise me. I have seen this in many other instances. I become invisible, almost like he lifts himself out of my presence and travels to a space that I cannot go, where distractions are eliminated, so that he might accomplish the task he's put before himself. How is this undisturbed effort conceivable for anyone under the threat of obliteration? And how is it possible for a five-year-old?

Chapman utilizes a tool I'm not familiar with. It's not a screwdriver, and it's not a wrench, rather a small

round disc, fitting in the palm of his hand. He vigilant-
ly runs his palm over the surface of the fishborn. The
commander part of my brain shoots out analysis of the
situation: Hands steady. Expertise with the tool. Acute
ability to detect weapon activity. The mother part of me
evaluates the future: My only a child. Needs his mother.
Destruction foreseeable.

The back of Chapman's hand lights up, glowing
from the tool he presses to the metal end of the weapon. I hear a vibration, not gentle, but violent, alarming.
My body tenses, but Chapman's does not. With his free
hand and with ambidextrous accuracy he punctures the
pointed front of the weapon with the nail of his thumb.
This, I have never seen—the ability to use his hand as a
tool upon command. So much I do not know about my
own son. The vibration ceases.

And then I feel the presence of people around me.
There are maybe thirty in number, all children and
led by McGinty, moving steadily over the dirt floor of
the Concourse, their eyes on the side of the fishborn.
McGinty holds up his hand, directing his apprentices
to stop. They are all cautious, incredibly aware that the
motion of their feet may bring a belligerent shout of violence from a weapon controlled by a monster of a commander, standing smugly in the underwater launch car
of the Dark Market. Did Pasha authorize this horror to
stave off Dorsey, to satisfy him momentarily so that we
might eventually breach the city by air? Would she risk

our Energy Concourse to avoid destruction of all the rest of Colony G?

McGinty and I are feet away. We say nothing, imagining the sound waves of our voices might activate the destruction of the Concourse, knowing that would be the end of everything we want to call our future. I can see it in his eyes. *Trust me. We must risk to save.* McGinty and I do not ever have to discuss "life sacrificed." Our willingness is like breathing. Necessary. No need to clear or check with a commander to weigh the risk of annihilation if the payload explodes. We have rehearsed our death on a daily basis for many years. This is simply the performance. We know the curtain may be falling, final act unfolding. Discussion unnecessary. Action required.

McGinty activates the chipster in his arm and then stealthily approaches the tail end of the fishborn. Without a flinch, he places one hand on its fishlike tail and uses the other hand to work his chipster, triggering a hologram featuring Morris face, not Pasha's. I'm not surprised that Morris had the foresight to provide contingency instructions for disarming. We hear Morris say in a perfect monotone, "Release the seal on the control lever." McGinty frees the cover. It falls toward the ground, intercepted by a child whose hands are cupped to catch it. "Rotate the lever to the left." McGinty is steady. He's practiced his game face hundreds of times before. He swirls the lever, and an unearthly groan is emitted from the weapon as the side panel swings slowly open, revealing hundreds of slots filled with solar cells and wind blocks.

Nausea begins, like a prize fighter just took his best shot at my stomach. I doubt our survival. McGinty remains at the rear of the weapon, gesturing to the children to come forward, motioning them to lift each cell and block out of the weapon in an attempt to eliminate the fishborn's energy supply. Have we trained them for war, as the Catalonian ambassador accused my mother and father? We trained them to mine energy, not for war, but they contribute to the fight when war requires it. And it does. As if they'd practiced this choreography for months, they move like dancers, gracefully raising their arms and extracting the energy source, then backing carefully away from the payload, stacking the cells and blocks, creating a hill of deactivation.

Almost half done with the removal, the children still exhibit a steady gentleness. Then Chapman shakes that grace to the core, dropping his palm tool abruptly on the ground. He jerks his body up to a sitting position, facing the rest of those trying to save our colony. "I got this!" he screams. "I don't need you." The children ignore him and do not falter, looking straight ahead at their task. McGinty and I lock our attention on Chapman.

"We will continue to dismantle," McGinty speaks to the children with a perfectly level voice. "Ignore distractions."

"I am not a distraction. I don't need you," Chapman says with steel in his voice.

"We're all needed, Chapman," I say, trying to mediate with this crazed alternative to my child. "Stay still. Don't move." I feel fear seizing my lungs, and I have little breath left. My inhalations are shallow, my exhalations shallower. I see the stubbornness inside Chapman as it is with children, wanting their own way, knowing they must obey someone else. But unlike other children, I also see in his eyes a message to me. Perhaps he intends to mask it, but it slips into his stare for a second or two. I read him with accuracy, as only a mother can. He's saying: *I'll be still if it serves me later. It is my choice to be still. Not yours.* I can't help but wonder if his deceit runs deep from the genes of his father, a weaponized GEB of The Third, or deeper from his mother's human failures in my attempt to be a commander fit for battle.

"That's it," says McGinty. "No longer activated." He sighs a relief with the others and weaves his fingers, right hand to right hand with one of the children. That one gesture signals to the others to run to McGinty, draping themselves around him, over him, in one big mound. I rush to the nose of the weapon, pulling Chapman downward by grabbing his heel, catching him in my arms as he falls before he hits the ground. How good to feel his warmth, his body unharmed, not blasted into thousands of pieces, but whole. The relief is short lived when I realize there is no reciprocal embrace. Chapman's body is purposefully lifeless in my arms. I stiffen and set him on the ground. He stares at the dirt, but then a transformation ripples through him as he raises his eyes to meet mine. His are filled with tears. He is crying child's tears. He reaches his little arms to me, grabbing my neck. This is the one whose heartbeat matches mine. The one I love so unconditionally beyond explanation. Chapman is the one who's made me look past the present to hope for a future that goes beyond his childhood.

A balloon-tech is only three feet from my face before I realize it's there, and I see Checkmate through the face-space, smiling. Setting Chapman down, I say, "Would you stop sneaking up on me?" Then I notice we are surrounded by scores of balloon-techs, more than I have ever seen before. I know I must find the time to develop relationships within this b-tech culture, and I need to uncover other unknown colonies living in their corners of what's left of the world. The necessity of joining forces with the balloon-techs and the urgency of aligning with other unidentified colonies must take a high priority. It should be my urgent agenda. Some of these colonies aren't even known to The Third, aren't under their tyranny and may be willing to rally with us and fight against the enemy. I need to find these groups and have these conversations, but time has not yet afforded the pursuit of these discussions. We are forced to rely only on our loyal ones, building a fleet of zooms to attack by air and consume Commander Dorsey's world with the righteousness of only The 28 United.

I can see Checkmate talking continually to himself through his face-space, as he hovers before me. Opening the sliding panel so he might speak to me, he says, "Do the children need a lift back to the colony past the danger zone?"

"Danger's over for the moment," I say, "but they'll take a ride from you. Do I have to trade for that?"

"No," he quips. That's the shortest thing I've ever heard him say, and I'm thankful for both brevity and kindness. I look at the children who remain here, the same thirty that disarmed the fishborn. "It's okay. Take a ride," I say to them all. "You showed bravery. As your Commander, I'm proud of you." All their eyes connect with mine. "Ride home tonight in the balloon-techs. Go with Shaw and the Council. Sleep."

"And you?" Clef asks.

"McGinty and I will take the horses back." I look down the length of the fishborn. "Tomorrow we'll figure out how to get this thing out of here." I can see their demeanors relax and their spirits seem to rise as they clamor into the b-techs. The length of a four-mile concourse would be a depressing journey and an exhausting conclusion to this frightening night. They wave at me through the face-space of each b-tech, their childlike personas stepping all over their warrior game faces.

Chapman peers out of a face-space too. He doesn't wave goodbye. He stares at the fishborn. He doesn't blink.

Looking up at the hole in the thin-skin, McGinty and I try to follow the progress of the b-techs sailing off, but they are quickly camouflaged. We are left alone under the sky that, tonight, seems to proclaim justice. McGinty holds the reins to both Dapple and his stallion, offering Dapple to me. But I don't take the reins. I slide down the side of the fishborn and sit on the ground, leaning against its powerful metal casing. McGinty ties the horses' reins to the tail of the weapon and comes to sit with me.

His fingers lace through mine and we stare upward through the chicken-poo blast site, our backs against the empty energy slats of the prototype weapon. Dorsey meant to test it and damage us in the process, a distinct forshadow of our future. Pasha's energy supply in this fishborn showcased the potential of what a fully armed weapon stash might do in the hands of Commander Dorsey. And now it is truly a race. Will we arm our fleet, be the first to attack and control The Third—something we've never done before? Or will The Third secure the energy they need to take us out with endless fishborns, destroying life and crushing what we've built—The 28 United?

The crisp of autumn air makes me long for my sleeping mat and a pile of blankets that might just keep me warm enough to drift into the sleep I desperately need, but McGinty's arm around my shoulders brings warmth too. Desire springs from his gentle kiss on my cheek, but is uncomfortably interrupted by my unexpected laughter. I don't intend to laugh, but I can't help it. I say, "How can you kiss me right now?" He seems surprised by my reaction. "We're sitting right here in death's arms."

"Exactly," he responds. "How can I not kiss you? In a world like this, every moment must be the best moment." McGinty opens his chipster and turns the music on. How ridiculous it all is. I kiss him. I do not believe it is our last. I don't believe justice has taken its final breath. The music is from a World War II song that McGinty liberated from the History Labyrinth. Its melody catchy and its sound tinny, the song's lyrics jive with images of bugle boys and companies of soldiers, but we are too tired to dance. So, we sit in the shadow of a weapon and think about tomorrow.

Chapter 15
SUBTERRANEAN DOZEN PASHA

He'd called her in for an analysis of fishborn #1's deployment. Pasha entered Commander Dorsey's strategy room, and a livid curiosity spread with a thickness through her veins. Morris had arrived before her and was standing next to Dorsey at the holographic map that covered the wall and showed a cross section of the entire Dark Market. Raghill sat on a chair slat in the corner, manipulating his own hologram, looking comfortable and every bit his father's son. Pasha knew this kid had wanted to be a subterranean when he, Morris and Annalynn rebelliously followed her inside The Third, but the mesmerizing power of a missing father overtook Raghill. He was not to be trusted. She only hoped for Raghill's loyalty, for the sake of what they'd been through together, and that he would keep the subterranean status of

Morris, Annalynn and herself hidden from Commander Dorsey.

The thirty-one cars, loaded with four fishborns each, were displayed on the screen in an enlarged fashion. While the fishborns seemed innocuous on the hologram, Pasha knew they contained the explosive power to end all life to the south and west of Erie. Her scalp glistened with sweat droplets that she swore earlier she could control. Foolish.

Just moments ago, the entrance archway had rolled up and then back down again, muttering a quiet purr. Pasha knew that noise made both Morris and Dorsey aware of her presence, yet neither turned to acknowledge her. No wonder she was sweating. Fine. She'd take this moment to memorize the holographic map. Each of the fishborns had their own firing tube, and each was aimed at a separate target. Florescent lines from the fishborns to their targets graphed the projectiles and their destructive paths.

"Hmm. Dr. Lutnik. Late as usual," said Dorsey while his hand traced one of those connecting lines, demonstrating to Morris the results of a potential hit. Pasha didn't even receive a nod from the Commander.

"I wouldn't call it late, if the time I was given was the wrong time."

"Was it?" His smirk enraged her, and when he turned to her, always sizing her up with a verdict of *ineffectual*, he said, "Analysis of deployment—fishborn #1?"

Complete Sentences. Pasha reminded herself. *You know you can.* "Analysis? A raging success." Sarcasm was her best expression.

"How can 'not exploding' equal success?"

Pasha marched to the map. "I'm not in charge of explosions. That's your job." Without looking at Dorsey, she reached inside the hologram and experimented with repositioning the fishborn firing tubes to angle back at Ash. Dorsey grabbed her wrist, tight.

"Evaluate—and whisper." He held one finger in his ear. Morris stood awkwardly behind Dorsey, and Pasha saw the fear in Morris' eyes. She knew he must be thinking of his own father, Borden, and all the commands he had given to get rid of her and Avery. Morris had seen his father give the command to set the flame and burn a library full of boys, himself included. He knew what this Commander was capable of. Much more.

Yanking her wrist away from him, she continued to play with the angles of the fishborns while he looked at her and not the map. "My part of the launch was a triumph," she said. "We provided the energy to send your fishborn at the target Raghill selected." She switched the hologram and captured the video-audio trails, showing coverage of the arrival of the fishborn at the Energy Concourse. The images were tight, a close shot of the fishborn after it left the water, speeding just below ground level. "Bam," Pasha sneered. "Made it—not just out of the water—but when it hit, it had the energy to ride the earth until gravity stopped it. Not our fault there was no kaboom. We're in charge of energy, not the 'kaboom-count.'" She made sure "kaboom-count" was nowhere near a whisper. Looking at Morris, she said, "Thank you, Morris, for assisting Raghill with a great launch." She saluted him with a flare of cynicism. He would know she was thanking him for more than being good at launching a fishborn. He was being thanked as a subterranean for avoiding a hit on the quarters of the colony, and for somehow delaying the blast until someone in that Energy Concourse disarmed the resting fishborn. Gravity had nothing to do with it. The video-audio trails had gone black after fishborn #1 came to a stop. The salvation actions of Avery and her team were not recorded and left to Morris and Pasha's imagination.

"Think 'future,'" Pasha said. "Think ingenuity. Your weapons being launched one after another with my energy resources..." She flipped the hologram back to the map where she'd been manipulating the routes of the other fishborns. "...that is, *if* you can ever get your fishborns aimed in the right direction." She crossed to the exit archway as Dorsey turned to see every fishborn repositioned and aiming directly at Ash. He motioned abruptly at Morris to fix it, and Morris complied immediately.

"Tomorrow at nine, Dr. Lutnik," said Dorsey. Pasha faced him, as the archway ascended for her exit. She saw Raghill had not moved. He was staring at her now, and she did not recognize a subterranean. Rather, she recognized a commander's son. "We have an appointment first thing in the morning." She turned her back on the Commander and Raghill and left without a response.

Morris continued to work on repositioning the fishborns Pasha had corrupted and said to Dorsey, "You couldn't have deployed that weapon without her energy sources." Morris now held Dorsey's attention. "She'll be able to get you as much energy as you want in the next few months."

"Whisper!" was Dorsey's only response.

Pasha raced along the side of the Dark Market in a glide, followed by Annalynn in a glide of her own, submerged and streaming through the Waters of Erie, the greenish brown colors encasing the rectangular transports, sealing their transparent walls off from a watery death. They traveled eastward to the docking bay on the shores of Ash. Many ideas came to mind as Pasha considered how to ditch Annalynn.

Pasha knew she needed a visit to her private lab, a place unknown to anyone but her and the subterraneans in The Third. She'd hoped the subterranean group would grow larger once inside The Third, but to date numbered only seven, not including herself, Morris and Annalynn. No one really counted Raghill anymore, and Pasha had started keeping info from him even before the secret lab was functional. Danger poked briefly at her conscience as she thought about the underground area of what used to be a surgery center before it was cordoned off after the Deadlies came to town. Outdated medical supplies, heavy x-ray equipment and surgical tools obstructed the hallways that led to Pasha's domain. She'd created a zig-zag series of items, a pathway known only to a few of them, that camouflaged the passageway, the items looking like they'd been tossed haphazardly by anyone needing storage. A subterranean coming to work in the secret space knew the way, but their steps of entry would not be detected, as the strewn storage items always looked undisturbed.

The glides docked. Pasha opted for the direct approach, standing unswervingly in Annalynn's pathway to the outskirts of the city. Pasha tried her best to be convincing, professional. "Annalynn, you're needed at the meeting."

"Boatload of bull, *mamasita*," said Annalynn. "You're the one that's needed."

"I'll be there soon."

"We're already late. I'm not going without you."

"You go. Let them know I'm coming." Annalynn didn't move. "I'm in charge."

Annalynn adopted Pasha's firm stance, mimicking her attitude. "*No one's* in charge. Morris has his game-face set so perfectly he scares me. Raghill's in Dorsey-land. And all you think about is giving the world back their memories. *No one's* in charge."

"I'm in charge. I'll make it work."

"Not if they kill us all off with a bunch of fishborns first!" Pasha didn't flinch. Annalynn did. "Go ahead. Stare me down with those hollow eyes. Tear my heart right out of my chest."

"Don't start."

"Okay. Okay. I'll go." Turning to a pathway heading north of the city, Annalynn said, "But you owe me—"

"Wrong. Never owed you anything. Never will."

"It's just an expression."

"Leave quicker," said Pasha, and she departed in the opposite direction.

———

Through a hologram in her private lab, Pasha, in a trance-like zone, spun a new hypothesis for improving reverse-*locasa*. Beyond the sight of The Third and past the point where anyone might hear her, she made the minutest adjustments to reverse-*locasa*, hoping they might be the key to fitting all the resurrected images she'd experienced into the memories that would form her past. *The soldier with skin like midnight. The infant. The lentils spilling from a sack. The gibberish letters swirling in the air. Letters, please collide.* She begged. *Slam into readable words. Language. Story.*

She kept track of the newly imputed data and the results, but weeks ago, she'd stopped numbering her attempts at finding the adjustments needed to complete her project. When the sum of the attempts began to equal failure, her irritation mounted, and she eliminated the double-digit count located at the left of her entries.

Tonight might be different. She needed to step on a stool to reach the expanse of the hologram, and as she did she winced at a sharp pain in her hamstring and noticed the drag of her right leg. She reached down to her quad and lifted her leg with both her hands. The adjustments to the device were intricate, and when she was finished she stepped down from the stool and sat on a chair slat, ready once again to perform experiments on herself. However, tonight there was another variable. Comparison. After reverse-*locasa* came in contact with her skull and led her into ghostly encounters with her past, she was determined to make new adjustments and try it out on someone else. A volunteer, she hoped. After all, this meeting tonight with Avery and the other subterraneans would be a collection of a small group of loyal ones who were confidential and controllable. If there were problems with the device, they could easily be contained, maybe sent back to the colony instead of returning to Ash. Would Avery allow her to use one of the subterraneans in a comparison experiment?

By now her fingers knew the way to the button that launched another journey into her extracted memories siphoned off by The Third, the ones who never played fair. The familiar convulsions began. The sporadic slams against the floor and the jarring of her body—her necessary ticket to the past.

She expected maybe it would begin with the items on the floor that she'd remembered—the garden tools and torn bag of lentils—but it didn't. The images were frayed on the edges, faded in the center and waterlogged all through. *Two strong hands. Each clasped a child's hand. Boots, attached to a body, but the body indeterminable. The boots stood apart from the hands, distant and walking backwards. More space between the hands and the boots. Then, so much space. The hands disappeared. No sound in these distorted fragments of memories. Written words flew through her field of vision, mixing with floating pigeon feathers. Tattoo ink spilled slowly across the boots.*

Pasha heard yelling, over and over. Someone shook her. It hurt. Someone yelled her name. "Dr. Lutnik! Dr. Lutnik! Answer me."

Pasha's eyes opened in slits, a fog covering everything in her frame of reference. Someone pulled her to her feet. She knew this voice. "Maven?" she barely articulated his name.

"Dr. Lutnik, I can call emergency personnel—"

"Don't." She grabbed his arm and forced her eyes to concentrate on his face, grateful it was Maven who had found her, and not some other Elite guard that might have observed her in her out-of-control state where she was unaware of her surroundings. Thankfulness did not last long. Pasha was captured by her data, by the necessity of a comparison that might lead to complete success with reverse-*locasa*. She allowed Maven to help her up. Unintentionally he lifted her off the ground, her body so light and his so bulked up, but he quickly righted her and stepped away.

"How did you find me?" she asked.

"You all right? I could get water—"

"How?"

He looked incredibly guilty and hesitant to answer, but he said, "I followed you." She knew she had the truth. This was not some Elite guard out for advancement in the ranks of The Third. This was a man who was smitten by her. He turned his back on Pasha as if it would be easier to get the words out. "I thought maybe we could—discuss—reminisce—about that awkward moment—memory we shared…"

Maven didn't have time to finish. Pasha had silently returned to the top step of her stool, standing right behind him. Quickly she placed the device on the back of his neck. As Maven slid to the floor Pasha felt a flash of human hesitation, but then desperate science took over. She opened the hologram, setting up the data for her comparison, but as she did, Maven started seizing.

Pasha dropped to his side, rolling his huge frame over to his back, checking his pupils. The seizure stopped abruptly. Dead? *No, please, no.* And this time she wasn't hoping for the sake of her experiment. She placed her ear below his nose, listening for life. She heard it. She felt the beat in his neck. Slow. Steady. *Coma is a good thing. He will rest. I'll be back quickly, and he will be ready for healing.* From a shelf she lifted a military blanket and covered Maven up, securing the edges under his chin and tucking the remaining fabric tightly around his body.

Her window of time to meet with Avery and the others was almost gone. She'd return to the lab, return to Maven. He would be here. She could fix this. Yet, the voice of reason said "don't go," presenting substantial arguments against her rationalizations. Uncontrollably she rubbed her head—with both hands. *Created chaos. Thought I was the one to end The Third. Thought I was. Made a mess. Here. Everywhere. Must fix it. End the chaos.* And for a moment this woman who'd professed to be the self-centered genius of the remaining world—this doctor who'd been touted by both The Third and The 28 United as beyond brilliant—suddenly this woman wondered if maybe she wasn't so smart after all. She jerked reverse-*locasa* off the counter where she'd left it, fitted it behind a stack of stored lab equipment on a shelf, and set out to the rendezvous with Avery and the subterraneans.

Once she was gone, Degnan stepped out from behind the antiquated stacks of lab equipment, picked up reverse-*locasa* from where she'd placed it and began an experiment of his own.

———

Pasha stepped through the doorway of an abandoned butcher shop in the back alley behind a forgotten cluster of stores. She attempted to focus, adjusting to the dim surroundings that momentarily obscured some of the objects in the deserted meat locker. Looted long ago, there was nothing left for a thief to pilfer, and no one would come searching here for anything at all. A flame burned from a torch at the center of the room, and she could barely discern Avery's form.

As her eyes adjusted, she saw the subterranean dozen dressed all in black, including Avery, Shaw, McGinty, Morris, Annalynn and the seven subterraneans currently working inside The Third. Shaw and McGinty stood near Avery, and the other seven subterraneans were positioned with Annalynn and Morris in a semi-circle facing Avery. Morris squatted near the flame while some rested against crumbling walls. The darkness of the room camouflaged their undeniable intent: the destruction of Ash from the inside out.

Avery directed her comments toward Morris. "What about Frederick? He was with us barely a month after we left Reichel, and he was only the second one we'd ever used reverse-*locasa* on. We have no idea how it affected him. When he got his memories back did he try to get home? How did he get back with The Third? Is there any way we can use him inside?"

Morris was firm: "No. We've seen no evidence that there are any holes in his loyalty to The Third. He hasn't contacted us, and contacting him might risk our subterranean status and jeporadize any connection with Dorsey that we've built so far."

Avery squatted next to Morris. Pasha thought Avery was almost confidential, yet everyone in the room could hear each word she said. Pasha had seen this urgency in Avery many times through the years that they had been connected. The years they occasionally misspoke of their relationship, calling each other friends. Everyone in the butcher shop was trusted, with the exception of herself. At this point, Pasha was sure there were cracks between her and all of these loyal ones. *Cracks—an understatement. No trust for the stirrer of chaos.*

Avery continued, "What about Raghill? Where is he?" Pasha, now accustomed to the subdued lighting, could see the discomfort and pain on Morris' face.

"Not coming." Everyone waited in silence for the explanation. "I blocked his eye-readers last week. He didn't get the message." Morris walked away from the flame and Avery followed. He finally faced her, and in the quietest voice Pasha had ever heard him speak he said, "Avery…his hair is gone. He wears the uniform of The Third now, and he looks like his father."

"Good call blocking the eye-readers, Morris." She placed her hand on his shoulder for a brief moment. "Good call." She turned back to the group and spoke, "Time is gone. The Third rammed a fishborn through our Energy Concourse."

Shaw said, "Whether we're ready to launch the Fleet of Zooms and attack or not, we have to, or everyone in the colonies and all the energy we've mined could be obliterated by a herd of fishborns."

Pasha looked across the shadowed room, and realized there were more than twelve of The 28 United she'd originally counted. She caught sight of the face-space of a balloon-tech floating outside the gaping hole where the window of the butcher shop used to be on the back side of the building. She thought it might be Checkmate exiting the craft and climbing in the window. Then she recognized his irritating voice when he said, "You're so proud of your energy mines, yet you're going to spend every last wind block and solar cell on destruction." Carrying his chessboard, the hoops of braided hair jiggled on top of his head. The subterraneans drew their Z-Colts from their shoulder holsters, but McGinty gestured them to stand down.

"We don't have a choice," said McGinty to Checkmate.

"Choice? We've been living in our colony for a decade and a half—self-sustainable and hardly a conflict. We don't even have jails. You've got jails with kids in them. We made choices, and we didn't choose war." He talked twice as fast as every other human being Pasha knew.

Avery said, "You might not be at war, Checkmate, but you definitely have the market on spying. Listen to me, your assessment of us isn't fair." Avery's attempt to control her ire was something Pasha was familiar with. Avery had finally managed to get a grip on her defensive flare-ups that used to get her into trouble. "You've been hidden away in your little section of the world where The Third has had no reason to find you. They've breathed down our necks for years with a viciousness you can't imagine. It's just a matter of time before they come after you with *locasa* at the base of your skull, sucking out your families, stealing your memories. And just when you turn around and figure it out, you'll see a caravan of fishborns swimming up the center of your colony."

"Then *kaboom!*" said Shaw with his usual bottom-line sarcasm. "And, maybe you'll wish you'd trained for war."

"Not worth the risk."

"I have a five-year-old son," said Avery. "It's worth the risk."

Checkmate argued, "You're bringing us into war."

"No." Avery walked to Shaw and took the map he held and turned to face Checkmate. "War's already here." She rolled the map out flat across a 55-gallon storage container weathered from fifteen years of no use. "You don't want to help? Fine. Leave. But I need to know now, 'cause as of this minute anyone who stays is committed to the plan." Checkmate opened his mouth. Closed his mouth. Opened it again, closed it once more.

Said nothing. Then sat on what was left of a window sill torn apart by the looting of desperate people and the severe storms of *Jurbay* years ago.

McGinty laid out the first part of the strategy. "We need two days to get the launch ready."

Pasha stepped from the dark edges of the room into the dim light. "How many in the fleet?" They all responded with a jerk of tension, raising their weapons, but then they recognized Pasha and stood at ease.

"Sixteen," answered McGinty. Pasha walked closer, looking at the map.

She pointed at a location. "My lab is right here, next to the government offices—"

Avery rushed to Pasha. "Keep your mouth shut. You don't get to say what you think anymore, and your Council position has been revoked."

"No one could've got inside The Third but me—"

"You acted on your own without consult. The Energy Concourse suffered in your absence, and you sent a fishborn to the Concourse that almost destroyed it and hundreds of our citizens."

"That was Morris, not me."

"I don't care. He's under your command inside, and you've messed it up. So keep your mouth shut." Avery gave her commands with abruptness and resolve. "Checkmate and the balloon-techs—you infiltrate immediately, tonight if possible. There's no one in Ash that even knows what a balloon-tech is. They won't be looking. Keep your observations on all entrances to the Dark Market."

"What are we looking for?" asked Checkmate.

McGinty answered, "Anything that looks like an unusual amount of troops headed into the market or building up on the shore of Erie. We think they'll start by sending the fishborns south and west of Erie."

"In the meantime," Shaw continued, "We're fitting out the Fleet of Zooms with energy. We'll have enough for one pass over the city, and then we'll land our planes on the far side of the hollers where we'll convert our efforts to the ground."

Avery pressed. "Pasha. You need to find a way to keep those fishborns without energy until we can launch."

Pasha yanked her fists from her head, stepping into her new persona, the one she used in front of Dorsey. She spoke in complete sentences. "Dorsey and I have an appointment in the morning with a scalpel, a laser and a lot of heavy-duty drugs. I can give you a day delay, but not two."

Maven announced his intrusion by stumbling in the abandoned meat locker with no regard for secrecy. All arms—the DR93s, the Z-Colts, and the SE454s—were raised in unison and pointed directly at Maven.

"Who are you?" asked Shaw, then turning to Avery he said, "We can't let him live. He's from The Third." Maven did not have his own weapon raised. It was slung over his left shoulder. Transfixed on Pasha, he edged toward her, exhibiting a slight limp. All bullets locked in chambers together, ready.

Maven laughed, making the others cringe from the robust sound of his voice. They were sure it traveled indiscreetly for blocks outside the covert and crumbling butcher shop. Maven held up his arms in surrender fashion and chuckled this time. "I didn't follow you to capture or report," he said. "I just came—to find my wife."

Chapter 17

REMAINS OF THE BUTCHER BLOCK

AVERY

In the seconds of silence that follow Maven's proclamation, I watch tears trickle from the corners of Pasha's eyes. She doesn't wipe them away. None of us had ever seen her cry, and all she says is, "I've been waiting for you." For Pasha, reverse-*locasa* will no longer be necessary. Maven fits all the missing pieces together, and at last, for her, the picture is complete.

I feel relief beyond any expectation. To see Pasha acting, even if it's briefly, like a human being and not a self-absorbed neurosurgeon who considers herself the solution to our salvation, well, that's as settling as anything could be right now. She embraces Maven for minutes. Him, gently stroking her bald head and her, stretching both arms as far as she can reach around his soldier's body. It doesn't seem right that we all stand around an abandoned butcher shop and watch this intimate reunion. There's a decade gap in their relationship, and together they will try to build a bridge to traverse the space between them. We are all aware of what this moment does for us, without any of us murmuring a word. As I watch them hold one another, restoration ignites within me. The lid that covered their kidnapped years and lost memories is pried open, and that stirs my heart, lifts my soul and prompts my spirit to rise. In a world on the precipice of more destruction we cling to this sweet time of redemption, so brief but so empowering. *Of course* we can't help but watch Maven and Pasha, for their embrace, in some way, throws a thimbleful of grace on our own gaps and holes. And maybe it even threads a stitch or two in the gaping wounds we've come to live with. I think, *There needs to be a celebration and a honeymoon of sorts*, but instead there will be front line decisions and a battle strategy that will violently rip apart everything this man Maven has worked for as an Elite of The Third. But love will hold on tight, despite Maven's spotless uniform belonging to our perpetual enemy.

I try to convince myself that we will be flying for peace when we attack Ash from the air, but an ironic awareness spreads inside me, as I stare at a butcher block in the corner of the room. Still stained with red blotches here and there, it serves as an intimidating reminder that there were cattle carved into buyable packages right here in this room. Our Fleet of Zooms must be airborne before The Third's fishborns are released, or we will be packaged too—sliced, pared, chopped and whittled into feeble challengers no longer worthy of the title "enemy." This reunion between Pasha and Maven may simultaneously be a tender "hello" and an aching "goodbye."

Maven pulls Pasha arms-length away from their embrace, confronting her with his eyes. "How much do you remember?" he asks.

"What? I have to pass a quiz to prove I'm your wife?" While her sarcastic response, typical for Pasha, hangs in the air, the moment changes abruptly when she spontaneously reaches up to touch Maven's cheek with her hand. "I remember Jett," she says. Tears ease out of Maven's eyes, glistening as they find their way to his uniform.

"He would be ten now," Maven responds.

"And Beckett thirteen. I expect her to be caring for her brother."

"Enough," I say.

Pasha turns to me, and I expect her usual cutting wit to be hurled my way, trying to slice into my composure. Instead with a barely readable smile on her lips she says, "We're both mothers now, Avery."

"We're both *warriors* today, Pasha." I'm ashamed of myself when I answer way too quickly. I see Maven hold tight to her forearm, probably thinking she might pounce on me for my insensitivity, but she doesn't. "The surgery's in the morning?" I ask.

"Said it once already. Weren't you listening?" Yeah, there's the Pasha I know. I knew she hadn't gone far.

"How long will Dorsey be out of commission?" I ask.

"As long as I want him to be."

"Two hours?"

"I said I can give you a day."

"Of recovery time?"

"No. Once he's awake, there's very little recovery. He'll be back in commission immediately." I think she looks nervous, and I wonder if it's because she thinks she might fail or if there is a certain terror in operating on the ruling Commander of The Third.

I look at the timepiece in the cuff of my sleeve. "How long do we have to get our fleet ready for attack and airborne?"

Pasha says, "Dorsey's expecting to load the energy source to the fishborns as soon as he's back on his feet and in command again. That will take twelve to thirteen hours. So, including the surgery and recovery..."

I glance at my timepiece. "From right now we have a twenty-four-hour window—tops." I look at Maven. "You're a subterranean now. You're part of The 28 United." Maven and I clasp forearms in a grip of solidarity. "No one can know about reverse-*locasa*. You can't look suspicious. Keep the illusion of complete loyalty to

The Third intact. Neither of you can be—in any way—aware of the other."

Pasha storms to the crumbling window hole. "I'm the smartest doctor in The Third and in The 28 United. You don't really think you need to give me an order?"

Shaw says, "You did end up inside The Third without the covering of your command."

Maven chuckles at Shaw's comment, and I see Pasha offer a grin to Maven. I like the effect this man has on her. He directs his comment to me. "I just got back the life I lost. I won't risk losing it again."

"Then leave now," I say. "Everything must be completely normal until the fleet attacks. Then you do all you can from within to stop The Third."

"Civilians?" asks Maven.

Shaw steps from his place behind me and says, "There are no civilians in The Third."

Maven advances a couple of threatening steps toward Shaw, the two hulks looking like admirable adversaries. "Those people are like me. They had no choice when *locasa* took their memories and they gave their allegiance to The Third. They'd be willing to fight for The 28 United if they could—if they knew."

McGinty holds Shaw back, addressing Maven. "We know that. We'll do the best we can with civilians, but it is war."

"Reverse-*locasa* gave me my family back, but it didn't take my training from me. I get it. We'll do what we can from the inside."

I speak to the other subterraneans who've assembled with us tonight, such a ridiculously small contingent of loyal ones. "Our attack from outside must be vigilant and mighty to allow you to help accomplish destruction from within. The assignment's the same for all of you. Life as usual—until the attack."

"We can't waste any weapon drops," says Shaw. "Energy is limited. To make this work we have to hit each target on the first attempt. Any ideas on how to do that?"

Pasha tries to inch herself taller by straightening her spine and improving her posture. I can always tell when she thinks she's the one with the ultimate answer. "Always have an answer. In my lab that no one knows about—"

"It's cool. Hidden. Secret," blurts Annalynn with her thirteen-year-old's smile that has no place in a war room. Pasha shoots her a look and Annalynn's face turns solemn immediately. Usually Annalynn ignores Pasha's input, so I know even she senses the urgency of this moment.

Pasha continues, "Some idiot years ago overordered dozens of white lab coats. They're in small boxes strewn around my private lab. The subterraneans come get them from my lab—couple boxes at a time—they won't be noticed. Then they spread them around on the target roofs."

Shaw smirks, "Laughable, marking war targets with lab coats." Some of the subterraneans join in the joke.

Pasha stares them all down. "Better ideas?" No one speaks. "Of course not."

"Mark the roofs of the buildings that have government officials or military inside," I say. "Some of them we know already—their congress, Dorsey's home—but others only you can mark, depending on the activity of the moment."

"We have to get to the fleet now—right away," says McGinty. "Checkmate? Can you spare a couple b-techs to get us there? Waiting for a glide or running behind the Warrior Strip's too slow."

Checkmate babbles, "Maybe. Yes. I don't know. I think so. Today? Tomorrow? Yesterday. Not sure—"

"A ride. Yes or no?"

"Yes. Although I'd have to think about—"

McGinty interrupts, "Once we've hit the targets, we land the fleet wherever we can—rooftops, streets, city square—and we secure the entire city."

"We'll need you for that," I add, addressing each of the seven subterraneans. "Liberate as many weapons as you can and don't hesitate to use them to lock this city down.

The subterraneans murmur in agreement, and then one man who looks fit and a bit older than most Elites, steps forward to speak. "Commander," he says. "I don't like giving incomplete intel—"

"Go ahead, soldier, we'll judge the truth of it. We don't discount anything."

"We've been working on mapping every car in the market since we got here. We've made a lot of progress. But this morning there were eight additional cars in the count."

"Is that unusual?" asks McGinty.

"Not really. Degnan is always adding or taking something out of his market."

"Then why the concern?"

"These eight cars are right in the middle of the weapons cars."

I look to Morris and Pasha. "You two know anything about this?" Pasha and Morris both shake their heads, surprised.

"I've heard nothing like that," says Morris.

Annalynn adds, "Must be flyin' under the radar. Just adding more fishborns."

"Quiet, Annalynn. Not another word," I say. "Pasha, you're in there with Dorsey constantly—nothing's suspect?"

"I don't know how he could hide it from me—or Morris."

"He's Dorsey," I say, then turn my attention to the subterranean with the information. "I'm the only one available to check it out. McGinty and Shaw are going back to the Concourse and the fleet. Where do I go?"

The subterranean answers with confidence, "The last recorded car ready to launch is #110, then come the eight new cars, unnumbered. Then, car #111."

"Okay. I'll head out."

"The Warrior Strip might be in place," says Morris, "but new cars aren't going to have two-way mirrors. You'll need to see what's in the cars from the cars themselves."

"So, I can't use the Warrior Strip. I'll have to take a glide, and enter from the outside."

McGinty is by my side. "I'll go with you."

"You'll come with me to prep the fleet," says Shaw, and McGinty throws him a menacing warning to stay out of his business.

"We only need one person to check this out," I say. "I'll go. You're both needed to prep the fleet. I'll figure out a way to get in, do it quickly and be back to the Energy Concourse within an hour.

The seven subterraneans exit the butcher shop, each nodding my way, affirming their support. In spite of the light of only one small torch, I'm suddenly aware of how much I'm able to distinguish. I guess I've learned how to see in almost total darkness. Running does that to you.

In their faces are glimpses of fear, determined to cloud eyes of courage.

Watching the subterraneans file out of the butcher shop, I have no need to issue further orders. They know what to do. Pasha and Maven exit last. I allow them to move down the alley before I tap my temple and engage my infrared chipster which locks in immediately. I follow them.

Outside I take note of where Pasha and Maven are, and deftly blend in to the deserted surroundings. Maybe my intent is to determine where they're going—see if they are following orders. But instead, I move quickly to overtake them, and when I'm close enough to be heard, I whisper, "Pasha." She stops immediately. She and Maven face me, weapons on the ready.

Maven says, "Commanders should be more careful."

"Maybe I'm not a commander right now." Pasha and I stare at one another. I advance to her, imagining my commander boots abandoned on the ground. We embrace, tight, holding on to all the years we've hesitated to call each other friends, yet knew that was the name for it. I feel like I might break her, my embrace so strong and her frame so slight, but she returns my hold with a robust one of her own. We let go of all our angry competitions, our misunderstandings, and our bull-headed obstinacy that have driven our relationship to the brink of disillusionment, especially since she left the zoo. I say, "I'm so glad you found him."

She whispers back into my ear, "Won't lose him again."

"I know."

"Got to find our kids."

"Of course." I pull back from her, aware once again of my commander boots and how tight the laces feel right now. "But first let's get this tyranny dismantled within the day. Then, no matter how long it takes with reverse-*locasa*, we'll get the people reunited with their families."

"Don't know if I can wait," says Pasha, childlike, her warrior persona sagging on the ground.

"It's an order." I wish I didn't have to say it, but I know I do.

Pasha raises her hand to rub her head, but her wrist is caught midair by the man she loves. She says to me, "I know it's an order."

"Being able to say you 'know' gives me no assurance you'll do what we need you to." I feel the rift opening again between us.

Maven steps between Pasha and me. "We'll do anything to take down The Third. You've got our commitment."

I believe him. "Journey mercies," I say and head back to the butcher shop.

———

When I return to the butcher shop, Annalynn is inspecting the mastery of Checkmate's balloon-tech, through its open door. "Keen," she says. "How about a ride?" Morris grabs her arm and starts walking her out the door and toward the interior of Ash.

"What part of 'life as usual' don't you get? We've got less than a day before the attacks. Can you just wait until we've secured the city before you have a playtime with a b-tech?"

She yanks her arm away from Morris. "I was kidding. I know my assignment. You just better know yours."

"I got it, Annalynn."

"Yeah, you always do."

I glance at them and every part of me wants to send them back to the zoo with The 28 United, where all children should wait in hopes they might escape the coming attacks, but I know that can't happen. When they chose to follow Pasha inside The Third they stepped into a subterranean status that now requires everything of them, including the willingness to feign normalcy when the world is about to come crashing down.

Chapter 17
HOLLER #9
PASHA

Maven half-carried, half-dragged Pasha through the outskirts of Ash by holding on to her upper arm. Her muscles were taut and fit but the frame of her body small, and yielding to his grasp was the only way to keep up with Maven. Yes, they had sworn to Avery "business as usual." And of course, they had said they understood the word "command," and obviously, they had promised there would be no acknowledgement of one another in the midst of The Third. However, when they came to a Y in the street, one choice leading back to Ash and the other way following a crumbling road into the darkness, Maven spoke, "I've heard there's a place in the hills where we might look." No discussion needed. They chose the route to the darkness, avoiding the city streets, in hopes of finding their children, missing for a decade.

Back in Ash, Morris was taking care of Pasha's absence, covering it with a lie to Dorsey who writhed in pain, desperate for the morning surgery. Maven took care of his absence by registering as "off duty" through the portable hologram he carried to report his hourly roll call. This luxury was reserved for Elite soldiers held in the highest regard by The Third.

Their bodies moved like a compass's needle, pointing north to "discovery," their parental adrenaline kicking in immediately and fueled by the ache of lost years. "I've heard talk," panted Maven. "Children living in the hollers up beyond the City of Ash. Training camps. Guess The Third scoops up the smart ones, those with an aptitude for battle, and brings them to the hollers where they're sorted out and placed in an area of training."

Pasha shook her arm away from Maven's hold and faced him, gasping for air, but calling on her newly trained ability to speak sentences. "I'm capable of keeping up, and I do much better when I'm not pulled." For a brief moment they stared at each other, and again the smile in Maven's eyes kindled. Then he turned suddenly, no longer dragging Pasha, but still leading the way up a barely decipherable trail and speaking over his shoulder.

"If we get to the hollers, Jett and Beckett might be there."

"But there's all sorts of children being raised by pocket-watches in the units of the city. How do we even know they're in a holler or even where to start looking once we get there?"

"Even though we'd lost our memories of what went on—The Third knew. They knew our background—both of us are Elite-trained—and they knew the DNA our kids had. It's likely this is where they are." Pasha listened intently and liked the logic Maven brought with his analysis. "You left for Elite service right after Jett was born. They put kids in training when they turn nine years old. So, at their age they wouldn't still be in a housing unit. They'd be training somewhere, and most likely they're up here for military purposes, not in the city preparing to be factory workers." Maven's hand reached behind him and held Pasha's, but this time he wasn't dragging her along. She kept up.

"Can't look forever. Got to be back for Dorsey's surgery, or The 28 United's plan disintegrates," Pasha said, forgetting the sentences.

"You'll make it. The hollers are right over the crest of this hill." A crumpled piece of paper expanded in Maven's hand as he unfolded a crude map. Moving forward, Maven explained to Pasha, "Morris sketched it. We're here." He pointed to the map. "There are eleven hollers."

Just over the hill, the first holler appeared—a long, narrow swath of land, meadow-like and a hundred and fifty feet wide, framed by two cliff-like sides, facing each other and extending upward at sharp angles. Pasha checked the Z-Colt Maven had fitted her with after they left the butcher shop. The steep terrain demanded sturdy boots, and she was glad she was prepared for the climb. "So this is #1?" She asked.

Maven studied Morris' sketched map. "No, this is #11. Morris said #1 is on the far side, further up the mountain. They started the camps up there five years ago, and they were much smaller. The ones down here—this latest one—just built—larger."

"Building toward the city."

"Maybe they didn't think there would be this many when they started putting kids up here."

"Another monumental miscalculation by The Third." They stood for a moment, taking in their first view of the strange hovels that lined the cliff-like sides of the hollers. Terraced on both of the valley walls, huts had been carved out of the thick trees, underbrush and dirt. Each about seven feet long and five feet high. Twelve rows of terraces ascended up the hillside. All the hovels were opened to the elements, but many had skins and pelts hanging, covering their entrances. Pasha thought on a miniature scale, she might have expected a pigeon to emerge from one of the openings. Soon, she and Maven might be climbing these holler terraces to find out just what was roosting inside the holes.

The further they travelled through the gorge, the more Pasha's observations expanded. Dots of light flickered on the hillside. Some of the hovel openings that had no coverings on their entrances allowed Pasha to see kids sitting around campfires. Four or five children encircled each open fire. This was most likely their home unit, and Pasha wondered how she and Maven would ever find children they hadn't seen in ten years.

Pasha glanced at Morris' map. "Which holler?" she asked. "There's eleven."

"I have no idea."

"Okay," Pasha said and started to hike ahead of Maven. "Then #9."

"How do you know? You're not a guesser."

Sentences took over. "Percentage of likelihood. The Third would have started these training camps five years ago when they settled Ash. If #11 is recent then they would have begun each new holler approximately every six months. That would make Jett nine years old when holler #9 was built. That's the age kids start their training. Yeah. Holler #9."

"I knew it wasn't a guess. Lead the way." Pasha thought it strange that Maven would even bother to say "lead the way," since she'd already started. Ever since Pasha had left Colony G, her rebellious confidence and passionate, but impatient, choices to destroy The Third had grown. Yet lately, she'd been second-guessing herself, allowing her goal to perfect reverse-*locasa* to cause some missteps in judgement and cracks in the normally strong facade she'd presented to Dorsey. Solving the scientific puzzle of reverse-*locasa* and filling in the gaps of her missing life dominated everything. So, maybe Holler #9 *was* a guess more than the law of averages. No, not possible. That's not how her brain worked. In spite of the misgivings, brilliance still prevailed.

"Keep up," she said. Maven followed, chuckling behind her. He'd learned long ago to step out of the way when Pasha was on a crusade. That part of his memory had returned quickly.

———

Even though they'd passed through two hollers without incident, Pasha wondered aloud why these training camps were left unguarded. Maven commented, "There's no need for protection. There's been no attacks on the city, and everyone within its borders are loyal to The Third. Why waste guards on a bunch of kids in training? No threat."

Holler #9 looked identical to hollers #10 and #11. At first Pasha thought Maven was mumbling. Then she realized he was chanting. "Boy, eyes of blue, skin like midnight. Boy, eyes of blue, skin like midnight."

Pasha answered back with a chant of her own. "Girl, onyx skin, spray of freckles cross her nose. Girl, onyx skin, spray of freckles cross her nose." And on it went as they woke up hovel after hovel asking if any of the children knew the kids they described. Each hovel displayed their housing number burned into a small piece of wood hanging off the side of the roofs. Not exactly like the holograms Pasha was used to, dealing with Dorsey in his strategy room, plotting an attack with stockpiles of fishborns.

She and Maven had the search down to a routine and were only taking fifteen to seventeen seconds to question those in each domicile and then move on.

Pasha came to a halt, unable to break her gaze as it locked on to the number at the right of the next hovel, 961. 961—Degnan's number. He'd spit the number out at her when they were in the Warrior Strip and entering the glides. He'd spewed it toward her as a curious talisman, and now she knew: this carved-out barracks for some reason belonged to Degnan. Without asking, she entered, and was met by four pairs of eyes, filled with questions and fear. Maven remained by the entrance, unable to stand inside, the ceiling height threatening collision with his forehead.

Unsure of what to do or say, Pasha stood in silence for a moment. "961," she said and waited, but there was no change of expression on the children's faces. "Boy, eyes of blue, skin like midnight. Girl, onyx skin, spray of freckles cross her nose. Know them?" Nothing. Then Pasha blurted it out. "Degnan." The tallest boy stood, his hair brushing the ceiling, and he crossed to the far side of the hovel, lifting a stack of branches that extended from his mattress made of the same greenery. He lifted a crate and brought it forward to Pasha.

Pasha felt a rush of dread-filled curiosity as her hands prepared to open the lid of the crate. *A scorpodart ready to attack?* Even after five years, she could still feel the viper fangs on her shoulder. But what she saw in the crate, she never expected. Twenty-four carefully placed devices, each set in a foam-lined rectangle. She did not have to guess their purpose. She'd worked years and made countless mistakes trying to create reverse-*locasa*, and here before her was a gift of twenty-four. Degnan had duplicated her design, the one that brought Maven back to her. She let out a yell that reverberated off the walls of holler #9, guttural, primal. Then, silence. The children in the hovel staring, hardly breathing, and Maven waiting patiently by the entrance.

She grabbed one reverse-*locasa* and stuffed it in her pocket, asking Maven, "You know what these are?"

Maven dipped his head inside the hovel and said, "I do." He took one too and placed it neatly in the weapon-proof vest of his uniform.

Then Pasha heard someone outside and recognized an annoying voice she had no desire to hear.

"We're here on a rescue of sorts," he said. It was Checkmate, and in the background Pasha hear an irritating giggle, of the thirteen-year-old girl who never took directions. Pasha rushed past Maven to the outside and looked through the opened face-space of a hovering balloon-tech, seeing both Checkmate and Annalynn, side by side, staring at her.

"We're here to evacuate civilians," smirked Annalynn.

"Avery know about this?" Pasha asked.

"She said, 'Go for it, with my blessing,'" said Checkmate.

"I bet." Pasha scrutinized Annalynn. "See you're as good as ever at taking commands."

"Right back at you." As always, Annalynn didn't hesitate to wage a war of tit-for-tat with anyone, especially Pasha. Two years ago, Annalynn wouldn't have dared to have this conversation. Today she always dared.

Maven stepped forward, running the palm of his hand over the curvature of the camouflaged flying machine that had worked its chameleon charm in the light of the moon. "Can he be trusted?" Maven asked, nodding at Checkmate.

"They," Pasha replied, pointing at Annalynn. "Can *they* be trusted?"

Maven squinted into the night. "Okay. Can *they* be trusted?" He turned and faced Pasha. "Can they?"

"Depends. Got any patience for incessant rambling?"

"You should talk, sista," yelled Annalynn from inside the balloon-tech.

"Trust them," said Pasha. "But we don't have to like them."

"Hey," said Annalynn. "Take it easy with my psyche."

"Open the door," said Maven. Checkmate responded and Maven handed in the crate of twenty-two reverse-*locasa* devices. "Each of you take several of these. Start here in holler #9. Find the pocket-watches for each holler." He turned back to the children, "How many caretakers per holler?"

"Five!" They shouted in unison.

"Place the device on the base of their skulls," explained Pasha, "and activate with the green button. Annalynn can distract the pocket-watches while you work the magic."

"Hey," yelled Annalynn, "that sounds dangerous."

"Dangerous? Like leaving the protection of The 28 United to follow me inside The Third?"

"Not the same." Annalynn looked at Maven, seeming in awe of his size. Then she saluted him. "I'll take any order from you!" Pasha had the feeling that, if it had been a different time and place, Maven would have laughed uncontrollably at Annalynn. Pasha loved that sound and hoped one of their children might laugh like their father.

"Don't we have to use these things on the kids too?" asked Annalynn. "There's a lot of kids."

Pasha hated to spend the time answering irrelevant questions, "No need."

"*Locasa* was never used on kids," Maven said. "After it was used on their parents and they left, The Third felt kids were too young to remember families. Maybe most were."

Maven's final instructions were given in haste. "Leave a few of the devices with some of the pocket-watches for protection. Tell them what to do if they should run into an Elite."

Pasha said, "Then the balloon-techs will start the evacuation. Don't have very many b-techs to get this done. Don't have very long to do it."

Checkmate and Annalynn scanned the sky. "Oh, we can do it," said Checkmate with a smile. "There's more up there. You just can't see them all," he said.

"I believe you," said Maven. "I hardly saw you."

Pasha pulled the Z-Colt Maven had given her from the waist of her pants, saying, "Taking too long. We'll never make it. Speed this thing up!" She emptied the clip of the Z-Colt, blasting it at the sky and yelling, "Everyone out of the hovels and meet down below." Children leaped from their huts, filing down to the flat meadow of the holler.

Maven and Pasha met the kids, gathering them together. It took only a quick minute for a couple hundred to assemble. Pasha asked in a clear, loud voice, "Boy—eyes of blue, skin like midnight? Girl—thirteen, onyx skin, spray of freckles cross her nose?"

Like a wave, the circled-up crowd washed back, leaving a lean boy, his skin blending into the darkness, staring at the ground. The boy looked up with piercing blue eyes, connecting first with his mother and then his father. "Jett." Pasha pronounced his name.

A girl from the crowd pointed up the hill to the other hollers, yelling, "She's up there. Older than us—onyx skin. Freckles." Maven linked his hands into the b-tech's opened face-space and yelled at Checkmate, "Go! Go now." Maven didn't bother to enter the balloon-tech. There was no room for him with Checkmate and Annalynn filling the seats. He simply held on to the side. At the same time Pasha ran to her son, Jett, encircling him with her smallish arms. He did not resist and held her close.

Pasha and Jett watched Maven sail up the hill on the side of the balloon-tech. She heard a barely audible whisper in her ear. "Mama." She looked hard at Jett. He appeared to be no more than seven or eight years old, for the bones that framed him were slight. But she knew his age and hoped his form reflected her genes more than the possibility of the malnourishment in these training camps. "Mama," he said again.

"How did you know?" she asked, her voice a whisper too.

He didn't hesitate for a moment and said, "I've been waiting for you." That took her breath away, but only for a moment. Inside her mind she was already celebrating the foolishness of The Third for never using *locasa* on kids. What idiots they were for believing children, even at an early age with constant indoctrination, would not remember. In this surreal moment where time perched upon the doorstep of the sun, looking down and wondering how to restore the days and years and months withdrawn between a mother and her son, all Pasha could think of was the gap. That hidden spot in her where *locasa* effortlessly abducted a husband, two children and memories, leaving in their absence an empty hole. That mysterious area that she could not explain or define or even talk about to someone else. It seemed to gnaw away from her insides, fester deep in the intestines and burrow in the walls of her heart. That gap, that empty hole, stirred when The Third's Commander walked near her. The loneliness jabbed each time the top button of her gray uniform was corralled by a buttonhole. And sometimes, in the still of a curfew, when the time for sleep was commanded but unreachable, sometimes she heard the whisper. It spoke. The whisper always seemed a foreign language, confusing to her, until now—looking into the eyes of Jett—when, suddenly, it was perfectly clear. It spoke: *Family*. It spoke: *Home*.

———

Employing reverse-*locasa* below the chin or at the nape of the neck on out-of-shape pocket-watches seemed, to Pasha, an easy task. She watched her husband Maven's eyes tear up every time one of these caretakers gained a lifetime of memories back. Fear often appeared, accompanying those realizations, and sometimes a hesitant joy or quiet weeping emerged from those who'd been released from the dirty spell of The Third. There were lots of questions from those who were restored, and Pasha's reply was always the same, "No questions now. Later."

After all the caretakers from the eleven hollers had been released, the children living in the hollers, who'd trained for military positions, lined up. Maven's voice boomed from the top of the holler hill and he said, "Load two of the children in each of the balloon-techs." Expressions of confusion appeared on every child's face, and the eyes of pocket-watches skimmed the dark skyline, lit from below by the glowing fires of the hollers. Yet no sign of aircraft was visible, signaling the success of Checkmate's chameleon fleet. "Look carefully," said Maven. "Let your gaze rest on one place for several seconds." Then one by one, as they squinted upward, the recognition came, and the caretakers moved swiftly, loading the b-techs as directed.

Pasha couldn't believe how many of the unique flying machines there were. Hundreds. She climbed further up the hill of the holler to where Checkmate's vehicle hovered. "How many?" she asked.

"What, can't see them well enough to count them? Ha! That's the idea," said Checkmate.

Pasha persisted. "How many?"

"Three hundred. Gonna have to make two trips. There's twelve hundred up here in the hollers."

"How do you know that?"

"Been flying here for awhile. Collecting. We call it 'invisible information.' Get it? They can't see us so—"

"Shut up. Where are you taking them?"

"Avery said you'd be impossible to work with." A few hours ago, Pasha's hands would have reacted in anger, targeting her bald scalp with a vicious rubbing action, but instead she couldn't help but look around the front of the b-tech, engaging Maven's eyes, hoping war would end and family would begin. Checkmate continued, "There's an abandoned stadium ten miles north. We'll get them there. We'll keep them safe." He stared at Pasha, and cleared his throat as she started to walk away.

She didn't turn to face him, but mumbled, "That'll be chaos. No food. No water. Chaos."

Checkmate shouted after her, "You should've prepared for that. No foresight. You only think about winning. I, on the other hand, am a prepared person. I have foresight. I have…" And on he went, spewing the attributes of his society, all the while loading the kids for an escape.

Jett was one of the first children to sail away in a b-tech, flying off to the closest thing to safety they could find right now. Pasha kept her eyes attentive, studying the face of every child waiting in line to board their ride to a momentary sanctuary. In her search to reunite with Beckett, Pasha had a checklist. She mentally eliminated any girl Jett's size or smaller. Beckett was three years older and would be bigger than her brother.

Pasha didn't look at any child with skin lighter than brown. Maven helped by scrutinizing a line further up the holler, guaranteeing the two of them wouldn't miss any possible match for their Beckett. Occasionally she glanced his way, and if Maven's eyes caught hers, she saw a brief smile, indicating the search should continue. They would find her.

Pasha had expected they might need to do some crowd control. She didn't have a lot of patience with children and had anticipated much noise and confusion, but these kids approached their departure with discipline and single-mindedness. In her spirit, Pasha felt (and she hadn't felt much in her spirit for a very long time) that these children were doing more than obeying orders. That sentiment was confirmed as she heard a young girl's voice speak out.

"A mother and a father came up through the holler..." Her voice was joined by several younger voices. "...looking. They were looking." Then all of the children in Pasha's line joined in. "We know what a mother and a father are. We've heard stories of them from travelers carrying music up the hollers." This chorus of storytelling—this oral tradition—wrapped its tentacles around Pasha's reason. Hundreds of voices became one. Pasha thought, *This voice will not be silenced. Not by preprogramed eye-readers or demands of submission from The Third.* No one could deny this power, and a sudden awareness spread over Pasha. With these children, the ranks of The 28 United just expanded, and that lifted her soul to the point of hope.

As if on cue, all those standing on the hill above her, waiting to be loaded in the line checked by Maven, continued the chant-like story in unison with the others. "We wait for the mother and the father." Pasha remembered how Clef and the minstrels would tell stories with one voice, assembling the context from the worn and tattered pages of treasured books.

The balloon-techs sailed away with load after load of children, who were promised protection and refuge, and all the while the b-techs blended seamlessly into a star-splattered sky.

The children's story continued, now half as loud, their voices decreased by many who had flown off in the first wave of b-techs, "The mother and father were looking for someone who belonged to them. And we wondered: 'Is it me?'" They paused in synch for several seconds. "But no one knew."

Pasha scanned the line. Her eyes rested on a group of children, perhaps the same age as Beckett. They pointed. Before Pasha could look in that direction, others pointed too. Then, abruptly, hundreds of children pointed, and inside Pasha a force rose up, yanking her forward to follow as directed. Running toward the end of the line, she stopped, looking at the only group of children that were moving at all. The girl in charge, the one with the onyx skin, herded a group of younger kids, encouraging them to stand strong, be brave. She faced Pasha, looking over the heads of those she rallied. This girl was a warrior, not malnourished—not small—but looking every bit her age and older. She did not flinch, her muscles taut and clearly defined, stance confident with stability and—a spray of freckles cross her nose.

"Beckett?"

And the girl replied in her warrior way, "This urban myth that we've recited to each other for years… well, you've finally come. The sound of your voice hasn't changed from when I heard it last." How brief the seconds were that connected the span between them and their embrace.

The older children continued to load but watched with intensity. One of the kids called out, "Was there only one mother and father?"

Pasha could hear the disappointment in the girl's voice and broke away from Beckett's hold. Pasha said, "More will come." Maven hurried down the holler hill and scooped Beckett in his Elite arms. She hugged back with all her strength. The three stood together, hands clasped in a tight triangle until it was time to load the last child into a b-tech. That was Beckett. Both Maven and Pasha kissed her cheek before her pilot adjusted the controls and the b-tech door sealed shut.

As the balloon-tech's camouflage intensified and made its silhouette impossible to find, the boots of Pasha and Maven were already jogging down the holler hill, their voices discussing strategy for the fast-approaching morning in the surgery room where every move was instrumental in carving out the future of The 28 United.

Chapter 18
PLAYING WITH BABY AVERY

Outfitted in the protective gear of an Elite soldier, I appear to be just another of The Third's well-trained troopers on assignment. My hands shake, sending a zipper on the shoulder pouch of my vest bobbing against the metal of the DR93 slung over my shoulder. It is a faint clicking sound, but seems like a loud announcement of my presence to those who stand with me at the glide transport dock, waiting for a lift. I readjust my fingers, positioning them so their tremors will not disturb any other piece of metal I'm wearing or carrying. Like the hands of an ancient clock ticking off the seconds and minutes of a day, the glides sail in with regularity, efficiently opening their doors, each releasing three passengers in exchange for three more who wait for a return trip to the west end of the Dark Market.

Fifteen or so of us stand together in the semblance of a line, in hopes of catching the next glide that docks. They are strangers to me, but I keep my knit face mask in position, exposing my nose, mouth and eyes, hoping others do not recognize me. I am, after all, a valued target. I'm third in line for a ride. I need to be alone in my glide to attempt a breach of one of the eight mysterious additional cars, storing what we believe to be stockpiles of weapons unknown even to Pasha and Morris, who've been working inside for Commander Dorsey. At least with the cars of fishborns we know what we're dealing with, but it sounds like Dorsey's created something that could derail our attack before we even get our zooms in the air.

I don't let fate force me into the first glide that arrives. My place in line dictates that I should be in that glide with the two Elites in front of me. Conveniently dropping the lid to my water canister, I chase after to retrieve it, allowing the two soldiers to load, and the woman behind me to step into my spot and take the third opening.

I quickly enter the next glide and watch the upper-tier teens that stand behind me shove one another forward to the glide. It's obvious that none of them want to split from their group and fill the empty two spots in my transport. Disguised as an Elite soldier, I wonder if they have something to hide from me, should they share this tiny transport space encased by water. My hand hovers for three seconds over the holograph lock pad, and the door closes, abruptly leaving the arguers to wait for the next glide.

I am alone. I do not extend my hands to the bar above my head as McGinty and I did on our first glide trip, lifting our feet off the ground to avoid the iron ankle-bracelet that attempted to encircle our ankles. That action would be suspicious to these guards and passengers who watch my glide thrust forward on the track that propels me to the depths of Erie. I cringe as the protective iron circle secures around my ankles with an ominous clack that locks its hold.

Even through the thickness of the transport walls and even with the rugged fabric of the uniform I wear, I feel the cold assaulting my bones. How clever of Degnan to insulate his Dark Market with water, hoping to shield it from what is soon to become a war zone on the land above. Was he in savior-mode when he designed our Warrior Strip behind the market, protecting us and allowing us firsthand information instrumental to The 28 United's attack plan? I think not. He knew he'd have to offer me something big in exchange for our defense of his Dark Market when our two warring forces went to battle in Ash. Ironic—me agreeing to protect this market when The Third's weapons fill launch cars, suspended and ready to destroy and defeat The 28 United.

The numbers on the side of the cars whiz by so quickly I can't read them, and I depend upon the digital counter next to the iron cuff that holds my ankle and my body safe from the jar of docking. I finger the buttons of reverse-*locasa* in my pocket, a copy of Pasha's prototype made by Degnan and given to me by him when I left the subterranean meeting at the butcher shop. I can only imagine Pasha's indignant anger when she finds out Degnan has been working on duplicating her prime experiment that she's been pursuing for the last decade. Should I feel lucky he chose me to try out his duplication? Maybe if it works, I'll feel lucky. I have no intent or need to use this device on myself, but just as when I entered Reichel eight months pregnant and on a discovery mission to end The Third, this device is a weapon unlike the one I carry on my shoulder.

The slightest wisp of a breeze floats through the glide, encircling me and my overactive mind. *Must be my imagination*, I think. *Nerves kicking in.* I breathe deep, forcing emotional control. This glide is sealed tight. There is no breeze. 108, 109, 110—the numbers click off digitally on the counter, and I raise my palm to the hologram strip, indicating I'm getting off at the next transport dock.

I feel the deceleration. The speed of the car breaking reverberates through my body. Gravity demands I fall forward, and training reminds me I won't. I stabilize myself by holding on to the bar overhead, and watch the guards swing my glide into the grab mechanism of the small transport dock. Morris promised two guards.

There are four. With two I might stand a chance to disable them both. With four there's no way I can keep all of them from sounding the alarm or aiming weapons at my head to dismantle the threat I pose.

The front panel of the glide opens. I step onto the transition platform, prepared for my most convincing performance, all the time clasping tight to reverse-*locasa* in my right hand, inside my pocket. One of the Elite expects to scan my palm for identification, and I extend my arm. Just before the Elite connects her scanner with my hand, I begin my dramatic seizure, falling to the ground. She leans over me and rips my helmet from my head, to evaluate me. I capitalize on the brief moment when her back is to the others and her face is to me, placing the tip of reverse-*locasa* on the open patch of skin under her chin. She rolls off me. I see the confusion on her face, realizing what *locasa* took from her and what reverse-*locasa* has returned. She is probably wondering why she's holding a military weapon. I continue my seizure and the second guard steps forward to help me, still having no idea that I am a threat. Reverse-*locasa* finds another target, and now two are out of the way, weapons inactive on their laps.

I swing my DR93 from my shoulder simultaneously with the third guard, each of us aiming at the other. The fourth Elite places his palm on the hologram, activating an alarm bell. Guards one and two have readied their weapons, now pointed at the third dangerous guard. He has no chance of firing. The first two guards take him out. Before the fourth guard can ready his weapon, he too becomes a target, and I strike between the small gap between his face mask and his neck armor.

I yell to the man and woman, guards one and two, who have instinctively defended me the moment reverse-*locasa* took hold of them, "Come with me! You'll find your families later." In half a second this man and woman's loyalty to The Third is yanked out of their beings. What is it that, after probably a decade of service to the current government, suddenly catapults their allegiance to me? If they knew I was the one whose name they chanted in a death hunt for DeTornada—would they follow me then? I think "yes." 'Cause they aren't following *me*. They're chasing the images from the past that are now firing on overload in their brains. The snapshots of their babies and their childhood outings by late night campfires, when leisure still meant family time and included more than work, and peps, and roll call at the beginning of a shift. I shout, "Names?"

The woman says, "Coleman. He's Hendrix."

"Hendrix, Coleman—help me out. Do you know what's in this car?"

"More weapons—stash—stockpile. More power in there," says Hendrix. They follow me into one of the eight unmarked cars between car #110 and #111.

It is a weapon stockpile, but why does this car look different than the other identical weapon cars? I say,

"These fishborns are half the size as the ones we're trying to stop before they're deployed." Both Coleman and Hendrix are examining the mini-fishborns.

"They'll probably launch these first," says the man. "It's half the energy for twice the bang."

"How long before they're armed?"

Coleman looks up from her analysis. "They already are."

Every problem has a solution, and almost always more than one. It is my father's voice I hear, and I try desperately to believe him, running my hand over the nose of the weapon. "Where's the warhead?"

"Don't need one," says Coleman. "Electromagnetic railgun launcher."

"Uses the Lorentz force," the Elite Hendrix comments.

I say, "Just tell me who launches this weapon and when."

"The kid—whenever he wants," the man says.

"The kid? You mean Morris?"

"No, the other boy."

Raghill. When I finally make the connection, I simply cannot imagine Raghill in the uniform of his father. The only images in my mind of this sweet boy are the ones of him standing in the middle of the sunflowers in the garden of the library, as a child abandoned by his father in command and hungry for a family. Or the images of him and Morris at ten years old arguing a philosophical thesis from their memorized library books and flying float cars in escape through the forests of Red Grove. I cannot distinguish between the grief and anger I feel. One emotion is not stronger than the other. I mourn the loss of Raghill from The 28 United. I grieve that my family is diminished in size by a valuable soul. Yet, I rage at his desertion. I am indignant that when the most important choice of Raghill's life stared him in the face—he chose *traitor*.

I run my fingers horizontally over the exterior of this weapon, from the front to the back. Three quarters of the way to the tail, I stop my investigation. I look at Coleman and Hendrix. "It says 'conversion switch.' What's that mean?" They have no answer. I don't have time to develop a hypothesis. I flip the switch. A gear produces a high-pitched, barely-audible whine, pronouncing the opening of the fishborn's nose. Unfolding like a mechanical flower, a circular-shaped flying capsule unfurls, surrounding the fishborn, encapsulating it and giving it wings for flight. Not unlike the balloon-techs, it is a design that allows this fishborn to be airborne in seconds without relinquishing its payload. Our biggest nightmare. We were counting on no opposition in the air. That's been our territory, our strategy.

"It's like the drones of decades ago," I say.

"Drones don't need pilots," says Hendrix. He points at the section inside the capsule's transparent covering, directing my attention to the dash, covered with dials and controls, demanding human intelligence.

"So they send these fishborns out, they stream along the ground toward a target."

Coleman says, "Then, in the launch car they determine to switch it to an air attack."

"They remotely flip the conversion switch, and that puts it in the air," says Hendrix.

"But that does no good," I point out, "'cause there's no pilot to fly it." The high-pitched whine drops an octave as a horizontal slat on the left side of the fishborn snaps open, revealing a cave-like, six-foot cavity. A muscular leg swings out of the hole with the power of a trained combat soldier. Only a GEB could remain in storage like this. Surprise fires fear at every part of my body, and my commander persona shatters just for a moment, confronting the unexpected, like an arrogant general proud of his strategy and the next minute jolted into reality by an unimaginable enemy blindside. I remind myself: I am prepared for anything.

I grab the iron bar by the railgun launch chute for stability, preparing for a fight, reaching for my weapon. I see Coleman and Hendrix shrink back against the wall of the storage car. They are no longer warriors of the The Third, and look unsure as to what their role might be in this coming confrontation. Battle-ready and horrific, the GEB slings a second leg out of its coffin-like storage slot and extends itself to a height well past six and a half feet.

I surge forward to the conversion switch, but before I can reach it, I am backhanded by the GEB's powerful right arm, flinging me across the car. I land in a heap. I hear the weapons of my two newly-claimed guards engage and I shout, "Don't fire! Distract it! If Dorsey suspects anything, our surprise air attack will be over. Distract it!"

Coleman rushes to the entry alcove and Hendrix moves to the opposite side of the car. The GEB's eyes turn from me and try to focus on both moving targets. It seems disoriented as to what to do. "Head toward me," says Coleman, and Hendrix does, causing the GEB's focus to narrow. As it finally sees both of them together, and has its back to me, I ease up to a standing position and slowly make my way toward the conversion switch, flipping it to its original position. The GEB's back arches like it's received an electrical charge at the base of its spine. It backs up until its calf muscles touch the hole from which it emerged. That touch triggers a reaction, and it begins to fold back into its storage space.

Just before its head swings inside, its mask repositions off its face, rolling into the helmet, allowing it a more retracted position. I scream. I cannot help it. The face on the GEB is Raben's. The hate I feel for Dorsey boils over, and my heart skips more than one beat. *This is not Raben, it is Dorsey's message to me*: *"I will find you,*

DeTornada." I am convinced that every GEB I encounter from here on out—every weapon they've developed in the form of a genetically engineered being, every genetic mess they throw at us—will have the face of the man I once loved. The face of the man I married, and the father of Chapman.

The slot closes to the fishborn, shutting away the nightmare. If an Elite enters to scope this car out, they will never know anyone has entered here or discovered their secret. Our grandiose plans of launching our only air fleet in the eminent battle suddenly seem petty and irrelevant. Success, once deemed highly likely, now appears distant and remote.

The alarm bell increases its urgent blare, deafening any further conversation. I count the mini-fishborns. Eight. And there's eight cars that were previously unknown to us. So if Dorsey releases his sixty-four death-wishes, right now we'd have no way to stop him. My sixth sense rises to quiet my doubts. It's unlikely that Dorsey will let Raghill launch while he, as Commander, is under Pasha's knife. Dorsey will wait until he can watch his own son assume the command of our apocalypse. Then suddenly, the design plan hanging on the wall of the Warrior Strip looms in my mind. McGinty and I studied it our first trip into the Dark Market, and now I clearly remember Degnan's explanation. After every fifty cars in the market, in the right corner of car #50 and #100 and so on, there's a palm-coded escape hatch, allowing those of us in The 28 that have been palm-coded in to exit from the Dark Market to the Warrior Strip undetected in emergencies. We have never had to use them. We are rarely in disguise in the cars. Usually, we are in the Warrior Strip, watching. Our trips to the Warrior Strip have always involved collecting information about The Third and their strategy. And while these escape hatches were marked on the design plans, there were no details as to what they looked like or how their secrecy would be maintained.

I race out of the weapon car and hardly touch the transition platform, leaping in the glide. Hendrix and Coleman, now free from *locasa*, stop on the platform, waiting for instructions. I gesture to Coleman to come close, and I place my mouth by her ear, trying to top the volume of the alarm. "Clean up on the platform, get rid of the bodies. Give the coming guards a story about where the other two Elites are, and then business as usual."

Coleman locks eyes with me, calling me by name, "Yes, Commander DeTornada."

"How'd you know it was me?"

"Your wanted poster in the city square is forty feet high. It's hard to miss."

"And here I thought it was my commanding presence," I say as she backs out of the glide, already dragging a body out of sight.

"That too," she says. I don't hear her over the alarm, but I read her lips.

"Yeah, right." I reach my hand to the hologram and the glide door slams shut. With a thrust from Hendrix against the side of the glide, I am sailing off. I figure the safest entry point will be car # 50, which would be the last escape hatch opportunity before the west end of the Dark Market. I lower the eye shield from my helmet. I wear the uniform of The Third, and no one will recognize me with my knit face mask and eye shield in place. We're in the middle of an alarm warning. No one will know my identity.

Never has 200mph seemed too slow. I tap the indicator control with the toe of my boot and instruct the hologram with my hand. When the door slides open at car #50, I move quickly from glide to the transition dock to the interior of a store car that displays winter coats of a very expensive variety.

The place is crowded. All customer eyes find their focus on me, and I read a flash of apprehension on their faces, but it disappears quickly when the alarm bell suddenly stops, and they go back to their selection process. I grab a coat from a section of garments that hang suspended in air at the center of the shop, as if an invisible rod holds them all in place. A store clerk nods toward the back corner of the car.

Holding her palm to a hologram, a dressing room materializes. I step through the entrance and palm code it shut. The gray silk coat's wide collar has long black strands of shiny hair in perfect order. A tag on the first buttonhole reads, "Human." I let it drop from my hands to the floor and push it to the door with my boot. I'm not remotely interested in being kept warm by the scalp of another human being.

I sit on the floor facing the corner of the car dressing room, wanting to believe the hatch will materialize just like the dressing room did. I know if the palm code for the Warrior Strip works, it will be because of my DNA that Degnan cleared along with the other nineteen 28 United soldiers approved by his security. I lay my hand on the corner of the floor, not knowing exactly where to begin. Nothing. I slide my hand around the corner to the right of the wall. No results. Then I retrace the space I just covered and try the left side of the wall. My fingers linger a moment, causing a hatch to open. It is big enough for me, and I point my feet inside the tube-like escape and slide through at a slight downward angle under the wall that separates the store from the Warrior Strip. Then I push myself at an upward angle into the Warrior Strip on the other side of the hatch. By now, I imagine, the dressing room has disappeared, no longer needed by a customer. The store clerk will be convinced she just didn't see me leave amidst the many patrons crowded in the upper tier car. She's probably cursing me for leaving the expensive garment on the floor.

I scramble to my feet, and begin a steady jog through the remaining forty-nine cars that will eventually lead me to the exit in the water. I'm anxious to leave behind any thought of a carload of elaborate attire designed to include a human scalp, yet my imagination runs wild as I recall lessons from the History Labyrinth about the scalping ventures of the Romans in battle and the similar exploits of Germanic tribes. Was Dorsey raising citizens to provide hair for the coats and collars of the wealthy's wardrobe? Were these materials harvested with the scalp or without? I would hope without, so hair might be regrown for another season. With each step I take I memorialized the names of the library boys and the brutality of their deaths, commanded by Dorsey and enacted by Borden. Scalping fits Dorsey's portfolio.

I palm code through the end of each car, entering the next one, and I'm shielded from the view of the customers through the security of the Warrior Strip. I have no other way to get to the water exit. If I were to take the glides to the end of the market, I'd be stuck in car #1. I guess that's the disadvantage of designing something that's never been used before. After tomorrow we shouldn't need another exit anyway—one way or the other.

My pace is quick through the first thirty or so cars. I try to avoid glancing through the two-way mirror into the market cars, but I find my curiosity leads my eyes to collect information as I travel. We have not been able to map all these cars, so much of this is new to me. I note the irony of some of the vendor's shop titles. *Restoration*—a room where mostly teenagers lie suspended on transparent slabs with needles hooked in every vein available. Their eyes are closed but the movement of their bodies indicates hysterical laughter. No audible sound has been turned on, but I see the mania, and I wonder how hysteria and a needle-infused state can be restorative. Only Degnan knows. *Hybrid* offers a standing cocoon with animals on one side and on the other side of a divider a human counterpart. Between the two runs a blood infusion, and I can't tell if the human is giving blood to the sleek greyhound dogs or the dogs are donating to the humans. I'm nauseated at the risk of bizarre experiments for the thrill of dangerous results. I'm sure these victims are exhilarated at the prospect of undiscovered horrors.

The next several cars assure me that dogs are not the only donors. There are veins to be found in reptiles, eagles and rodents. Has Degnan fostered a community of perverted scientists who invent the demented and are rewarded for the macabre?

Just seventeen cars away from the exit of Degnan's vile collections, I have to stop. *Is this a nursery?* I press my nose against the two-way to get a closer look. The shop title reads: *Leftovers*. Babies of the crawling stage move everywhere within the car. More storekeepers are on duty than in the other cars I've passed. An assortment of upper-tier teens play with the babies. No, wait. This is not play. They fill small vials with unusual substances, and on the end of the vial is a punch-stem. They place the punch-stem into the babies' shoulders. The infants seem unaffected by the prick, but begin to act wild, flinging themselves in all directions, bouncing off the padded car walls, to the pleasure of the upper-tiers who seem to race one baby against another until one falls lifeless on the floor, sending one group of teens into cheers as their baby wins, but then it too promptly falls on the floor as well, no movement evident.

A claw shoots up from the floor and just before it grabs the limp forms, I see that on the chest of each baby's shirt there is a number. On one it says *GEB 10,083* and on the other *GEB 10,341*. So now, The Third no longer brings GEBs into the world as adults? They're experimenting with genetically-engineered babies. Part of me screams in protest to this inhumanity, yet after Raben, with the exception of Ulysses and Pepper, I can have no sympathy for GEBs that only imitate life as weapons for The Third. So, these leftover GEBs that didn't work out so well become playthings for the upper-tiers? I'm thinking the upper-tiers can't even recognize the difference between a GEB toy and a real child, and that makes me insane. I contracted with Degnan to protect his market when war comes, but I can find no rationale to prevent me from breaking that contract and giving the command to the Fleet of Zooms to sink Degnan's ventures and put evil to rest in the waterlogged grave it deserves. He gave me access to The Third's strategies through a Warrior Strip in exchange for my protection of his market based on half-truths. I had no knowledge of the weapons and their launch cars when I contracted with Degnan. And my mind could never conjure up the horrors he's capitalized on here to feed the upper-tiers repulsive desires. Tomorrow, when we fly into this city, I have every intention of blasting the Dark Market out of the water.

I begin my jog again, and when I reach car fourteen I once again see children. I do not want to become aware of more unsettling details belonging to Degnan's ventures, but there are more children in this car, and my own motherhood compels me to stop. My commander status allows me to pause for a minute or under. Through the two-way I see all ages of children seated in chair slats and accompanied by their pocket-watches who mostly doze, probably relieved they are only watching one child instead of dozens.

A curtain, suspended in air, draws back, exposing a man in a white coat—a doctor, I think—and a pocket-watch with a child who skips and twirls past the doctor and out into the waiting room. The doctor is different from the emotionally nondescript store clerks, his face displaying a tired but readable smile as he watches a waiting child examine the leg of his joyful patient. The pocket-watch and child exit the car while the next child in line, distinguished by her missing arm, amputated just below the shoulder, enters the cubicle. As her pocket-watch steps in to accompany her, the curtain draws shut.

My allotted minute drifts into two and the curtain swings open again, the child with a new arm, seemingly perfect in every way. She leaves the curtained area, her eyes wide, her new limb swinging quite normally at her side. She stops in front of the waiting children and their pocket-watches. One of the children seated in a chair slat stands, then pumps his arms above his head. The child with a new arm mirrors the action and smiles when the arm-pump works for her too. Spontaneously all the other children jump to their feet, everyone pumping their arms above their heads in a wild dance of discovery. I feel my arm doing a bit of a pump at my side and continue my jog to the Warrior Strip exit hatch.

The paradox of Degnan jabs at my conscience. Using the dead GEB parts to enable healing in the maimed, this resourceful devil plundered evil to finance the accomplishment of good. Does that make him an angel? I gag at that thought. I try to imagine what he would have been like with a wife and a twelve-year-old son before *Jurbay* fell. Remembering the family picture I saw in the horseshoe tunnel hideaway beneath the factories of Reichel, I think about Degnan, a father once who smiled without malice and nurtured without a deviant purpose in mind. Is he trying to reconnect to an anchor of morality? I know he thinks he is. This man, who lost his way in the middle of the night when half the states submerged, now wants to take a detour. Perhaps he desires to veer off the vile path and find his way to wholeness. So he uses leftover baby parts from experimental GEBs to regenerate an arm or a leg or a malformed face, thinking that will baptize him into the light. It will take much more than that.

I move again and finally raise my hand to the hologram entrance of car #1. I slip quickly into the Waters of Erie, exiting the market and swimming to the colonies in a desperate effort to tell my story of an airborne GEB with a face like Raben's, and a fleet of flying fishborns that will give our Fleet of Zooms a battle they never expected.

———

I push the manhole cover up and exit the tool shed in the cul-de-sac. My clothes drip with the water. The vacuum sucks have become less and less effective with no one to maintain them. My head collides with something unseen. "Checkmate!" I speak his name like a curse word and locate the face-space in his balloon-tech, glaring at him through its opening. His smile offends me, considering the fact we're about to annihilate or be annihilated. And of course, he's speed-talking without ever pausing for breath. Grating. "What now?" I yell at the face-space.

He flips open the face-space and speaks without the aid of periods. "I'm just saying I think we could work together—you and me—you seem to be convinced you need to make a war—and I am definitely of the mindset that the fewer people in a war the better—so, I say I'll take my balloon-techs—we're practically invisible now, you know—"

"I know," I say, rubbing my head where the b-tech collided with it.

"…and we go in there—to Ash—which you seem to believe you're going to make a warzone—and the pacifists among us—noble as we are—will whisk civilians away to the north—out of the city—and we'll leave the bad guys for you—and our pilots with their balloon-techs—will make this great, big semi-circle—up at the old coliseum." Checkmate is demonstrating the escape path, with his arms waving in several directions. I can make no sense of it. "Well, we're not really making a semi-circle. More of a 'G' really. Get it? 'G'—Colony G." He stops for a moment, using a very long dramatic pause, seeming to have lost his train of thought. Tilting his head in one direction, he asks, "Want a ride?"

"Look," I say as I climb in the b-tech, "You *are* noble, but you're a colony that's completely eluded the two major powers in the remaining 28 states." Checkmate makes adjustments on his flight panel to close the door, ascending at the same time. "Right now, we need to get to the Fleet of Zooms and the hangars by the wind orchards. We'll make one quick stop on the way to pick up Chapman."

"Okay. So, pick up the cute kid who isn't always a kid."

"Been spying again?"

"Yes. Don't you think yourself just a tiny bit arrogant, Avery DeTornada, naming yourself as one of the remaining powers? You didn't even know we existed. How do you know that there aren't other colonies out there that are bigger than you, smarter than you, more peaceful than you?"

"That's not hard to imagine."

"Let us help the civilians of Ash."

"You don't need my permission."

"It's your war, Avery. You're in charge." He waits for my response, but I am done with this dialogue and need to focus on finding Chapman, in hopes that my five-year-old prodigy might not be spinning in a circle somewhere without breath.

"Checkmate, go. Go to Ash and save those you can. Just remember, citizens swear allegiance to The Third. Don't expect to just fly in there and lift people away."

"Children, not people. Children up in the holler. Lift children away. It's different, you know, not the same. They've never had *locasa* used on them—they'll come willingly—"

"Done talking, Checkmate. Just go. Drop me off and take your thirty balloon-techs and do what you can for the civilians. Just don't mess it up for us. No one can know we're coming."

"Self-absorbed is what you are. Ought to get some eye implants for better vision. Ought to use that infra-red chipster of yours. Some night you ought to take a little trip past your own colonies and into ours. You are foolish, Avery. Multiply by 10." And before I can ask him what he means by "multiply by 10" he says, "Glad we made your 'permission' official. I had to come and ask. The kids' evac is partially complete already, and the guilt I was feeling—saying you'd approved it—and it wasn't true—I was, well, ashamed about my deceit."

I should have known he'd already done what he thought he should do. After all, he's under no one's authority but his own. Checkmate brings the b-tech to a halt in front of my quarters.

Immediately I see Fortnight, Chapman's caretaker, lying face down at the front of the entrance. Running to Fortnight's side with Checkmate, I turn Fortnight over to his back and his eyes wander in confusion, trying to find a focal point. There's a deep gash on his forehead, already clotted and caring for itself. "Chapman—where is he?" I ask.

The gray-haired man whispers from his haze. "Used the butt of one of your weapons to bash my head. How's a five-year-old lift a weapon that big?"

"Where is he?"

"Can't say." I sit him up. "Don't know. Can't say."

"Okay. If he comes back, send him to the fleet hangars. We need him."

"He's not comin' back here. He just cut my head open. You oughta keep a weapon pointed on that kid."

"He's not always like this."

"My head says otherwise."

"You going to be okay?"

"Yeah. You go," says Fornight. We rush back to the b-tech and climb in.

Fortnight calls after me, "Commander?"

"Yeah?"

"Your Z-Colt—keep a bullet in the chamber."

"Always." We're off in the direction of the hangars, expecting to reach the Concourse in two minutes' time.

Chapter 19
AS PERMANENT AS IT GETS
MCGINTY

When *Jurbay* fell, McGinty and his father were bent over the engine of a Catalonian float car, tinkering, grease to their elbows, in an attempt to restore the aircraft to the strict safety standards enforced by the government. Even at ten, McGinty had come to appreciate how his government worked and the fairness with which they treated his father. The shake of the asteroid's power crossed the Atlantic, rattled the populations' nerves and brought the surprised child and his father from tinkering to fear. Their preservation instinct caused them to reach for and hold onto the beams at the center of the work shop, more out of emotional motivation than a physical danger. There was no damage to their country until the ash clouds circulated later, but they had a sense that something out of the ordinary was going down, and they had no control over it.

McGinty's father was a national peacemaker in the coveralls of a mechanic. Many times, the two of them would be called upon to visit with the President and his closest advisors in the flower-draped exterior court-yards of the President's private residence. The contrast between his father's greasy work clothes and the other five men's spotless, branded business suits went unnoticed through the eyes of a child. Later, McGinty would reflect first on the memory that these men, his father and the President had grown up together, and second that he'd wished his father would have bathed before attending meetings like those and had thought to wear his Sunday clothes. McGinty knew these men, and he knew their children. The fathers had been boys together on the coast of the Catalonian countryside and had all attended the same university. As married men with families, their children had played beside one another in the courtyards, on the rolling hills and in the backyards of family homes nestled in the small towns of Catalonia.

McGinty had one slipshod recollection from his childhood of Carles and Quinn DéTornada leaving the Catalonian President's home as he and his father were entering. Clips of the scene flipped up on the screen of his mind. The DéTornadas were heavily guarded as they exited the residence. McGinty remembered shocked parental faces when they realized their little girl was missing and anger from the mother's mouth when the girl was spotted playing with a puppy in the dahlia gardens that lined the austere driveway. McGinty and his father entered the home before he could catch a glimpse of the girl's face. Maybe that's why now, since he was forever glimpsing the face of the grown-up girl and watching her steer a course through motherhood, that he was captivated.

———

McGinty stepped into hangar #5 at the Energy Concourse, a repurposed reptile display tank from the zoo. It held the smallest of their sixteen aircraft that made up what they called the Fleet of Zooms. McGinty checked out the wind blocks, secure in the energy cavities on the side of the plane. Checkmate followed him, each word out of his mouth racing to overtake the next. McGinty, as usual, ignored Checkmate, tuning him out, directing his own comments toward a couple teenagers, apprenticing as mechanics. "This plane is pretty ridiculous," McGinty said to those in training. "So small it might as well be a b-tech. It's going to be hard to fly it into battle and carry explosive planters to drop on Ash." When he noticed Checkmate was quiet, which was never the case, McGinty tried to take his foot out of his mouth. "That's not to say b-techs aren't valuable and—" But before he could finish, Checkmate had flown away with his balloon-tech and his pack of pilots. McGinty didn't see him again for a week, and thought hard about using the same insult regularly to avoid the constant one-sided conversations.

McGinty prepped for the takeoff that would begin the attack of Ash, testing and assessing every weapon stored in each plane. All soldiers in The 28 United carried their personal Z-Colts, but the Snake Eye 454 and the DR93 were weapons already loaded on the Fleet of Zooms. He was meticulous in his inspection, but he knew there would be no surprises. The men and women flying these planes and the ones releasing the planters on the target sites were well trained—weapons clean and on the ready.

During the hours he performed these checks, he thought about *the end*, and it permeated everything inside him. As his hands went through the rote of each weapon check, he obsessed about it. *The end* might embody everything they'd hoped for, obliterating the power-hungry government of The Third and finishing the reign of atrocities the 28 United had lived with and fought against for so long. Yet, if they couldn't get back to the zoo after the attack on Ash, and if they were trapped in the city, then that might be the *end* of him, of Avery, Shaw, Pasha, Annalynn, Morris and all the rest. He had to stop this ominous consideration of *the end*.

McGinty flipped open the chipster in his bicep and coded in his own personal diversion. Music. It was flamenco, and for more than a step or two his feet danced without permission. A soldier preparing for battle didn't dance, although he knew Clef and the minstrels would praise his action. His movement was passionate beyond limits, and he missed Avery with an ache inside that no explanation could define.

———

Ten years ago, in Elite training, the four of them first met—McGinty, Pasha, Shaw and Avery. Each received a visit from a pigeon that perched on their shoulders, calling them to the undercover subterranean status for The 28 United. For McGinty, his first response was to brush the dirty bird away, fearing it would leave disgusting evidence that he'd provided an unwilling roosting location. In seconds, the pigeon was back. This time McGinty stood and abruptly moved a few paces away, but it was on the third flyby that he spotted the tattered edge of a slip of paper tucked into a metal band around the bird's leg, easy to recognize when paper was scarce and even non-existent in certain areas. Curiosity urged him to reach his hand around the pigeon's chest and unlock the hidden message from its leg. *Subterranean status confirmed. Elite training with The Third begins tonight at* La Trucada. *Find the stage.* McGinty knew the name of the flamenco club written in the message. It was a back-alley haunt that was always packed with locals, and hard to get to without knowing your way around the intricate web of streets that really had no grid.

Two hours into his waiting stint at the La Trucada club, he'd worn out his welcome by camping out at a table by himself, drinking *vermut* long past evening and keeping his eyes on the stage, mentioned in the pigeon's note. The switch to *cerveza* brought a full table of strangers with no other place to sit than his half-empty table. Still no clue as to where his training might begin and who would make contact with him and tell him how to proceed. A seat closer to the back wall opened up, and he took it immediately, hoping for a better visual of his surroundings. There was a child next to him, with a pigeon feather stuck in her frizzy black hair. She said, "Stop staring at me." McGinty had barely given her a glance.

"Stop with the paranoia," he replied, but kept his eyes poised on the passionate dancers performing on the stage, their heels engaged in a full-scale assault of the marred wooden floor.

"I didn't say you could sit at my table."

"Maybe I asked your mother."

"I'm short. Not a kid. Brilliant beyond your best dream." Something cooed in her bag.

"Tell me that's not a pigeon in your bag."

"It's not a pigeon in my bag. It's two." Neither talked for a few seconds, McGinty continuing to scan the room.

Finally, McGinty said, "Pigeons stink. You think it didn't smell enough in here with all these bodies packed together?"

"People smell. Pigeons don't. What? You don't like pigeons?"

"Had a nasty run-in with one today." He noticed the orange slice in her *vermut* was soggy and wondered if she was old enough to sit in a club and drink with adults, but the longer he sat with her the more he realized she was every inch an adult and didn't waste any of her size. The club opened the stage to dancers from the audience. Each one was allowed a minute or two to strut their version of flamenco. Then the performers would try to lure the drunk and inexperienced audience members to become a part of the show, hopefully leaving generous tips they may not have considered in sobriety.

"I think it's under the stage," she said. McGinty wondered if he dared imagine this petite, ebony smartmouth was also a subterranean. "Can you dance?" Still he kept silent. "You know where they hold them? Those that wait for their moment to join the dance?"

"In the pit in back. I've been here—lots of times." He stood and wove a path just big enough for himself to travel to the backstage pit, but he sensed before that path closed up behind him, with the raucous crowd filling in the gap, that the pigeon girl tagged close in his wake. That was confirmed when she stepped on the heel of his boot. He tried to reach around and bat her aside, but resiliently she clung to his jacket and would not be deterred.

McGinty found his way to the pit behind the stage. Like a small mass grave, this waiting room was dug in the dirt about five feet down and held the only space in the club where someone could line up and enter the stage from behind. A burly guy, with long hair hanging over his sinewy shoulder, like a highway to his six-pack, twirled a ten-inch blade in his left hand. McGinty wasn't sure if he was the bouncer that kept too many people from entering the pit, or if he was the guard that prohibited someone already in line from leaving until their commitment to dance was fulfilled. In any case, McGinty thought it best to try to remain invisible, but that was tough since there was only him, his sidekick and an athletic woman a little younger than himself, waiting for their time before the audience. He liked the fact that the woman was dressed in fatigues, when every other woman in the club wore a miniskirt, taking the focus off the dance right away. He appreciated the auburn highlights in her hair that was pulled up in a messy bun. She looked anxious, and he wondered if the anxiousness was motivated by the coming dance or something else. Their eyes met for a moment in which he saw a bit of mockery, but he was unsure why. Then the call came to take the stage and Mr. Burly leapt through a human-sized crevasse at the base of the pit that looked like a digging mistake, leading to a dark hole, a doorway to nothing. He was gone. *Okay,* thought McGinty, so *he's not the bouncer.*

Just as the girl in fatigues took the stage with McGinty, the pigeon girl tumbled down the black hole after the burly guy. McGinty thought he knew now that was the entry point of his training and not, like he'd previously thought, the stage itself. However, not wanting to arouse suspicion, he was now committed to finish this improvisational encounter with the girl in fatigues in front of a couple hundred people.

Several outdated spotlights heated up the stage. Sweltering. Didn't matter. He'd learned the dance from his relatives who lived above their family flat—a grandmother, a grand uncle and two sisters. When the dance began, the heat didn't matter. Nothing did. The ghostlike cry of the flamenco musicians, as they called forth the dancers, stilled even the drunkest in the audience. For a moment, it was quiet. Like an animal deserted, the guitarist's guttural cry urged McGinty and the girl to come forward and join the dance. Right away McGinty found his right heel stomping out a rhythm all his own, spontaneous in nature, traditional in legacy and predictably sensual, considering his stature and his understanding of the rhythm. His left foot followed the right. The audience cat-called, hooted praises and hollered out their desires to frenzy-up the pace, and let the passion spill from the musicians, to the dancers, to the audience and back again. McGinty felt that raw abandonment to his feet that led him into the ultimate moments of the climactic plunge to the finish of this tribal moment.

On his climb to the full momentum of the rhythm, a twinge of compassion interrupted. He saw the girl in fatigues struggling awkwardly to catch an inkling of what she was supposed to do. In that single moment, he knew her subterranean status. He knew because no one would place themselves in this humiliation if it weren't for a higher purpose—either that, or they were incredibly drunk. She didn't act drunk. He was suddenly consumed by protecting her possible subterranean identity as well as his, and scooped her up in his arms, pulling her close and trying desperately to guide her around the small stage, attempting to cover her inadequacies. He thought he did a rotten job of this, but the crowd was so consumed with him they hardly noticed she was there.

After one awkward and relentless minute of their sweat mingling and their eyes locked solid on each other, he swung her off the ground in a circle. He could tell she was making every effort to hold her legs in the position of a soaring finale. They came to rest in a tableau that was really more of a clump. He pushed her toward the stage exit and into the pit, and then followed her with grace, swooping down the pit and right into the dark hole of the crevasse. Then he popped is head back up, and said to the girl in fatigues, "Coming? It's a lot less scary down here than it is on the stage." Then he was back down the hole, followed by Avery DeTornada, not realizing then that in a few years *he* would be following her.

———

His weapon-check done, he replaced the final anti-brainy in its storage slot and turned to go, trying not to juxtapose the thought of the inevitable conflict over the semblance of a family he and Avery had built through the last five years. Through those years, an occasional strand of permanence tempted him to imagine a home with Avery and Chapman without military boots by the door and weaponry always on the ready. He hadn't come very far in the realization of that dream and had to be content with small victories here and there. He lightly rubbed the tat of the entwined vines that circled the ring finger of his left hand. Barely a week old, it still itched, reminding him that it was as permanent as it gets these days.

———

Several days ago, McGinty and Avery had journeyed to the outskirt colonies to get an accurate grasp of just how trained the new recruits of The 28 United were. Avery expressed her approval to a young general when he showed her the training methods for his troops. "You've come to the point of readiness very quickly, general. I'm pleased with your results."

He responded without tact when he said, "Well, it's been a while since you've been here, Commander..." Then, realizing he might have just tossed an insult her way, he clarified, "...but we simply followed Colony G's training routine."

"I have seven colonies out here, general. We're in the final planning stages for the air assault on Ash, and one of the most influential people under my command has gone rogue to try to solve all the problems of the world. I come when I can." Avery headed deeper into the tent-city, similar to most of the other colonies' housing set-ups. Before McGinty followed Avery, he nodded at the general, perhaps in support of his work, perhaps trying to cover her abrupt response. McGinty knew well that when Avery got this defensive it was never due to anger, but to an abundance of insecurities. The toughest measuring stick for her command was herself.

By her side, McGinty kept a quick pace with Avery. "I can't be everywhere," she said. "There's only one of me." He knew her commander's exterior continued a battle with her mother's interior. He guessed the mother just wanted to have a week of nothing but sleep and stories with Chapman when the day broke.

"Yes, I know there's only one of you. And it's a good 'one,'" McGinty responded. "A very good one." He noticed the corner of one side of her mouth headed upwards, and hoped the other side might join. An actual smile would be welcomed. Avery allowed her hand to brush against his and gave it a quick clasp, then released it. They'd become used to these brief connections, usually hidden from those around them. A kiss when finally alone after a fleet inspection, an embrace in the morning before they went their separate ways, and the many nights he slipped from his mat outside her quarters' door to lay beside her, holding her as together they watched Chapman spin. For ten years they'd called their friendship "best," even when Raben stole her heart, but these last five years they'd stretched the boundaries of friendship and claimed the territory of a deeper bond.

They continued their walk toward the training grounds where they would meet more colony troops, but long before McGinty actually saw the activities of the men and women of The 28 United, he smelled the strong aroma of birch sap mingled with the smoke of campfires and heard their robust laughter. As he and Avery drew closer to the group, he noticed the wine flowed freely and some of the eclectic assortment of cups, mugs and canisters picked up the light of the fire, projecting shadowed images on the sides of tents much larger than the size of their reality.

When finally reaching the perimeter of the circled soldiers, McGinty saw the source of their attention. Three tat artists inked the same section of skin on three separate clients. A circle, perched right below the left shoulder, extended to the area above the heart. The artists were all in various stages of completing this emblem of allegiance. McGinty had seen the image first in Red Grove, hanging on a canvas draped two stories high in Pasha's lab. It was a visual representing what was left of their nation, after *Jurbay* had taken its cut of the formerly united states. The jagged coastline of the 28 remaining states, painted clearly and running vertically up the canvas, was labeled by lettering etched beside the coastline. It read, *The 28 United*. McGinty's eyes traced the edges of the encampment. Most of the soldiers had abandoned their outer jackets, and the tattooed emblem that symbolized The 28 United peeked out from below the fabric of their sleeveless shirts. None of these men and women expected subterranean status. They boldly proclaimed through a permanent ink: *We are united*. And tonight, shouting from the shoulders of these warriors, the moon and stars heard *justice*.

"Commander DeTornada?" a soldier recognized Avery and stood to her feet in honor of her Commander. "Up in Colony G—you wear the sign of justice?"

"Just a few soldiers do," Avery said.

Another soldier stood in respect and said to Avery, "So you come here for a tat, Commander?"

McGinty watched Avery from a couple steps behind. He could feel her hesitation. "Yeah," she said, surprising him and taking off her outer jacket. "Yeah, I came for a tat." She took the place of one of clients and sat on a battered barrel. She pulled her sleeveless shirt off her left shoulder, exposing a new canvass for the artist to work. The artist handed her a tin cup filled with birch sap wine, and she took a healthy swig as the crowd stood to their feet, raising an odd combination of cups and glasses to their Commander.

Hours later, only a few soldiers remained around the glowing embers of a dying fire. McGinty and Avery sat with their backs propped up against the trunk of a peeling birch tree, him tracing the newly recorded circle on Avery's shoulder with his fingers. "The artists are still working," he said.

"Looks like they're almost finished. Should we take them back to Colony G with us?"

"They'd have weeks of work to do back there." He picked up her hand, gently rubbing her ring finger. "For what purpose?"

"What?"

"The tat. For what purpose?"

"Proclamation," she said. "'Till our dying day, nothing can take this commitment from us."

"Not even death." The silence between them was comfortable, like it always was nowadays. "A vine woven around the ring finger..." McGinty looked at Avery, not really expecting her to finish his sentence, but she did.

"...proclaims a lasting devotion."

"Friendship amplified by love eternal."

"Even though eternal may only be tomorrow," said Avery.

"Let's get in line."

"Let's send someone for the general."

McGinty laughed, "I'm sure he'd like that. Sealing a marriage is probably outside his job description."

Avery moved to her feet, holding McGinty's hand and pulling him along with her. "We've all expanded our job descriptions. And I don't think we've seen the end of it yet."

And as the night grew longer, just below their shoulders, an emblem marked their lives with a circle of allegiance to the dreams of justice hanging on a cliff's edge, and on the left finger of their left hands, a vine entwined, unbroken, displaying their willingness to be marked for each other. It was permanent, and McGinty understood that "permanent" sometimes meant only a day.

———

McGinty marked the hour and minute of the completion of his weapon inspection on a small pocket hologram. Right on time. He used his chipster to turn off the music, and approached the exit of zoom #5. The glinting eyes waiting for him at the aircraft door jolted him from his sentimental moment, sending his hand immediately to release the Z-Colt holstered on his shoulder.

"You shouldn't point a weapon at a kid," the voice said.

McGinty now had the target in the crosshairs and said, "If you'd act like a kid, I wouldn't have to point my weapon."

"Wanna dance?"

"Your mother's worried about you."

"Silly. She knows I always come back," Chapman said.

"Five-year-olds don't usually run wild spying on soldiers."

"I'm just playing."

McGinty lowered his Z-Colt. "I don't think so. Go home."

Chapman backed out the door and down the short ladder to the ground. "Got things to do."

"I bet."

Chapman brought his head back in the door, challenging McGinty. "Don't trust me?"

"Not today." McGinty placed his foot on the first rung, barely missing Chapman's head, forcing him to scoot down the ladder to the ground.

Chapman ran off in the direction of the wind orchard, screeching back at McGinty. "Families are supposed to trust each other. That's what you said."

"Stop flipping back and forth between a man my age and a kid who's supposed to be five." He thought about abandoning the weapons inspection in favor of following Chapman, thinking maybe he could discover the source of his mistrust. His internal father-type voice insisted the boy might get injured, but the soldier's voice inside him argued an injury to Chapman may be necessary in the line of duty. In the end, the urgent deadline of the takeoff for the Fleet of Zooms won out. *Mind on the task*, McGinty repeated to himself, and that task was the defeat of Ash.

Chapter 20
ETCHED IN A CIRCLE
AVERY

Checkmate lowers our b-tech through the blown-out roof of the Energy Concourse, then steers us east to the hangars just beyond the wind orchards. A light breeze skirts between the edges of the face-space and my cheek, reminding me that Checkmate still has some perfecting to do on these machines. An odor wafts in, riding on the back end of the draft, confirming that the children are still below making sure the chickens do their job for the future of energy.

For our Fleet of Zooms, sixteen aircraft hangars dot the landscape at the far end of the Concourse. None of the hangars look the same, but the one assembled at the center of the rest of the hangars is a towering, rusted grain silo. A fleet had always been Shaw's goal. From the moment he had secured one stolen float car from The

Third at the landing dock of Red Grove and paired it with his own repurposed aircraft, Shaw had envisioned a convoy of planes to do more than defend the 28 United. He wanted the float power to go after The Third. I took him seriously. No one else did until he and his mappers uncovered an old air base out past the colonies.

Shaw taught his map team discipline—how to use the ten-inch blade, and the specifics of mapping the terrain on the outskirts of the colony with detail—but he also instructed his topographers in the art of mechanics. Once he'd determined that there were two workable aircraft on the defunct base, he made sure their daily mapping route took them in the vicinity of the base at the end of the day. When the team's daily routines were complete, Shaw and his crew worked a dedicated two hours on fixing the grounded planes. Of course, it wasn't mandatory for the exhausted mappers to stay on and help him, but Shaw drove their only mode of transportation back to Colony G—a four-wheeler from the garage of someone they guessed had once dealt in antiquities. Their other option—a walk home at the end of a challenging day—seemed more daunting than staying for a practical lesson on engine repair. Besides, Shaw had lots of battle stories that kept the hours rolling.

Each time Shaw returned to the Concourse with his latest resurrected aircraft, it was under heavy guard, and since he wanted to make sure nothing happened to send his flight babies back to their damaged state, he also brought back deconstructed materials to repurpose as hangars. For the float car, it was a collapsed grain silo which he'd positioned at the center of the other hangars on the Energy Concourse. The float car's ability to fly vertically and horizontally in tight situations made the silo a perfect match. "Zoom!" said Annalynn the first time she saw the float car zip out of the top of the silo. "I never pegged Shaw as the creative type." Later that day, she convinced him to give her a flying lesson that would begin with guiding the float car in and out of its hangar. Morris said they made at least fifteen practice exits, which meant the same number of returns.

Each time Shaw flew into the Concourse with a new type of aircraft, Annalynn greeted him with her scheme for test rides of her own. "Zoom, that's the best one yet, Shaw. Where'd you get it? Can it be powered by poo-balls? Let me help you reconstruct that hangar." And then always her inevitable question, "Will you teach me to fly it?" I don't know if her curiosity compelled Shaw to teach her pilot skills, or if he just let her participate with his other students to shut her up. "Zoom! Got another one, I see," Annalynn greeted him with enthusiasm. "Zoom, that's nasty. Gonna need some serious cleaning."

Annalynn thought Shaw's fleet needed a name. When someone joked, "Here comes Shaw with another addition to his Fleet of Zooms," the name stuck on Shaw's reconstructed air power. Of course, Annalynn thought Shaw had named the Fleet of Zooms after her, when, in fact, Shaw never named anything.

Shaw's protective hangars ranged from the silo to metal storage garages to wooden structures comprised of weathered barn wood, and a huge tank once used in the zoo to house reptiles. In our squatters' paradise at Colony G, Shaw took mappers and repurposed them into mechanics the same way he repurposed a grain silo into a hangar for one of his fleet in waiting.

"All the planes are rolled out," said Checkmate as we approached the hangars. "Are you planning on starting this war today, Commander?" I try to ignore him, swinging my legs out of the side of the b-tech and mentally reviewing how each worker prepares and readies the fleet. I look for McGinty. "Hey, Avery. Did you hear me? Is this the day that goes into the History Labyrinth as your war to end all wars?"

"Depends on whose history labyrinth you access—ours or The Third's," I say.

"Hey, we have one too. *Balloon-tech History for the Future.*"

"Oxymoron."

"Don't call me names."

From across the other side of the hangar area I see what's left of our Council approaching in a clustered group of wise, brash risk-takers. Some more brash, others more wise, but all of them risk-takers still finding their way, forging an evolving government that began in the basements of pre-*Jurbay* homes and extended across an ocean to protect a Catalonian leader and a device of healing. With Pasha and Morris rogue and Quinn MIA, we're down to just five of us on the Council—McGinty, Shaw, Clef, Old Soul and me. Through the last five years, we've done our best to be consistent, though our meeting places have been anything but constant. Once we met in a grove where trees spread thick-leaved branches over us, as we stretched justice between the limbs and whispered equality above to the canopy. An abandoned parking lot provided anonymity for our Council. There, weeds pushed through cracks bigger than the chunks of cement that still remained. Circling around a modest fire, we lifted carefully-crafted words into the air as a model of fair-mindedness, forged from our memories of history and our own ignited passions.

Recently, we've sat on the banks of a dried-up watering hole in the middle of the savanna grasslands of Colony G's abandoned zoo, solidifying our future hopes in the form of confessed dreams and debates on moral code. This Council's tenacity to hold our vision, as if it were a framed document, hanging firm on the wall of a history labyrinth, invigorates me. These men fight with me, reason their cases, walk out in anger, return with compromise, and they hold me together, the only lighthouse in a dangerous sea. And I hope, as they sit themselves in a semi-circle at the base of Checkmate's b-tech, that I, in the smallest of ways, hold them together too.

"One last time?" asks Clef, his empty sockets turned in my direction.

I answer, "One last time, we meet as a council before the attack." They all nod in my direction. I see Checkmate peeking out the open passenger door of his b-tech, and I can't help but speculate as to what government in his colony might look like. I hope I find out.

Old Soul begins, his ancient hippy glasses perched askew on the bridge of his nose. Through time and use they are now lens-free. "We can expect to find resistance, even with the surprise of attack," he says.

Shaw stands, saying, "No resistance. Not by air." Defensiveness spread thick upon his shoulders, anxious to get this battle on.

"Old Soul's right," I say, barely audible. "There may be resistance by air." They all look at me, expectant of an explanation. "They have more than fishborns. Smaller ones that, when activated, will fly and attack." I'm aware that all the hangar pilots and mechanics have begun moving in our direction, curious about the coming mission. They do not set their tools down, bringing them along, walking toward us silently. I don't stop them from approaching or try to end their eavesdropping.

"How did they know to develop a defense against our air attack?" asks McGinty. "Degnan?"

"No, not Degnan," says Old Soul. "He's been on our side—or his own side—but never Dorsey's side."

Clef adds, "Dorsey must have sensed, with his uncanny abilities, that air assault *might* come. That's why he's retained his power for this long. He didn't know specifically we were coming by air. Just that someone might, sometime."

Shaw stresses, "Well, then The Third's kept this under-under tight wraps. Our subterraneans didn't even know." The crowd surrounding us is close now. Near enough to hear our voices. No one moves to exclude them from the Council's discussions. They have a right to know that this threat, that endangers their existence, just got a lot more deadly. They are a part of the unknown climax to this unfolding strategy. There are no secrets here.

Shaw continues. "If they're controlling air fishborns from a launch car, all they can do is try a direct hit. Without pilots their damage will be minimal. We can out-fly them."

"They have pilots, Shaw." I'm direct.

"How? If they're launching from the market, and they don't know if they'll need these things or not..." Shaw pauses, maybe beginning to answer his own question.

"What flies these aircraft, Avery?" asks McGinty.

"GEBs," I say. Shaw groans at my response and walks away from the Council, staying within earshot. "I ran into one, coming face-to-face with it."

"Still—," says McGinty, "that doesn't mean they're expecting us."

"It does when the GEB has the face of Raben."

The look I see in McGinty's eyes has a sprinkling of hurt but quickly flashes to anger. He asks, "Did you see more than one?"

"I saw the one that was activated, but there's eight cars of them. There's over sixty air fishborns."

"All with his face?"

"Highly likely." I say. "Dorsey knows we're coming."

"Then we have to change our plan," says Shaw.

"No." I look out at the crowd that hasn't moved since they circled around us. I direct my orders not just to the Council, but also to these pilots. "We don't change a thing." I step up on the edge of the b-tech to be seen and heard by all. Checkmate shrinks back inside his invention, making room for me. "We don't change a thing. We have a plan to take down the major government buildings we know about and the ones that the subterraneans mark with lab coats."

"Lab coats? Not that again." Shaw responds, and he doesn't need to step up on the b-tech to be heard.

"These GEB pilots are capable of air battle, but they don't have full reasoning skills. I used reverse-*locasa* on two Elite guards, and together we stopped the GEB's attack on me by outwitting the GEB with a movement diversion. If they're activated in the air, we fight them off."

"We only have enough fuel for the attack—not side-battles on the way."

"Exactly. It is 'on the way,' and we'll strengthen our ground attack by sending in more troops to meet us when we land."

"If we land," says Shaw.

I know he's right, but there's no other plan. A fleet by air is still the only chance at surprise. So I say to all of those waiting for my explanation, "Continue to load the energy into the fleet. There's no time to waste." At my command, Shaw doesn't budge, but the rest move immediately, and I know they'd rather follow hope blindly then to stop and consider the alternative.

———

Minutes later, I spot McGinty directing a work crew primarily comprised of the children from the prison. They all wear tinted-orange metal bracelets. I wonder, what's the appropriate time to palm code those bracelets off their wrists and give these kids a second chance? I foresee some of these boys and girls being master mappers, mechanics, pilots, and some may end up being healers or minstrels. If only we can teach them there's more than war.

Touching the back of McGinty's shoulder, I say, "Last time I saw you with a group of kids, you were disarming a live fishborn."

"We removed its power source," he says as he turns to me, gently placing his hand on my cheek and then removing it immediately. He knows the limits between a top weapons soldier and a commander. Both of us would like to remove those constraints, but neither of us knows how to do that. As his hand moves away, I grab it midair and hold it tight in my grasp for the briefest of moments.

"How much longer?" I ask. In spite of the fact that there are many varieties of aircraft here, the loading of the solar cells and wind blocks is quite the same as it was for the fishborn that came after us at the other end of the Concourse. Side-loading, the cells and blocks are slipped into slats in uniform rows.

"How much longer for loading?" McGinty asks. "Three more hours, maybe three and a half."

"Then we're airborne?"

McGinty notes one of the children has stopped the loading process holding the wind block in her hand, staring. "August?" McGinty asks the child. "What's wrong?" Forlorn, August looks at him then turns the wind block over.

"It has a hole," she says. McGinty reaches his arm out encircling August, reassuring.

"Stack it with the other duds." He points her in the direction of the pile of reject blocks and cells that won't be making the journey to Ash for one reason or another. August follows his directions, and he turns and says to me, "There's no additional energy for a return trip."

"Yeah, I know, and there's no extra energy to fight the air fishborns. I know. Every strike has to be accurate.

We won't need a return trip to Colony G. We'll be staying in Ash. New government and all that." For a very long minute neither of us moves. Neither says a word. Both of us desperate to believe what has quickly become a fantasy.

McGinty takes my arm and leads me behind the silo. He cups my hands in his, drawing them to his lips and kissing the delicate tattooed circle of vines that entwine around my left finger. I kiss the same spot on his left hand. "It's been a week," I say, thinking back to the unannounced commitment we made to each other by the campfire under the stars in the presence of a tattoo artist and a few soldiers from the colonies beyond G. It's a marriage built on fierce, opposing opinions and a never-ending respect for the character of one another. The unspoken attraction was always there, even when Raben became a powerful force in my life. Raben cast a passionate spell on me, and I yielded for the sake of pleasure and convenience. Raben and I celebrated a marriage of revolt, a slap in the Third's arrogant face. McGinty and I committed to a marriage of love, knowing that when there's so much risk and danger in the world, love and faith become our only hope. The artist wound the ink around our fingers in a most enduring way—a ring etched deep in skin, never to be taken off, or lost, or exchanged for one that might look more appealing. Our intent was everlasting, yet in just hours from now, "everlasting" may find its end.

I open my mouth to speak, but he kisses me, and I have no words. We embrace, and I feel the heaviness of wishing Chapman were beside me with Quinn's version of grandmother close at hand. And I desperately want to renovate one of the decaying houses in the decrepit cul-de-sac, outside of the zoo. I want to make it into a place called *home* where the four of us would never have to speak again of a savior fleet that may not have the energy to accomplish the plans we've made for it.

McGinty says, "Don't worry about Chapman. You know he can survive anywhere."

I pull away from him. "He can—if he's not the five-year-old Chapman."

"Yeah. Well, he wasn't five when he paid me a visit not long ago."

"Here?"

"Oh, right here. He was spying on me. He threw an adult tantrum when he recognized I didn't trust him."

"Was he hurt?"

McGinty grabs my arms in confrontation. "Avery, you do get it, don't you? When he's not Chapman the five-year-old, *he's* the one that does the hurting. We all have to be careful of him."

I stiffen and step away from McGinty. "I get it."

"Yeah, but will you get it in the moment you have to choose between his life and Shaw's, or Annalynn's, or… mine?"

"I got it when we discovered Raben was a GEB."

"Quinn pulled the trigger on him—not you."

I turn my back on McGinty and walk away, ending the conversation, but he has more to say. "No matter what happens today…this might be the last chance for us to say—"

I rub the tattoo on my finger and face him once again. "McGinty, we don't need more words. At the end of the day, if we get a chance to whisper *home* when this is all over—we'll be blessed." The reins of the Commander intrude on my private moment, slinking up my spine and placing a stranglehold on my neck, but I won't choke. I imagine myself prying off the reins and holding them securely in my hands where I can offer direction. I still do not see myself as the most likely candidate for Commander, but I am better than I was five years ago. And if destiny affords me the opportunity, then in five more years I may see my father Carles when I look in the mirror. August scoots around the corner, the same despondent look on her face. "Excuse me, sir," she says to McGinty, "but we're out of blocks and cells, and zoom #16 is only part way loaded."

Rushing to zoom #16, we find Shaw loading poo-balls in the aft of the aircraft. I never knew there was storage there, and especially not for energy in the shape of the poo-balls. A sudden sentimental twinge surprises me, as I think of Pasha and her wit. We don't have a successful way of using these poo-balls yet, but she had the confidence—or arrogance—to think we would. She planned accordingly, and I see those plans embedded in the aft of this plane—round holes waiting for the moment poo-balls might be loaded and used as energy the way solar cells and wind blocks are.

"Are we ready for these?" I ask Shaw.

"There's been a lot of tests done," he says.

"Results?"

"Mixed reviews."

"How mixed?"

"There's been a lot warriors through history, Avery, who went out not expecting to return."

"Thought you always turned the eye-readers off when required history was broadcast."

"Yeah, I did, but Morris is always spouting history. Don't need eye-readers to get all the facts." August helps Shaw load #16 and several children join. He recites what he learned from Morris. "There was the pilot out of fuel—coasted into enemy territory, fended off the enemy troops then hid for eight months until the allied forces arrived. There was a Union soldier caught behind the Confederate line—stripped off the gray uniform of his dead opponent and traveled in those clothes with the southern patrols for weeks, until he could escape and find his own troops. Then, a survivor of Auschwitz—"

I stop the history lesson, saying, "I get the point. Just promise me you'll land this thing if it's out of fuel instead of diving it into the side of a building. We'll have boots on the ground too. You'll have a better chance—"

"Don't worry. I'm not going all the way to Ash without dropping this payload, even if I have to fly through a sky full of Raben-faced GEBs to do it."

I smile at him. "I order you not to kill yourself."

"Yes, sir."

Chapter 21
CAVES STAY STANDING
AVERY

I tick off my options at a rapid rate, while I try to evaluate how a commander's time might best be used in the last hours before war begins and time runs out. I'd spent forty-two minutes at the hangars by the wind orchards. I'm not needed to load the energy in the planes. Shaw had that organized and in full production. And while I'd like to spend the last moments I have, before our fleet lifts off for Ash, holding Chapman and McGinty, Chapman is MIA and McGinty is assisting Shaw in the energy load. I never thought, during the hours that pass before an attack, that, for me, there would be intervals of waiting. Now there is a stint of time where all our loyal ones know their jobs and accomplish tasks with efficiency, their training now rising to the surface with a fierce necessity that might allow our preparation to be our salvation. Since everyone is doing what their Commander wants them to be doing, this Commander isn't really needed. And so, "goodbye" rests on the tip of my tongue, trying to form the word on my lips, trying to send it into the atmosphere, finding those I hold dear and delivering a final pronouncement.

I stand at a distance in the Energy Concourse, my eyes fixed on the mishmash of zoom hangars, wondering whose idea it was to take Ash by air—to take Ash at all. Suddenly that eerie awareness prickles through my scalp, and I sense I'm not alone. Checkmate hovers in his b-tech above me. I have tutored myself to detect his camouflaged aircraft. That sixth sense that constantly roams around my being rises up, allowing me to sense his close presence. Then, once I am aware, if I look carefully, I can see the outline of his face-space. I open my mouth to speak, but, of course, he beats me to it. "Drop you somewhere, Commander?" he asks.

I hesitate, thinking I would like to embrace the quiet of the next hour without his random babblings, but instead I pull myself up through the open door on the side of his balloon-tech and say, "To the caves," and off we sail.

It only takes a couple minutes to arrive near the caverns' entrance. I contemplate thanking Checkmate for assuming the job of my own personal cabby, but the drums of battle beat up my insides, and I just don't have the breath for an extra word. Maybe later.

Checkmate flies me to the door of the caves, his balloon-tech transforming seamlessly through the changing environments that meld from energy orchards to savanna grasses to a gentle knoll covered with a wild overgrown mix of Rose of Sharon and Russian sage. Flat, satiny blooms of brilliant, untamed blue tangle with the silvery edges of the sage, crowning the rise, protecting what lies underneath with the royal cover of anonymity. We land.

I've become quite successful at tuning out Checkmate's droning monologues, but when he wants to get my attention he yells my name, and that's my cue to concentrate on what he's saying.

He shouts, "Avery! Notice that balloon-tech parked by the entrance of the caves?"

"No."

"That's the point." His machinegun-cracking laugh grates on what nerves I have left.

"Heard that one before. Thought all your b-techs were in Ash, locked into rescue mode."

"Hey, you're the one that authorized me to do some trading—"

But before he can finish, I am fully aware that the biggest trade of my life may be going down right now. One that I had intended to negotiate, 'cause after all I'd already traded Checkmate some energy palettes for a b-tech. But the jumbled priorities of command took over the one demand of my friendship with Pepper.

I am out of the b-tech, sprinting for the caves with all my plans for battle forgotten, and the only thing left in my non-commander brain right now is a hope for— Pepper. If Checkmate bargained in my stead on behalf of Pepper, when I failed to do so because my mind was on war and not birth—well, I might be obligated to listen to Checkmate ramble 'till the end of time. And if he's been successful, I would not complain.

The threshold of the caves is more than a symbolic barrier between the grit and terror of a post-apocalyptic world and the healing notes of minstrels. I should know, for I have felt the healing. I took the medicine of the flutes playing, the drums pounding and the artists painting pictures of serenity, and I received the prescription for a cuddle from a gazelle named Gizzie. Nature has fashioned this entrance with a drapery of evergreen shrubs, not appearing as a doorway to anyone unfamiliar with their existence.

The minstrels' melodic tones of comfort reverberate off the cavern walls in a counterpoint to the droll of water droplets, dripping their way down the slimy sides of the cavern to its floors. My father's namesake, Carles, approaches me timidly, his eyes cautiously examining my face. He seems like he wants to tell me something and yet hesitates to share his information. Carles' whole body lists away from me, in a conflict with his feet that move him forward in my direction. "Avery," he says, "Degnan's here." At his name I bristle, my muscles

335

tense. The tiny hand around mine urges me to stay, and Carles says, "Pepper wants you to come." I summon a smile, nodding in agreement. He leads me quickly across the slippery floor of the cavern.

We weave through groups of children in various stages of healing, all focused, craning their necks to see something ahead. Clef stands guard before a curtain of woven feathers, agates and dried berries, encircling something hidden on the other side. Clef senses my presence, his smile communicating when his empty eye sockets cannot. He urges me forward just as a baby's cry rings through the peaceful music of the caves, but the tiny wail does not disrupt the peace. It only adds to it. The agates bump back and forth, clacking as I part the curtain and find the source of this new voice. Cradled in the arms of Pepper, her tiny baby screeches to the heavens, *I am here! I have arrived! Nothing will ever be the same!*

For Ulysses, who stands at Pepper's side, and for Pepper, the waiting is over, the trade complete. Degnan got his b-tech, and Pepper and Ulysses got their baby. Hardly a fair trade, I think. And suddenly I wonder if Degnan would have gotten around to facilitating this birth without Checkmate stepping in to trade the b-tech I'd acquired from him for this very purpose. Degnan built the Warrior Strip for The 28 United, yet even with all the good Degnan's Warrior Strip has done for us, he's allowing Dorsey to keep his stockpile in the Dark

Market. Without the b-tech trade, my guess is that Pepper would have been perpetually pregnant. I will never trust him.

Degnan steps through an opening in the quiet crowd, straightening his shirt and then slipping his arms in his jacket, buttoning the front. He appears every inch a market owner, but I know, just moments ago, he played the role of genetics expert and midwife.

Pepper waves me near, and I kneel next to the pallet of savanna grasses she rests on. I reach my hand to gently touch the bald head of the first baby created by the only two GEBs who swear allegiance to The 28 United. Pepper's bow, perched on a small tuft of a blonde wig, is soaked with sweat. She says, "You did it, Avery. You made the trade. You gave us this baby. You did it."

I laugh and brush a few unwanted tears from my face, "No, Pepper, *you* did it. You and Ulysses." She places her newborn in my arms, and I feel a jumbled mix of joy for the birth and guilt for the fact that I did not make this trade. It was Checkmate who made it.

"Say 'hello' to your auntie," says Ulysses. And this child looks human only in the sense that many newborns look like GEBs—pale skin, no visible eyelashes, bald. He's not crying. His eyes are opened, unlike Chapman who squeezed the world away with tightly clamped eyes for days after he was born.

"What's his name?" I ask.

"Rummy," says Ulysses.

"*Her* name is Rummy," says Pepper. "In honor of Degnan. You know how we always beat him at gin rummy—how he always refused to say he'd lost—"

"That's because I always won," says Degnan.

I lean closer and kiss Rummy's head, an identical match to both mother and father.

Degnan retreats in the direction of the cave entrance, and I gently place Pepper's babe back in her arms. I chase after Degnan.

I run past him, placing myself in his way, walking backwards and confronting him with an irritation that consumes our every meeting. I say, "I see you got your balloon-tech."

"And Pepper got her baby," Degnan says. "Can't you just say 'thank you' for the trade?"

"Would she have gotten her baby if you didn't get a trade?"

"Probably. I've always been a bit partial to that matched set of GEBs. Even though they cheat at rummy."

"You like them 'cause you taught them everything they know."

"Not fair. You taught them too."

"I taught them humanity has value. You taught them to cheat at cards."

"Well, I guess everyone got what they wanted."

He is smug as usual and my next words come with assault. "By the way, *our* deal is off."

"You mean the one we sealed with a glass of Hennessey?"

"Yeah, that one. The only deal you and I've ever made. I will not be protecting your market that has all Dorsey's weapons aimed at our colonies and any other colonies beyond the Waters of Erie. They're ready to take us out at any minute—at Dorsey's command."

"Oh, you're wrong—Raghill's going to make that call, but Dorsey wants to watch it happen." He takes a long look at me, as he always does, as if he's evaluating my fitness status as a commander. Then, he says, "Your father wouldn't have broken a contract."

"A contract's not a contract if it's built on lies in the first place."

Degnan laughs, "I never lied."

"You deceived me."

"When Dorsey moved into his space in the market, I didn't know there would be weapons."

"You know everything."

"I didn't know, until he'd already started stockpiling. By then, I couldn't tell him to get out."

"It's your market," I say.

"It's his city."

I see the musicians and the children inside the caves all raising their fingers to their lips in an attempt to quiet our debate. The hostility between us is very incongruous with the mission of the caves. I whisper with no less anger, "I won't defend your market."

"You won't have to. I have a security force of my own, you know. You, of course, remember my competent warrior, Miranda."

"She's a trained guard."

"She's been promoted, in charge of hundreds."

"Your own security force? So, you never intended for me to protect your market?" Degnan remains silent. "Then why offer me the contract? The deal was the Warrior Strip so I could access information in exchange for my protection of your market. That's what you said. That's what our contract was. Why do that?"

"Because you won't take gifts from people you hate." In that moment, in spite of the fact that I despise him, he rips apart my heart, and I hate what I see inside me. Am I really the one who wouldn't take the gift of the Warrior Strip if it were offered with no strings attached? If I didn't have to pay or exchange or trade something with Degnan in return for using the Warrior Strip to obtain The Third's secrets, would I really have rejected the gift and withheld the life-saving information from The 28 United? Why? Because I hate the giver? Hypocrisy stinks.

"Avery, our best chance at taking Dorsey down is to defend the market together—not blow it away. I protect it from below the water, keep Dorsey from launching anything. You take the city by air, and then we dismantle the weapons and the launch car piece by piece from the inside. We work together, and we both get what we want."

I laugh. "We don't need your market. You think I care if your human hair coats sink to the bottom of Erie or your GEB baby factory goes down with Dorsey's weapon cash?"

"What about those GEB baby parts giving human babies new arms or legs? You going to send that to the bottom of Erie too?"

"You think we're on the same side? That's ludicrous."

"We're on the side that takes down Dorsey. Our reasons are different. Mine's personal."

"Personal? Still have some of those pocket-watch memories kicking you in teeth, when Dorsey declared you incompetent to lead anyone but a bunch of ten-year-old kids shacked up in a library?" I see Degnan straighten just a little, like a familiar barb burrows deeper in his skin, and I can't help the satisfaction I feel. I hold the barb.

"What's *your* plan?" He doesn't wait for my answer. "I mean, besides flying your limited fleet into Ash and dropping every bit of your payload on the buildings with white lab coats strewn all over their rooftops?" He really does know everything. "You blow the market apart, with all those fishborns sleeping in their hideaway, you take the city of Ash and miles around it down too. You won't even have a place to land your planes." So, this too is what he meant by not needing my protection. He doesn't need it not just because he has his own security force, but because he knows we won't fire at the market—we can't fire. He knows I'm not willing to murder a half a million innocent citizens along with Pasha, Morris, Annalynn—even Raghill. I could never. I'd be no different than Dorsey.

"I can help you from inside the market—where the weapons wait to find their mark. I have full access. You direct your fleet away from us, and I'll find a way to keep those weapons from deploying."

I realize, once again, I have an unintentional alliance. I'm reluctant, but can't turn down his offer, or none of us live. "Okay, the market won't be one of our targets. We'll have the ground troops of our colonies on the ready when the government buildings fall, and McGinty and I will get to the market when Ash is secured and help you dismantle the weapons—give you support if you need it." I expect another of his cynical slashes, but he is quiet for a series of uncomfortable moments.

"Good," he says. "Then at last we agree on something." I move a few steps from inside the cave to the outside where I watch him slip into his newly traded b-tech. Looking through the window, I see Gizzie curled into a ball, causing her to look smaller that she actually is. Degnan, realizing I am watching him, mumbles as he swings into the b-tech, "She might not be safe here." I have nothing to say to that. I'm stunned that there's a cave full of minstrels and children and GEBs loyal to the 28 United that are at risk of being blown into oblivion, and Degnan chooses to save a gazelle toward the end of her lifespan. I want to be done with trying to figure Degnan out, but he's wrapped himself around my life with a throttlehold of necessity, and right now I can't escape it.

Chapter 22

WITCHING FOR POWER

DORSEY

In Dorsey's private quarters, he lay on his sofa in a drugged-out state. On the floor beside him, a leprex squatted on its haunches, licking Dorsey's face. The other leprex, comprising the pair, was nowhere to be found. A twitch possessed Dorsey's right eyebrow, hopping from the arch down to the corner of his eye and then back again, not defined enough to call "pain," yet still poking on the perimeter of his unconscious state. Alone, with Elite guards outside the entrances, Dorsey's mind, lolling in the Degnan-induced drug, took a slow roll backward to his younger self when he first felt the pricks of power tap on the back of his shoulder.

———

Dorsey, an arrogant commander's son, breathed each moment of his existence under the training of his father, unlike the other officers' sons who were often sent away as young children to decommissioned government buildings, unused confinement facilities and deserted libraries, where caretakers—the pocket-watches—provided the essentials of life and nothing more. When Reichel and its surrounding forests were finally cleansed from the remnants of the Deadlies, allowing the city to house most of the remaining citizens in the area, there was a water shortage that drained the reservoirs and parched the throats of the inhabitants.

During his officer training lessons where Dorsey should have been studying how to turn the salt water of the New Coastline into palatable liquid for the benefit of the citizens, his eye-readers drew him to the Reichel History Labyrinth. The mystification of the pioneer era and the settling of the West, when the West still existed, captivated him. Something about hoisting a wagon train over virgin mountains spoke to him of power, achieving the unattainable. Who stood at the base of those mountains motivating the travelers to winch the primitive wooden wagons up sheer cliffs and severe inclines? More important, who stood at the top and gave the order to heave and ascend? He could picture himself with an oiled wide-brim leather hat, the rain of the Northwest dripping from its brim, a buffalo hide coat swinging mid-calf, its dark brown color almost black from wear.

The image was so clear he felt the ache in his bones from the cold as he imagined standing at the top of the cliff, issuing the command to winch oxen upward.

Dorsey's father had introduced his namesake to the trappings of the pioneers when Dorsey was only ten. They walked frequently down the narrow, dimly lit corridors of the History Labyrinth. But at eighteen he came alone to the Labyrinth's empty halls. He stopped directly in front of the glass window that shielded the groping hands of what used to be hundreds of curious visitors. Encased in a rectangular six-foot by ten-foot cubicle of history were the implements of the pioneers' hard-fought, rugged life. An oxen's yolk with a heavy, wooden, bow-shaped piece that connected the two beasts, allowing their chins to rest in secured leather straps. An iron block and tackle, split and rusted. A barrel butter churn constructed of pine slats, encircled and held together by large steel rings. Next in the exhibition line, another butter churn—tall with a plunging stick extending upward from the hole at the top of the marred wooden cylinder. Carved tally marks ran up its side. Dorsey counted one hundred and eight marks dug in crooked rows, reflecting what? How many times the butter was churned? Number of barn cats born to do their job with the mice? A memory of storms that threatened to level the house? Times the Cheyenne or Pawnee might have stared in a window then retreated without incident? Or maybe it was a tally that kept track of the only ones who made it up the mountainside, who blazed the trail from East to West. Or perhaps it was a record of those who didn't. This remaining ghost tally meant someone back then was well enough—alive enough—to count something relevant. And then, beside the butter churns, lying on a square of canvas with the gradation of dried mud, rotted food and droplets of blood—lay a stick, Y-shaped and roughhewn. Below it, neatly printed in faded black ink and written on parchment paper, its edges curling, were the words: "Dowsing Rod." The label also said: "From a willow tree."

Dorsey placed his hand on the glass barricade that separated him from touching all the items the pioneers had handled, leaning so close his nose touched the glass and his breath left a mist, momentarily obstructing him from reading the information. He held his breath, and as the fog dissipated from the glass he read: "From ancient days, rods have been used to locate water, minerals and graves." He stepped back, took a breath and scrutinized several black-and-white photographs, diminished by time and featuring the images of men in well used farm clothes, holding the Y-shaped stick in their hands. The pictures showed one hand on each side of the stick as if they were handles, allowing the other part of the Y to aim forward, pointing at an unknown *something*. Dorsey gulped air, held it in and stepped back up to the glass, reading the final words on the label. "The end of the Y-shaped stick will dip or uncontrollably flail when the hunt is completed. The person using the rod is often called a 'diviner.' Not all who use the rod have the power to divine."

Dorsey's father's words to him when he was a kid came back to his remembrance, challenging the legitimacy of the dowsing stick, the divining rod. Mystical. Folklore. Community ramblings. However, at the end of that disdaining list of adjectives, his father said, "They swore by the stick's accuracy to find water. Some still used rods like this a hundred years after the pioneers settled."

Dorsey exhaled, moving several feet away from the display, taking in the entire scope of the pioneer tools, but his eyes continued to settle over and over again on the dowsing rod. *Not all have the power.* He took off his uniform jacket, its insignia showing a much higher rank than others of his age who didn't share his father's name. Then he pulled his form-fit gray shirt over his head, wrapping his right fist in it like a boxing glove from the twentieth century. *Not all have the power.* Dorsey beat upon the glass case with his covered hand, busting through the aging material by the time he'd struck the seventh blow.

Shards clung to the edges of the circular hole, and he brushed them away with his bound hand. Unwinding the shirt, Dorsey let it fall to the ground and plucked his gloves from his weapons belt. The gloves fit like skin, and he reached through the hole, securing the rod and twisting it sideways to slip it through the opening. Dorsey set it gently on the floor, then he threaded his arms through the armholes of his uniform jacket, leaving it unbuttoned, exposing his fit, bare chest. None of the Elite would dare question the Commander's son for having his uniform askew. And when they watched him exiting the labyrinth, perhaps they thought he was crazy—uniform failing and holding a stick, pointed forward, like it was directing him somewhere. Dorsey thought, *I have the power.*

Later that day, when most citizens were working in the plant and military officers were attending to their duties in government buildings, Dorsey let the rod fit into his hands and guide him from the roll call square outside the Plethora Plant to the forest edge. At first, when he tripped on a half-buried rock and caused a movement of the rod, he believed it was his abilities, but after another forty minutes of no more action, he felt relieved to be in the forest by himself where this absurdity could be seen by no one else. Yet, the quest for power drew him on.

A full hour passed before the dowser went berserk, shaking sporadically then dipping its Y, pointing up and down like a horse unwilling to be broken. This simple willow stick became a maniac in his hand, and when he realized it was quieting, settling its erratic behavior, Dorsey backtracked to find the point of ultimate intensity. It was there that Dorsey stacked seven rocks together in a miniature tower to mark the spot, and only then was he sure that he should gather a crew together and give the order to dig.

After he found the water, on the west side of Reichel just beyond where the terrain blended into forest, thousands of citizens were called to surround him while he stood by the thirty-foot deep hole in the ground that his crew had dug over a twenty-four-hour period. The crowd cheered him on for his success, and it was his first experience as a hero. It wouldn't be his last. Dorsey knew this heroship was real, palpable. The way the crowd in their gray uniforms pressed forward to touch him, reach their hands in his direction for his approval. The people were thirsty, and he had an answer to their frantic quest for the sustenance of life. But he would later wonder, as the years went by and his father passed the ultimate Commander role to him, at what point the adoring cheers turned to the nauseating platitudes that merely hoped for a better position in the plant or additional food and water peps to be added to their monthly allotment.

Today, after twenty years, Dorsey still believed the stick had power, gave him power, and not just for finding of water.

———

The stabs inside his ears left Dorsey with no protection against the pain. He cursed Degnan for his inability to develop a drug that would permanently keep the torment from returning. He flung his hands up to his ears and had to let the brittle willow stick that rested in his arms, like a pacifier for a young child, drop to the ground. He cupped his hands over his ears, squirming in agony on the sofa of his private quarters.

The leprex by him whimpered as it looked at its de-clawed paws, the result of a surgical action taken after Dorsey had shot the other leprex with his Z-Colt when it had been curled on the sofa, kneading its claws and perpetually digging at the couch fabric. The brain-swapper's sounds proved more than Dorsey's ears could endure. He grabbed a puncture vile from the medical bag Degnan left him earlier and jabbed it into a vein on the inside of his arm.

The pain subsided. He knew it would be short-lived, and that this vial that Degnan had provided would not, like some of the others, cause him unconsciousness. To the contrary, he was filled with a heightened awareness. For the moment.

Chapter 23
A LITTLE SOMETHING FOR THE PAIN
QUINN

Dorsey entered the strategy room on the arm of Quinn. The dress she wore fit her form, gray with burgundy accents that he had chosen. Quinn detested his bent of demanding color when it suited his whim. The hem of the mid-calf skirt met the top of her black military boots and swung with grace, as she walked him around the room for its inspection. Now a sterile surgical environment, the converted strategy room did not eliminate the noise from scuffing feet, like a debilitating drum inside his head, intolerable. The surgery could not come quick enough for him.

"Where's the ear inserts?" she whispered.

"Stopped working last night," he whispered too, and his voice sounded crotchety, matching his slow, hesitant gait. He looked like an invalid. He was. The last thing Dorsey said to her the night before, when the inserts had still allowed him clarity and focus, sickened her. His mounting arrogance became more offensive and intolerable by the moment.

"Quinn, I'm a bit of a diviner, really. When Avery comes after us—and she will—everyone under her command will be face-to-face with my fishborns. There's no victory in their future. It was prophetic, me moving the weapons stash and the launch car into Degnan's market. They'll sneak in around the perimeter of my city, thinking they'll defeat us boot-to-boot, hand-to-hand." Quinn heard the realism in his voice. Yet she hoped Shaw's dreams of an air fleet attack might still be a possibility, turning Dorsey's bragging into miscalculated imaginations. "They'll come after the government buildings," he continued. "They'll think we're unprepared. Then, when they least expect it, we'll launch from the market and wherever they've established their colonies—the ones we haven't been able to find—the fishborns will find. They'll find their mark."

"Sit for awhile," said Quinn, and she guided him over to a chair slat and helped him sit. He seemed to alternate from an intense state of awareness to a disconnected distance where his consciousness lapsed. His head bobbed down to his chest, and he was still.

Quinn knew Dorsey detested the steadiness with which she gave advice, but he appreciated her intelligent correctness. Her assurance and confidence often caused his skin to crawl, but in a high-threat moment he craved her presence by his side. In the past, Dorsey shared her same demeanor. Ten years ago, there had been a healthy competition that raced between them. Who would have the ultimate control, the stony command or the unflappable response? But the sounds in Dorsey's ears wouldn't stop, and he was both desperate to escape her and insane to keep her near. A year ago when she returned, with her own self-proclaimed subterranean status, she'd seen him from a distance, speaking to his citizens or attending the roll call at the plant. He often carried a thin branch in a Y-shape. As she grew close to him in the last weeks, she quickly perceived it was a symbol for him, an icon of what he felt was instinctual power. Dorsey's real power, Quinn observed, was his ability to convince himself that anything he wanted to be true—was true. Quinn, on the other hand, discovered her legitimate sixth sense years ago, and she had trained it well.

Decades ago, when the title of "Commander's Wife" spit in the face of Quinn, wanting to be a commander herself, and long before Avery complicated and enriched Quinn's life, the intuitive sixth sense emerged in Quinn with a gentleness, in the smallest of ways. Maybe it was on her first trip to Catalonia to meet Carles' family that the perception-beyond-normal tickled her brain in recognition. And oh, what a family they were—maybe a hundred of them, cousins, aunts, grandmas in a matched set, uncles with pasts that caused suspicion and those that did not, and all talking non-stop. Quinn's natural tendency toward the winning of arguments urged her to join in, let her voice escalate to the top of the noise meter and win the always-heated debates about the best kind of sea salt or the most volatile political candidate. However, a slight hesitation lapped at the edges of her voice, and she found herself reining in her disagreements, even the ones she knew she could win. And oddly enough, after holding all her debates at bay, when she *did* comment it seemed the minimal words she offered were never wasted in the power of persuasion.

Quinn honed her newly discovered ability, and soon others noticed her discernment went beyond the volume of the family rabble and extended to the late-night roundtables at the presidential residence. To Quinn, this sixth sense was a gift, and she delighted at passing it on to Avery, who both questioned and used it simultaneously. But the idea that Dorsey had his own version of her ability to intuit the unknown or unexpected merely because he carried a three-pronged stick around, feigning himself a diviner with a prophetic insight, that repulsed Quinn. This was an abuse of a gift meant to align with justice, and Quinn determined that Dorsey's folly and arrogance would be his downfall.

Dorsey's head popped up from the lulling position on his chest. How long had he been in that state? Minutes. Now he was suddenly aware it was just the two of them inside the room.

"Where's the workers—where's my guards?" he asked, but Quinn tightened her grip on his arm, linked with his, and quelled his anxiety.

"They haven't been here since we arrived. They're noisy. I sent them away," she said. He seemed grateful for a moment but then shook that thankfulness away, and she remembered he'd told her many times before that appreciation usually ended up as a fatal flaw.

Quinn saw him reviewing the transformed strategy room. The room attached to Dorsey's quarters had been outfitted and prepped with all the essentials for an efficient surgery. He believed he needed to be in Degnan's market instead of the hospital, for quick access to the launch car and the weapon stash. The tables, draped in sanitary white, were ready, and the instruments lay in a row with military precision, like marching troops standing at attention, awaiting the inspection of the top officer. The implements of surgery sat on a miniature dais, encased with a glass cover, like an old-fashioned cake sitting on the counter-bar of a historic diner. Quinn thought Pasha's preparations for the surgery site seemed perfect, and surely Pasha, who may be thinking herself capable of single-handedly taking down The Third, must have her own secret plans for Dorsey's operation. Perhaps it might be delaying the surgery time or finding something else wrong with Dorsey to add to the surgery schedule. Quinn sensed something was brewing.

"Does the room meet with your approval?" Quinn asked. He did not muster an answer, and Quinn watched his white-knuckled fists clamping two sections of the Y-shaped stick. He turned his back on her, and her eyes moved quickly from the rear of his head to the chipster buried under the skin of her middle finger, designed to indicate "truth" or "lie" when facing questionable situations. The glance that settled on her finger was more of a habit than a need to determine Dorsey's deceit. Quinn, one of the first to allow the chipster to be implanted by Pahsa, was the only one with the integrity chip in her finger. Now that so many people in both The Third and The 28 United had chipsters buried in various places under their skin, hers seemed archaic. The chipsters of today were advanced and multi-purposed, unlike hers invented with only one purpose. But her chipster had served her well as a subterranean for so many years in the high command of The Third. She *never* trusted Dorsey, so she had no need to use the chipster on him in her current situation, but she wondered about the loyalty of others. Without Pasha's knowledge, Quinn had scrutinized Pasha with the chipster. It revealed a consistency in Pasha to lie to Dorsey, and Quinn finally abandoned its use, convinced Pasha was operating as a true subterranean for The 28 United. Only someone with Quinn's keen perception might also notice that Pasha's dialogues with Dorsey were subtly manipulative and full of pretense. However, Quinn couldn't imagine that Avery would have entrusted an entire covert operation to the hands of a scientist urgently needed for the continued development of the Energy Concourse. Pasha wore the label of "subterranean" well, but whether she was inside The Third under the command of Avery or had gone rogue and was under her own authority was debatable

Then there was Morris, who seemed to be following Pasha and at times leading her. Was he still with The 28 United? After all, Raghill now wore the uniform of allegiance to his father, so perhaps Morris had made that commitment too, and was keeping his traitor's decision from Pasha. Yet every time Quinn used the chipster face-to-face with Morris, it flashed "truth." She trusted him.

Dorsey remained quiet until the entrance to the strategy room opened and Raghill entered, unannounced, his hair spiked like his father's, but his presence nowhere near the threat. "I've been to the launch car, father."

Dorsey stood with Quinn's assistance and took two feeble steps toward his son, "That's 'Commander.'"

"Commander. Do you want me there so I can launch the minute I hear you're out of surgery?"

Dorsey flinched, and Quinn thought it was as much at the sound of his son's voice as at the pounding in his ears. Then Dorsey uncurled his invalid demeanor. His posture assuming another three inches in height. "I want you at the surgery. We'll go together to the launch car when it's finished."

"But I will give the command?"

"On my command, you will give the command."

Raghill could not stop a slight smile from creeping onto his face, but quickly pulled it into check. "A transfer of power—"

The enfeebled man by Quinn's side transformed into the power-fiend she'd always known. He bolted forward, slapping Raghill on the cheek. "There's no transfer of anything. This is training."

"I understand," said Raghill, looking like a disciplined child.

Quinn believed Dorsey might have been disappointed that his son did not strike back. She saw in Raghill's eyes a curious expression, and she knew that after all this time, in spite of what The 28 United had done for him—saved his life more than once, given him protection, welcomed him into a family—in spite of all of that, Raghill still had hopes that he might find a father in the command of The Third.

Raghill straightened himself in an attempt at control, but as he left the newly outfitted surgery center, Quinn watched his shoulders slump just before the archway closed.

As soon as Raghill was gone, Dorsey crumbled to the ground, and the low moan arrived. The one that announced a semi-conscience state, preceding the moment all pain killers became ineffective and he became enraged by uncontrollable agony.

Quinn rushed to Dorsey's side, squatting, moving him to a position that she thought might be more comfortable. Odd, these daily facades she kept up in an effort to guard her subterranean status in hopes of finding some piece of information that might help Avery and The 28 United. A slight gag reflex knotted her throat the moment she tightly rolled her jacket and placed it under his head. She hated making this man comfortable.

In the year since she'd deserted Avery and Chapman for the greater good of The 28 United, Quinn had planned what it would be like to return to Dorsey, and in the recent weeks that she'd been close to him, he'd prodded her with jibes about her grandson. Should she have expected anything different? The nerve connected to family in Quinn's life had always been one Dorsey manipulated to evoke a crack in her control. But Dorsey, facing the rage in his ears, was vulnerable. Quinn had learned how to tame her fury at him and what he stood for, so she might wait for the precise moment she could push him in a direction she called her own. But his incessant comments drew her into an unwilling review of the last year of her life—the year she chose to leave The 28 United, abandon her daughter Avery and desert the grandson she loved, Chapman. The power of her fierce commitment to the cause she and Carles had lived for would always supersede her desire to become the missing link in a dysfunctional family she'd always loved, but never held together. If there was ever to be a matriarch in the DeTornada family it would have to be Avery, not Quinn. Nonetheless, isolation inside The Third had been merciless, and she frequently retreated to her four years of memories, during the time she ran from The Third under Avery's command. The years she was a warrior and Council member. The years she had held Chapman in her arms as a grandmother should, as she wanted to. While their lives were anything but normal, the sense of "family" had begun to take shape within her.

Yet a year ago, just when her status as subterranean seemed ancient history, and her new title of "grand-mother" appeared to be fully cemented, it began—that gnawing sensation of unrest, eating so deeply into her stomach wall that she couldn't eat. Her physical strength began to dwindle. Others noticed.

"When I look at you," said Avery, "all I see are moun-tains of bones protruding from under your skin."

Quinn brushed back the unkempt hair from Chapman's face, and shifted him from her right hip to her left. Pressure anywhere on her body hurt. There wasn't enough skin or muscle to protect her from her-self. Quinn said "Running from The Third's kept me in shape."

"No. *I'm* in shape. You're frail and sickly."

"We've always defined things differently," said Quinn

Avery picked up Chapman from Quinn and set him next to Gizzie, who promptly licked his face. Chapman licked back, wetting the hair behind Gizzie's gazelle ears. Avery stepped close to Quinn, placing one hand on each side of her face. "You're valuable to The 28 United. We need you. I need you. And so does Chapman." She turned away from Quinn to locate Chapman, but he was gone.

"I'll find him," said Quinn, as she slipped away at a slow jog through the streets of the abandoned city where they'd been settled for a few months. But even as she moved, the ache in her joints met with her discernment and together they both screamed, "Go. Leave tonight."

And now, a year later, she felt the conflict of the strength she'd gained by turning subterranean once again, fighting with the loneliness that consumed the empty pit that should have housed a heart.

Dorsey's scream yanked her from reflection. "Make it stop!" He writhed on the floor and Quinn was unable to contain him. "That noise! The rattle! Stop it!" She heard it too—of course, not to the magnitude of Dorsey's audio perceptions.

The sound vibrated. Quinn stepped back against the wall of the strategy room so she could get a visual of the entire area in an attempt to locate the sound. A metallic sheet hung over a small stand, ready to provide warmth for the patient, if needed. Under it was movement, quick and sporadic, accompanied by a disconcerting, skittering sound. Quinn raced to Dorsey's side, unholstering his Z-Colt from his shoulder and pointing it in the direction of the moving sheet. Dorsey seemed unfazed when Quinn disarmed him, and continued his shriek of pain, his own voice melding tightly with the threatening rattle.

The entrance from Dorsey's private quarters opened, and Quinn heard the voice before she saw the person. "Don't shoot the little buggars," Degnan said, then stepped through the entrance. "I've become quite fond of them." He looked at Quinn, with cool control. "And for the sake of my market, put down that weapon."

Quinn lowered Dorsey's weapon, and Degnan opened the messenger bag by his side. Racing out from under the surgical drape scurried Telson and Dart, scorpodarts with a purpose. The little monsters dashed across the floor, stopping momentarily to stare down Quinn, then they sped up Degnan's pant leg and leaped into his bag. Dorsey's scream shifted to deep hyperventilating breaths.

From the pocket on the outside of his messenger bag, Degnan withdrew a syringe-punch and a vial, popping the lid off the vial with his teeth and filling the syringe-punch with the ease of the surgeon he was. A half-smile teased the corner of Quinn's mouth. She knew what he was up to and couldn't help but admire his devious tactics. The strategy he'd cultivated to give him access to anywhere he wanted to be in his market—even in Dorsey's private quarters and the makeshift surgery center in the strategy room where Dorsey would soon regain the competence needed to fulfill his command and lead The Third.

Degnan squatted by Dorsey's side, gently placing his free hand on Dorsey's shoulder and holding the syringe aloft. Dorsey croaked a raspy objection. "Don't."

"Be sensible, man. You won't make it to the morning surgery in this kind of pain."

Dorsey grabbed Degnan's forearm with desperation. "Stay with me through the surgery." He pulled Degnan's face close to hear his whisper. "Pasha can't be trusted."

"I know that."

"I'll pay you anything you want—"

"Oh, you've paid me quite enough." Degnan placed the end of the syringe-punch on the top of Dorsey's hand and pushed, releasing a dose that made a snapping sound.

"Just make sure the surgery's a success." Before Degnan could answer, Dorsey fell into deep unconsciousness.

Quinn laughed. "Really? He trusts you?"

"Oh, I think you'll discover that the desperate find me quite endearing."

"I would never be that desperate."

"Spoken like a true DeTornada. Your daughter has the same wit—if you can call it that." He touched the back of his ear and communicated orders with someone unseen. "Send Dorsey's Elite guard in here to get him to his quarters." Degnan roamed around the strategy car, checking out the instruments and arrangements, while Quinn stood still, following him with her eyes. "How about you?" he asked her without turning. "You need a little something for the pain?"

"No," Quinn answered, not taking her eyes away from him.

"Oh, I didn't mean the kind of pain he has," said Degnan, nodding his head toward the floor where Dorsey lay. "I can offer many choices from the market that can make you forget the word 'grandmother.' Or maybe you have already."

"Not your business."

"No one's seen you in over a year. Whose side are you on?"

"There's never been a question."

"Oh, I think your daughter would say otherwise. You disappeared without an explanation. That grandkid of yours doesn't know what a grandmother is."

"Again, not your business.".

"Not true. You might be needed to calm that maniac five-year-old down, so Avery's plans can proceed. But then—if you're *with* The Third—"

"I'm not. And you're not? *With* The Third?" asked Quinn.

"After what they did to me? Hardly."

"So, you're saying you're with The 28 United now?"

"I'm saying I don't want anything to happen that would sink my market."

The entrance to the car opened and Frederick led two other Elite soldiers in. The two soldiers laid a stretcher by Dorsey's side, and one placed a medical air-lift device flush to Dorsey's temple. Without effort, the device lifted him off the floor and laid him on the stretcher. The two soldiers carried him out the other end of the car to his private quarters, leaving Frederick with Degnan and Quinn. Frederick stared at them for much longer than necessary, the entire time his finger flexed on the trigger of his weapon. "Degnan? You'll be all right here?"

"Fine."

"I could leave a guard outside," said Frederick. Degnan looked directly at Quinn.

"Might be a good idea." Frederick nodded at Degnan and left the room.

"You'll see Avery, soon?" asked Quinn.

"Only when necessary.

"And is *now* necessary?"

"I just saw her at the caves. I don't think she needs my help right now. Why? Do you have some little love message you want me send to—what's his name? Charlie? Chuck?"

"Chapman. And, no—no love message."

———

An hour or so had passed. Degnan had left, and Quinn sat in the chair facing the sofa where the guards had laid Dorsey in his unconscious state. Soon, pain would begin its tireless dig in Dorsey's ears, stirring him to cognizance. The only drug available before a surgery was short-lived, designed to give a brief respite so the body might regroup, in hopes the patient might exhibit management instead of hysteria. Quinn knew Dorsey's body would revolt against the idea of steady control and fall head-long once again into a painful spiral. Today, watching Dorsey rage at his disability and flail against the injustice of a fit commander succumbing to the one not-so-fit, Quinn faced her own sadistic muse. The swordplay of voices in her head weighed the pros of Dorsey's murder for the sake of The 28 United against the pros of her sixth-sense, cautioning her to let time stir Dorsey's command into a muddled stew that might eventually spill into chaos.

"Need quiet," he whispered, quivering in renewed consciousness and once again on the verge of pain.

"This is as quiet as it gets," Quinn said.

"I need the place—quieter."

"Where? Tell me where to take you." Quinn asked. He fell still for a second, but his fingers still convulsed, anticipating the noise of his answer.

"Get me—to the—Confinement Circle." He gulped for air. "There's a room…" He barely exhaled before whispering his command. "Get me to the Divining Room."

Chapter 24
COSMIC PULSE
QUINN

Quinn chose not to ask Dorsey any questions about where they were going. She knew another of her whispered queries would cause him more pain throughout his head and deep inside his ears, radiating to the rest of his body. At this point she just needed to console him long enough to get him into surgery in the morning. From there, she'd follow Pasha's lead. Quinn didn't even know if Pasha trusted her. Did Pasha know Quinn was once again a subterranean of her own accord? Or did Pasha, like Dorsey, think Quinn was simply resting comfortably in the arms of The Third, biding her time for when she might once again stand by Dorsey as second in command? In just a few hours Pasha would hold the Commander of The Third under a scalpel she controlled. Pasha's plan had better be a good one.

The private guard of four Elite, led by Frederick, had accompanied Dorsey and Quinn through the glides, to the exit of the market and down the streets of Ash. Now the guards surrounded Dorsey and Quinn in a rectangular human box that shielded them from any potential danger. The trip from the glide transport station to the main government buildings took less than five minutes on a back street, and by the end of that five minutes Dorsey was in a dead-man's carry over Frederick's shoulder, Quinn directly in back of them. The Elite were experts at moving noiselessly in any environment. The grassed pathway they traveled behind the buildings curved, following the circular shape of a cluster of buildings.

Quinn visualized the layout in her head. She'd lived incognito in the outskirts of the city for almost a year, a lurking phantom highly proficient in discovery, and driven by the urgency of an unnamed calling that had drawn her away from Chapman, Avery and the rest of The 28 United. After months of unearthing the schematics of underground escape routes in the Mock Courts and stumbling into Elite training facilities, Quinn had decided to position herself as close as she could to Dorsey. She'd hoped this decision to separate from Avery's command and the Council without any warning would be worth the sacrifice. The piece of information that might turn the course of the coming war in the favor of The 28 United was hiding somewhere in Ash. Quinn was propelled to find it, and daily her sixth sense, while cata-pulting her into danger and placing her at Dorsey's side, also calmed her with patient purpose that promised results. Yet none had appeared.

Everything on the backside curve of the government buildings was manicured with the same attention to detail as the front. Beautiful greenery sculpted in rounded hedges edged the pebbled paths. Without warning, their cubicle of Elite protection turned toward a building wall and ducked beyond the hedge and through a palm-coded back door that Frederick had no problem accessing. Though Quinn could not see the signs on the front side of the buildings, she had counted the structures as they passed by the perimeter and knew positively this was the Confinement Circle, a three-building grouping referred to by The 28 United as the "Mock Courts." In these buildings the prisoners of political dissent were kept, locked away and unable to express opposing thoughts to The Third. Most of the cells inside were empty. Very few chose to defy. Many times in the last year, inside the Confinement Circle, Quinn, in disguise, had sold homemade breads and jams to the guards. In each building there were six circular floors consisting of small cubicles that housed those of guilt and those of innocence. There was a reason Avery named these national structures the "Mock Courts." These prisoners would never see a judge, and a jury hadn't been called since right after *Jurbay* fell.

Dorsey's Elite protectorate had to break apart their rectangular unit and jog single file down a narrow hallway, the sounds of their footsteps mixing with the moans of Dorsey. By this time, he was almost catatonic, trapped in his pain like a pig stuck through with a spear on route to the roasting pit. *Just a few more hours*, thought Quinn. Surgery at Pasha's hands offered many options, and Quinn hoped there would be one for Dorsey that did not include recovery and healing.

Frederick activated a hologram to access a small, unassuming door off the hallway. When Quinn entered, the darkness consumed her. While she heard the muffled boot-steps of the others thudding on the floor, she focused intently, trying to establish her bearings without sight. She intuited the others advancing and felt the beat of their footsteps. Quinn progressed in sync with them. They halted. Stillness. A fading groan from Dorsey and then a deep-from-the-core sigh, ending with a steady, relaxed rhythm of breathing that she thought out of context, considering his pain level. The faintest of light appeared. She could not recognize the source. From above, she guessed. This darkness should seem oppressive but it was not. Some variations in the light source occurred— maybe a blink or a flicker or a glisten.

Quinn heard the shuffling of the guard. The light shimmering, hardly measurable, but brighter. She recognized the sporadic silhouette of a circular formation in what she perceived to be the center of the room. The glimmer intensified, this time from the sides of the room, and she definitely saw enough of Frederick to recognize how carefully he rolled Dorsey from over his shoulder to the rounded platform, the size of three sleeping mats, covered with lounging pillows. Even in the dim light she could see the rich color of the fabric, nothing gray. Instead of curling in a fetal position, Dorsey lay on his back, arms extended, outstretched from his body, as if ready for crucifixion or perhaps an expectation to be raised from the dead. He stared upward. An undeniable presence consumed the room. Every tentacle of Quinn's discernment prickled and pulsed to attention. Their Elite contingent was not alone.

And then an eruption of fire-like pinholes burst across a planetarium canopy. It seemed like she was outside, under the night sky, yet she was not.

The blast of sprinkled light and the power of the visual aura sent Quinn prone to the ground, and when she righted herself, turning upward to get her bearings, she saw a sky like no other she had ever seen. Each burst of starlight ignited several more around it until the display above her radiated. Forcing herself to locate Dorsey amid the spectacle, she found him to be fully lit in the glow of the universe, lying with his face illuminated and his eyes soaking in the shining glory of the galaxy. A look of peace consumed him, a look Quinn had not seen since she had reconnected with him in his quarters weeks ago, holding the pink ear inserts in her hands as a provisional peace offering of temporary healing.

A living, breathing planetary system encompassed them. A flicker of movement sparked across the room. Quinn's eyes adjusted to the contrast of the brilliance above and the dimness around. An officer stood and came toward them. Raghill. He held the Y-shaped stick in his hand. He placed it in Dorsey's palm and manipulated his father's fingers to curl around the divining rod. "You have the power," Raghill whispered to the Commander.

"I always have," said Dorsey, his voice almost indecipherable. There was a silence hanging there, and Quinn's normal steadiness seemed dizzy, her balance dancing with the splendor of the universe. Dorsey pronounced, "The Divining Room."

Raghill no longer spoke with the jests and jibes he traded with Morris and Annalynn when they were children, but his voice stung with logic and touted the teachings of an unfamiliar father.

"It is here we find ways to redirect the universe so it does not redirect us," he said. It would take faith far beyond what Quinn possessed to believe Raghill or Dorsey could control anything above. There had been no control of *Jurbay*. *Jurbay* had carved up their world with its own domination, and still its memory lurked, like an unforgotten nightmare intruding into daylight hours.

Each minute, the dome of darkness triggered alternate splatters of light even more stunning than the ones before. As the brightness increased, Quinn became aware of a hologram control station at the edge of the room, and she saw Raghill sit in a chair slat, placing his hands within the hologram. Dorsey thrust his arms high above his body, and while he mimed movement in the air, Raghill responded in a puppet-like fashion, directing the actions of the night sky. But the night sky was no hologram. Did she detect a breeze from the north or was this view of the sky so authentic she imagined it? This was not a duplicate of planetary pathways and patterns of stars or a record of waxing and waning moons. This was the real-time universe.

Raghill manipulated the interior of the hologram and zoomed into close-ups of the asteroids hanging in the vicinity of the sun. He then swung around behind the sun for a one hundred eighty-degree close-up of its backyard, where meteorites played in stunning rotation.

Frederick settled on one knee, ready to spring to his feet if needed, and the other three guards followed his lead, like ordinary men hoping to be knighted. For these highly-trained Elite, the fireworks of splendor seemed to edge through their frozen, nondescript faces, bringing cracks of momentary humanity and inquisitive pleasure to their eyes. Quinn saw the slightest of smiles on all of their lips, and the younger one's hand, that rested on his knee, flexed upward in praise of an unexpected starburst, then returned to his knee, checked into submission. And Quinn felt they all breathed, even Dorsey, with a rhythm in unison guided by a cosmic pulse that she thought breathtaking and frightening all at once.

Raghill used his fingers to alter the hologram controls, and they disappeared, winking the dynamic performance into darkness. Dorsey spoke, and Quinn found his voice, which was previously a whisper of weakness, now mesmerizing, alluring. He said, "Quasars loom with massive intensity projecting energy throughout celestial ceilings." Was he rambling or spouting scientific commentary? "They hold open their unmeasurable black holes, like a waiting womb, the birthplace of an unborn galaxy." Quinn heard no pain in his voice.

Every sensory nerve within her shouted, "Caution. Danger. Alert." And while she longed for Raghill to lift his hand again, manipulating the shots of space to capture close-ups and wide angles of the iridescent jewels in the ever-changing cosmos, the unrest of the hunt inside her called her to heightened consciousness. She'd let down her guard a bit, and now she forced herself to raise it.

Dorsey's voice once again shriveled into the invalid ramblings she'd heard before they entered the Divining Room. It seemed the calm and strength he'd exhibited laying on his dais was fleeting, and the pain meds from Degnan were barely hanging on.

She sat with the others in the darkness, trying to categorize every iota of information she'd obtained through her year inside The Third. No leads had paid off yet.

Nothing earthshaking to provide solid intel that might help in The Third's defeat. In the hours remaining before the morning surgery, would Dorsey keep them here? When would they return to the surgery center so carefully set up by Pasha? And what about this real-time galaxy? Was it entertainment for Dorsey to divert his focus from his ears and reiterate the power he felt he held as a diviner? Or was this access to the heavens part of some ultimate plan beyond the market and the fishborns to bring down The 28 United? Even as she forced herself to analyze, she felt it, constant—the palpitating cosmic pulse. And her sixth sense said, "Listen."

Chapter 25
FINAL SUNRISE
AVERY

From a distance, flying with Checkmate in his balloon-tech, I see the sixteen eclectic aircraft hangars emptied and abandoned in the field next to the wind orchards of the Energy Concourse. Shaw has assembled his fleet at the far end of the field, in position for takeoff. The gigantic thin-skin covering of the Concourse has been peeled back, revealing the world beyond—the route to Ash—where the offensive attack will begin.

Checkmate lands his b-tech smoothly as always. While he may be a lousy conversationalist, he's an excellent pilot. The noise from various engines, in the middle of testing and fine-tuning, deafens. I touch the minis-cule button behind my left ear, activating the ear-seals that edit out part of the sound. McGinty glances up from the rear of a cargo plane, sprinting toward me. The wind from the rotors of the only float car in the fleet whip his pants, pressing them so tightly to his body they look like skin.

His hand touches my ear, and I hear him say through the ear-seals, "Zoom."

"Zoom," I respond with a quick smile, using the word Annalynn had coined as an eight-year-old kid, living in the same housing unit with McGinty, Shaw and me. Annalynn lived down the hall, and I thought back to the tenderness McGinty showed her, so very out of context for our lives on the edge. While we joked with her and welcomed her into our limited social life, providing the only dysfunctional family scenario we knew how to give, she wheedled her way into our hearts as well. It's true that we provided the human contact she needed when the pocket-watch-caretakers only gave her food peps, water and a curfew, but she gave us what we needed, too. A child who, in spite of the unemotional, restricted life of the children in The Third, retained a sense of humor and exuberance for life that none could squelch. I try to silence the memories of all the laughing we did at clichés she used in everyday conversations, but the injustice of her being undercover at thirteen inside The Third stirs my fury at Pasha. And the image that presses against every part of my mind is the one of three kids following Dr. Pasha Lutnik blindly into Dorsey's lair.

I hear McGinty through the ear seals, but the roar of the engines still permeates the background. We are not alone with our words. All pilots, copilots and soldiers are linked when ear-seals are used, but there is a connection between McGinty and me that goes beyond the words of war. He leads the way to a vast cargo plane. Through the window I see Shaw, tipping his helmet at me. He says through the seals, "Commander. Told you I'd have a fleet someday."

"Never doubted it," I said, and I see him smirking. We both know he's about to take off and accomplish what he's never lost sight of in the last five years of preparation to take down The Third.

I follow McGinty up the enormous entry plank at the base of the plane. The cargo hold is lined on each side with seats completely filled with our warriors—men and women well-trained and on the ready. It's powerfully breathtaking to see them all suited up in an assortment of military gear, scrounged with nothing matching, assembled from a variety of sources over the past years. I notice right away that, although we don't have uniforms, there is something very uniform about these loyal ones and what they wear. On their left shoulders, just above the heart, is sewn the patch. The 28 United patch. A duplicate of the one many of us now have tatted in the same position on our skin. And once again I remember the first time I saw the images of this patch, hung by the artists of Red Grove and hanging two stories high in a dominant statement that we are all one as The 28 United. I command that memory away, assuring my game face stays intact and does not give way to sentimentality. These two hundred men and women are all watching me. Eyes on my face, unwavering in their commitment. I pause for a couple seconds and take it all in, then begin my walk to the front of the plane. Just before I pass where they are seated, they stand, one from each side of the plane, like a tsunami wave amassing power before its landfall, they roll to attention. No salutes required like a century ago, just an incredible exchange of respect.

As McGinty and I reach the front of the plane, we sit in the two remaining empty seats by the bulkhead that separate the pilot from the passengers. On the floor of the cargo plane, I tap my commander's boot in a recurring message of nerves. On one side of me sits the most competent weapons expert in what's left of the world. A man who steams up a room when he dances the rhumba. The man I love. On the other side of me stands the presence of my father. I hear him say, *Avery, you are on the ready. Go.* And this time I don't argue with him. But missing from the empty spot on my lap is the child I long to hold. I try to convince myself that the five-year-old Chapman will be cared for by Clef and compassionate workers, and that the other Chapman, the one arising much more frequently now, will care for himself. Is he running through the forest trying to locate and chase down Gizzie? Or is he spinning in a circle, setting a record for time without breath? As much as I've had some success as a commander, I'm not sure if I've had any as a mother. A vice in my stomach squeezes a confusing mixture of anxiety and courage that feels anything but stable, anything but strong.

We lift off the ground, no ancient runways needed anymore, and I try to imagine the hundreds of wind blocks and solar cells loaded on the outside slats of this aircraft. Hundreds. I know there are no refuels waiting for us in Ash, only trained Elite soldiers of The Third, always on the ready. Waiting. Thirty-one cars of fishborns, noses planted on the targets, and clusters of flying-fishborns anxious to release Raben-faced GEBs that may meet our Fleet of Zooms with a vengeance.

———

We fly low in the sky. Our cargo plane originally flew heavy equipment, so our load of soldiers utilizes minimal fuel. The moon shines like a phosphorescent invitation to travel her direction and not toward combat. I'd like to imagine ways to do that, but Ash is approaching on the horizon. In the first breath of dawn, the east end of Erie appears a grayish green, and I think of all the sunrises that mark the timeline of my life.

When I was six years old, before *Jurbay* had set its mark on our civilization, we camped in the Redwood forest on the Pacific coast. I could never sleep. While other children rested in their family's rented trailer pods, exhausted from hiking adventures, my father and mother hiked across a footbridge, me on my dad's back, to the otherworldly grove of twenty-five-hundred-year-old monster trees. This grove provided an anonymous haven for the secret meetings of the emerging 28 United. In the still dark of the early morning hours, my luminary light stick traced the burned-out holes of tree trunks struck by lightning. I crawled inside the gigantic cavities, my mind creating an imaginary fighter plane or a transport flying to a distant planet. All the while, Carles' and Quinn's voices nearby, spinning plans with allies that I tucked away somewhere in my memory, to be recalled when I was older. Their language, rolled around the strategies of war, wanders back, confronting me right now. I watched those Redwood dawns without the benefit of sleep, my body desperate for rest, my child's mind already plotting a return trip across the footbridge.

And when I was seven, to the east of the New Coastline, I stayed up to see a sunrise, but *Jurbay's* residue of smoke and ash and putrid smells confined me to an inside window, staring out in hopes I'd see our sunken continent rise again someday.

By fifteen years old, Pasha resided permanently in our home, her sleeping chamber next to mine. In those days, I lived for the sunrise. While she would sleep, exhausted from days of setting up challenges only she could meet, I'd sneak out to greet the morning. By this time the sun had found its way past the darkness of *Jurbay*.

And suddenly I was twenty-two. Daybreak, in the boots of a hesitant and inexperienced commander, I awoke each day hoping to find clarity, a strategy, a way to avoid decisions that were unavoidable. And half a year later, cooped up in a horseshoe tunnel underneath Reichel, with my three closest friends, the defunct doctor—Degnan and a few bottles of Hennessey, I saw no sunrises for months.

Twenty-seven: I held Chapman in my arms for so many sunrises in our quarters at the zoo, watching the emerging daylight with a story on our lips. I always knew how the story began. Now, I fear how it will end.

Chapter 26
SCALPEL PLEASE PASHA

A contingent of Elite marched into the Divining Room, led by Pasha, with Morris and Annalynn close behind. None were able to hide their awe as they looked up at the real-time display of the throbbing, one hundred and eighty-degree universe. Each man and woman in the group carried containers of supplies to outfit the room for Dorsey's surgery. Pasha had not seen this room before. She felt an ilk rise within when she saw Quinn standing by Raghill, who sat deeply involved with some sort of work at a hologram station to the side of the room. How ironic that Quinn, who'd abandoned her connection to The 28 United for a distant chance of acquiring a position of power in The Third, should be privy to this hidden space, when it was Pasha making the sacrifice to bring The Third down. Quinn turned to acknowledge

Pasha, but she intentionally moved away without meeting Quinn's eyes. Pasha said, "We already set up this surgery center once. This is a waste of time."

"Schedule stays the same," the frail voice of Dorsey rasped. "Peaceful here." *Peaceful?* Pasha thought, *More irony.* It was only then that Pasha's eyes adjusted to the light in the room and she became aware of Dorsey, lying face up on a dais at the center of the room. The ridiculous divining rod, that so frequently accompanied him now, lay to his side. There seemed to be a stillness in Dorsey's tortured being. He looked more like himself, his face lit by the glow of the heavens. But it was short-lived, and she watched pain clutch Dorsey by the hand and agony return him to the fetal position that had become so common to this Commander. Even his dowsing stick and the splendor of the cosmos could not pacify his misery.

Pasha heard his low moans spilling into the room. It prompted her memories (she wished she had more time to enjoy them) of Jett as a baby and his fussy digestive system that required the occasional use of the archaic pacifier for comfort and distraction. It was Pasha's memories of Jett and Beckett and Maven that momentarily appeased her desire to pursue Dorsey's end at this very moment, not waiting for the air attack. Pasha wanted Time to captain a reunion journey between her and the family she'd found. No time—until the final page was placed in the history books of the labyrinth. A page captioned: *Ash Defeated. 28 United Reigns.* She knew the role she played in this page of history. She must finish it.

With a seemingly calm reserve, Pasha directed the re-creation of the surgery center that had been disassembled from the strategy car in the market. She said to Morris and Annalynn, "Surgery table here." She pointed, and her finger, on its way back to a relaxed position at her side, joined the others on her hand, rolling into a fist and making its way to her skull. But before the anxiety rub began, Annalynn yanked Pasha's fist away from her head.

Annalynn said in a most confidential way, directly into Pasha's ear, "Let's not reveal our annoying neurotic mannerisms at the exact moment the Commander of The Third's fate is in your hands."

Pasha's entire body tightened, like one big muscle preparing to retaliate against Annalynn. Pasha whispered, "Your only job is to make sure you have access to the roof." She stared at Annalynn, who was immoveable and doing her best mirror-image-imitation of the surgeon in charge.

Annalynn rubbed her own scalp with her knuckles, mocking, and said with her irritating brand of sarcasm, "Scalpel, please," holding out her palm as the surgeons used to do when expecting their nurses to provide the right surgical tool.

"Out," Pasha shouted, and when Dorsey responded with a more intense groan, she pulled her volume down and said again. "Out. Now. Roof. You and Morris take the lab coat packages by the door with you. You know what to do." In the darkened environment, with the pageantry of the galaxy above, and the surgery items being carted in and arranged, no one noticed two teenagers carrying boxes out the door. Pasha thought Morris was probably more suited to assist her in the surgery instead of littering the roof with white lab coats. However, inside Pasha there was a hope that if Morris and Annalynn were up there on the roof and saw the Fleet of Zooms approaching, maybe they could get off the building before the attack. Was there a way Pasha could get herself out of there and leave Dorsey and Raghill in the building? She'd think of something. Maybe not.

Annalynn followed the order, but Pasha still raged, acutely aware that Annalynn had once again recognized Pasha's inability to be consistent in her subterranean behavior. For a moment, Maven's laughter-filled eyes flashed before her, and she regrouped her composure. Anything she could do to delay Dorsey on the surgery table—take his command away for as long as possible— let The 28 United strike in a most unexpected way—that responsibility was on her and her alone. No one must suspect this surgery was taking longer than expected. Everything must seem legit. Pasha could feel her confidence puffing up within her. Of course she could do this. She'd camouflaged the Red Grove command center in the thin-skin she alone had created. She'd built an Energy Concourse and mined solar, wind and chicken poo for flying an attack fleet. She'd reversed *locasa*. This is what she came for, and this is what she'd do.

In under an hour, the team had the surgery center assembled and sanitized, and by that time Dorsey's moans had turned to angry, desperate commands. "Start the surgery now." He looked pitiful, draped in sterile garb, lying on the surgery slab. Yet in the pristine presence of the makeshift surgery center, his stick lay beside him, like kindling ready to start a campfire, waiting for the flame to begin the burn.

Pasha reached for the button that controlled the release of the anesthetic, but her hand was intercepted by a man's hand and she instantly sensed who it was. She faced Degnan, and he whispered underneath the volume of Dorsey's cries, "Need an assistant?" She would never see him as an ally, but she did know him as someone who did not support The Third, and he might be the vital element that could facilitate her plan, working in these final hours before the attack.

"Can you keep that kid and the traitor with him out of my way?" Pasha spoke quietly and indicated Raghill and Quinn who were still located by the hologram center, but now stood, craning their necks to see every detail of the surgery.

"Oh, I can run an interception for the most difficult of—"

"Save it. Sterilize yourself—if that's possible—and get ready to assist." She lifted her finger once again toward the anesthetic, but Dorsey's hoarse voice, erratic with agony, commanded her.

"No anesthetic." He said it like a curse hurled directly at Pasha, and panic burst into her shrouded plans. She opened her mouth to respond, but Raghill raced toward her.

"I won't see him suffer," he said, staring into Pasha's eyes with a strength she was unaccustomed to. Dorsey rolled to his side with a violent push, but before he could interrupt Pasha's reach to the anesthetic pump, she had pushed the button and administered the dose that knocked Dorsey out immediately. She hoped Raghill hadn't heard her sigh in relief. She saw him try to control the smile sneaking around the edges of his mouth as he grabbed his father's divining rod and swiftly took his place by the hologram station.

Degnan slipped into the sterile drape held by Frederick. He spoke to Frederick. "Get everyone out of here. Dr. Lutnik's going to need complete silence and focus. Guard the door from the outside." Pasha wondered if Degnan knew her plan. Never. He would never expect this kind of boldness, but she knew he would not be surprised if her plan ended in stupidity. It wouldn't.

Degnan motioned Raghill toward the door, but he resisted and said, "No way. I stay with the Commander." His hand moved to the Z-Colt on his shoulder, and while Degnan seemed to present an attitude of submission to Raghill, Pasha knew Degnan always had weapons of his own, and thought she saw a faint movement in Degnan's messenger bag that sat propped on a chair slat by the wall. Sometimes scorpodarts found it difficult to remain still, even when trained by the most experienced in brain-swapper technology.

Quinn stood fast by Raghill. "I won't be leaving either." *Not going to argue with that*, thought Pasha, but she would keep eyes on Quinn. She was an uncertain equation in the coming surgery and an untrusted element in the attack Pasha knew was eminent. Quinn, at the moment, stood seemingly disconnected from the action that surrounded her, very uncharacteristic of this woman who years ago had served as second in command of The Third, holding a subterranean status so important to The 28 United. She stared, transfixed, at the universe displayed above them all. For now, the cosmos would babysit her until the Fleet of Zooms released their surprises and consumed Quinn's attention.

Degnan opened a small hologram control toward the foot of the surgery table. He activated the surgery lights, and the white glare forced Pasha to remember why she had come, taken this risk. Avery was not moving fast enough to take down The Third. They needed to fall. This was the exact position Pasha had always thought she'd put herself in, once she'd decided to go inside The Third. *So, you wanted your ears fixed, did you?*

Pasha thought as she prepped herself mentally for the steps to come. *A most reasonable request.* And she had absolutely no desire, no impulse and no reflex to rub her knuckles across her skull.

Forty minutes into the surgery, Pasha and Degnan worked in sync to accomplish the promised results for Dorsey's hyperacusis. Raghill busied himself at the hologram center, mumbling "Scale in, scale out" as he manipulated the controls of the firmament above. Pasha had forced herself during the surgery to occasionally glance up and see past the glare of the surgery lights to the dimness of the surrounding room. Raghill occasionally snickered, reciting the numbers of asteroids that hovered behind the sun. He chanted, "Brown dwarf versus white. Fail, brown dwarf, fail." Pasha found him strange, childlike, consumed with entertainment, some game he'd invented, yet bent on assuming the role of Commander. All the while he held tight to his father's divining stick, clutched in his left hand.

Quinn inched ever closer to the perimeter of white light encircling the surgeons' area, yet she kept her distance just outside the sterile circle. Pasha glanced at her momentarily and was startled by the intense look she received back. An eeriness hovered around Quinn, and it seemed she was transforming before Pasha's eyes from a traitor and Dorsey's confidant to a warrior of confidence and power. Pasha wished the com behind her ear, that five years ago allowed her to communicate only through thoughts to Avery, could be hooked up right now between her and Quinn. For Pasha knew Quinn was trying to tell her something with her eyes.

Suddenly Quinn turned her glare from Pasha upwards to the expanse above. Pasha followed Quinn's gaze and fixed on what she knew Quinn wanted her to see. It was impossible for Pasha to tell if it was Quinn who stopped breathing or if Pasha herself was unable to take a breath for the moments that followed. She hesitated in the operation procedures. Her hands quivered to the point no progress could be made. Ever so slowly she reached across to Degnan's arm and clutched it so tightly she was sure she interrupted the beat of his pulse. Degnan, looking first at Pasha, then at Quinn, then upward and back at Pasha, took her hand from his arm with a steadiness. An understanding passed between the two. Pasha knew he would not impede any unexpected action she might take.

"Quinn, I could use your help," Pasha said with unflappable reserve. Raghill glanced over, but seemed intent on watching the universe divulge its secrets. Quinn stepped into the halo of white light at the head of the surgery slat. She was breathing again, rapidly this time, and while Pasha and Degnan held their hands above Dorsey, in surgery position, no operating was transpiring. Their eyes, so wide in search of answers, while they waited for Quinn to speak.

Quinn's voice, dry, like a wisp of wind unable to gust on the hottest of summer days, resonated just above a whisper. "We can see everything that happens up there," she said and nodded her head in the direction of the real-time cosmos images. "You can't let Avery take this building down. We're going to need it."

Both Pasha and Degnan continued the surgical procedure, Pasha unwilling to let the unexpected divert her from her goal. Quinn repeated, "The 28 United can't take this building down."

"Then someone needs to get to the roof and get rid of those lab coats," whispered Pasha.

"Shut up!" yelled Raghill. He pushed away from the hologram station and ran toward the surgery slat, but was stopped abruptly by Quinn who stepped in his way.

"It's fine," she said and ushered Raghill back to the spot of his previous entertainment. But while her hand stayed reassuringly on his shoulder, her head turned back to Pasha and Degnan with what Pasha deemed to be a desperate plea, punctuating their collective need to stop the Fleet of Zooms. Plans had changed. Pasha looked toward the expanse of stars above, collected herself and allowed the laser scalpel to hover around Dorsey's right ear.

———

Degnan ran the magnetic sweat-collector across Pasha's brow. Never could she remember sweating so profusely. Her leg, the one that had developed a limp since she reversed *locasa*, had cramped an hour ago. She stepped back from the surgery slat, letting her sterile drape fall to the floor and whisking off her surgery cap, dropping it as well. Raghill dozed in his chair slat, his head collapsed on his arms. "I'm finished," she said.

Raghill jerked awake. Taking no time to recover from his nap, he staggered to the head of the surgery slat directly above his father who was half conscious from the short-lived anesthetic. "It's done?" he asked Pasha.

"Yes," she answered and dreaded another question. She heard a distant hum and a slight vibration under her feet. The faces of Maven and her kids flashed repeatedly in her mind.

"You fixed his ears?"

"No." Pasha paused with a stillness, only her lips moved. "He has no ears." All Pasha could think about was the rising noise that turned the vibration she felt into the distinguishable engines of aircraft. Her choice was not Dorsey's death but the perpetual pain he would always feel from having his ears amputated. Sentenced to silence and holding a dried-up, Y-shaped stick. A perfect plan, really. This would cause intense confusion. The death of Dorsey would have made Raghill Commander. Missing ears posed the question: Who's in charge now?

Raghill screamed: "He has no ears!" Dorsey's eyes blinked open, and he rose erratically from the table in a flailing attempt to grab Pasha, but she stepped away and let him fall on the floor. As Dorsey fell, Raghill drew his Z-Colt and, without a flinch, aimed at Pasha's head.

With a lightening kick, Quinn brought her boot up under Raghill's chin, disarming him and securing the weapon. The Divining Room rattled as the hum Pasha heard seconds ago was now a steady buzz, like the bees of a hundred hornets' nets had been released. The Fleet of Zooms arrived.

"Guards! Guards!" Raghill called for help, but none came.

"You can't fight an air attack with fishborns," mocked Degnan.

"You think this attack by air is a surprise?" Raghill smirked. "Surprise on you." He rushed to cradle Dorsey in his arms, but the Commander stumbled away, tearing at the bandages that bound his ears. The covering on his left ear, now dangling, blood-soaked and torn, exposed a line of laser-placed elastic, woven into the skin and sealing shut the hole where there used to be an ear. Raghill stood under the dome of planetary brilliance, fighting to control his anger and dredge up some ability to show management in a crisis, but instead the childlike fear from a long-ago-rescued library boy took over.

Degnan said, "I've got security so tight on your weapon's command car in the market that you'll never launch those fishborns."

Raghill spoke sporadically, like a child on a playground fighting to be king of the mountain, "You think I'm stupid and inexperienced in command?" He laughed in a way Pasha had never heard before. "We have our own version of subterraneans here, Degnan. They're called 'Mirandas.'"

Pasha saw a crack in Degnan's normally flawless composure, and then he raced for the exit, touching the activation button behind his ear, communicating with his guard in the market. "Purge the launch car. Purge the launch car." He turned to Pasha and yelled, "My guards say the the Elites got off one fishborn on the ground and a couple dozen in the air."

Pasha threw a quick look back at Quinn while running to the exit. "You got this?" she asked.

Quinn tightened her grip on Raghill's arm and swung Raghill's Z-Colt to include covering Dorsey and said, "Oh, I got this."

Raghill screamed at Degnan, though he was long out of sight, "You wanna watch this finale? Be my guest."

Pasha heard bombs close by, and the vision of white lab coats scattered on a roof, begging for attack, drew Pasha's fists to her skull. As she ran for the roof her knuckles bore into her head, calling forth little rivers of anxious blood.

Chapter 27
BIRD'S EYE VIEW
AVERY

My reflection on the past blurs, the edges diffusing then fading to total darkness. I open my eyes, hoping for more memories, more mornings, yet I realize it is *this* moment and *this* morning I must focus on. I thrust my hand into the controls of the hologram on the bulkhead of our cargo plane. It grants me enough light for a bird's-eye view of the surface of Erie. I am aware that suspended below hangs the Dark Market, like a weightless line of butcher shop display cases, waiting for consumers to point at their selections. Degnan's creation. Miles and miles of underwater cars, containing an offering of excess pleasure and weapon cars ready to launch more devastation on the people and country I love. Yet, juxtaposed and deftly designed in the same market are the technological miracles of healing and options for children to walk again or have an arm where there was never one before. Destruction and redemption cannot hold hands. Degnan can't have it both ways. Yet, he has entwined the two and only he can sever their connection. Enough, enough.

Dawn draws the curtain of darkness back enough to see the outline of the rooftops of Ash. We are flying low. As planned, white lab coats dot the tops of designated buildings, and I know the subterraneans have just proven their worth to anyone who doubted that a small group of men and women might have a powerful impact. Shaw's strategy unfolds on schedule, and the float car from behind our cargo plane passes us, steadying itself above the roof of the first marked building, dropping its explosives and severing the top stories off the structure, like a decapitation from a terrorist of the past. The float car ascends momentarily then banks toward the hillside hollers further north where the pilot will land and wait for our remaining aircraft to hit their targets and assemble in the hollers. We then convert to the ground assault.

Next in line to attack is a long, sleek, needlelike aircraft, able to carry only the pilot and the bombardier. They hit their mark too, but this building is leveled, transforming a steel structure into smoldering rubble. I try not to think of the body count inside the mess below and promise to mourn them later, at the same moment I celebrate the children's lives that Checkmate rescued just hours earlier.

It is our turn to attack, and suddenly the risk of our potential annihilation becomes more personal than ever before. What is ripped away at this moment from Ash and Dorsey will also yield a collateral damage list of innocents, and it will all be directly tied to *my* hands. No amount of the sixth sense can chase away that terrifying realization. No common sense, no logic, no battle plans, no rules of necessity and no survivor's mentality can turn off the prophetic remorse that consumes me. And I long for a negotiation table that works. When the lion, like Morris would say, lies down with the lamb, and the word "enemy" becomes a fantasy.

I see McGinty stand, his hand moving mine aside from the hologram, and taking the control. From the underside of the cargo plane I feel the shake of the eyelid-like covers peeling back, exposing the explosives ready for the trigger.

A violent smack rams the starboard side of our cargo hold. The murmurings of soldiers from the aft of the aircraft float forward, showing cracks in their courageous exteriors for only the moment of surprise. I search for the source of the attack out the window, and a miniature fishborn saddles up beside our plane, ridden by an enormous GEB like the one I'd come face-to-face with in the weapons car. Its pilot's face, hidden in a protective guard on the front of its helmet, seems, even through I cannot see through the covering, to be staring at me. These fishborns are small, no longer than six feet, compact, and within five seconds our plane is encircled by a dozen or more, all piloted by the GEB duplicates.

The fishborns fly dangerously close, and I can see five or six flirting with the aircraft, zinging right up to the windows, using the tips of their wings to scratch and mar the glass, then dipping away. My breaths quicken and sweat saturates my body. I think about slowing my inhales and stabilizing my exhales, but the plane shakes as another half dozen GEBs dive at the windows on the opposite side of the plane. They are playing with us.

McGinty yells at Shaw, "Set this thing down before they crash us."

I stand, calling to the front and holding on to the bulkhead, "Drop the explosives on our target first. There's not enough fuel to come back. Dorsey or some of his top military are in that building—the Confinement Circle—the Mock Courts. How far?"

"There!" points Shaw, directing the nose of the plane toward the Confinement Circle and increasing our speed.

"Wait! On the roof. See it?" I ask and press closer to the window through which I see Annalynn and Morris waving at us wildly while Pasha, in a sea of white lab coats, tries frantically to collect them all. Their faces upturned, arms flailing and heads shaking hysterically "no." "Are they trying to stop us from dropping the explosives?"

"Looks like it," says McGinty.

"We're running out of fuel," says Shaw. "We either drop our load now, or we don't drop it at all."

I say, "Now would be the time for Pasha's experimental poo-balls to kick in and fuel this thing so we can land it."

"Yeah, well, it was an experiment," says Shaw, and the plane is shaking like a pneumonic cough, vibrating the floor of the aircraft.

"Experiment failed," says McGinty. "Fire now? Or get to the hollars? Your call."

"Just head to the hollers," I say. "Land it there. Pasha's got to have a reason for calling off this attack."

"And waste the payload?" asks Shaw. "No way—" But before our argument finds an end, and I claim rank over friendship, our sightlines are obstructed by the flying-fishborns, lining up before the forward section of our plane. From the front, the GEBs look like the rodeo riders of the past, the fishborns their steeds and the steerage controls their reins.

The fishborns are flying full force, and, just feet before colliding with us, they abruptly stop. Even though we advance, they appear to be in a holding pattern. In unison, these GEB pilots use their left hands and lift their helmet masks so that the Raben-faces are revealed simultaneously. It is then I realize I have never been far from Dorsey's mind. Their eyes hone in through the window on me. Adrenaline pumps, but my heart rate steadies, thanks to the Elite training I regained over the last half a decade. McGinty moves in a slow-motion-steadiness, strapping himself into the empty copilot seat.

I cinch myself to the bulkhead and draw my SE454 from my back across my shoulder into firing position. I activate the com at the back of my ear. "SE454s," I say with conviction, and I don't need to look over my shoulder to see the men and women in the mismatched uniforms of The 28 United drawing their weapons in synchronized perfection. I know they have my back. Then one GEB from the herd of fishborns drops its holding pattern, letting go of the top of its fishborn, flinging itself out and splattering against the side window in front of McGinty. Then, grabbing tight to the ridge around the window of our cargo plane, it bashes its feet through the window. A horrific splintering apart of the glass, like the magnified sound of my father's ax, splitting wood at a campfire, only louder—much louder.

Flying shards cover the pilot's cockpit, but shattering glass and the spinning plane do not stop Shaw from trying to gain control of the descending spiral. McGinty and I fire over and over at the GEB as it enters the window. The SE454's microwave bursts attach to the face and body of the GEB, incinerating it, the air assimilating its ashes.

The force of the downward acceleration begins the dismantling of the plane, sending crushing pressure through the aircraft, through me. I'm sure my skin will rip away from my bones. Two more GEBs hang on the open space where the plane's window used to be. All the fragments of glass have been shaken away. These GEBs too have let go of their fishborns, which will crash below, and I realize these GEBs have been programmed to kill me first above everything else, even above using the explosives inside their fishborns to take our plane down.

I'm out of ammunition. McGinty fires his last into the head of one GEB as the other clings to the window, perched to spring at McGinty. There is so much quaking of the aircraft that I struggle as I lean forward and release the 10-inch blade from Shaw's waist. The knife comes free in my hand, and I hold on with the strength Pasha gave us all through her ridiculous exercises for palm strength, which now don't seem so ridiculous. The GEB takes a leap in the window, lurching and landing on top of McGinty. I simultaneously release my attachment to the bulkhead, falling knife first on the back of the GEB. McGinty throws his arms around the dead GEB from the underside as it inches closer to falling out the window, and I embrace the thing from above, our bear hugs the only way I'm going to stay in this plane until it lands, if it lands. This sandwiched GEB, my lifeline to the aircraft and to McGinty, makes me the subject of a tug-of-war between accelerating speed and the man I love.

We are in a freefall of tonnage, racing toward the earth, metal parts flinging through the universe. I hear the shouted prayers of soldiers, ascending through the rattling, disassembling cargo plane.

"We're gonna hit," yells Shaw. I feel the plane rolling to its side in Shaw's direction, and then a slam so powerful it renders the cargo beast still. At the same time, I have been wrenched away from McGinty. My eyes close, and I am hurtling through the darkness.

———

I've smelled it before in Elite training. The nauseating odor of fire on metal so hot it liquefies, mixed with the flesh of human beings so charred I do not want to open my eyes. I am being carried, a constant jostling of my body. Pain. All-over pain. A blanket of ache. Stabs escalating down my hamstring and prodding away at my knee. "Commander," someone shouts at me, urgent. His voice is close to my ear. Carried. "Commander." This time he speaks in a comforting tone.

My eyes pop open to the bloodied face of a 28 United soldier, missing a cheek and his clothing torn past recognition. I find a spot of focus and try to settle the spinning in my stomach, the pounding in my head. Dawn still hangs at the edge of morning, but there is light enough to read the damage.

All vegetation is burnt black or powdered with ash. Outcrops of flames fuel hotspots over the vast crash sight. I breathe a sigh of thanksgiving that Checkmate rescued the children from these hollers earlier. I look into my rescuer's eyes, and I should say "thank you" but I can only say, "McGinty." The soldier's eyes speak to me, and I follow their direction to the crumpled plane, I throw myself from his arms and run toward the jumbled mass of metal. Stumbling over a muddle of soldiers' legs, twisted weapons, bloodied parts, unrecognizable. And heads. There are some heads. I do not stop to honor their sacrifice or identify their corpses.

The ground is slippery, making it difficult to progress with any steadiness. When I tumble down to one knee I recognize the "sticky" as red. Blood. The air, so heavy with wet blood it works its way into my taste buds, sickening sweet and tinny. I want to vomit it away, but I press forward to the plane. Without warning, it looms above me, staring me down. The entire left side is flattened. Shaw rolled it before we hit, allowing his side to absorb the biggest impact.

From the scorched frame of the remaining right side of the aircraft I see movement, life. A form backs its way out of what used to be a door, carrying a heap of something. It is a man in pursuit of recovery, not rescue. Standing, he cannot negotiate the steep decline to the ground of the upturned side of the plane, so he lays his body down, with what's left of the soldier on top of him in his arms, and slides to meet the ground. I want to run to the living form, but I can only move in slow motion, trancelike, not wanting to see who each one might be.

My legs find strength from somewhere propelling me to reach them, in spite of the throbbing pain throughout my entire body.

Twelve feet from the soldiers, the grit of ash coating the inside my mouth, I recognize the man who carries the other. It is McGinty. He holds the form of what used to be a man, and who I know now was once our Shaw. McGinty's face turns up to the smoke-black sky, and he wails like a wounded wolf. He knows there is no justice, only regret. Right before I reach them, my foot tangles with a mess on the ground. A GEB quite dead in the mix of our soldiers. I trip, catching myself, regaining my balance, but not before I see the torn-up face of a Raben-GEB, staring blankly up at me.

Shaw lies in McGinty's lap. McGinty lifts his arms to me. I fall in his dirty embrace, then push away, and place my hands as gently as I can on the seared face of my fallen comrade, Shaw, one of my dearest friends. My cry to the heavens remains within, and I force myself to a standing position, using McGinty's shoulder for support. I say, "You do what you need to for Shaw. I'm headed to the Confinement Circle." McGinty doesn't say a word.

As I run in the direction of Ash, I shout to those on the crash site, "If you can walk, follow me." The further I get away from the plane, the more the ground begins to breathe with whatever life is left in broken soldiers. Some move to their feet, slowly, and begin to jog next to me, their gait like mine, irregular and finding a new pace to accommodate their wounds. Other soldiers hold each other up, and two become the strength of one and that's enough. I'm driven by the image of Pasha, Morris and Annalynn on the roof. There is a reason we preserved that circle, and Pasha will lead us to it.

The closer we get to Ash, the more I'm aware that, while all sixteen planes didn't make it, Shaw's fleet did its damage. Debris laces the streets in piles deeper than me. Some buildings are now merely cauldrons in the ground, and the ones destroyed but partially standing will comprise a very different skyline in the days to come. Now, we enter this city to clean up the rest of the garbage, and I hope Dorsey's ears are ready to hear the power of The 28 United taking back our world.

A thud sounds from behind me, clanking as it hits the ground. It is a DR93, and I think it has fallen from above. I flatten myself against the side of a crumbling building, hoping for some protection, then look up. Like the Cheshire Cat in the literature section of the History Labyrinth, Checkmate smiles down on me. He's surrounded by the camouflaged balloon-techs, hundreds of them, only visible because their doors are open and their pilots are dropping weapons from twenty feet up. I remember thinking Checkmate only had a fleet of thirty, and now I feel my foolishness comprehend his comment, "multiply times ten." "Thought you didn't believe in war," I shout up at him.

"I believe in ending war," Checkmate yells back. "You owe me." I laugh at the absurdity of ever paying back anything owed.

I cannot hear most of what Checkmate is saying, but I can tell it is a steady stream of one-sided conversation, probably a string of anecdotes about the balloon-tech territory, and why we haven't discovered it yet. I am quite sure I've heard it all, in detail, many times before. I pick up the DR93 closest to me and hang the strap over my shoulder. All the soldiers with me do the same. Checkmate and his pilots have dropped more than one weapon. There's enough for all. I look back to Checkmate to nod a "thanks," but he's gone—or maybe I just don't see him.

Chapter 28
CHILDISH WAYS CHAPMAN

A month before Avery and her soldiers left with the Fleet of Zooms for the Ash attack, Chapman counted his mother's push-ups. "Twenty-five, twenty-six, twenty-seven." His form, small for a five-year-old boy, showed signs of unusual muscle development, especially in his biceps, quads and hamstrings. He clung to Avery's neck with his arms and held onto her torso with his legs, hanging on her front section like a baby primate secured to his mother's underbelly, causing her push-ups to be even more challenging. "Twenty-eight, twenty-nine, thirty—"

"Keep counting," Avery said. One might not notice Chapman's strength anomalies under the covering of his clothing, but his mother noticed when the child stripped down to swim in what was left of the savanna pools on the

African grassland of the deserted zoo. Chapman loved to see how much faster he could swim than Annalynn, Morris and Raghill, but he never bragged. His mother told him boasting was not an appreciated quality of leadership. Was he a leader? He only knew his mother was, and from stories he'd heard of his grandfather, Carles DeTornada, Chapman knew there were others in his family considered leaders—great leaders. "Thirty-one, thirty-two, thirty-three."

———

Avery DeTornada's arms quivered in a feeble attempt to break her own record. I was embarrassed that she called me "son." I refused to call her "mother." When necessary, I would call her "mama." I released my arms just enough to let my hands—not my arms—do the holding around her neck. "Thirty-four..." I positioned a stranglehold with perfect pressure. "Thirty-five..." I tightened. "Thirty-six..." I squeezed with the vice-grip I'd developed.

———

Avery fell on top of Chapman, coughing, gasping for air, unable to continue with the push-ups. "Stop it! Chapman! What are you doing?" With an unexpected power, Chapman pushed his mother off of him.

———

I pushed her off my body, thinking, I will not let this woman's weakness affect my plans. *She had fallen, unable to maintain control when I tested her strength. With genius, I bolted to a standing position in the middle of her sleeping mat in her private quarters at the zoo, expecting the man McGinty to sprint through the door the moment this woman, exhibiting another weakness, called out for him. I accurately predicted most human behavior. From the standing position, I spun. I focused, stopping my breathing. The mother hated it when I did that. She showed fear. The man McGinty drew back the curtain to her quarters, and she didn't even need to call. To twirl without breath provided a strategic place for me to formulate my plans, my actions necessary to...to...to...*

———

Chapman heard Avery and McGinty whispering. Chapman was on the bed, standing and feeling dizzy. He tried to breathe, and he could not. Panic set in. He exerted the effort again, gulping for the air. He needed help and called, "Mama? Mama?" He collapsed on the bed and felt the comfort of his mother's arms around him, drawing him close. He loved the beat of her heart. An awareness set in. There was another set of arms enfolding both him and his mother. It was McGinty. Maybe he would invite Chapman to come with him today and check the weapons in the storage lockers of what used to be the monkey cages. That was one of Chapman's favorite activities, other than the stories he and his mother told at dawn most mornings.

———

McGinty thought our trip to the weapon storage lockers was a bonding time to enjoy each other's company. Unknowingly, he took all the necessary steps to put me right in the middle of the information I needed. At some point in the future it will be vital for me to know the weapon count for The 28 United, and he will help me get it. McGinty's hand reached out and did that action that I could not stand. That rubbing of my hair, affectionately. It nauseated me, as did the necessity of my pretense. They still believed I was a part of their family, even with my occasional lapses into what they claimed were glitches in my DNA. Again, the man McGinty's hand descended on my hair. I tried to put up with it, but even those destined for power have their limits. I pushed his hand away.

I waited until after we visited the storage units, and as he took the lead to take us on an examination of the wind orchards I slipped away, arriving at the aircraft hangars inside the Energy Concourse.

When I reached the hangars, the area was deserted. An air fleet to defeat Ash. They had little understanding of how one attacks a major power. They had a high learning curve ahead, and no time to achieve it. My intercession would eventually save them from themselves—not that I care about their unintentional demolition of everything they've built, but it would get in the way of me pursuing the strategy I have in place.

I climbed the ladder to the top of the silo that Shaw converted to an aircraft hangar. Pushing myself, I used only my arms to climb, leaving my legs swinging free. After reaching the last wrung, I readied myself to descend through the hole that gave entrance to the hangar.

———

He hung upside down on the outside of the silo-hangar. The heel of his boot stuck fast in a sturdy metal loop used to close the entrance to the hangar. Chapman was barely conscious and whimpering, no longer struggling to right himself. It was Annalynn who heard him crying. Shaw had been teaching her all about the float car, its hangar and the entrance and exit to the silo, and she was somewhat delighted to demonstrate her knowledge to Avery's son.

Annalynn crawled up the ladder with stealth, all the way comforting Chapman with her words. "Hey, little man. Don't worry, this superhero of a woman is on her way to get you out of hangar-trouble and into the arms of your loving mama." This made Chapman cry louder in full voice. "Little man, you know you'll be okay. So stiff upper lip and all that." Chapman let out a wail so loud Annalynn almost lost her grip. "Shut your face, kid." Her patience was gone.

———

Mama. Mama. Scared. I want my Mama. Get me down from here. Story. I want a story, Mama.

———

Right after The 28 United arrived by air to attack Ash, Chapman, dressed in the gray uniform of the officers of The Third, slipped into the Divining Room unnoticed. Though his size was unusual, the uniform waited for him. Quinn's back was to Chapman. The Z-Colt in her hand firmly controlled both Dorsey, whining on the floor in a pool of blood, and Raghill, pouting on the chair slat, twirling his hand in a nondescript way through the hologram controls. The recent explosions, destroying buildings near by, had left their mark on the Confinement Circle, even though it had not been targeted directly. The flooring curled up from the holes left by blasts, but the hologram station and the planatery dome above remained in tact.

"I left my childish ways," Chapman said in a voice that, in the few previous hours, had passed puberty and marched into the voice register of a man, his body still suspended on a timeline at five years old. He held his own Z-Colt without difficulty, his over-developed muscles begging his small frame to catch up. The barrel of his weapon pointed with unquestionable accuracy at Quinn's head. Chapman knew Quinn weighed her options, as to where the Z-Colt she held should be pointed. But as she turned and shifted position to lock eyes with her grandson, he saw she chose to keep Raghill and Dorsey in her sights. After all, he was just a boy, and Chapman thought he saw the softness of a grandmother around the edge of her eyes.

"I haven't seen you in over a year," she said. "I hardly expected our reunion to be weaponized."

"Any other kind of reunion would be a childish choice."

And now, Chapman saw those grandmother eyes turn to immoveable steel. "Don't give yourself credit for 'choice' or being smart or wise or decisively grown-up. You left your childish ways because you're a GEB, and you had no options. What you were created to become you became. Your arrogance offends me."

"*You're* calling *me* arrogant?" A childish tantrum seeped in to the man-child, then backed its way out. "You're the one who left your grandson to take a position in The Third."

"I don't have a position in The Third, you do."

"Stop talking. You left your daughter and your grandson. You don't get to talk." The tantrum tapped at the door again.

"Oh, I've got plenty to say—not to the grandson who I loved—but to the man-child with an ego far bigger than the brain that holds it." Quinn turned the Z-Colt she held from covering Raghill and Dorsey, directly to Chapman.

"Shut up."

"Disrespectful to talk back to your elders." He could hear the taunt in her voice. She was trying to throw him off his game. She'd never do it. She moved a few inches closer to him. "You know, we could get you help. You don't have to dismantle your family person by person."

Chapman backed away from her. "Stop. Shut up and stop."

"You don't have to choose to side with The Third."

"Choose? I'm not siding with The Third. I'm part of it. Always from the first."

"You're Avery's child. She's loved you. Your father was the only 'Third' in your life. Don't choose to be more GEB than human."

"That's not a choice." The tantrum boiled over, and Chapman pulled the trigger, penetrating Quinn's fore-head faster than she could get a shot off at him. The hole through her skull was clean and fatal, forged by the hand of the child Quinn had saved five years before with her own shot to destroy The Third's weapon—Raben. Raghill stood and stumbled backwards, covering his face, taking a few shocked gasps, or maybe he was crying. Dorsey's painful moans turned momentarily to a perceptible laugh and then fell into wails of agony.

Chapman still held the Z-Colt in his hand, unwavering, pointed down at Quinn where she lay dead on the floor of the Divining Room. No tantrum left. He liked control. He said aloud, to his audience of two—a bleeding commander and a frightened teenage boy, "Now *that* was choice."

Chapter 29
THE VISITOR
AVERY

The jagged fragments of the metal door grab at my jacket as I plunge into the Divining Room, followed by McGinty and a contingent of our wounded soldiers, our weapons on the ready. Shaw had called off the target on the Confinement Circle before our cargo plane went down, but apparently not before the zoom behind us caught the edge of the building while trying to bank away and drop the explosives on another site. The dome above us seems untouched by the attack and palpitates with the power of space, but the floor has buckled and the room looks like an upturned fall garden, everything in a dead, random, disorganized mess while smoke swirls through the destruction, investigating the rearrangement. Alarms scream the announcement of our invasion, and I know we have only seconds—maybe a minute—to end Dorsey, and if Pasha, Morris, and Annalynn are still here, extract them.

I see Degnan's messenger bag laying on a chair slat by the wall. I know he must be somewhere near. Through the haze I see Frederick with six other Elite soldiers, weapons drawn, surrounding Dorsey, protecting what is left of his body. We spray them with a ballistic surge of ammunition from our DR93s, taking out four of the Elites, the others diving for cover as they return fire. The guards are quick and excellent specimens of Elite training, but our warriors are shaped with the expertise of survival and the momentum of a last resort mission. Elite bullets go unanswered by our human flesh, bouncing off steel beams and buried in the ash of destruction.

Our warriors advance, but more Elites run in from the entrance behind us. I take cover, using the bent steel beams for protection. Through the small spaces between one beam and another I see a man, avoiding the fire by scrambling from one pile of rubble to the next until he reaches the messenger bag, grabbing it by the strap and slinging it over his shoulder. Even through the haze of smoke, I know it's Degnan. Just feet away from Dorsey, Frederick stands, guarding him. Degnan flings Frederick the messenger bag. Frederick throws his weapon over his shoulder at the same moment he catches the messenger bag, opening it for the scorpo-darts to poke their heads out. They leap from the bag to the shoulder of the fallen Dorsey. Seconds later they spring, one to his face and the other to his uncovered hand, proving their worth. Dorsey, with his bleeding ears gone, now writhes in a desperate attempt to stop the scorpodarts' poison from taking effect, but he cannot. I am once again in Degnan's debt for taking down the man I've stood against for so long, and I wonder what Degnan will ask for this time, in return for the services of Telson and Dart.

Frederick once again engages his weapon. Now he is with us. If we make it through this, Pasha will be gloating. Reverse-*locasa* did its job on Frederick, and it worked long-term.

I raise my weapon to my shoulder in another round of assault, but the bullet exchange dwindles. And through the sounds of chaos and the constant weapon release outside, a strange quelling of battle settles inside this room. I turn to check my back. Then, I hear it. The unmistakable engagement of a Z-Colt bullet charging into the chamber of a weapon. Raghill holds the Z-Colt's cold metal snout tight against my temple. I alter my position, forcing him to point the barrel at the center of my forehead. His hand shakes, and both his lips quiver as he speaks. I sense him trying to be the malevolent man his father had been, but Raghill hasn't had the practice. We trained this boy to be totally in command of firepower, yet he seems to have forgotten some of his education. The tremor in his hand intensifies, and he says, "Drop your weapon, Avery. Now."

Pasha runs into the room with Morris and Annalynn, but she slows when she sees Raghill with his Z-Colt pressed against my head. Her Z-Colt is already unholstered and in her hand. She takes aim at Raghill. "Put it down," she demands. Raghill doesn't budge, and I can feel the vibration of the barrel on my skull. He's a boy, not a commander.

Morris says, "It's not going to happen this way, Raghill. It can't."

Raghill responds, "It has to. It's what my father said has to happen."

My eyes have not moved from Raghill's eyes, even though his jet back and forth between Pasha, Morris and me.

"What happened to you, Raghill?" I ask. Now his eyes come back and rest on mine. Nothing is said for so many moments while the war unfurls its intended force outside this building and trigger fingers itch for fulfillment. "What happened?"

Raghill's lips move without sound, I think he's trying to formulate the words his heart has always battled with. Finally, a whisper comes, "I found a father."

"Dorsey was never a 'father.'"

"Easy for you to say, daughter of Carles DeTornada."

"We don't choose our fathers, but other choices are ours to make." Maybe I see a tear in Raghill's eye, but he blinks it away before I know for sure. "Stand with us," I urge him. From my peripheral I see McGinty, weapon poised and ready to take down our own Raghill, and I am painfully aware, without looking upward, that the universe pulsing above has no interest in our final arguments. The looming night sky covers us with constantly shifting splashes of light, like the blinking black-and-white images from the spinning reel of an old movie from the recesses of the History Labyrinth, twirling out its tale to the audience, waiting for a climax.

All our remaining soldiers have their weapons spotted on Raghill. From somewhere behind me I hear Degnan say, "Let's all take a break." I hear the sharp click of munitions loading into several weapons around me, and I am convinced no one's listening to Degnan. He tries again. "It's over, people." No one moves, and the Z-Colt against my skull continues etching a mark on my forehead. I fear Raghill will release the bullet in nervous error more than intent. "Raghill, you first, lower your weapon." Raghill staggers back in relief, shouldering his Z-Colt in its holster, and I'm convinced he doesn't know who to follow, so now he's following Degnan, God help us.

"Confusing," I say to Degnan. "I thought you had your own side."

"For a while there's not going to be 'sides,'" says Degnan.

Pasha moves through the wreckage toward me until she's inches from my face—focused—a look in her eyes I have never seen. I see desperate traces of fear and confusion usually foreign to Pasha. She says, "Morris, Annalynn and me—we'll never be 'with' The Third— but for a time we're gonna have to work with them."

A flicker from the smoky perimeter of the room draws my attention past Pasha. There stands the one I love more than any other. More than Quinn or Morris or McGinty. My boy. "Chapman," I yell for him, but my burst of speed toward Chapman triggers Raghill, who, for a teenager, has stunning strength from years of training with The 28 United. He yanks my hair, and then my arms, twisting them behind my back. Okay—so he *is* his father's son.

"Let me go!" I flip Raghill over my head, and he lands crumpled in a heap, the roles of aggressor and victim now dramatically reversed. I draw my Z-Colt on him, and neither my men nor the Elite troops move to stop me.

But I quickly abandon my target and run to Chapman, not letting the collapsed section of roof deter me from my goal. I wrap my arms around my child, hold him close, terrified that he is in the middle of a war claiming lives on both sides. There is no response. No reciprocal embrace, no breath of relief, nothing. Stepping back to catch a glimpse of his face, I see not the child I've nurtured for five years, but a seasoned, unemotional man dressed in the uniform of The Third. His demeanor that of a five-year-old, his nature that of a trained general.

This is what Raben has done, and I hate him for it. How could I have ever believed that a half-GEB child would be completely mine? And now I see the normal part of motherhood has all but disappeared, and the memory of Degnan's nasty challenge to me—*Will you hesitate in battle when it comes to your son?* That challenge booms in my head, running circles around my brain like I'm standing in a belfry with a church bell, bigger than me, and it won't stop ringing. I can't hear anything else. *Will you hesitate? Will you hesitate?* Until I hear my own son say, "Your mother's dead. I shot Quinn." Chapman's childlike voice, hyped up on the steroids of adultism, packs a punch, bashing a hole in the hope I'd had of relationship with my mother, already so fragile and under reconstruction. He stares off to his side. I see my mother, forehead marred by my son's own bullet. I stumble backwards, McGinty catching me before I fall. He eases me over, and I kneel beside Quinn, scooping her in my arms, pressing my lips to her cheek.

Chapman says, "After all, she was a subterranean." I stare at him, expecting some sort of explanation. "It was necessary."

"She was your grandmother!" I say.

"She was a threat to my destiny," I hear the condemnation tightly wrapped around his words and everything inside me wants to rail at him, but *I don't hesitate.* I stand to a commander's height, take the Z-Colt still clasped in my hand from the recent draw on Raghill and direct it to Chapman's heart.

"Don't become your father, Chapman. You have a choice. You're my child too."

Chapman stares right through me. "No more choices."

Morris runs to my side, clinching my arm and drawing me in his direction. He stares into my eyes and says, "We *don't* have a choice. Not now. We either work together or we all die." He directs my focus fifty feet above and steps to the side of room, activating the hologram that controls the view of the universe. He scales our view in tight sailing us behind the sun into the orbit of unnamed asteroids. Quickly we watch, as if we travel on the back of a meteor to the far side of the sun, and as we peer out, catching sight of earth again, a terrifying, whirling, scarlet, circular form spins on a collision course. I recognize this enemy. I am horrified at the direction it propels itself at a mighty speed—Earth.

All heads turn toward the cosmos and the pulsing live feed from space. Momentarily every weapon quivers in each soldier's hands, no longer on the ready. Morris says, "Avery, *Jurbay—Jurbay* just had a baby." The asteroid spins in a projectile toward our planet, dwarfing *Jurbay* in an attempt to minimize the terror of the past.

I see Dorsey's dead form crumpled on the edge of the shadows, his ears red with blood, the marks of scorpodarts upon him. No longer able to issue a command. Near his side stands Raghill, caught between the world of the dead and a man he thought knew everything, and the world of the living where he himself must strive to know anything at all. He moves his weapon from his right hand to his left and hesitantly extends his trembling free hand to me, waiting for me to clasp it and his forearm in the traditional exchange that might be shared by comrades, always is embraced by friends and never considered by enemies. Chapman picks his way through the debris to position himself at the side of the ruined Dorsey and quivering Raghill. Chapman directs all his attention toward me and then surprisingly clasps the hand of Raghill that was extended in my direction. Chapman, with his free hand, reaches out to me in an effort to link us all together, a triangle united. I look at the gap between the two of us. I no longer stare with compassion in the eyes of my young son. I gaze in the face of an enemy. And I say to them all—the mutilated, dead Dorsey—the traitor Raghill—my son, Chapman, the GEB I'd hoped would be more me than Raben. I see what's left of my friends—Pasha, Annalynn and Morris and the empty spots that should be filled by Shaw, my dear comrade, and by my mother, Quinn, the one I was just getting to know and love. I stare at the Elite soldiers of The Third and then at the seasoned warriors of The 28 United and finally at the man I love, McGinty. I say to them all, "I will not let a rerun of *Jurbay* take the remains of what it left of our states. The 28 United will stand, and if that means cooperation with The Third for a time—we will cooperate—with caution. But we will never, never join hands."

REMEMBERING
INSIDE THE THIRD

JURBAY

The asteroid that fell in 2067, severing 22 states, plunging them into the Pacific Ocean and drowning half the population in the course of a day.

THE 28 UNITED

A colony that stands against The Third. Originating under the leadership of Carles and Quinn DeTornada, now led by their daughter, Avery DeTornada. After Reichel was enveloped by sinkholes, The 28 United moved north to the New Coastline, finally colonizing to the west of the Waters of Erie. For the last five years, The Third has been unable to track them. The 28 United has been building an air fleet and is strategizing to attack The Third's new capital, Ash.

The Subterraneans
Those from The 28 United who work undercover inside
The Third.

The 28 United Council
Avery DeTornada, Quinn DeTornada, Pasha, Shaw,
McGinty, Morris, Clef, and Old Soul.

Standing for The 28 United

Avery DeTornada	Quinn DeTornada	Dr. Pasha Lutnik
McGinty	Shaw	Morris
Annalynn	Raghill	Degnan
Ulysses (GEB)	Pepper (GEB)	Clef
Chapman (Avery's son)	Carles ("The Littlest Librarian")	Old Soul
Herman and Orbit (pigeons)	Gizzie (gazelle)	Fortnight
Miranda	Checkmate	August
Minstrels	Mappers	Allegra

THE THIRD
The current government with Commander Dorsey in
power.

PLACES
Abandoned Zoo—The settlement of The 28 United to
the west of the Waters of Erie.

Anteater's Nose—A small section of the Waters of Huron, extending inland just before Huron spills into the seas of the New Coastline.

Ash—New capital of The Third, northeast of the Waters of Erie.

Balloon-tech Colonies—Colonies located somewhere to the south of the Waters of Erie.

Butcher Shop—Located in the outskirts of Ash. Where the subterraneans meet.

Confinement Circle—A collection of three government buildings housing the Mock Courts and prisons of The Third.

Dark Market—Underwater market designed by Degnan. Dorsey built the market for Degnan in trade for Degnan sanitizing Ash and the remaining country. The market is suspended forty-five feet below the surface, consisting of cars containing merchandise for the upper-tier patrons of The Third.

Divining Room—A room in the Confinement Circle where Dorsey goes to find peace.

Energy Concourse—A four-mile-long facility designed by Pasha to mine energy, covered and camouflaged with her thin-skin invention.

Healing Caves—Part of Colony G. Caves where children traumatized by war come to live and be restored. Clef, the minstrels and the artists are caretakers in the caves.

New Coastline—The remaining western section of the nation severed by *Jurbay*.

Warrior Strip—A hidden strip behind the merchandise cars of the Dark Market where Degnan allows Avery and The 28 United to collect intel about The Third.

Waters of Erie—The receded waters of a large lake.

THE UNUSUAL & BIZARRE
Brainy—A brainy fires more like a shotgun with a single pop, not like an assault weapon with a spray of multiple rounds. It will chase the target around a corner, up a tree, in a hole, even on the backside of a boulder.
Anti-brainy—Designed by McGinty and mounted on the back of a brainy. The two weapons ride in tandem: same weapon, separate barrels. When a brainy is fired by an enemy, the anti-brainy can be fired. It will track the brainy down and destroy it before it hits its mark.

Brain-swappers—Two animals who are genetically modified to create one being with parts of each. **Leprex**—A T-rex merged with a leopard. **Scorpodart**—A scorpion merged with a poison dart frog.

DeTornada—A Catalan (Catalonian) phrase for "on our way back."

14 Deadlies—Diseases created by Degnan on behalf of The Third. Sent worldwide to diminish the population, making it simpler to invade and control countries. The diseases also destroyed much of the population left after *Jurbay* severed the nation.

Eye-readers—Installed in the eyes of all citizens of The Third. Provide an opportunity for reading documents without looking at paper copies. The Third can alter material from places like the History Labyrinth, to give their own twist on facts. Avery and her team have eye-readers from being undercover subterraneans in years past.

Fishborns—Torpedo-like weapons with a fin on the back end. After a land strike, can be programmed not to explode immediately. Can run along land, just below the ground level, until it finds a specific target. **Flying-fishborns**—A smaller version of a fishborn that converts to a small aircraft during battle.

GEB—Genetically engineered being.

Glides—Transparent, rectangular transportation, designed to transport patrons to and from the Dark Market.

Locasa—Scientists developed *locasa* to remove specific memories from the brain with the intent of providing healing for those victims of heinous crimes or those with PTSD. The Third stole the device, using it on their citizens and deleting memories of family and home. **Reverse-*locasa***—A device still in the experimental stages created by Dr. Pasha Lutnik to return the memories *locasa* removed.

Sanitizing—A process created by Degnan (The Cleaner) to dissolve and disintegrate human, animal and plant decay caused by the 14 Deadlies.

Solar cells, wind blocks, poo-balls—Materials mined in the Energy Concourse.

Thin-skin—An organic material developed by Pasha. Has incredible strength and can camouflage anything.

ACKOWLEGEMENTS

To Katie Shaw, editor, who continued to read long past deadlines. I treasure your critiques. Thank you.

To those who edited in a variety of ways: Karis Melin and Daniel Melin. You always had my back. Thank you.

To Denise Mahoney, running partner, valued friend, and gifted artist. Thank you.

To Andie Avery Photography, for "Avery" and your creative photographic eye. Thank you.

To Sheri Miller, professional with values, trusted friend, cover and website designer. Thank you.

To my readers: Brian Whelan, Evan Peterson, Ellie Mansfield, Debbie Andersen, Teri Waag, Paige Walthall, Phil Mansfield, and Anna Flood. Your fresh eyes gave me encouragement. Thank you.

To the actors: Brian Mahoney, Anna Flood, Ellie Loney, and those yet unnamed in the coming launch parties and readings. You know how to tell a story. Thank you.

To my students who continue to inspire me with strong opinions, a passion for life, and incredible talent. Thank you.

To the knee-worn warriors. You know who you are. I'm grateful beyond infinity. Thank you.

And oh, this family! To Phil, Ellie, Natalie, Zoe. Stories rise in me because you have let them. To my mother, Norma; father, Robert Gibson; stepfather, Les; sisters, Gail and Sara; and to the aunts, uncles, nieces, nephews, and of course—the cousins. Your influence shows up in every book. Thank you.

To my Creator, the Giver of all gifts. You stirred the story in me. Thank you.

THANK YOU, TO MY READERS...

We may never meet in person, but once you've joined me in reading the Roll Call Trilogy, we are linked together in a unique way. My words become richer and more meaningful with each set of eyes that share my characters' adventures, conflicts, discoveries and journeys. Thank you.

I need a favor! Please take the time to write a review on Amazon. Most of us are pretty internet-savvy now and realize that REVIEWS MATTER. Please follow the directions listed below and take five minutes to express your opinions about *Inside The Third* or *Roll Call* or both. A review can be as short as one sentence, or a paragraph, or an extensive commentary. All of them are appreciated.

I'm looking forward to meeting you again on your Kindle or on the pages of your paperback as we share the final story of Book #3 in the *Roll Call Trilogy, Reluctant*

Warriors. Be blessed, challenged and surprised by the pages to come.

To write a review:

1. Go to Amazon.
2. Type in the name of the book and my name.
3. Scroll down to the bottom of the page where the reviews can be accessed.
4. Look for the directions on how to write a review.
5. Write the review!

ABOUT THE AUTHOR

Gwen Mansfield lives in the Northwest with her husband and children. She received her BA in Theatre from
Seattle Pacific University, MA in Theatre Production
from Central Washington University and MFA in
Creative Writing from University of New Orleans. She
is the author of the historical fiction *Experiment Station
Road*, the musical *Resistance* (based on the book *Tales
of the Resistance* by David and Karen Mains), and stage
plays: *Grace Diner, The Luggage of Ellis, Mrs. Boggart Says*,
and *Experiment Station Road, Stories from the Journey*.

Visit the website...

gwenmansfield.com

Visit the blog...

https://rollcalltrilogy.wordpress.com

EXPERIMENT STATION ROAD

a historical fiction by

GWEN MANSFIELD

In 1962 Ellen Merrill finds herself in the midst of a revelation: the townsfolk of Hayford, Oregon have two sets of standards—one for the Anglos and one for the Mexicans. Ellen says, "It was the only time I ever heard from God. He said, 'Prejudice demands an age of accountability—how old are you?'" Through the next decade of her life Ellen chases equality, and in spite of her parents and the heritage of a town's racism, she catches glimpses of justice. *Experiment Station Road*, a quirky but poignant coming-of-age story, invites the reader through a decade of discovery with Ellen Merrill as she slams into community prejudice, advocates for Cesar Chavez, and conceals a clandestine but sweet romance.

Ellen's revelation is clear: the value of a solo voice lifted in a community of clatter shakes up the world and allows the experiment to continue.

Experiment Station Road may be purchased through the Amazon.

Avery's World
2088

Balloon-tech
Colonies

Waters of Ontario

(receded waters)

★ ASH
(Headquarters of The Third)

(receded waters)

Waters of Erie

Dark Matter

(receded waters)

Waters of Huron

(receded waters)

Anteater's
Nose

Colony G Headquarters
(The 28 United)

New Coastline

Made in the USA
Middletown, DE
25 September 2021